CHAD

THE ANIMAL

*This book is dedicated to Belle,
the toughest dog I've ever known.*

"Do you like scary movies?"

−Ghostface

"   . . .   "

−Michael Myers

TABLE OF CONTENTS

MESSAGE FROM THE AUTHOR

Hey, this is Chad Nicholas. There are a few surprise bonuses at the end of this book that I wanted to mention, but first I wanted to personally thank you for choosing this book as your next read. The slasher genre has been one of my favorites for a long time, and there have been so many incredible stories told, from the all-time classic work of John Carpenter and Debra Hill with the *Halloween* franchise, to Wes Craven and Kevin Williamson's incredible *Scream* series, which is why I am truly honored that you decided to pick up The *Animal* and make it your next slasher story.

Years of work have been put into this novel, not just from myself, but also the input of various beta readers, the careful proofreads of my editor, and the incredible artwork and formatting done by my cover artists. All of it with the hope of giving you the best possible reading experience we could, from the bloody slasher scenes to the various twists and turns and the detailed artwork that surrounds all of it, telling the story without words.

So, with that in mind, I truly hope you enjoy it. This story was for you.

Now, I also wanted to mention a few bonuses that are included in this novel.

The first is called Oliver's Journal. Why it's called that will become clearer once you start reading the story, but it is essentially a suspect list: a series of character profiles with blank spaces where you can keep track of clues and evidence, in case you want to try and solve the mystery alongside the characters. Trying to solve the mystery before a book reveals it to me is something I've always loved to do, so I thought if readers were anything like me, they'd love a suspect list where they could write all of their theories regarding each and every character.

If that interests you, the journal can be found at the end of this novel.

You won't solve it in time, but you're welcome to try.

Don't forget, everyone is a suspect.

Finally, the first chapters of my two previous novels, *Nightmare* and *Shade*, can be found at the end of this book as well. I wanted to include them in case you liked this story and wanted to see what my other books were about. I hope you enjoy them as well.

With all that said, welcome to *The Animal...*

PART ONE

THE PREY

CHAPTER ONE

The animal stalked its prey.

Hidden in the grass, out of sight and yet close enough to smell its prey's blood, the predator waited: muscles tensed, heart pounding, sharp jagged claws leaving trails in the broken dirt below as it opened its massive jaws and bared its bloodstained teeth. Drops of red fell from its mouth, remnants of its last meal staining the green field with a trail of death even as its ears twitched, and it began to search through the silence of the field, listening for the subtle, rhythmic sound of its prey's breathing, evidence of a life soon to be taken. As it heard the innocent prey's gentle pant for air, the animal's eyes changed, losing what bit of life had appeared in them, replaced by mere darkness as its pupils dilated into black, lifeless holes, only focused on its next meal.

Mere breaths away, the prey stood, grazing peacefully, unaware of the horror that lurked within the shadows of the tall grass. Unaware of the predator seeking to rip it limb from limb and feast on the lifeless carcass that remained. But although no sound was made and no horrific sight revealed, instinct made the prey stop, a sixth sense revealing the truth as a mere feeling of dread, the sensation of a death soon to come, choking out all other senses and leaving only fear.

Something was wrong. A predator was nearby, and it had come for the prey's flesh.

As its legs trembled, the prey's eyes quickly scanned the grass, looking for any sign of danger, any sign of which way to run, even as monstrous images formed in its mind, fevered hallucinations of the creature whose teeth it could almost feel already sinking into its throat, draining the life from it.

What felt like an eternity of quiet dread passed, stuck in that frozen place between safety and slaughter, until finally the prey saw a pair of eyes hiding within the grass. Monstrous black eyes filled not with life but with hunger.

The lion pounced.

The gazelle tried to run.

In a single moment, every last nerve within the gazelle's small body erupted in a crazed, fear-induced panic, and it took off like a bullet. But it was far too late, for the lion's claws had already dug into its side, tearing through its shimmering brown fur and digging down to the exposed flesh below, cracking the ivory of its rib cage as the single strike brought the prey crashing into the dirt.

Still, the gazelle tried to fight. Frenzied, it kicked its legs in a sudden desperate attempt to find solid ground, anything to be able to run again. To escape. But when the lion's foot crashed down on its leg bone, breaking it in two, escape was no longer an option.

Screaming in mangled agony, tears of unimaginable pain streaming from its dying eyes, the gazelle began swinging its head, no longer thinking of survival, no longer thinking at all as instinct took over, the last remnants of conscious thought within a dying carcass, and it tried to push its razor-sharp horns into the lion's heart. The final hope of an animal too broken to run, too terrified to really fight, but still just alive enough to scream.

Its pain ended a moment later, when the lion's teeth ripped its throat in two.

"Yes!" Brandon screamed as he shot up off the couch, arms thrust upward in celebration as he watched the carnage unfolding on the television screen.

On the other side of the small sofa, Eric cursed as he slumped back into the cushions, defeated.

"The predator won," Brandon said, chest out and voice triumphant as he outstretched his open hand toward Eric. "Pay up."

Groaning, Eric pulled five dollars from his pocket and gave it to the victor of their little wager.

To their left, leaning back in a recliner, Kelly rolled her bright eyes in disgust. "What is wrong with you two?"

"Aww, let the boys have their fun," Britney said, leaning against Eric on the couch, grinning as he put his arm around her. "Besides, what's the point of a nature documentary if we don't get to watch animals kill each other?"

"Wow," Kelly said, acting too horrified to even look at them. "And my brother says I have issues."

"Where is your brother, by the way?" Brandon asked, equal parts mockery and actual question. "I mean, you said he was bringing us drinks and a movie, but we've been sitting here watching a nature documentary for the last hour. No offense, but I had higher hopes for this party."

"He'll be here," Kelly promised, despite being irritated with Rhett herself. What could possibly

be taking him so long to show? She'd planned
this party for four months. Not that it was hard
to do when her parents were never around, but
still, he was about to ruin it by showing up late
on the worst night possible.

*What could he be waiting for, a more dramatic
entrance?*

"You know Rhett loses track of time. He's
probably on his way now."

"I hope so," Britney said, "because Eric looks
way better when I'm wasted."

Eric grinned. "I have been told that before."

"Can we at least change the channel while we
wait?" Kelly asked. "All the blood is grossing me out."

"Why don't we ask the new girl?" Brandon
said, and soon their gaze focused on Megan, all
of them turning to her in unison.

Kelly sighed to herself. Megan had been sitting
next to Brandon all night, occasionally playing
with her jet-black hair, clearly trying to get his
attention. There was no way on earth she was
going to back Kelly on this, even if the gazelle's
death had made her visibly sick.

"I say we leave it," Megan said. "This is kinda
interesting."

"Besides," Eric said, sitting up at attention,
pointing at the screen, "it's about to get even better."

On the television, the lion had finished eating
the gazelle and was now approaching a small lake,

looking for a drink, something to wash the blood from its jagged teeth.

Unaware of the crocodile that lurked beneath the shallow waters...

"Round two! Predator meets predator!" Brandon howled. "Ten bucks on the lion."

"You're on," Eric responded, his last semilogical sentence before he began actually talking to the crocodile. "C'mon, Croc, you can do it. Avenge the gazelle!"

They waited in tense anticipation as the lion put its head down to the water and the crocodile moved closer. Any second now, one of them would move, and it would be a bloodbath.

The crocodile lunged.

The screen went black.

In an instant, darkness crawled over every inch of the house, enveloping the kids in a void darker than even the night sky, trapping them in its nothingness. Not a sound was made, not a heartbeat felt as suddenly they started shivering, imagining what could be watching them in the darkness.

What could have returned for more blood.

Anywhere else, it would have been brushed off: a simple power outage, nothing to fear. But in this town, on this day, the darkness could be felt in their bones, the memories of legends still spoken of. The thing that hid in the darkness of this town, waiting to hunt once more.

It happened so long ago...

A few minutes later, wax slowly creeped down from a dozen candles now scattered wildly across the room, illuminating the uneasy features of the five kids in a warm glow of flickering fire.

"Who's up for a ghost story?" Brandon asked, leaning forward so that his face hovered above the candles on the coffee table.

"I don't know if that's the best idea, considering," Kelly said, voice quiet. "You know what day it is."

"What day is it?" Megan asked, an innocent question from someone unaware of the nightmarish stories lurking within this town's history.

Kelly raised an eyebrow at the strange question. "It's the twenty-fifth anniversary."

"Of what?"

At first, not one of them dared answer her, as if whatever it was would rip them from their seats and drag them out into the darkness if they even dared speak its name. But finally, Kelly managed a hushed reply.

"The Animal."

Confusion creeped over Megan's face as she seemed to grow increasingly frustrated at their sudden secrecy. "What is the Animal?"

For a moment, each and every one of them looked at Megan in unsettled disbelief, as if not knowing about the Animal was the same as not knowing how to breathe. As if a piece of her was missing, a hollowness in her mind where the stories and the legends should have dwelled.

It was Brandon who finally broke the silence. "You don't know about the Animal?"

"No."

Still taken aback, Kelly found herself staring at Megan, wondering how it was possible. How could anyone in this town not have heard the stories, seen the houses still stained in blood, witnessed the forest where the beast had come from? The legend was a part of the town, a part of its people, a very real and monstrous myth that had changed everything.

To live in this town was to live in its shadow.

But then, Kelly finally remembered what should have been a simple explanation. Megan had only moved to this town a week ago. She was still an outsider, someone not yet marked by the legends. A single innocent soul amidst all the rest—probably the only one in the entire town who didn't know.

"Well, then, listen close," Brandon said, always the storyteller, shrugging off his unease as he jumped onto the coffee table, candlelight flickering softly beneath him as he shifted his voice to sound dramatic, prepared to tell his scary story as the dimly lit faces of his friends leaned forward with horrified interest. Most of them knew the story he was about to tell, but familiarity made it no less frightening. The horrific truth of what had emerged from the forest couldn't be dulled by something as weak as memory.

So there they sat, none more anxious than Megan, about to hear the legend for the first time, still naive enough to think that imagined monsters inspired more terror than those that truly existed. That nothing out there lurking in the darkness could ever be as terrifying as one's own imagination, when in truth, as she was about to discover with a trembling heart, it was the other way around.

Silence echoed for a second longer, frightened eyes glowing in the flickering fire, surrounded by nothing but shadows of a house, before Brandon began his story, fear creeping into even his voice.

"Twenty-five years ago, on this very night, the town was quiet. No sound could be heard in the streets, no bird could be found in the air. The light of a full moon cascaded down from the sky when an entire street of houses on the edge of the forest fell asleep, unaware of the horror that had escaped.

"That was, until the first family started screaming."

Tension filled the room as the words were spoken with such magnitude that even the candles' flames seemed to dim, as if attempting to retreat from the savagery once witnessed. As many times as Kelly had heard it, it still caused her heart to race, her breath to quicken in anticipation of something she knew wouldn't come and yet had feared all the same.

However, as she looked over at Megan, who was hearing the legend for the first time, Kelly felt a tinge of sympathy. The girl wasn't just nervous, she was terrified.

"What happened next?"

"The screaming stopped. For a few brief moments, the silence returned. Until the darkness moved into the next house, and the screaming began once more. On and on it went, an unspeakable horror moving from house to house, bringing with it screams of agony and death.

"When the police finally arrived, they found seventeen bodies, torn to shreds, most barely recognizable as human. In the end, though, the most terrifying thing wasn't the bodies left behind. It was what the police couldn't find. What had vanished without a trace. They searched the forest for weeks, trying to find any sign of what had killed the victims, any answer for what had caused the massacre. But they never did. The monster was gone."

Megan leaned in closer, jaw trembling as she spoke. "Did anyone survive?"

Brandon grinned. "Yes. A single victim. An eight-year-old girl who lived in the last house on the street. The police found her hiding under her bed, surrounded by her parents' blood and dismembered bodies, crying and twitching violently, repeating the same word over and over.

"Animal. Animal. Animal."

At that, Megan shuddered with fear, just as the rest of the town had ever since that night, hearing the only description ever given to the monster: the frightened words of a child who spoke a truth no one else would ever understand, for they hadn't seen what she had.

The Animal revealed.

"The legend goes that she didn't speak another word for months, her mind still lost in the horrors that she witnessed. Even when she did begin speaking, she never once spoke of what she saw in that house."

"What was it?" Megan asked, now visibly shaking.

"To this day," Brandon said, his voice growing solemn, "no one knows. Some say it was just a man, dressed in a costume, deranged and homicidal. Others, however, told stories about the monster that haunted the forest. The screams that could be heard there, even before that night. A few old hunters will swear on their life that they saw a werewolf in the woods that night, massive, with black fur and blood dripping from its mouth. But in the end, the only real evidence for what killed all those people is the single terrified word of an eight-year-old girl. *Animal.*"

The anxiety-inducing dread that had once merely been felt now grew until it was all-consuming, as did the silence. For a moment they didn't even dare to blink, wishing more than anything that they had more than candles left to provide light. Because even growing up in this town, hearing the legend over and over again, could never really take away the horror of not knowing what had truly happened. Not knowing what could still be out there, in the forest, ready to devour.

More than the rest, Megan looked as though she might cry. "What happened to the girl?"

Brandon lowered his voice, once again trying to invoke fear. "The story goes that she still lives in that same house where it happened and never comes out. Some say she has gone insane, afraid of a monster that could be lurking outside. Others say she is the werewolf from the legend, and that she locked herself in a dungeon of her own making for fear of what she might do were she ever to be unleashed again."

"This story isn't true, right?" Megan said, no longer trying to hide her terror. "You guys are just messing with me?"

"It's true," Britney said. "Every word. You can still see bloodstains on the carpets of where it happened. The cleaners did what they could, but there was so much, and no one else has dared to live in the houses since. No one except the little girl."

Kelly piped in, feeling sorry for Megan but unable to resist at least mentioning it. "The forest that the Animal came from is the same one that rests behind this house. Legend has it the Animal is still in there, stalking its prey, waiting for its next meal."

"Let's go!" Eric said, suddenly excited as he leapt off the couch, pointing to the back door. "Let's see where it lives!"

"What?" Megan asked, terrified.

"C'mon," Britney said, following Eric to the door, brushing aside her unease. "It's the anniversary of the Animal. Live a little."

Both Brandon and Megan looked to Kelly, to see what she would say, to see if she would follow. Everyone always did that, looked to her to be the example, the leader.

Kelly shrugged. "Why not?"

They all stood on the edge of the porch, too afraid to step closer to what lay beyond the yard, merely fifty feet away.

The forest.

It was massive, stretching out for what seemed like forever, twisting through the entire town, corrupting everything with its endless expanse of dried dirt and dark trees. Looking at it now, at how the trees' dying branches choked out the moonlight, making the forest seem as though it wasn't even there, as if there was nothing alive behind the trees but instead merely shadows of things once living, Kelly couldn't imagine walking into it. Sure, she had gone in before, but not too far, and always during the day, never when it got dark.

Never at night.

Just like the rest of the town, a twenty-five-year-old story kept her from wandering through the trees for fear of the uncaught monster. The waiting beast.

The stalking animal.

"Okay, we've seen the forest," Megan said, quivering. "Can we go back inside now?"

"Don't you want to see inside it?" Britney asked, giggling. "See if the Animal is really out there." She turned to Eric, giving him a subtle grin and winking. "Go check it out."

Her smile made him blush, but he hesitated. "I don't know. I mean, looking at the forest is one thing, but actually going out there... I'm not sure."

"You don't have to go out there," Kelly said, trying to help give Eric a way out, even if she knew it wouldn't matter. Britney was her friend and all, but she had a bad habit of doing things like this.

Pushing guys into doing stupid stuff, just to see if she could.

"Aww, come on, be brave," Britney said, once again giving him that smile of hers.

Eric looked into the woods, and as the darkness within it filled his eyes, he gave a slight shudder. "I don't know, Brit."

"What are you so scared of?" she asked. "The story of the Animal might be real, but that was twenty-five years ago. Whoever it was who killed those people is long gone by now. Besides," she said, adding the last bit to mess with his ego, "Dylan would go out there."

"Dylan's an idiot with no concept of danger," Kelly said. "He would jump in a shark tank covered in chum just for a laugh."

"Or," Britney continued, turning Kelly's point into her own, "he would go into the woods to impress the pretty girl. It's not even a full moon."

Kelly rolled her eyes, but she also knew at this point it wouldn't matter. Nothing could stop it now as Eric took a deep breath and, given no choice, he started toward the woods, his path faintly lit by thin traces of moonlight that escaped from the clouds above.

Step by step he grew closer to the vast expanse of darkness that seemingly lay behind the trees, the darkness that had once held a monster, and as he grew ever closer, his hands trembled.

"You don't have to go out there," Kelly said, loud enough for him to hear across the yard.

The rest of them watched in complete silence, waiting for something to happen. For some creature to reveal itself at any moment and charge at Eric with twisted teeth and broken claws, wailing and snarling as it left the deceased shadows of the forest and attacked those still breathing.

But nothing came.

At least not yet...

Fighting the urge to run, Eric took another step, and his outstretched hand pressed against the rough bark of a hollow tree, long dead, its rotting corpse held up by twisting roots, unwilling to let it fall, to let it rest, instead keeping its carcass standing as a reminder of the death that lay within. As Eric's palm scraped against the bark, he felt the fear it instilled flow across his skin and bury itself within his bones. He was on the edge of the forest now, only a single step from entering its depths and facing whatever lay within.

Suddenly, Kelly saw something move in the forest.

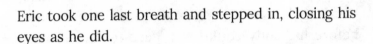

Eric took one last breath and stepped in, closing his eyes as he did.

"Eric, come back," Kelly said cautiously as she searched the forest for the movement that caught her eyes.

As Eric's foot hit the ground, the gravity of the forest faded for a moment, and relief washed over him as he turned around to see his friends watching him from across the yard. Standing within the forest, he held his hands up in victory, the last happy moment he would ever experience, before he heard something: a faint noise coming from the woods, coming from behind him. It almost sounded like...

Growling.

"Get away from that tree!" Kelly screamed as her eyes saw the horror.

Growling echoed throughout the forest as the thing hidden within the trees leapt at Eric, bringing him to the ground in an instant, and before his body could even gasp for air, Britney was forced to watch in shocked terror as the unnatural thing still shrouded in darkness, looming over Eric, began to claw at him. Soon it drew blood from his chest, the shimmering splatters of red contrasting the darkness of the creature, signaling the death it had brought. As the forest grew painted with crimson, the new victim wailed in torment, unable to leave the forest he had entered, forced to die within its cold grasp.

Eric's screams of agony were soon silenced when his body went limp.

It was only then, after its prey was slaughtered, that the creature finally stood up, slowly turning its gaze to them as though it hungered for more blood. Covered by the forest's shroud of darkness, it stepped closer. It walked almost like a man, though hunched down, but its body was distorted and covered in something inhuman. Something grey.

Britney's body froze in terror.

What is that thing?

"Run!" was all she heard as Kelly grabbed her arm and pulled her backwards toward the house, like a desperate shepherd trying to drag its lamb to safety, knowing that safety wouldn't come, for the wolf had already tasted blood.

Yet still, they ran.

The creature followed.

"It's coming," Britney screamed as she saw it run, wild and frenzied, its horrific growling only echoing louder as it grew closer. Her mind began to panic. How could it be real? How could something like that exist? Something so... inhuman.

"Get in!" Kelly screamed as she pulled Britney through the door and shut it behind them mere moments before the creature crashed into it. But while the door might have kept the monster at bay, its bloodthirsty growl still echoed through the cracks, filling the house with the sound of its hunger.

It wanted in. It wanted *them*.

"The car!" Kelly cried as they moved through the house toward the front door. "We have to go now!"

As they ran, however, fear took hold of Britney once more, and she collapsed on the floor, too paralyzed to move, even as her mind begged for an escape, forcing her into a wretched state of distress and terror.

Knowing they couldn't stop, Kelly motioned for Megan to help Britney up as Brandon made it to the front door.

"Ready?" Kelly asked, now beside him, both staring at the wooden door in fear, imagining the creature that lay beyond it, still stained in Eric's blood.

"You stay here," Brandon said, voice shaking. "I'll go first, in case it's still out there. Then I'll back the car up for all of you."

Kelly looked to him, clearly stricken with fear, but still trying to be brave, to do the right thing. She respected him for that. "Are you sure?"

"No," he admitted, choking back a nervous gulp as he ran out the door into the cold night air where no walls could protect him, moving desperately toward the lone car revealed in moonlight.

For a few brief seconds, it looked as though he would make it. Even Britney stopped crying as she watched him run, giving them all a fleeting hope of survival, until he was less than five feet from the safety of the car, and the creature with grey fur revealed itself on the other side, rising from the darkness like a wraith, a symbol of death itself, before leaping over the hood and tackling Brandon to the ground, growling viciously as it cut into his chest. The boy's screams were silenced in mere seconds, but the creature didn't relent, lashing out in a frenzy of grim, bloodied slashes.

As though it was losing control.

The night was dark. Clouds covered the sky like a black veil, blocking out any trace of light from the stars. But as the monster stood hunched over the boy's corpse, the moonlight that escaped the clouds was just bright enough to make out one single aspect of the creature's face.

It wasn't human.

Britney began screaming.

The creature turned its head toward the sound.

Kelly slammed the door as fast as she could, not waiting to see what it did, not waiting to see if it would attack the sound or continue to mutilate its already disfigured prey.

"We're gonna die," Britney cried, and Megan began weeping as she paced the floor, wishing she was already dead.

"No, we're not," Kelly said as she ran frantically around the room, checking the locks of every door and window, before finally sitting on the floor beside Britney, taking her head in her hands, and looking into her eyes.

"Listen, we are going to be okay, but we have to stay calm. We can't call the cops because we don't get reception this close to the forest, and we can't go back outside. So, we have to stay in here and hope that it can't get in."

For a moment, it looked as though she might get through to Britney. But then something crashed into the upstairs floor, echoing throughout the entire house, a sign of what had already entered.

Britney tried to scream, but Kelly covered her mouth. That didn't stop Megan, though, who screamed so loud that the police might have heard it from across town. A scream that caused birds from the forest to scatter into the night.

But far more haunting than the scream were the footsteps echoing from upstairs, each one in quick succession. Whatever was above them, it was running.

"How'd it get in so fast?" Britney asked, terrified.

"I don't know," Kelly said, trying to think. "There's a knife in the kitchen," she said, dragging Britney and motioning for Megan to follow. As they ran, the creature could be heard descending the stairs.

They didn't have much time.

In the center of the kitchen was an island, just tall enough that it shrouded the other side in darkness, even when there was light. Resting atop it was a single knife. There were more in the drawer, but the footsteps from the stairs stopped, and they were out of time. Kelly went for the knife, but as she grabbed it, she caught a brief glimpse of something inhuman moving through the darkness by the kitchen doorway, and she dropped to the floor, bringing Britney and Megan with her. They hid, crouched down behind the island, hoping the creature wouldn't find them.

The image she'd glimpsed burned in her memory.

The creature, it wasn't just inhuman.

It wasn't natural.

Footsteps grew closer.

Britney didn't allow herself to breathe, thinking if she did it would hear her. It would kill her. She didn't want to die. Not like this.

She heard growling. It was coming from behind the island, a monster hidden in the shadows of the house, and it was moving toward them. Her heart started to race. The creature had found her. *No!*

The creature leapt onto the island, and through the darkness, Britney saw an outline. Legs bent, poised to pounce, arms reaching down to the island's granite top, body bent over them, moving unnaturally, almost agile. Face-to-face with the three of them now, it tilted its animalistic head, and for a single moment, it didn't move at all: a predator waiting to pounce, staring at prey who were waiting to be slaughtered.

It lunged at Kelly first, striking her in the head and stabbing something into her stomach. She squealed in sudden pain before moving to bring the knife down in its neck, but it caught her arm and struck her again, knocking her back into the cabinets behind her, the impact cracking them. Then, her body simply fell to the floor below, head bruised, sight fading.

Dizzied, Kelly lay there in agony, clutching her bleeding stomach, as the creature turned its attention to the other girls.

Megan screamed as it stabbed something that looked like a bone into Britney's stomach, and then her throat, killing her in an instant. But death didn't stop the creature's torment, and it kept stabbing her, over and over, until blood covered every inch of her once living skin.

Frozen in horror, Megan looked at the monster, still partially cloaked in the shadows of the house. Grey fur, a beast's head, feral movement. But the way it stabbed her. The cruelty of it. That part seemed almost human.

"Run!" Kelly screamed as she pulled Megan away from the monster, still clutching her side, and grunting in pain as blood streamed from the wound. "She's already dead. We have to run."

Finally, a resolve grew in Megan's eyes, and they took off through the house, Kelly frantically grabbing a flashlight from a drawer as they did. Before they could even think, they were out the door, through the driveway, and onto the road, running so fast they couldn't feel their legs, desperate to get away, adrenaline kicking in as they tried to fulfill their most basic instinct.

Survive.

They had to have run almost a mile, feet dragging against a gravel road, surrounded by the forest on either side, when Megan's body finally gave out and she slowed down, lungs bursting, barely managing to stay upright as she looked behind her, expecting to see safety, nothing but an empty road and a hollow forest.

But the beast was chasing them, less than thirty feet away.

How had it gotten to them so fast?

It ran on two legs, arms flailing wildly as it growled. The sound sent a sudden shiver down Megan's spine as she cried, pleading with anyone who would listen to save her.

A blood-curdling shriek echoed through the air.

Kelly turned in terror to see something on top of Megan, slamming her head into the ground, attempting to crush her skull. Instinctively, Kelly shined her flashlight at it, and for the first time on that dark, horrific night, she saw the beast clearly. It was massive, covered in grey fur that held distorted eyes, a long nose with sharp teeth, and an expressionless face now drenched in blood. As the light hit it, it looked to the moon and howled, standing over its fallen prey.

Then its eyes turned back to Kelly.

In a flash of movement, she ran down the country road as fast as she could, clutching her bleeding side, waving her flashlight in the air. In desperation she searched for anything, anyone at all, all the while wondering how far away the monster was.

Wondering when she would hear it growl.

Then she saw it. Headlights.

She dropped to her knees in the middle of the road, holding up the flashlight, blood streaming down her stomach as well as her head, screaming at the top of her lungs.

"Help me!"

The car stopped beside her, and an elderly man stepped out in shock, seeing the blood as she began to cry. As he approached her, the two of them alone in the light and surrounded by darkness, he asked her a single question. "What did this to you?"

Her voice quivered as tears streamed down her face.

"*Animal.*"

CHAPTER TWO

She hid under the bed.

Closing her eyes, she tried to focus her attention on the footsteps. They were faint, almost nonexistent, and yet they echoed all the same. The thing that hunted her must have been on the other side of the house. But it was moving closer.

She looked to the closet door, about five feet to her right; it was only a thin piece of wood, old and creaking, paint chipping off, and yet it called out to her, begging her to enter within its depths, as if it could protect her from what was coming. A beautiful lie, and yet she believed it all the same.

Suddenly, she could feel her heart pounding inside her chest, sending blood and adrenaline through her shaking body with every second that passed, as her eyes focused on the closet door, and the empty space that lay behind it, a darkness that was reflected in her own panicked eyes. Should she go to it instead? Or would she be safe under the bed, hidden out of sight?

The footsteps got closer.

Emma stayed quiet, deciding to stay under the bed, hidden beneath its cocoon of safety as if it were an old mother owl shrouding its young within its massive wings to hide them from the vultures that circled. The closet was too risky; the footsteps could reach the bedroom door at any moment, and she could be caught. *Never second-guess yourself out of panic*, she thought, remembering the words of her mom. *Just stay calm, and try to focus.*

The bedroom door creaked open.

Emma opened her eyes to see the feet of her hunter, stepping through the door slowly, a predator stalking its prey. She held her breath just like she had been taught, staying in total silence even as her lungs cried out for air, forced to watch the hunter's feet move across the floor, listening to its menacing footsteps slowing approaching the closet door.

In a sudden swift movement, the closet door swung open, slamming into the wall behind it, making a crashing noise as it did. Emma used that brief moment of sound to hide her own as she took another breath, savoring the final seconds spent resting beneath the bed unseen.

It would be over soon. Either she would be found, or the thing that hunted her would pass by, unaware that she lurked only a few inches away from its grasp, and she would escape.

The feet turned from the closest, taking a step closer to her.

Emma wanted to gasp for air as her heart raced once more, but she didn't allow herself to. Had to stay quiet, not give herself away. The hunter was too close. She could hear its breathing now, slow and methodical as it searched for her. *Just a few more seconds*, Emma thought to herself. Only had to stay quiet a few more seconds, and then she could get away, finally escape the hunter's grasp.

But then, like a flash of lightning, the thing bent down, finding her underneath the bed. Emma flinched in shock as she saw the origin of the footsteps, the thing that hunted her. Hazel eyes focusing on her, long brown hair falling to the floor as it bent down to be at eye level, and a warm grin spread across its mouth as it prepared to speak.

"Gotcha."

Emma giggled as Riley pulled her from under the bed and hoisted her in the air, laughing as she did.

"You did so good," Riley said, eyes beaming with pride as she held her daughter in her arms. "I almost didn't find you. Locking the door across the hall so I'd check it first was so clever!"

"How long did I make it?" Emma asked, still giggling.

"Almost fifteen minutes."

"That's all?" Emma asked. Disappointment rung in her voice.

"Trust me, sweetie," Riley said, placing her daughter down on the bed and kneeling down in front of her, "it always feels longer when you're the one hiding. But fifteen minutes is a long time. You did really good."

Emma grinned, unable to contain her happiness at her mother's praise. "How'd you know I was under the bed?"

Riley cracked a smile, leaning over and whispering the secret into Emma's ear.

"I used to hide under the bed too when I was your age."

Emma giggled again, and they shared a brief moment as Riley reached over and adjusted her hair, holding back the tears as she looked at her daughter, so young and sweet, so much like her father. Riley leaned over and hugged her tight, wishing she could never let go, never let her daughter leave her arms. Wishing she could keep her safe forever, protect her from the horrors that lurked in the shadows of this broken town.

But eventually, she did let go.

"Get washed up, breakfast is in ten minutes. And since you hid for so long"—she saw her daughter's excitement grow—"we'll have waffles."

"Yay!"

Emma rushed off the bed and down the hall, leaving Riley alone with the memories of this room, memories that seemed to crawl toward her even now, horrific flashes of pain mixed with screams of agony.

Drawn to the image, Riley walked over to the dresser and picked up a picture resting on top of it. She sighed in pain as she looked at her parents, smiles on their faces and her in their arms. She remembered being upset that day, not wanting to sit still long enough for the photo to be taken. She longed to go back to that moment, let them know how much she loved them. How much she missed them. How every moment that passed, she wished she could make Emma feel as safe and protected as they had made her feel. A tear fell from her face as she remembered them hiding her under the bed, telling her not to come out no matter what.

The wounds from that night might have healed, but the scar tissue was still there. Haunting her in the back of her mind every day, the thought that the horror might have survived, that one day the screams of the innocent would echo in the night sky once more, calling out to the moon to save them from the beast hungry for blood.

The horrifying thought that one day, the Animal would return.

Her fingers ran over the photograph, over the faces of those she'd lost, as she took one last look before placing the picture back on the dresser and starting out the door, ready to leave this room and its memories behind.

But before she could make it, her phone rang. "Hello?"

The voice on the other end was familiar but shaky, almost nervous. "Riley?"

"Hey, Hank, what's up?"

"Riley," he said again, the tone in his voice making her anxious. It took a lot to shake the old man. "Something happened last night, and I'm on the scene right now. I... I wanted you to hear it from me first."

Suddenly she couldn't breathe as a lifetime of fear came back in an instant.

As Emma walked back into the room, Riley was slipping a sliver knife into her boot and holstering a small pistol behind her back, hidden by her black leather jacket.

"Hey, sweetie," Riley said, trying to hide the dread in her voice, trying to make sure Emma still felt safe. "Sorry, but we're going to have to wait on breakfast for now."

"Where are we going?"

Riley forced a smile, trying not to think of what could be waiting for her. What could have returned.

"We're going to go see Uncle Hank."

Every deputy in the town had to be there, dozens of them wandering around the house like hungry scavengers, shifting through the broken bones and bloodied flesh left behind, forced to search through remains of a massacre they hadn't caused and yet were bound to all the same.

But Riley's focus was not on the living souls surrounding it, or the ghost left behind, but the house itself as she looked on from a distance. It was massive, with faded white paint and a roof in tatters, beaten from the wind. But more haunting was the large backyard that fed directly into the forest, just like her own house. Just like the town itself.

For a moment, it was the forest that held her gaze, the dark shadows within its trees, the lifeless silence that echoed from within, seeming to grab hold of her even now.

She felt a slight sense of comfort as Hank walked up to her, gun on his hip, greying hair on his head, sheriff star on his chest.

"Uncle Hank!" Emma said, hugging him, as Riley caught the fleeting glimpse of a grin on his face. He tried to hide it, but he liked the nickname.

"Hello, Emma. You've gotten so big." His eyes then moved up to Riley, his expression changing, saying without words how scared he was. How serious this must be.

Gently, he patted Emma on the head. "I've got to talk to your mother for a little while. I need you to stay here and keep watch for me, alright?"

"Okay," Emma said, grinning, as Hank motioned for a deputy to keep watch on her.

Riley leaned down and whispered into her daughter's ear, just in case this was the real thing. Just in case she never got the chance again. "I love you."

With that, she walked with Hank toward the forest.

As they approached it, her heart felt like it could burst. The moment was getting close: the moment when she would see the body and her fears would be confirmed. What if it was as bad as she remembered? What if the true monster really had come back?

As they walked, Hank explained everything, from the power that appeared to have been cut to the number of victims left behind, before finally he pointed across the backyard to a teenage girl wrapped in an ambulance blanket, still quivering. The girl's forehead was bruised, her blond hair stained red, and it looked like she was clutching her side. Beside her was a boy that looked about her age, a little taller, with black hair, who was holding on to the girl, as if to protect her.

"The girl's name is Kelly. Her brother, Everett, is the one holding her. She's eighteen, going to graduate in a few months." Hank sighed. "She's the only one who survived."

Riley stared at the girl, watching her quiver, still in fear or shock from whatever had happened. Sympathy stabbed at Riley's heart, and she wished she could tell the girl that it would be okay, that the bloodshed from the legends wasn't real. But that would be a lie.

"She gave a description of what she saw," Hank continued, pausing as he spoke, not wanting to say it, but having no choice. "She said it had dark grey fur, and that it was massive. She said..." Another pause, dread choking his voice. "She said that it looked like an animal."

Riley hesitated. "She spoke?"

"Yeah," he said, sensing her hidden implication. "She spoke."

Soon, the girl noticed Riley staring, and they held each other's gaze for a moment, survivors seeing the same scars in each other's eyes, even as Riley thought over the new information. The girl had spoken. Described the monster. It seemed impossible. To see the Animal and be able to describe how it felt, what it was. Even now, Riley could barely speak of it, almost unable to even say its name, reveal its true nature.

Animal.

They reached the woods, and Hank pointed to something within the trees, hidden by the police tarp that rested on it.

Riley walked over to it, hands shaking as she did. This was it. She would see the body, the aftermath left behind. Then she wouldn't be able to deny it, wouldn't be able to run from the truth. All her fears, her lifetime of terror, would be confirmed. She swallowed the lump in her throat, preparing herself for what she was about to see, as she lifted up the tarp and saw the corpse.

It was a boy, looked around seventeen. His chest was filled with holes, torn open, his entire body drenched in its own blood. Lifeless eyes stared up to the sky, forever staring at the monster that was no longer there.

It was all wrong.

The stab wounds were too close together, and the entry wounds looked too clean. Whatever had done this had used something sharp, perhaps a knife of some kind. It was the type of bloodied corpse that should have shaken her to the bone, but it didn't even send a chill down her spine.

"Do they all look like this?"

Hank motioned his head for her to follow.

They looked at the body inside the house next. It was the same. A corpse littered with stab wounds, bloodied flesh torn open, but it still didn't feel right. Neither did the body by the car.

Finally, they began walking down the road, toward the final corpse left behind.

"Do you really think this is the Animal?" Riley asked, doubt in her voice. "The real Animal?"

"I don't know," Hank said as the forest on either side of them seemed to reach out, attempting to drag them back into its dark depths. "The crime scene, the bodies, they don't look like what I was expecting. But I don't know if that is reality speaking or if I'm just too afraid to admit that something like what happened twenty-five years ago could happen again. Too afraid that the Animal never really left but just went into hiding."

In truth, it was the same notion that worried Riley. Was she doubting the Animal's return because she truly believed it, or because she was too afraid of what would happen if it had returned? If the thing that haunted every dream she'd ever had, the nightmarish memories she had tried so hard to forget, was back?

"This one is worse than the others," Hank said as they approached the body. "The girl was running alongside Kelly when it got her. Kelly said she saw the animal slamming the girl's head into the pavement, which matches the wounds. Apparently, it was attempting to crack her skull."

This was it, Riley thought. No more stab wounds, no more precise cuts, but pure, brutal violence, the attempt to break a skull in two. If it was really the Animal, this would prove it.

She knelt down, lifting up the police tarp and looking at the girl's body below it. Her head was covered completely in horrific purple bruises, to the point of no longer resembling skin. Blood filled her mouth and stained her face, her left cheekbone looked broken, even caved in, and the skin around her eye was almost entirely scraped off, revealing the pale bone below it, the girl's face trapped forever in an expression of pure terror.

Riley breathed a sigh of relief. It was nothing.

She had seen a crushed skull before. A real crushed skull. She had seen it fall down not two feet from her face, a mound of broken bones and distorted flesh that no longer looked human. Something that couldn't have an expression of fear because there was nothing left. No body, no corpse, only *remains*.

Somewhat calmed, she stood up, noticing how Hank was staring at her.

"You don't think it's the Animal, do you?"

She didn't answer, instead staring into the forest lurking on the edge of the road, its withered branches cracking against the wind, brittle dying leaves falling slowly to the ground.

Hank sighed and started to walk away. "One last thing," he called back. "The girl, she says it growled."

Riley acknowledged that with a subtle nod but continued staring into the forest, lost in thought. It was a horrific crime scene. Multiple bodies, mutilated, a terrified girl still shaking, telling stories of a monster, of the animal, that had done it. This should have been enough to make anyone run away in fear, but she didn't. Because she had seen worse.

Much worse.

Whoever had done this, whether it looked like a monster or not, it could be a man. There could be a face hiding behind the mask, behind the creature the girl described. This was violent, terrifying, cruel, but it was still human.

The real Animal, the one she had witnessed for mere moments twenty-five years ago, a few seconds forever ingrained into her mind, into her nightmares—it wasn't human. There couldn't have been a man inside that thing, that monster.

This wasn't it, she kept telling herself, hoping it would eventually calm her down. That eventually the dread she felt would go away. But it wouldn't. No matter what this new thing was, it was bringing back scars from her past, and memories she had tried to bury were resurfacing.

She shuddered as she thought of the first moments after the gunfire. The single thought that had coursed through her, causing a lifetime of fear and terror.

Animal.

CHAPTER THREE

The deer was about twenty feet away, illuminated by the morning sun, peacefully grazing on grass, surrounded by the beauty of the forest.

Clyde was crouched down, hidden next to a tree, sitting in complete silence. He'd spotted it through the woods a few hundred feet back and wanted a closer look. A content smile slowly crept onto his face as he watched the deer, being careful not to alert it to his presence, not wanting to scare it away.

It was a doe, no horns to be seen. Remnants of its faded white spots from youth were still barely visible, contrasting with its bright brown coat and the solid white hair beneath its tail.

It was rare, quiet moments of nature like this that Clyde appreciated. No running animals, afraid of a predator, no violent winds or strong rains to disturb the peace. Nothing to signal distress or fear. Just a young doe, grazing in a forest, at peace.

The doe saw him.

Its eyes stared in sudden shock, and its ears twitched, pointed toward Clyde. He remained perfectly still, smiling as he waited to see what it would do. At first it looked confused, as if trying to figure out what had snuck up on it, what had gotten so close. Its ears twisted back and forth, trying desperately to find a sound, but there was none.

Finally, it turned and ran away, but slowly and gracefully, merely leaving the scene because it was startled and didn't know what else to do.

Clyde remained next to the tree for a few more moments, still taking in the quiet calm of the forest.

The melodic singing of a blackbird echoed through the trees as Clyde continued walking, running his hand alongside the fence that separated his land from the rest of the forest. Twelve feet tall, silver steel bars interlocking with one another in perfect rhythm, the game fence stood high above him.

As his hand felt the steel, Clyde felt sympathy for the animals trapped inside. It was a massive game ranch, taking up almost a fourth of the entire forest, stretching out for miles on end. The animals inside were no longer hunted, and most days they enjoyed the same peace that was present outside the fence. But still, it wasn't their home. It might have been big, might have had everything the real forest had, but it wasn't where they belonged, wasn't where they should be.

It was still just a cage.

A deformation in the dirt caused Clyde to stop walking, and he bent down to investigate it, running his fingers over the mark left behind.

Tracks.

They looked canine. At first glance, he thought coyote, but the tracks were far too large, too deep into the dirt. He sighed as he thought of the reason he couldn't open the fence and let the animals join the rest of the forest. The predators that would escape with them.

Wolves.

Large, vicious timber wolves, most with dark grey fur that blended in with the shadows the trees created. They had roamed the forest, trapped inside the fence for as long as Clyde could remember, how they had gotten there a complete mystery. All that was known for sure was that they hunted the prey trapped inside with them, and if he opened the

fence, he would unleash them on the whole forest, allowing its dirt to run red with the blood of their slaughtered prey.

So instead, he merely sighed, feeling the cool ground as his fingers traced over the tracks, not yet filled by dirt or distorted by the wind. The tracks were fresh, which meant he'd better move.

For the wolves were close.

Later that day, Clyde walked up the creaky wooden steps to the top of his porch and stepped inside. It was a log cabin. Small, but enough room, hidden within the trees in a small open area, almost a mile from the ranch's entrance. The TV inside was still on from when he'd left that morning, the reporter's voice loud and distracting. He muted it and took off his camouflage jacket, still thinking about the deer he had watched and the tracks he had found. It had been a while since he'd found tracks, especially ones so close to a deer.

At least, a deer that was still alive.

Clyde sat down in a chair, resting his head in his hands, growing anxious, but unsure of why. It was just a feeling, the same one he always got when he was inside the cabin, when he was safe. The feeling of discomfort, of restlessness, of waiting for something bad to happen but having no idea what, or when it would strike.

It was then that his eyes caught something on the news. A drawing of something, some creature. Behind the reporter holding the drawing he could see the outside of a house, crawling with police, sullen faces full of dread. Confused, he turned up the sound.

"This is a sketch of the creature, as described by the sole survivor of the night, who claims to have seen the animal which took the lives of four of her classmates."

Clyde leaned closer to the TV, unsure of what to make of it. The sketched drawing was clearly exaggerated, but at its core, with the grey fur and sharp teeth, it almost resembled a wolf.

Clyde's mind returned to the tracks he had found by the fence. Timber wolves. Nervously, he considered the possibility for a moment before dismissing it. He had walked the length of the fence this morning and there had been no holes, no way of escape.

No, he decided. Even if they could have escaped, there would have been something left at the crime scene, something for the cops to find. Wolves were hunters, exceptional at stealth, even better at killing, but they would have left a sign that they were there. They were still animals, and all animals left tracks.

"The sheriff declined to comment on whether this is being treated as an independent case or

if the police believe it is somehow connected to the infamous massacre that took place twenty-five years ago."

Twenty-five years ago? Clyde thought to himself in shock. *This happened before?*

"However, the similarities are unsettling," the reporter said before holding up another sketched animal, this one's fur much darker, more black than grey, and teeth dripping with blood. "The similarities between the two sketches, as well as the trail of bodies left behind, have many townspeople worried that, after all these years, the Animal may have returned."

A chill crept down Clyde's spine as he looked at the drawing of the old monster. The Animal. It couldn't have been one of the wolves, it wasn't possible. But if it wasn't a wolf...

Then what was it?

Clyde twitched violently, awoken by nightmares of an unseen horror, always stalking, always hunting. Rising up in the bed, he felt anxious again but didn't know why. He was in his bedroom, the doors were locked, and nothing could get in. He was completely safe; nothing was hunting him.

So why did that feel so wrong?

Getting out of bed, he rubbed his hands across

his face, his mind still going back to the tracks he had found, and the animal he had seen on TV. It was then, with the thought of that horrendous sketch, that he made up his mind: he'd check the fence again tomorrow. It was impossible, it couldn't have been the wolves, but he had to check again to be sure. Make sure they hadn't escaped.

As he stood, he looked out his window and into the forest, barely fifty feet from where he stood. Sometimes it calmed him to see the shadows hiding behind the trees, the vast expanse of a forest hidden from view.

But tonight was different. Tonight, it caused his heart to race, and his breathing to stop, as he saw something else hiding within the trees. A massive figure, standing perfectly still, features hidden by the darkness.

Was that a wolf?

In a panic, he reached for a flashlight, shining it out the window, attempting to make sense of what was out there. But the light wasn't bright enough, the animal's black features still hidden, revealing no trace of its true form.

But its eyes...

They glowed in the light, two small specks of yellow in a vast sea of darkness, and they were staring right at him.

Clyde dropped the flashlight as the realization hit him. The eyes watching him, they were too

high off the ground, and spaced too far apart. Whatever that creature was, it had to be massive, twice the size of a normal wolf.

Dread crept into his bones as he picked the flashlight back up, once again shining it at the woods, afraid the yellow eyes would appear closer, but as the light hit the forest, he saw that the animal was gone, vanished in the night. Clyde wanted to feel relief, but he couldn't. It might have gone back into the forest, might have disappeared from his view, but that didn't change anything.

The eyes, they'd belonged to an animal.

Something was out there.

CHAPTER FOUR

After what felt like an eternity, the police finally left the house, leaving Kelly inside, still in her brother's arms.

"It's okay," Rhett whispered as he wiped the tears from her face.

She winced, no longer shaking badly but still a little unsettled. Even so many hours later, the screaming faces of her friends were still fresh on her mind, and no matter how much she tried to ignore it, to focus on the present, she couldn't. The horrific image of the beast was burned into her thoughts, forever present in the reflections hidden within her eyes.

"There was just so much blood. And it happened so fast. I don't know, it just..." She paused, looking over the blood once more. "It just doesn't feel real. Feels like a dream, like it happened to someone else."

"I know." Rhett nodded as he too looked over the bloodshed, the carnage left behind as a reminder. Bloodied outlines where corpses had once lain, their bodies taken by the cops and yet their wailing ghosts still remaining. "I could see it in the cops' eyes too. They felt the same way, that this whole thing wasn't real, that the Animal couldn't have returned."

"They kept staring at me," Kelly said. "The cops. They just kept staring, but they weren't actually looking at me. It was like... like they were trying to see the monster through me."

"That's what's wrong with this town," Rhett said as he looked around at the pictures framed on the wall, a hint of malice growing in his voice. "No one cares about anything other than the legend. Unless you're the Animal, unless you are the predator everyone is afraid of, they just look right past you, like you're nothing. Like you don't even exist."

After a moment of silence, he continued, looking over the wounds on her head with concern on his face. "But I care. I don't know what I'd do if you got hurt, so please be careful."

She sighed as she punched his shoulder, a small touch of life entering her voice once more as for a moment she let go of the pain and became just another sister who teased her brother. "Look at you, still trying to protect me."

He smiled. "Always."

"So," she asked, hesitating as she spoke, afraid that she already knew the answer. "Were you able to get ahold of Mom and Dad?"

Rhett sighed, clearly not wanting to tell her the truth and hurt her further.

Kelly grimaced, wiping away a tear. "They didn't even pick up their phones, did they?"

"I'm sorry," he said. "Maybe they–"

"Don't," she interrupted. "It's okay. We've seen them three times in the last year. I don't know why I thought almost dying would make them want to see me."

Rhett didn't say anything at first, instead placing a hand on her shoulder gently. When he finally did speak, his words shocked her. "Screw them. It's just me and you, always has been. Together to the end."

Kelly smiled. "Together to the end."

They remained quiet for another moment as they looked at the broken furniture and shattered glass, a home destroyed, a haunting stain of bloodshed never to be forgotten, merely covered up, buried deep within a dark ocean of regret and pain. Eventually, Rhett broke the silence, asking the question she had known was coming.

"What did it look like?"

Noon came fast, as did the school's lunch break.

Kelly walked down the halls, through the lockers, trying to avoid the faces of the kids who turned to watch her, being anything but subtle about it. She didn't blame them. The Animal was a legend, a very real ghost story that the town was obsessed with. As she walked, she saw the insides of several lockers hiding little sketched images of a wolf's face, the original drawing of the creature that had become the symbol of this town's legacy. With this new attack, some clearly thought the story was repeating itself, and this time, they wanted to see the aftermath for themselves, wanted to see the victim left breathing in the monster's trail of slaughter, hoping to see the hollowed eyes of fear left behind.

Kelly just sighed as they all stared right at her, desperately wanting to ask questions but being far too afraid. As if she were too broken to even be spoken to. As if the slightest sound would stop her heart. And as much as she wanted to, she couldn't blame them. In their shoes, she probably would have done the same thing.

After all, everyone in town was obsessed with the legends.

That included her.

As she stepped into the next hallway, less packed than the last, she saw a familiar face leaning back on the lockers, waiting for her.

"What kind of psychopath," Dylan said, rising up from the lockers to greet her, his voice light, almost joking, "comes to school after something like that?"

"What was I supposed to do?" she said, not liking the joke. "Stay at the house where it happened?"

"I guess not," Dylan said, joining her as she walked toward the door, toward freedom from this zoo where she had become the main attraction, even as a creepy smile grew across Dylan's face. "I have to say, you're not playing this victim part very well. You're too stoic."

She rolled her eyes. "Shouldn't you be annoying Gabriella?"

"Wish I could, but she's busy over at the gym. Besides, I'm serious. Where's the crying, the screaming? The *Oh no, what if it's still out there?*" he said in a shrill dramatic tone, holding up his hands like a frightened child. "I mean, what's the point of getting attacked if you don't play it up?"

"What's wrong with you?"

"So," he added, ignoring her question and leaning in closer to whisper in her ear. "How scary was it? Did the Animal look as terrifying as the legends describe?"

She started to get upset, him talking about this crap so soon after it had happened, in the middle of the school no less, with her still clearly bothered by it. But then again, there had always been something off in Dylan's head. As long as she'd known him, he'd never so much as jumped or even been startled. It was like something in his head kept him from understanding danger, and therefore he couldn't understand it when other people were afraid. Couldn't empathize.

Honestly, had he been there last night instead of Eric, he would have walked into the woods just because they were there and probably would have laughed when the monster tackled him.

So instead, she held her tongue. "Not now, Dylan, okay?"

"You're the boss." He grinned as he pushed open the door for her, and they both stepped out of the school.

Outside, she took in the fresh air. The fact that the kids inside could no longer stare at her calmed her nerves somewhat as she walked toward the usual spot.

Right behind the school was an additional lunch area, about a dozen tables spread out over the grass. It was only meant to be used for school-specific activities, so no one was ever around, but technically there was no rule against eating lunch there, and right now Kelly didn't feel like staying inside and having every single pair of eyes watch her every movement.

As they walked, Rhett joined them, asking Kelly if she was okay before Dylan started bombarding him with questions. Apparently he thought that if Kelly wasn't up to talking about it, Rhett might be.

"What's up!" Dylan finally shouted as they approached the lunch table, hidden from the sun below the shade of a tree, the massive forest in view behind it, always present, always haunting.

"Hey," Luke said, already sitting on the table. It always amazed her that he and Dylan were such good friends. Dylan was outspoken, loud, bold, while Luke was reserved. Not shy by any means, but he held back more, like he was constantly afraid of being judged for his every move. Kelly guessed that was what happened when your father was the sheriff.

At the moment, he was motioning his head to the left, warning them about who was lying down on the table beside him, a kid wearing a dark brown jacket and writing something down in that small notebook he was always carrying.

"Crap," Rhett whispered under his breath, seeing Oliver. "It's the conspiracist."

Kelly shot Rhett a glare. "Would it kill you to be nice to him at least once?"

"Probably."

As they reached the table, Oliver sat up and offered a sympathetic smile to Kelly. To her surprise, he didn't immediately ask about what had happened, instead asking how she was doing.

She grinned, then sighed. "Already getting tired of people asking me that."

"My dad didn't grill you too hard, did he?" Luke asked. "He can be kind of mean when he's in cop mode, which is pretty much always."

"No," Kelly said, shaking her head. "He was actually really kind."

"Hmm," Luke grunted, more to himself than any of them. "That's a first."

"So!" Dylan exclaimed, sitting down beside Luke and resting his elbow on Luke's shoulder, if only to annoy him. "Based on the looks we were getting in the hall, I'd say our Kelly is now a local celebrity." He held a hand out, emphasizing the words as he spoke. "The girl who survived."

Rhett looked ready to pummel him. "You just don't know when to shut up, do you?"

Dylan noticed Rhett's body language and laughed it off. "Please, don't be so dramatic. I'm just messing with you. Besides, it's not like everyone in the entire town isn't saying the same thing. I heard three separate people talking about it on the walk to school this morning."

"Really?" Kelly asked.

"Sure," Dylan said, having to lower his elbow back down as Luke moved further away. "Whole town is already wondering if the reports are true. If the Animal is really back."

Wow, Kelly thought to herself. After it had happened, she'd expected the looks she had gotten at school, but for the whole town to be talking about it already, only hours after it had happened—that shocked her.

"I even heard reports that the fabled recluse showed up at the crime scene," Dylan continued. "Is that true?"

Kelly nodded. "Yeah, she was there. She actually looked at me for a few seconds, like she was wondering what I had seen." As Kelly spoke, they all leaned forward with interest. The Animal was the legend, but the girl was the survivor, the victim on that fateful night, and everyone in town was fascinated with her. Everyone except Luke, who ground his teeth and leaned back, ignoring the conversation. Kelly had never understood why he hated her so much, given he'd never even met her.

"What did she look like?" Dylan asked. "Was she all frail and scary looking?"

"No," Kelly said, thinking back over the stories told of her. They all made Riley out to be some kind of reclusive hermit, a withered shadow of something once living, too terrified to go outside into the light. But when she'd seen her eyes, Kelly had seen something else. "She wasn't like that at all. She seemed calm, tough, actually kind of pretty."

A creepy smile spread over Dylan's face. "Really?"

Kelly gave him a disgusted look, and it shut him up, even if just for a moment. "I don't know. She just wasn't what I was expecting."

For another few minutes, they talked about random stuff; all the while, Kelly watched the expression on Oliver's face. It was so obvious that he wanted to ask about what exactly had happened, pry out any information he could about the attack, and the creature responsible. It was practically eating him up inside, yet he held his tongue, trying to be polite, not wanting to upset her.

She almost felt sorry for him. To spend so much time, so much of his life investigating the legend of the Animal, and then be this close to new information but unable to ask about it. She even noticed his fingers start to twitch with anxiousness.

"Oh, for the love of—" She sighed. "Just ask me, Oliver."

Not giving Rhett time to object, Oliver asked his question. "What happened?"

She told him the story. How the Animal had attacked, how it had killed four of their friends, how it had struck her face, stabbed her, and shoved her into the cabinets. She even showed them the bandages still on her stomach, covering wounds still fresh, still bleeding. Her voice cracked as she reached the end of the tale, telling them about how she had seen it trying to break Megan's face, and how she'd collapsed when the car had arrived.

After she was done, no one dared say a word for almost a minute, either out of fear or sympathy. But then, as expected, Oliver was the first to break the silence.

"You said it stabbed you," he said, writing something in his notebook. "With what?"

"I don't know. It almost looked like a bone, but sharper."

"What did the creature look like?" Oliver asked. "Like, specifically, did you notice any details, like seams of a costume or anything like that? Did it look old?"

"It was dark." Kelly shook her head. "It was hard to see."

"What about its face?" Oliver asked, pushing it. "Did the face itself move, or was it stuck in one expression, like a mask?"

"I don't know. It was dark."

Oliver started to ask something else, but then Rhett glared at him. "Dude, back off."

"Sorry," Oliver said, holding up his hands as an almost mocking apology to Rhett before looking to

Kelly and offering a more sincere one. "Really, I'm sorry."

Kelly nodded that it was okay. She couldn't blame him for asking. She didn't know why he was so obsessed with the legend, especially since he hadn't even grown up here, but at the same time she knew how fascinating legends could be, how they could grab hold of your very being and pull you down into their terrifying depths.

As Dylan and Luke started arm wrestling like a couple of idiots, Oliver looked back to Rhett. "What about you?"

"What about me?"

"What did you see last night?" Oliver questioned, voice surprisingly sincere, and yet the look in his eyes told Kelly that he already knew Rhett wasn't there. He just wanted to make him admit it himself. This was what Oliver did best, question people, make them upset and more likely to slip up. It was also why he wasn't exactly beloved in this town.

"I wasn't there," Rhett finally answered.

"What?" Oliver asked, faking confusion. "Your twin sister throws a party and you weren't there. Why?"

Rhett grimaced, trying not to let Oliver get to him. "I was running late, okay?"

"Why? Where were you?"

Rhett breathed deeply, muscles tightening, flashes of anger spreading across his eyes. "Look,

I feel like crap that I wasn't there. I don't need you reminding me, okay?"

"Okay," Oliver said, writing something in his notebook. Kelly closed her eyes for a moment, knowing what was about to happen.

"What'd you just write?" Rhett demanded, moving toward Oliver, his demeanor clearly threatening.

"Nothing."

Rhett grabbed the notebook in a burst of anger, a sudden look of confusion hitting his face as he looked at the pages, flipping through them in disbelief. Eventually, he held it up, showing it to them, revealing what had been marked within. Oliver had told the truth. There wasn't a single thing written in the entire notebook.

Sighing, Rhett threw the book back at Oliver, muttering under his breath. "Crazy freak."

Oliver, however, merely shrugged and moved on to his next interrogation, not missing a beat. "What about you, Dylan?" Oliver asked, lying back down on the table, looking up into the clear sky. "Why'd you miss the party?"

"What about you?" Luke snapped, also getting irritated by Oliver's questioning, which Kelly figured was because it reminded him too much of his father. "Why didn't you go to the party last night?"

Kelly sighed. Oliver hadn't come because she hadn't invited him, and like a clueless idiot,

Luke had to bring that up right then. But, to her surprise, Oliver laughed it off.

"Guess I just got lucky."

The bell rang, and it was time to go back. Time to feel the eyes watching her as she walked into the school. Just another carnival attraction, a lion burned by fire, that everyone wanted to see but was too afraid to actually speak to.

"One last thing," Oliver said, giving another one of his sympathetic smiles and speaking directly to Kelly. "You know to be careful, right? Whoever this new creature is, he's not going to like that you made it out."

Rhett raised an eyebrow. "You're saying you think that it will come after her again?"

Kelly's hands visibly began shaking, and Rhett held her close as Oliver offered his response.

"I would be extremely surprised if it didn't."

CHAPTER FIVE

Emma ran as fast as she could, trying to escape her mother.

Riley smiled as she watched Emma duck and roll underneath the table, increasing her lead by five more feet. Barely eight years old and the girl had almost done a perfect combat roll. Her father would be so proud.

Riley placed a hand on the table's surface and used it to anchor her weight as she picked her feet up and slid over it, gaining a few feet back in her pursuit. But it didn't help her for long, because before she could reach the kitchen door, Emma was already through it, locking it behind her.

CHAD NICHOLAS

Leaning her head against the door and sighing, Riley tried to think. Emma had gone through the kitchen door instead of going outside, which meant she must be planning to escape based on location, rather than pure speed, and there were only two places in the house that Riley wouldn't be able to get into if Emma was already there, not even with a key.

The thought of it made Riley laugh. The girl was smart, she'd give her that. Smiling for a moment longer, she pitied the friends that Emma played tag with at school. But then, with a burst of speed, Riley was through the other door and heading up the stairs.

At the top, she looked both ways. Both directions led down hallways, which in turn twisted and led to more. So many rooms and so much space, she had never known what to do with it. Apparently, her parents had planned on having a big family one day, but in the end all they had gotten was her.

Riley forced the thought from her mind and concentrated. At the very end of the hallway to the right, there was a safe room, hidden behind the last wall, fortified by reinforced wood. Once entered, it could only be reopened from the inside, and it had an emergency exit that led to the basement.

To her left... well, at this point it didn't matter. Emma would have had enough of a lead to get

76

to either side in time. But then, just as the very thought crossed her mind, she saw Emma step into view from the left hallway and stop in sudden shock.

Riley sighed. Emma had doubled back, questioned her hiding spot. Why did kids always do that? Leave their perfectly safe hiding spot out of fear, only to get caught in the process.

For a moment they looked at each other, each deciding their own next move, before Riley chased, and Emma ran.

Riley gained about seven feet by the time she reached the turn. By the time she was halfway through the next hallway, she had gained another three. Only five more to go, but the end was close. Emma only had fifteen more feet to go before she reached the door.

As she ran, Emma's footsteps echoed on the floor, pressing down firmly on the wood and activating the hidden switch. In a mere second, a hidden tripwire rose from the floor and would have caught Riley's legs had she not expected it.

Only a few feet separated them now as Emma reached the end, and Riley knew that it would be close. Had it been any normal door, Emma wouldn't have enough time to get through it and shut the door behind her. But it wasn't normal, and Emma knew it.

She opened the door in an instant and slid her small body between the frame and the now cracked-open door, held by a thick chain, bolted to the wall. Riley had designed the door herself. The chain held it open just enough for Emma to barely fit through but closed enough that no one else would be able to get more than an arm through at most.

Riley slammed into the door and pushed her arm through the open crack as far as she could, but she couldn't reach far enough to grab Emma.

Defeated, she pulled her arm back and waited for her daughter to open the door. A few seconds later she did, and Riley lifted her up in her arms. "Good job!"

"But I doubled back," Emma said, her voice almost sad, afraid her mom would be disappointed.

"Yes, you did," Riley said. "But you still got away, and you used your size as an advantage to roll under the table and get through the door. I'm so proud of you."

"Really?"

"Really," Riley affirmed, leaning her head down to touch noses with her daughter before making a strange face so that Emma would laugh. Even if she had her own reasons for teaching her daughter how to survive, she still wanted to make it fun for her, preferring to see her laughing rather than afraid.

"Now," she said, setting her back down, "go get ready for school."

Later that day, Riley paced the floor, trying not to think about what had happened, what she had seen the day before. The new bodies, the new killings. But most of all, she tried not to consider the possibility that it was the same animal as before. That the same predator had come back, that it had survived.

Grunting in frustration, she went to a closet and pulled out an old cardboard box before dumping the contents over her living room table. Old photographs, sketched renderings of the creature, and any shred of evidence that had ever been recovered.

She began arranging everything according to what house it had been found in, starting with the photographs of the scene. She winced as she looked at them. Bloody piles of broken flesh that, had she not known, she wouldn't have recognized as human. A tear fell down onto the photographs of her house.

Even her own father was unrecognizable.

Taking a deep breath, she continued. The houses within the photographs were filled with blood, but within them, a few bullet holes could be seen cratered into the walls. Some of them had tried to kill it.

A few footprints revealed themselves in the bloodied carpet, but every one had been traced back to a victim whose body remained in the house, as had all of the blood: a haunting reminder of those who couldn't escape, whose screams had been silenced within the confines of their own homes, never to see the light of day again.

No footprints, no blood, no DNA evidence. No sign whatsoever that anything had ever been in the house, other than the corpses, the bullet holes, and a few broken walls into which some of the victims' bodies had presumably been shoved.

Riley sighed as she thought about the new crime scene. The remnants of a footprint had been found in the mud where the first boy had been killed. It was too distorted to use for a match, but it was there all the same, a sign of the monster that had attacked.

The girl, Kelly, had tried to fight back but had been shoved into the cabinets and stabbed through the stomach. Yet she had survived, escaping with her life, with breath still in her lungs.

Next, Riley observed the two different sketched descriptions. The first, the one meant to describe what she had seen, was nothing more than a shadow of the monster it was supposed to represent, a mere image that could never capture the terror she had felt at the first sight of the Animal, the first time she'd felt its presence.

The looming shadow of death itself.

The second image, however, was nothing more than a hollow, reskinned version of the first, similar to the point of being a blatant copy, and yet the small details were still wrong. The fur wasn't quite black enough, the teeth weren't quite bloodied enough, and, as strange as it felt for her to even think, the face was too mean. Almost like the cruel expression was forced, meant to scare, a cheap illusion to frighten its prey. What she had seen all those years ago hadn't looked mean, hadn't looked cruel. Its expression was far worse. Wasn't manufactured, wasn't purposely terrifying, it just was.

What stuck in her head the most about this new case was the last thing Hank had said to her. That the girl had heard it growl. Riley had relived that night over and over in her head for twenty-five years, every horrifying moment etched into her mind in perfect detail, a scar that would never heal. She remembered gunfire, bones cracking, flesh ripping, and most of all, she remembered the cries of agony.

So much screaming...

But the one thing she had never heard was growling.

It was a detail no one else could have known, but she was sure of it. The Animal hadn't growled, howled, or made any noise whatsoever. She hadn't even heard the sound of its footsteps, which she had seen with her own eyes.

Once again, her mind settled on the same truth: that the Animal hadn't returned. That this was most likely just some guy in a costume who had grown too obsessed with the legend, seeking to recreate its horror.

Knowing that, however, caused her blood to boil in ways she hadn't expected. How could someone do this? What kind of a person could take something like this, that caused suffering to so many people, so many families, and make a legend out of it? A monster to imitate. The thought made her sick.

One last photograph caught her attention, a picture of her sitting in the back of the ambulance, pale as a ghost, all signs of life having left her face, as if she was nothing more than a propped-up corpse, traumatized forever by what she had seen.

The night her life had changed forever.

When she'd learned what real monsters looked like.

Riley shrugged it off and began putting everything back, hoping to trap her memories in the box with it. Emma would be home soon, and she couldn't see this.

The last thing she wanted was for Emma to be afraid.

She hit the bag, grunting as her body grew more exhausted with each passing second, but she didn't stop, striking it again and again.

It was the middle of the night, and she had desperately tried to sleep, but sleep wouldn't come. She couldn't escape her own thoughts, her own anger.

She struck the punching bag two more times, grunting as her body dripped with sweat, teeth clenched, eyes furious.

How could someone do this?

The question filled her with anger she had not expected. For all the years that she'd spent living in fear of the Animal, in constant terror that one day it would return and find her, find Emma, she had never hated it. At least, not the way she hated this new monster. Whatever it was, it wasn't human. She could live in fear of it, scream at it in her thoughts, imagine one day killing it and removing its bloodstained soul from this world, but she didn't despise it in the same way, as if fear crippled her hatred.

But this new thing, this monster who wanted to give rise to the legend, who thought its destiny was to be the new Animal, who didn't care what horrors it brought up from the past, she wasn't afraid of it.

Which meant she could hate it.

Three more strikes, and she held back a scream.

She could despise it for the pathetic thing it was, the unfeeling psychopath it had to be. She could hate it to its very core, but no matter what she did, she knew that it was only distracting her from her own memories. Memories that would never reside in a box in the closet, never be locked away from her every waking moment.

"Hide," her mother pleaded, with tears in her eyes.

Riley screamed as she continued to beat the punching bag, putting everything she had into every swing, letting adrenaline and hatred keep her from passing out in exhaustion.

"No matter what, don't come out."

Riley tackled the bag, breaking the link that held it up, landing on top of it as it hit the floor.

The Animal stepped in, and in a moment she heard her father scream before something broke, and his lifeless body fell to the floor, blood splattering everywhere, including on her. But still she hid.

She struck the bag over and over, a lifetime's worth of anger coming back.

"No!" her mother had screamed, causing her to hide her eyes, a child too afraid to even look as her mother faced the monster.

Riley slipped the knife out from her boot and, losing control, stabbed the bag over and over again, trying to ignore the memories, ignore the tears.

The next moment, she heard her mother's body hit the floor and opened her eyes to see what little was left, wanting to crawl to her, bury herself in her arms.

But still she hid.

Riley dropped the knife, no longer able to fight back the memories as she collapsed onto the floor, crying. For the longest time she lay there, weeping in agony as she cursed herself, hating her parents for leaving her, hating the Animal for taking them, and most of all, hating herself for hiding as they died.

She was still weeping on the floor when Emma walked into the room, eyes also filled with tears.

Sensing her fear, Riley managed to sit up and look at her daughter, wiping the tears from her own eyes. "What's wrong?"

Emma's voice was hesitant, afraid. "I had a nightmare."

Hiding her own pain so that she could comfort Emma, Riley forced a smile and motioned with her hand. "Come here."

Soon, they both lay down on the floor, and Riley held her daughter in her arms as tight as she could, feeling how much Emma was trembling. "It's okay," she whispered in her ear. "You're safe."

As she held her daughter, never wanting to let go, wishing she could stay in this room with her forever, she finally fell asleep.

CHAPTER SIX

This wasn't possible. There had to be something, some trace left behind.

The light of the morning sun cascaded down through the branches above him as Clyde knelt in the forest, desperately checking the ground for any signs of what he had seen, any trace of the creature that had stalked him in the night. Yet his hand ran over the smooth undisturbed dirt, free from any markings.

No, Clyde thought in frustration, remembering how the unnatural yellow eyes had glowed from the light of his flashlight. How big the creature had appeared. Something like that, an animal that massive, it would have left some kind of markings:

deep tracks in the dirt, pushed-over grass, or even a broken twig.

But there was nothing.

The forest itself almost seemed different as well. Clyde had brought an old hunting rifle, with wood chipping off the stock and a rusted metal bolt, just in case he found the thing that had stalked him. The creature attached to the monstrous eyes. But so far, he hadn't found anything at all, except for a few birds nestled in the branches and one or two squirrels running up a tree. Not nothing, but also nowhere near as much life as he normally witnessed within the forest.

Pushing against his rifle, whose stock was set in the dirt, he stood up, shaking off the strange feeling. The missing tracks. Maybe he was in the wrong spot; maybe it had left tracks somewhere else. Determined to find it, he walked through the forest, checking every single inch that surrounded his house, every single foot of the fence line, and as much as he could in between, finding the tracks of deer, rabbits, hogs, coyotes, and even one or two wolves.

But nothing that matched the size of what he had seen. It was like it had vanished completely, disappearing into the night. Clyde shook his head, confused and desperate as he continued to search. Every animal left tracks. There had to be something, anything to signal the animal had really been there.

In the end, he found nothing.

Clyde had finally given up and gone back to his cabin.

Yet before he even had time to wash the traces of mud from his hands, someone knocked on his door, revitalizing his memory. Last night had unsettled him so much, he had forgotten she was coming.

Opening the door, he was greeted by an elderly woman with tied-up grey hair, thick glasses, and an old white coat, who was currently holding shopping bags. "I haven't seen you in town for a while," she said as she stepped in, "so I took the liberty of bringing groceries."

"Oh," Clyde said. "Thanks, Doc."

"How many times have I told you? Call me Linda." She smiled as she set the bags on his table and eyed him curiously. "You forgot I was coming, didn't you?"

"Yeah." It had always amazed and just slightly annoyed him how perceptive the old woman was. It was like she could see every aspect of her life in perfect focus, something he desperately envied.

Clyde motioned for her to have a seat on his couch as he sat down on the chair opposite her. She took her glasses off for a moment to wipe her eyes,

revealing the wrinkled skin behind them. Sometimes wrinkles told a far grander story than scars ever could.

"Why is there mud on your hands?" she finally asked, tone like a mother trying to find out why her child had made a mess.

"I've been in the woods all day."

"Ah," she said, nodding, not fully accepting his answer but also not pressing the topic. "So how have you been?"

"Okay."

"You've got to give me more than that, Clyde," she said, shaking her head. "I'm an old doctor who doesn't have anything better to do. At least give me something. Any headaches?"

"Some."

"Sleeping okay?"

"No worse than usual."

She grinned. "You say that like it's something that can't be changed."

Clyde just shrugged. He didn't know what she wanted him to say. Sleeping had never been something that had come easy for him, and it probably never would. Something about the way the bed felt, the calmness of the cabin.

"What about the woods?" she asked. "Was there a particular reason you were out there today?"

Again, he shrugged.

She rolled her eyes, muttering to herself. "Just like your mother. I swear that woman would never

talk to me either. I'd hoped that would be the one thing you didn't get from her."

After a few moments, she continued. "Have you thought about her recently?"

Clyde tilted his head, thinking. "Yeah. Mostly just scattered thoughts, but yeah."

"That's good," Linda said, nodding her head.

"How about you?" Clyde asked, purposely changing the subject.

"I'm doing good," she said. If she noticed the deflection, she didn't mention it. "Just a little tired is all. Getting old stinks, don't let anyone tell you different."

"What about Hank? Is he doing okay?"

To his shock, for the briefest moment before she answered, Clyde saw hesitation in her eyes, but she tried to dismiss it. "Hank's doing fine. He's been really stressed the last couple of days, normal police stuff, but it's nothing to worry about."

Clyde rubbed the back of his neck, growing more uncomfortable as his mind started to wander back to the eyes that had watched him from the forest. "I saw something on the TV about some attack that happened recently. It said that some kids were killed by some kind of animal?"

"Oh, yes," she said, sighing as she spoke. "Well, the news tends to exaggerate these types of things. But from what I understand, a few teenagers were

attacked by someone in a Halloween costume, and the girl that survived was pretty shook up."

"Did Hank say anything about it?"

She shook her head. "Not to me at least, although it's probably what has him so stressed. But it's not something you should be worried about."

Clyde went quiet for a moment, thoughts going back over the timber wolf tracks he had found by the fence, before speaking, almost to himself. "They said it happened before."

"Excuse me?" she said, leaning forward to hear him better.

"The Animal. They said it attacked before. Said it killed a lot of people."

"Oh, yes." She leaned back on the couch. "It has happened before. But that was twenty-five years ago. I'm certain this new attack is something else."

"What about the sketch?" Clyde said. "It looked like a wolf."

She scoffed, brushing it off. "The sketch might, but artists can only draw what they are told, and stories are always exaggerated."

Her voice was light, but something in her eyes made Clyde think she was holding something back, like a quick glimpse of a tragic, pain-inducing memory that entered her mind. He wanted to say something, but she spoke before he had the chance.

"Why are you so interested in this?"

Clyde started to lie but knew that she could tell if he did. Besides, part of him wanted to tell someone, to get it out there, make him feel less crazy.

"Last night, I saw something in the woods."

Curiosity spread across her face. "What was it?"

"I don't know," he said, thinking about the haunting yellow eyes. "But it was watching me."

"What?" she said, curiosity becoming concern. "Someone was watching you?"

"No, it wasn't a person," Clyde said, remembering in perfect detail how its features had bled into the darkness of the forest, hiding its true nature from view. "It was some kind of animal, maybe a wolf? But bigger. *Much* bigger."

For a moment, as he looked into Linda's eyes, he saw something in them that he never had before. Not just fear, but abject terror, appearing as though she might have a panic attack on the spot.

But just as soon as it came, it also went.

"You know," she started, "yesterday, I had a terrible nightmare about snakes. I dreamt that one slithered up into my bed, coiling itself underneath my covers and digging its fangs down into my foot. I woke up frightened, of course, but then remembered that earlier I had seen a grass snake on the hospital lawn. Sometimes our mind

can play tricks on us and turn some small fear that we experienced during the day into a more serious fright at night, whether it be a bad dream or your eyes catching a shadow and creating something more out of it. That's all this was."

"No," Clyde said, shaking his head. "No, this was real. I saw it."

"I don't doubt that you did, but let me ask you this. Had you been thinking about the sketch of the Animal on TV that night?"

"Yes, but—"

"And," she said, pointing to the dirt still on his hands, "I see you looked for tracks. You didn't find any, did you?"

Clyde sighed, knowing where this was going. "No, I didn't."

"Okay, then. If you want an old doctor's opinion, let it go. You're safe. Even if this new killing is as serious as the news claims, no one is walking through a mile of trees just to get to your house." She smiled. "Except an old friend with bad knees."

They both laughed quietly for a moment as he thought it over. She was probably right; it had just been his mind playing tricks on him. After all, he'd walked back and forth through the forest for decades. If there was something else in there, he'd have seen it by now. Shaking his head slightly, he decided to take the doctor's prescription and let

it go. There was nothing stalking him from the woods.

Clyde smiled, at peace for a moment, as he continued to talk with his friend.

Where was it?

Night had fallen, and with it came restlessness. Clyde had tried to forget it, tried to make himself feel safe, but that in and of itself was the problem. He couldn't sleep because his bed, his cabin made him feel safe, and that was a lie. Something was in the woods. It wasn't his imagination, and he had to find it. It might vanish in the daytime, but he had seen it at night, so he decided to hunt for it at night.

Carrying his hunting rifle, he weaved between countless trees, looking for tracks in the dirt, for eyes illuminated by the moonlight, or even the brief glimpse of a shadow moving within the forest.

But he found nothing.

Moving further into the vast expanse of withered trees, he began growing desperate. It had to be here; he had seen it, watching him. Hunting him.

Suddenly, the sound of wood breaking echoed through the forest, and Clyde turned, aiming his weapon at the sound and the creature that had

made it. Nothing more than a simple raccoon, yet its eyes seemed different as it saw him. Not shocked, but something else, as if it was scared of something it couldn't see.

Unnerved, Clyde progressed further, walking for what felt like hours, stepping on dirt, hiding behind trees, trying to find a single trace of the animal that had stalked him, anything to put a body to the eyes, a creature to the stare. But eventually, even that hope was shattered.

Defeated, hours of searching giving him nothing, he found himself next to a dried-up creek, choked by the lack of rainfall in this town. On the other side the ground was higher, rising about ten feet above his head. It was there that he fell to the ground, knees in the dirt along with his rifle's stock, his hand still on the barrel to keep him steady as the truth set in.

It was over.

No amount of time would ever make him believe that the eyes that had watched him the night before weren't real. But so long as he couldn't find the animal they belonged to, he'd never know for sure, never be able to let it go: the feeling that always haunted him. Of being stalked, being hunted in the dark by creatures whose teeth snapped together with vicious hunger, having been left alone within their grasp.

But then, all at once, he saw it.

Something dark, moving along the ground. The thin trace of a shadow creeping toward him, caused by the moon above him and the monster blocking its light. Something was behind him. Something unnatural.

Slowly, he adjusted his position, bringing one foot up the ground and resting his gun on it, trying not to spook whatever was behind him, as the darkness started to move over him. Clyde couldn't breathe as the shadow enveloped him completely and he saw the outline on the ground in front of him. Wild fur, pointed ears, long nose. The shadow was the head of a wolf, standing atop the higher ground on the other side of the creek, revealed by the bright glow of the night's moon.

The features of the wolf surrounded Clyde as he realized in horror that he shouldn't have come into the woods.

The shadow that covered him in its darkness, the shadow that reached out and carved an outline of the wolf's features onto the ground, it was too big, even if the wolf was on higher ground. It had to be twice the size of a timber wolf, at least.

What felt like an eternity passed as Clyde steadied his heart rate, not allowing his body to make a single sound as he waited for the animal to do something. To attack him, kill him, rip his body to shreds. But it didn't. Instead, it simply watched

him, its shadow slightly moving as it bre
behind him.

Finally, when Clyde had stayed motionless
as long as he could, he brought his hand up
the bolt of the rifle, pulling it back and loading
a round. In an instant he turned around, letting
his back anchor into the dirt as he pointed the
gun up and fired.

Clyde had always believed in monsters. But
now, as the gun's flash illuminated the forest,
giving way to the slightest glimpse of the animal
that moved away, covered in black fur and what
looked like blood, he had finally seen one.

CHAPTER SEVEN

Never stop moving. If you stop moving, you die.

Russel kept repeating that same phrase to himself as he ran down the field, pursued by those much faster than he was, trying to make it to the goal.

The first to reach him tackled full force, but with a slight shift of weight Russel sent him flying backwards, crashing into the dirt over five feet away. Another student was in front of him, a big, overweight student who was built like a professional linebacker. Russel crashed into him, not even slowing down as the kid felt the impact and dropped to the ground in a moment.

The last kid left standing caught up from behind and leapt onto Russel's back, attempting to tackle him. Instead, he was forced to hold on as Russel continued to run, barely noticing the extra weight, and in a few moments, the touchdown was made.

"Again!" the coach screamed, sending more players onto the field, attempting to find out how many it would take to finally knock Russel to the dirt.

Russel took a deep breath and started running again.

As he crashed into the first opponent, Russel kept repeating the same phrase in his head. *If you stop moving, you die.* To most people, it evoked a sense of strength, of power, reminiscent of sharks. But to Russel, it meant something else. To him it was a reminder.

Another opponent crashed into the ground.

It was a reminder of what he used to be. Most everyone in this town only remembered him as he was now: massive, strong, over a head taller than the second-tallest senior. Some of them called him Giant or Goliath. Others called him John Henry, a strong man of mythical proportions. But they had forgotten what he was like before.

Another student fell, this one grunting in pain as he did.

They had all forgotten how small he used to be. How, when he was seven, his arms had been twigs and how the bullies had reminded him of it every day. How when he was twelve, he had been so uncoordinated that he'd often tripped while running from them, which had caused him more than a few beatings that he still remembered vividly.

Two more fell as Russel reached the goal, and the coach shouted, "Again!"

To Russel, *if you stop moving, you die* meant survival. It meant running until you escaped your tormentors: those who bullied you because you were small, because you were weak.

Three more tried to tackle, and three more fell.

Ever since the growth spurt, ever since he'd trained, worked his fingers to the bone to bulk up, to become the strongest kid in school, the strongest kid in the whole town, they had all forgotten what they used to do to him. Forgotten the beatings, and the times he had been forced to run. Now they all watched in awe whenever he played, getting the same satisfaction out of watching him beat down others as they used to get while beating him.

Two more tried, both giants themselves, probably two of the toughest players in the state. Russel grunted as he knocked the first down and then collided with the next, stopping him for a moment.

His feet dug into the ground as he pushed harder, not letting the sweat, the exhaustion, drop him. He was stronger than this guy. He was stronger than everyone.

If you ever stop moving, you die.

Russel shifted his weight and sent the kid flying down fast, body bouncing up slightly as it collided with the field, the kid screaming in pain.

With no more opponents in his way, Russel ran into the end zone, looking back over the field of bodies he'd left in his path. Pumping his arms, he screamed into the sky, victorious. They couldn't stop him. Nothing could.

Then he noticed the assistant coaches helping one of the players up. The kid looked hurt and was limping pretty bad, even with the coaches helping him walk.

Russel saw the coach's flash of anger, the fire in his eyes that scolded Russel without words. But Russel ignored it. Had the kid been able to, he would have tackled Russel to the ground the same way. That was what this town was, what it had always been. A jungle, survival of the fittest. And after years upon years of waiting, working, and training, Russel was finally the fittest.

Practice over, he threw his backpack over his shoulder, popped his knuckles, and looked over into the distance, to the gymnasium at the far side of the school, remembering who would be there.

Russel smiled as he walked toward it. While most kids at the school either used to pick on him or were now afraid of him, he did still have a few friends. Good ones too.

Focus, Gabriella told herself as she took a deep breath and started running, fast as she could. It had to be perfect.

She jumped in the air, hands landing on the platform in front of her, springing her even further upwards as she began flipping: once, twice, three times. Finally, she landed, feet hitting the mat, knees buckling as the impact hit her, and she fell to the ground, cursing as she did.

It wasn't perfect. Wasn't even close.

She stayed on the ground, hands balling into fists as she resisted the urge to strike the mat, angry at herself for failing, ignoring the other gymnasts looking at her.

"You gotta lighten up," she heard a voice say from behind her. "You just tried a Produnova vault and almost got it. You can't be perfect all the time."

"Tell that to my parents," Gabriella said, her tone lighter as she stood up. Something about Kelly always relaxed her, even now as Kelly's movement was slightly off. Gabriella stood up to hug her, wondering what the monster she had seen at the house had looked like. How terrifying the animal that had attacked really was. "You doing okay? I didn't think you'd be back at school this early."

Kelly just shrugged, still feeling the eyes of other students watching her, prying ears listening into their conversation, hoping to hear a whisper of the legend. So, rather than get into it, Kelly simply sighed. "What else was I supposed to do? Besides, Dylan called and said he had somewhere to be and that you needed a ride."

Gabriella rolled her eyes and jumped up to the rings, pulling her body up with her. "So, Dylan isn't coming. Why am I not surprised?"

Kelly laughed. "He doesn't deserve you, ya know."

"Who does?" Gabriella said, laughing as well.

"Your humility is truly inspiring."

"I know." Gabriella winked before twisting her arms and hanging upside down from the bars, arms behind her body, legs bent down, smiling as she saw Kelly's disgusted look of discomfort.

"How are you not in pain?" Kelly asked, rubbing her own shoulder as she saw Gabriella's unnatural movement. "My arms hurt just looking at you."

"Perks of being double-jointed." She dropped down, striking a small pose as she did.

"Bravo," Kelly said, half-mocking.

"Thank you." She bowed.

To their left, Betty walked up, using a towel to wipe the sweat off her neck. "You should see her when she hasn't trained for three hours straight. Thanks for that, by the way. I didn't have anywhere else to be tonight."

Gabriella shrugged. "Practice makes perfect. Besides, you could have left whenever you wanted to."

"Yeah, sure," Betty said, pointing back to the other kids still training. "So that we can all get embarrassed by you when the meet actually gets here."

Gabriella smiled. "I mean, let's be honest. That's gonna happen anyway."

Betty scoffed but cracked a grin. "Probably."

"So," Kelly said, looking to Gabriella, "ready to go?"

"Sure thing, boss," she said, knowing how much being called boss annoyed Kelly. It was fun to mess with her sometimes, upset the perfect smile Kelly was so used to carrying.

"Can I catch a ride?" Betty asked.

"The more the merrier."

"Sweet," Betty said, loading up her gym bag.

But then, all at once and too soon to react, the gym went dark.

That's when the screaming began.

At first, the screams were out of nervousness. The power had gone out, just as it had at Kelly's house, and the mere thought of the monster attacking was enough to cause kids to cry out in fear.

Kelly was in the middle of them, nerves firing, looking at the figures in the darkness, nothing more than fleeting, featureless forms, moving about in fear, the absence of light stealing away their appearance, their look of humanity, as they began to frantically move about, searching for escape.

But then another figure appeared, features too monstrous to be hidden even in the dark, and then the screams of fear became wails of agony.

To her left, Kelly saw the monster tackle a shadowed figure, bringing them both to the ground as the boy's screams echoed in the enclosed walls of the gym before a blade could be heard cutting flesh, and the cries were silenced, even as the echoes remained.

She started to move right, but another figure dropped as the monster appeared in its place, killing another victim mere feet away, and yet stolen from her sight by the consuming darkness.

On and on it went, blurred figures of kids, classmates, outlines of flesh being forced to the ground by an unseen beast.

Trying to focus, Kelly saw the soft glow of moonlight creeping in through the door and started to go for it. But then she saw the monstrous shadow moving toward it and knew she didn't have time.

So instead, she ran away, down the hallway behind her, venturing further into the gym, where there would be no escape, where she would hide just as all victims did, thinking the monster wouldn't find them.

But it always did...

In fear, Betty tried to run for the door, Gabriella beside her, but as they moved, the thing hiding in the darkness saw them, and having no more figures left to slaughter, it turned its horrific gaze to them.

In terror, they ran down the hallway that led to the lockers, stumbling in fear as they reached the point where it branched off into two sections. Not thinking, only running, they went through the door on the right, closing it just in time to hide their chosen location from the monster.

As the monster reached the hallway, it stopped in the middle of the two doors, tilting its head, trying to decide where its prey would be hiding.

Finally, it made its choice.

Inside the locker room, Kelly ran her hand across the little grooves of the lockers, feeling her way around the room. Small fluorescent decals of animals lined the walls: bears, foxes, a couple of deer, and various other wildlife. The edges were chipping off, and they weren't nearly as bright as they used to be, but with the power off, the decals were all Kelly had as she moved further into the room, being surrounded by what in the light would have been simply rows of lockers but in the darkness looked more like old concrete gates of a cemetery, trapping both living and expired souls inside, forever enclosed in the emptiness within.

Then she heard the growling.

Betty stayed close to Gabriella as they walked through the room, shivering in fear, afraid the monster would find them. Afraid it would know which room they had chosen to hide in and come for blood.

Betty's hand started to shake as a horrifying thought crossed her mind. When the monster had attacked, it hadn't come through the door.

It came from within.

She almost screamed as her foot hit something.

Kelly controlled her breathing, moving into a locker beside her, trying to hide within it, stay out of sight until she knew what to do. It was what all victims did, thinking they'd be discovered not by the creature but by the cops who'd come to search for survivors.

Often, there were none left to find...

As she steadied her breath, the growling got louder, and out of impulse, her hand gently pressed against the wound still in her stomach, wincing as she did. Seven stitches to remind her what had happened the last time she'd been this close.

Suddenly, slight glimpses of a monster were revealed by the open vents of the locker, and for a moment, it appeared as though the beast looked right at her: wolflike features staring in silence, no eyes to be seen behind its mask of fur.

But then, another sound echoed. A kid at the end of the room, unaware of what now lurked within the darkness, having been too far enclosed to hear the screams that had echoed just a moment ago. A kid who would now die because of the hiding victim who'd led the monster into the heart of the gym, where it otherwise would not have thought to go.

A kid who now saw the monstrous shadow illuminated by the decals of animals and realized too late the dark fate that awaited him.

Betty bent down, breathing fast, trying to see what her foot had hit. There was no light at all, so the only way to see was to feel. Slowly, her hand glided down, pressing against what lay on the floor.

Feeling its touch on her skin.

It was wet.

Kelly trembled as she saw it move like something possessed before hearing the muffled screams and tearing of flesh. As she heard it, as horrible as it was, she knew it gave her the only opening to escape. So, she burst out of the locker, looking in awed silence at the creature hunched down over the bleeding kid, growling as it wiped the blood from the kid's stomach onto its own face, staining its grey fur red.

Kelly froze.

Betty fought the urge to scream as she moved her hand, now covered in something warm, further down the object, until finally, her fingers ran over the features of a face, and she realized in horror what was on her hands.

Blood.

109

Kelly almost jumped out of her own skin as she heard Betty's blood-curdling shriek. In an instant, the creature turned its blood-covered face toward her, hesitating for a moment as it stared right at her, tilting its head in an exaggerated manner.

She was out the door in a second, almost running into Gabriella, who was dragging Betty, covering her mouth with one hand to keep her from screaming.

"It's behind me," Kelly said as they ran, not realizing just how close it was.

Suddenly, it caught Gabriella by the arm, causing her to drop Betty, who crawled away as fast as she could, looking back in disbelief.

Kelly moved to help, but in an instant Gabriella twisted her body and bent her arm, appearing to break her own shoulder and wrist but succeeding in escaping the animal's grip.

Perks of being double-jointed, Kelly remembered her saying as she watched Gabriella pop her shoulder back in and attempt to run away, but she wasn't quite fast enough, and a sharp bone stabbed into her back. Not a deep cut but enough to trip her, giving the animal time to get close.

Kelly ran to her friend's defense, catching the animal off guard and shoving it to the side, noticing how Betty looked at her like she was insane.

The attack gave them just enough time to move, and they hid behind the stack of blocks set up in the corner. As they sat on the floor behind it, Kelly waited for something to happen, to hear its footsteps, anything to get a sense of where the animal was. But a far more haunting sound echoed into the darkness as the growling started.

Horrific, vicious growling, moving slowly closer. It didn't know where they were hiding yet. Kelly remained still, as did Gabriella, but Betty was beginning to shake again.

Kelly looked at her, trying to make her stop, but it was no use, and the more she looked into her eyes, the more Kelly realized why she was shaking so much. Betty wasn't going to stay and hide; she was getting ready to run for the door.

A last-ditch effort to escape with her life.

Desperate, Kelly shook her head, but Betty didn't listen, and so Kelly started to panic. She shook her head again, trying to tell her it was too risky, that the animal would get her, but she wouldn't listen and instead turned around, bracing herself to take off in a sprint.

"Betty, no!" Kelly screamed as Betty took off, making it two feet before the animal found her.

The sound of her gagging echoed through the gym as the animal stabbed something into her stomach, then her ribs, and finally her chest, turning her gagging into full-fledged screaming as her body dropped to the ground.

It looked like she was still conscious, even as the blood poured out of her. Her eyes focused forward, watching the animal turn its head to face them. One more step and it would be close enough to strike, and so, confident in its victory, it began twisting the sharpened bone in its hand.

A loud crash filled their ears as the door swung open, and they heard running. In the darkness they couldn't see what it was, but the animal turned around, focusing its attention on this new presence.

Something massive tackled the animal to the ground.

"Get away from them!"

The night might have hidden the details of the massive figure, but Kelly instantly recognized the voice. It was Russel, on top of the animal, striking it in the face.

Their savior.

But then the animal slung its sharpened bone across Russel's chest, drawing blood, and then used the surprise to push Russel to the side, striking him as he hit the ground, drawing more blood from above his eye.

Kelly moved to help, but the animal growled, striking Russel again before turning and grabbing hold of her, throwing her aside violently.

Her head hit the floor. Hard.

Suddenly, everything felt like it was a dream as fire erupted in her skull. She heard screams, almost sounding like anger, as she tried to shake off the dizziness.

Where was she?

Something grabbed her shoulder, startling her at first, and she went to scream, until the dizziness finally faded and her eyes focused, seeing Russel kneeling above her.

"Kelly," he said, checking her head. "Kelly, are you okay? Can you hear me?"

"I'm fine," she said, grabbing onto his hand and pulling herself up. "Where?"

"Gone," Russel answered, chest still bleeding.

"Guys," Gabriella's cautious voice said, causing Kelly to turn and see her hovering over Betty, whose eyes had now closed as blood continued to drip from her chest. Gabriella's hand was on her throat, checking for a pulse, when suddenly her expression turned to shock.

"She's still alive."

CHAPTER EIGHT

She could still hear the screams of her neighbors, echoing in her ear, the horrific wailing trapped forever inside her head.

"Get under the bed!" her mother screamed, voice barely getting through to Riley as she covered the girl's mouth, keeping her from screaming. But it couldn't stop the crying. Nothing could have stopped the crying.

The door downstairs crashed open, and Riley waited in terror to hear the footsteps that never came. Her heart started to race, pounding inside her chest as she waited there, tears streaming down her face, almost hoping to hear it, to hear something, anything to tell her where the Animal was, to tell her this would go away.

The bedroom door shook, as did the house itself, as something slammed into it. The sound of the wood cracking was so loud, Riley almost felt it, as if the unseen force had cracked her bones instead. The door shook again, almost breaking in two. Riley forced her eyes closed at first, too scared to look at the monster. Wanting to stay underneath the bed, hidden forever, wishing her parents were underneath it with her.

One last crash and Riley felt splintered wood hit her arm as the door broke completely, solid wood shattered like fragile glass. And in a moment she would regret for the rest of her life, she decided to look, to let her eyes witness the beast that had come seeking its prey. Imagination was always scarier than the real thing. There was nothing that existed in this world that could be as terrifying as the monstrous animal she had pictured in her mind. It wasn't possible.

As her eyes opened, she saw the door, massive cracks running through the entire bottom half, the top half almost completely missing, with only a few broken pieces of wood splintering out from the sides.

The Animal was behind it.

Riley would have screamed if terror hadn't stolen her voice. She was wrong to look. She could feel its presence in her bones, see the image even when she closed her eyes. No monster she could have ever created in her head would have stolen the life from her eyes like a single glimpse of the Animal did.

It wasn't human. Wasn't even a monster. It was something worse, something darker. Something unimaginable, unkillable, an Animal with a thirst for blood, for hunting.

Her heart beat so fast she thought she was being torn apart from the inside as she heard the sound of bones cracking and saw her father's bloodied carcass drop to the floor, followed by something that had once resembled her mother.

She moved further back, still underneath the bed, not daring to make a sound. But somehow, she knew it still heard her. Still felt her, instinctively knowing where its prey hid.

The Animal moved toward her bed, and she screamed until she lost her voice.

Riley woke up screaming, crying, and everything in between. After all these years, so many dreams of the same moment, the same image, yet it never went away. The hopelessness. The fear.

Everyone had recommended therapy. Anything to talk about it, rationalize it, but none of them understood. The Animal might have become a legend in the town, a ghost story everyone was afraid of, but the stories were wrong. They could capture the facts: the seventeen bodies, the forest, the screams. They might even draw a rough sketch of what they believed the horror was. But stories, no matter how terrifying, how exaggerated, would never be able to capture the fear she had felt in that single moment: looking at an Animal, feeling its presence, knowing its true nature.

The monster the town thought existed was only a pale, distorted reflection of the real Animal that she had seen with her own eyes.

She wasn't sure how long she had been crying when suddenly the phone rang. She wanted so badly to ignore it, escape from the reality of the world, but if someone was calling her in the middle of the night, it was either Linda or Hank, and either would have an important reason. So, reluctantly, she picked up the phone and was greeted by Hank's strong voice.

"Riley, can you talk?"

"Yeah," she said, forcing the tears back as well as the memories as she left the bedroom, going to another where hopefully the memories wouldn't be as fresh, where the screams in her head couldn't linger in the air. "What's wrong?"

"There was another attack. This time it was at the school gym. Killed five kids, bodies mutilated in the locker room. It also attacked three more girls, one of whom is in critical condition right now."

"So," Riley asked, confused, "some of them survived?"

"Yes." Hank went on to tell her everything: how it had stabbed Betty, how Russel had shown up and managed to hit it, scare it off. Unconsciously, she began shaking her head.

Scared it off? This is wrong, all of this is wrong.

"There's one other thing," Hank said, hesitation in his voice. "One of the girls who was attacked is Kelly, the girl who survived the first attack. Whatever this thing is, I think it's following her."

This didn't really surprise Riley. She hadn't necessarily expected Kelly to be a continued target, but it made sense. This new imitation would want to finish what it started. However, what did surprise her was the little inflection in Hank's voice. He wanted to ask her something but couldn't bring himself to.

"What is it, Hank?"

"Well," he started, voice still shaky. "It's just, the kids, especially Kelly, they haven't spoken much, but they're terrified right now, even if they're trying to hide it. We're going to try to put them in a safe house, but that won't make them any less scared."

"Hank," she said, rubbing her eyes, "it's late, just ask me whatever you're going to, please."

"Okay. I thought it might help them if they could meet you. Maybe you could talk to them about this."

"No," Riley said immediately.

"Please, I'm not asking you to guard them or anything. I don't want you in danger. Just talk to them, show them how you learned to survive. I think it could help them."

"Hank, no." Her heart started racing again. "I can't get involved."

"Riley," he said softly, "I wouldn't ask if you were anyone else. But even when you were eight, you were different. Stronger. You've managed to survive it, let the past go, even if just for a few seconds at a time. You're proof that surviving is possible. I think the kids need that right now, before this gets any worse."

She didn't even allow herself to consider the possibility. It might be a new animal, and she might only have to talk to the kids, but she couldn't dare risk it. If there was even the smallest chance that she was wrong, that this new animal was the same one that had attacked her, then she couldn't be a part of it, couldn't involve herself in any way. Because if she gave it a reason to attack her, then it had a reason to attack Emma, and if it was the real Animal, she'd never be able to protect her.

"I'm sorry," she said, a tear falling down her cheek. "I'm sorry, but I can't."

With that, she hung up the phone and collapsed into the nearest chair, body shivering, trying to justify her choice, even if it meant lying to herself. Telling herself that if it was something new, then she wouldn't know how to help.

Soon, she looked up, seeing the antlers mounted on the wall at eye level in front of her, once belonging to a whitetail deer that she had hunted when she was nineteen. The antlers were huge, white, with sharp, jagged points jutting off in every direction, a symbol that reminded her of what she was. What they all were.

If the Animal was back, the *real* Animal, then she couldn't help the kids, because they were dead already. Because no matter what else, one fact remained constant.

It was an Animal, and everyone else was just prey.

CHAPTER NINE

"It was right here," Clyde said, kneeling down in the forest and tracing something in the dirt.

The morning sun was beaming down from the sky, casting far harsher shadows than the moon had the previous night. But the memory of the monster was still fresh in Clyde's mind as he finished his tracing, carving the image of the creature that had loomed over him, the grotesque features of an unnatural beast.

"I saw it," he continued, still kneeling in the middle of his makeshift dirt drawing, just like he had knelt in the real shadow the night before. "I think it's been watching me."

"Clyde," Hank said, tired and rubbing his eyes, "I'm sorry, but I really don't have time for this. There was another attack. There are kids back in town—"

"I know," Clyde said, having seen it on the news again. "I think that whatever this thing is, it might have something to do with the attacks." When he saw Hank was about to protest, he continued. "I know how this sounds, but just hear me out. Please."

Hank groaned but eventually relented. "Fine. So when did you first see it?"

"Two nights ago. It was watching me from the trees. I tried to find it the next morning, but it didn't leave any tracks."

Hank scoffed at that but didn't stop him.

"Then, last night, I came back out here looking for it when I saw this shadow come over me." He motioned to the drawing in the dirt, the monstrous outline of a creature that almost resembled a wolf, yet far darker. Then he pointed up to the higher ground across the creek. "When I turned around and fired, I saw it. Only for a second, but I saw it running away."

For a moment Hank stared at him, as if trying to decipher a secret only he knew, before he finally looked over to the higher ground. "Show me."

On the other side, Clyde knelt down, again running his hands over the cool dirt. "It was right here, watching me with its hollow, yellow eyes. When

122

I fired, it turned and ran. I only got a brief glimpse, but what I saw... it wasn't natural. It looked like a wolf, but twice the size, with fur so black it was darker than its own shadow."

"Where are the tracks?"

"There are none."

Hank ran his fingers across his forehead, sighing. "Clyde, you say that like it doesn't make you a crazy person."

"I'm not crazy," Clyde said. "I saw it, I swear it was right here."

"But without tracks—"

"The Animal didn't leave tracks," Clyde said, defensive. "I saw on the news. They said that there were no tracks left at the original attack."

"You think this is the original Animal?" Hank said, his tone implying he had lost patience. "Clyde, that was twenty-five years ago, and I don't know what trash they're reporting on the news, but it's all exaggerated facts about a real tragedy, just to fuel the local legend. They have no idea what actually happened. No one does. But I can guarantee you this: whatever it was, even if it isn't dead, it hasn't spent the last twenty-five years hiding on your property."

"But what if—"

"Clyde, think about it," Hank said, voice calming back down. "I have no doubt that you saw a wolf last night. I'm not sure if I believe the size of it,

but either way, it doesn't matter. The original attack was twenty-five years ago. Last I checked, wolves don't live that long."

"You don't know that," Clyde said. "They say wolves only live for fifteen years, but they can't know for sure how long they'd live in the wild. It's not impossible. And what about the new attacks?"

"The new attacks don't prove anything, because they aren't the same animal. It's most likely just some idiot too obsessed with the legend, trying to find an excuse to kill. The only people in this town who think the real Animal has returned are the ones who never saw the aftermath it left behind."

"But–" Clyde started again, not willing to relent. He had seen something, and it couldn't be a coincidence. It might not be the Animal, but there had to be some connection. There had to be an answer, something to explain why he had felt eyes watching him his whole life, even before he had seen them two nights ago.

Something had to be lurking within this forest.

Hank held a hand up, stopping him. "Last night, you saw a wolf. The moonlight played tricks with its shadow, so it appeared massive. The night before, the eyes you said were watching you–it was probably a trespasser, hunting illegally. They probably removed their tracks as they walked, so that they wouldn't be caught, and they stopped to look at your house because they were afraid

you might have seen them." Hank put his hand on Clyde's shoulder, voice becoming sympathetic. "There's nothing unnatural out here. No monster hiding behind the trees. You're safe, Clyde."

Somehow, Clyde did feel safe.

That was the problem. The feeling made him anxious, nervous, like he was trapped forever in the calm before the storm, waiting for the horror to arrive, knowing it would, but unable to see it, stop it.

"Okay," he said finally, considering Hank's explanation. Both he and Linda had told Clyde the same thing: that there was nothing to worry about, that this wasn't connected to the attacks, the killings.

"I really do have to go," Hank said, checking his watch. "Are you going to be okay?"

"Yeah," Clyde said, sitting down on the edge of the creek as Hank left, looking over to the carved outline of the shadow, the only remnant of the monster's existence. He kept going over Hank's explanation in his head, and so much of it made sense. Maybe he was just becoming obsessed, turning these simple things into something greater, something to explain why his entire life he'd only ever felt afraid when he'd been completely safe.

Maybe it was nothing.

But the eyes had glowed. When Clyde had shined the flashlight onto the animal in the forest, its eyes

had lit up, glowing in the darkness. Which meant it couldn't have been a trespasser, couldn't have been a man, because human eyes didn't do that.

Animals' did.

For another hour, Clyde stayed there, staring down at the sketched image of some inhuman thing resembling a wolf. As he studied it, imagining the real monster's unnatural features—the elongated mouth, the blood-covered teeth, fur darker than death itself—he made up his mind. He would come back here tonight and look for the wolf again. Even if it found him, even if it killed him, he had to be sure that it existed, had to have proof, if only for himself. Something was in these woods, and tonight he would find it.

It found him first.

Clyde's body froze in shock as he heard it from behind him, the low rumble in the animal's throat a precursor to something worse. No footsteps could be heard, no breaths echoed into the trees. Only the vicious growling escaping the beast's row of teeth, which began to grow louder, transforming into something unnatural, something dark and twisted.

Making no sound himself, Clyde slowly turned, somehow managing to keep his heart rate perfectly steady, his nerves perfectly calm as he saw it in

the light of day, standing within the trees as if it were a part of the forest itself.

Black fur. Massive head. Sharp teeth bared as it growled, stained in blood.

Clyde shifted his weight, getting ready to run. It was hopeless, he could never outrun a normal wolf, much less something whose legs were the length of most wolves' entire bodies, but he had to try. Better to die running than to just let it maul him right there.

As he took off, the monster behind him cried out, the sound so deep and vicious it almost caused Clyde to stumble in fear, but he kept running, even as he heard the footsteps, massive paws striking the dirt behind him, growing closer as it chased him.

Desperate and terrified, Clyde ran faster than he had ever thought possible, running along the creek through trees, over hills and dirt, followed closely by the animal, stalking him closer than even his shadow.

As he ran, his mind flooded with thoughts. If he kept going this way, he would run into the fence within minutes and would be backed into a corner. He had to go left toward his house, even though something inside him was screaming to go right, across the creek.

When he attempted to turn, the dark behemoth leapt to his left, screaming something between

a roar and a howl, moving its distorted tail and twisting its head as it dug its claws down into the dirt, getting ready to pounce, hunger flashing in its cold yellow eyes.

Panicking, Clyde listened to his instinct and jumped to the right, over the creek, his body colliding hard with the ground on the other side. He wanted to scream in pain, but he wasn't given time, as he saw the animal running for the creek as well.

Not waiting to see if it would make it, Clyde ran again, feeling as though his heart would explode inside his chest, spilling its blood and choking his lungs. The feeling grew worse when he heard the animal land on the dirt, the impact shaking the very forest, and the withered branches trapped within forced to watch from above as the beast grew closer to Clyde with every waking second.

It was going to catch him, Clyde realized in a moment of haunting dread. If it had wanted to, it could have already, but it was prolonging his suffering, creating the illusion of a chase, the veiled hope of a bloodied victim, nothing more than a rabbit thinking it could escape the wolf's fangs, thinking its body wouldn't be ripped in two in a single instant.

Footsteps bounded behind him, one right after the other in perfect rhythm, coming from a creature who no longer needed to hide its

presence, for the hunt was already on, and the footsteps were growing closer.

Just when Clyde thought he would collapse from running and the beast would feast on his bones, the footsteps stopped abruptly, and for the briefest second he felt relief. Until he turned his head and saw that the wolf hadn't left.

It had jumped.

His bones felt as though they were being shattered as the animal tackled him to the ground, its massive weight crashing down on him, the sound of its gnashing teeth so loud that he thought his ears were bleeding, and in that moment, he knew it was over. So he closed his eyes, waiting for it to kill him, instinctively covering his throat with his arm, a vain attempt to protect what would be a wolf's first target.

But the bloodshed didn't come, even as the horrific growling remained.

Cautiously, Clyde's eyes opened once again, seeing where he was. Trees still surrounded him, and dirt still lay beneath him, but something was different. Above him, there was a small opening in the trees, a glimpse of the sky revealed in a space between the twisting branches. In front of him was a large, jagged rock, which the beast had moved behind, its monstrous features hidden in the shadows of the forest once more, piercing yellow eyes staring right back at him.

Frozen in pure fear, Clyde waited for the attack to come. For the animal to lunge, dig its teeth into his neck, and rip him limb from limb with a single movement of its massive jaw, leaving his remains to rot within the forest's dirt. But it never did. Instead, it merely watched him silently, until finally it moved back within the trees, its eyes vanishing within the dark depths of the forest.

Only after it was gone from his sight did Clyde's body finally allow itself to react, hands shaking, muscles tensing, vision getting blurry and lungs gasping for air as he bent down, falling into the dirt.

Why hadn't it killed him? It could have caught him within seconds, so why had it chased? Animals weren't cruel. They didn't hunt for sport; they hunted to eat, to survive. It didn't make sense.

As Clyde stayed frozen on the ground, he kept waiting for the attack to come, almost wanting it to. If it attacked, he would know where it was, what would happen. If it came back, it would make sense, feel real. The true predator would be revealed, and there would be no more false safety, no more terror or anxiety, no more looking over his shoulder, expecting an attack at any moment. Then it would just be about instinct, about survival, and he would rather see the animal attacking than wait for it to appear.

But the attack never came.

CHAPTER TEN

"She's awake."

The doctor's words shocked them all, but most of all Kelly. She knew Betty was tough, she had always been tough, but this was different. The amount of blood she had lost by the time the ambulance had arrived—Kelly had been sure it was going to go a different way.

But then again, a lot of the older people in town said that Dr. Linda Parker was a miracle worker when it came to surgeries like this, so Kelly guessed it shouldn't have been too surprising. Still, three stab wounds, one of them to the chest—Kelly had to hand it to the girl. She was a fighter.

Kelly's hand unconsciously moved to her own wounds, to the bandage still covering her stomach, hiding the blood and the stitches below. She wondered if she would have pulled through had it been her, had she been the one stabbed three times rather than one. If she would have been strong enough to make it.

The doctor spoke again, this time directly to Kelly.

"She wants to see you."

Nervous, Kelly stepped into the hospital room. She wasn't quite sure why she was anxious, but she guessed it was nerves left over from the night before. That, and she had no idea what Betty was going to say to her. It was strange that Betty had asked for her specifically. They were friends, sure, but Kelly had never thought they were hospital bedside friends.

"Hey," she said as she walked up to the bed. Betty had been on the brink of death, and she looked it, especially her eyes. They were bloodshot and seemed to be twitching side to side, searching for a monster and simultaneously staring into nothing, as if she was already dead.

"Was...?" Betty tried to say, voice shaking, words unintelligible. "Was...?"

"What is it?" Kelly asked, leaning over the bed slowly, forcing Betty to meet her eyes.

In a sudden burst that made Kelly jump in shock, thinking it was an attack, Betty reached up and grabbed her, pulling her down closer, voice cracking with fear.

"Was it real?"

Heart now racing, Kelly nodded. "Yeah. It was real."

Hearing her darkest nightmare confirmed as reality, Betty sighed and released her grip, hands trembling. "I'm sorry."

"It's okay. I get it, trust me."

"Did anyone else survive?"

Kelly nodded. "Gabriella and Russel."

Betty closed her eyes and tilted her head down, grief-stricken eyes mourning friends she had lost. When she finally spoke again, her words surprised Kelly. "How do you do it?"

"How do I do what?"

"Not fall apart."

Kelly shrugged. "I don't know. I guess to me, this still doesn't seem real. It seems like I'm watching something happen, some horrible thing that crawled out of the darkness, with no control over it myself. As if I'm not there to die, only to witness the slaughter. It's strange. Plus," she added, "I didn't get stabbed in the chest three times, so that helps."

Betty gave Kelly one last surprise when she laughed. It wasn't a hard laugh, and the second she did it she clutched her chest in pain, but the smile was still there. Eventually, she spoke through the pain. "I bet it does."

A few minutes later, noises came from outside the door as Kelly heard doctors trying to stop someone from coming in. Evidently, they failed, because the door swung open and Rhett rushed in, going straight for Kelly and hugging her tight.

"Are you okay?"

Pressure built on her stomach wound as she pushed him away. "Stop, you're hurting me."

"Sorry," he said, checking her face for bruises, cuts, anything. "Are you okay?"

"I'm fine," she said, rolling her eyes and then pulling his hand down as he tried to look at the bruise on her forehead from when the animal had thrown her to the ground. "Stop it."

He sighed but put his hands down. "Okay. They said you got hit in the head pretty hard, and I was just worried. I'm sorry. I should have been there. I should have stopped it."

"Don't do that," Kelly said. "Really, I'm fine."

If he was about to say something else, he was interrupted by the sudden entrance of Gabriella, followed closely behind by Russel, who had to duck slightly underneath the door frame.

Gabriella smiled at Betty. "How on earth are you still alive?"

Betty shrugged. "I'm secretly immortal."

"I guess you'd have to be," Gabriella said before winking at Kelly. "How about you? Is our bad luck charm feeling any better?"

"Ha," Kelly said mockingly. "You're hilarious."

"Take it easy," she said, patting Kelly's shoulder. "You know we love you."

Behind her, Kelly overheard Rhett speaking to Russel. "The cops said you scared it off."

Russel smiled. "I tried."

Suddenly, all of their conversations were interrupted by Dylan, who walked in carrying flowers, proceeding to bow down in front of Gabriella as he presented them to her. "For you, m'lady. Something to make you feel better."

She took the flowers from him, rolling her eyes. "Seriously, what's wrong with you?"

He stood up, undeterred. "The jury is still out, but my therapist is leaning toward dementia. Personally, I'm hoping for schizophrenia."

Gabriella rolled her eyes once more, but Kelly spotted her sniffing the flowers and felt like laughing herself.

"What about you, big guy?" Dylan said, backhanding Russel on the chest. "I heard the animal dropped you flat on your butt."

Russel ground his teeth. "You heard wrong."

"Really?" Dylan questioned sarcastically. "So, if it didn't kick your behind, then why wasn't it apprehended?"

Russel sighed. "It got away."

"I bet it did," Dylan said, smiling like an idiot for some reason.

"Dylan," Rhett suddenly said, his harsh tone scaring Kelly, "can you shut up for one morning, please?"

"Easy, man." Dylan held his hands up. "What, your sis gets a bruise to the head and suddenly you get all touchy?"

Rhett's eyes flinched, and Kelly saw his hand turning into a fist. Not wanting them to get into a fight, she reached her own hand down, stopping him. "It's fine," she whispered. "Just let it go." It took a second, but his fingers finally straightened again.

As long as Kelly could remember, she'd had to do this. Rhett was smart and nine times out of ten would stay calm and make the right decision, but every once in a while, his temper would flare, and she'd have to calm him down. Of course, if their parents were ever around that might have helped his temper, but she removed the thought from her head before she got irritated too.

Outside, Kelly suddenly heard arguing, loud enough to be easily understood.

"This is not a debate. I don't want you involved in this," an older man said, voice dignified but angry.

"They're my friends, Dad. I'm going to see them."

With that, the door opened and Luke stepped inside, looking like he would snap at any moment. The sheriff followed with piercing eyes, and for a moment Kelly thought he was going to drag Luke back outside by force, but eventually he calmed down, allowing Luke to greet them.

"Hey," Luke said, nodding to Kelly, who nodded back. Luke then silently gestured to the rest of them, clearly too afraid of his dad to speak up more.

"So," the sheriff finally said, speaking directly to Betty, "I was told you had woken up. Are you alright?"

She nodded.

"Good," he said. "When you feel up to it, you'll have to give a report of what you saw to the police officer outside. For now, I just wanted to discuss options with all of you."

"Options?" Kelly asked.

The sheriff nodded. "Given that this killer has attacked twice now, it's clear that it wasn't just an isolated incident on the twenty-fifth anniversary. Whoever this new animal is, they're here to stay until we find them. And given that you"–he pointed to Kelly–"have been attacked both times, that's a coincidence we can't ignore. It appears that this killer is targeting you because you survived the first attack, and it follows that now his targets would also include Russel, Betty, and Gabriella."

Kelly wished Oliver could have been here to hear the sheriff say that. Oliver had known from the start that the new animal would immediately target her, something that the police only admitted after it had happened. Most kids in school, and adults for that matter, were annoyed by Oliver's paranoia and constant obsession with the Animal, but Kelly had always admired it. Sure, he could be way too paranoid, but at the end of the day he was a lot more clever than most people, especially the sheriff, gave him credit for.

"So, what are you going to do?" Rhett asked.

"Well, the first thing I want to do is move those attacked into protective custody. There's a safe house at the edge of town where everyone attacked can stay until we catch this new killer. Most of you can go tonight, and Linda"—he hesitated as he switched the name—"Dr. Parker said that Betty will be able to get more stitches in a few hours and can be moved there in a couple of days once she heals up."

"I ain't going to a safe house," Russel said, voice firm.

"It's for your protection."

"I can protect myself."

Kelly smiled as she realized Dylan's jokes had bothered him. Russel was so used to being the strongest, even a joke about something hurting him made him visibly upset.

"Well," the sheriff said, "I can't force you into the safe house, but I would strongly recommend it."

In the corner of her eye, Kelly noticed Luke rolling his eyes and grinding his teeth every time his father spoke. On the one hand she felt sorry for him, having the sheriff as a father, being watched and judged twenty-four seven, all the while hearing how amazing some woman was that you'd never even met, who your father had just happened to save twenty-five years ago.

But on the other hand, at least Luke saw his father more than once every few months. Even if his dad was strict, at least he was present, and Kelly felt embarrassed about how jealous she was of that.

"I'll go," Betty said, wincing from pain in her chest.

"Me too," Gabriella added.

All the eyes in the room then shifted to Kelly, who grew uncomfortable as she felt them staring. Eventually, she nodded.

"Good," the sheriff said. "We will move the three of you to the safe house tonight, and then when Betty is able to be moved, she'll join you. As for right now, Gabriella and Betty, your parents are here to see you. Russel, we called your dad, and he's on the way."

Rhett tilted his head and chuckled out of anger. "Let me guess, you couldn't reach our parents, could you?"

"No," the sheriff said, voice low. "But we'll keep trying."

Rhett ground his teeth. "Good luck with that."

Kelly hid in the dark hallway, trying to escape the noise.

After everyone's folks showed up, it got so loud and cramped that she felt like she was suffocating, everyone staring at her as if she had brought the monster down upon them, as if the monster was linked to her survival. She just needed a few seconds to herself to calm down, process everything. *Just a few seconds, that isn't too much to ask for. Right?*

Apparently it was, because she jumped as a voice startled her from behind.

"Come here often?"

"For the love of—" She swore, muscles tensed as she saw him. "You can't just sneak up on people like that."

"Sorry," Oliver said, leaning against the wall. "Didn't mean to scare you."

"I'm sure you didn't," she said sarcastically, sighing as she also leaned back on the wall.

"So, how are you holding up?"

"Okay, I guess. I just don't really know what to do. It's like I'm stuck in limbo and can't control anything that happens. I can only watch."

"Well," Oliver said, voice kind, "sometimes watching is the best thing you can do. It means you aren't just stupidly rushing into things."

"Look at you, trying to make me feel better." She pushed him on the shoulder. "Oh, by the way, did you mention your theory about the animal coming back for me to the sheriff?"

"Yeah, why?"

She smiled. "Because he just told us the same theory, only he did it after the animal attacked again."

Oliver laughed. "Figures. Well, at least he admits it now."

"Yeah, I guess that is a positive. Plus, he says he's moving us to some safe house at the edge of town, for protection."

"Really," Oliver said, voice suddenly curious. "When did he tell you that?"

"Just a few minutes ago, while all of us were in Betty's room."

"Hmm," Oliver said, thinking something over but not sharing what it was. "By the way, how did you end up at the gym last night? Last I checked, you weren't exactly a bodybuilder."

"Ha," she mocked. "Dylan was supposed to pick up Gabriella but couldn't make it, so he asked me to go."

"And Rhett didn't go with you?"

She raised an eyebrow at him. Most likely he had already found out that Rhett hadn't been there. So, if that wasn't his real question, then what was it? "No, I asked, but he was busy."

Oliver nodded and then wrote, or at least pretended to write, something in his journal.

"You know," Kelly said, "now that we know it's blank, it doesn't annoy us anymore. So what's the point?"

He smiled. "I would never dream of annoying you. Besides, that's not why I use it."

"Why, then?"

The journal snapped shut as he put it behind his back. "Story for another day."

Kelly heard the movement of police officers and figured that the sheriff was looking for her. "Well, I better get going."

Oliver nodded. "I'm glad that you're okay."

"Thanks," she said, winking.

As she started to leave, she heard his voice again. "Hey, Kelly."

She turned back to face him. "What?"

"About the safe house," he said, voice more serious than she was used to. "I wouldn't tell anyone else about it."

"Why?"

Oliver just shrugged.

She laughed. "You really should learn to be less paranoid."

"Can't be too careful."

She smiled at him as she walked backwards. "In that case, should I have even told you?" She meant it as a joke but was surprised by his response.

"I wouldn't have."

CHAPTER ELEVEN

How could she help them?

Riley asked herself that question as she stood in her living room, staring at the flag, once waving high in the clouds as a symbol of life, now folded solemnly into a triangle, bright blue with white stars showing through the glass of its display case. A symbol of something else, of a life sacrificed. She reached her hand out and gently pressed her fingers against the small letters etched into the glass, spelling out the name of a loved one now gone.

In her heart, she had hoped staring at the memorial would help reinforce her decision that helping the kids was a mistake, that she shouldn't get involved, because it only led to death, only led to more suffering. If she got involved, even if she could protect Emma, she could still lose her own life, and then Emma would be left all alone, just like she had been.

She couldn't let that happen to her daughter.

But the longer she looked at the flag, the more she began to wonder if she was wrong. If ignoring the kids who needed help wasn't right, but instead cruel. If there had been someone like her twenty-five years ago, with history and training, she would have given anything for them to help her, help her parents. She would have blamed them if they hadn't, whether it was fair or not.

She put her head in her hands, pushing the thoughts from her mind, repeating it to herself once more. She couldn't help them, and even if she could, it wasn't a risk she could take. Even if it wasn't the Animal, it could still be dangerous. It could still kill her, and she wouldn't leave Emma alone. She had promised to always be there, always protect her. That was the only reason she lived. Protecting her daughter was the only reason she still had for breathing, for enduring the memories, the flashes of bloodshed not forgotten.

"What's wrong?"

The voice of her daughter startled her, and Riley turned to see Emma standing across the room. She was rubbing her eyes, apparently sleepy.

"Nothing," Riley said softly. "Why would something be wrong?"

"You always stare at that when something is wrong."

Riley sighed but then smiled. "You're too smart for your age."

"So, what's wrong?"

Riley started to lie, but how could she? She didn't want Emma to be scared, but it wasn't fair to keep her in the dark about what was happening. She deserved to know.

So, Riley sat down with her on the couch and explained everything she could about these new attacks. At least, everything that she could tell an eight-year-old without scarring her for life. When she was done, she was surprised at how well Emma seemed to take the information, and she smiled as she realized the girl was tougher than she sometimes gave her credit for.

"So," Emma asked, "why were you staring at the flag?"

"Because Hank called last night and asked me to help the kids. And I want to, but I can't."

"Why not?" Emma asked, and Riley knew she was genuinely curious. She had always asked questions that Riley didn't want to answer, but did it so sincerely it gave her no choice. Of all the things to get from her father, why did it have to be that?

"Because I can't risk it. If something went wrong, then—" Riley paused, not knowing how to say it. "I just can't. It's too dangerous."

Emma stayed silent for a moment, seeming to think it over in her head before responding. "Could you help the kids?"

"I don't know. Maybe."

"If," Emma started before hesitating, clearly wanting to ask something but afraid of getting in trouble, until Riley nodded that it was okay. "If we can help someone, don't we have to?"

Riley smiled and, not knowing how else to respond, hugged her daughter. As she did, she glanced back up at the folded flag, which seemed to be telling her the same thing her daughter had, and knew that the only way to figure this out was to talk to him. Even if she was afraid of where it might lead, talking to him was the only thing since that night that had ever made her feel safe.

"You should see how big she's gotten," Riley said. "Fast, too. The kid can almost outrun me. She misses you so much, you know. We both do. I'm sorry I left her in the car. I promise I'll bring her next time, but I needed to talk to you alone for a little while."

Wind blew softly through the field. Sunlight seemed to pour out of the sky, drenching everything in sight with its warmth, like a gentle fire softly burning away the cold breeze, which swept across Riley's cheek as she sat in the grass, surrounded by the tombstones of strangers, leaning back on the tombstone of the loved one she missed.

"I just don't know what to do. For my entire life, I've been afraid that it would come back, and I've done everything I could think of to prepare in case it did, but now that I'm here, it feels like I'm being suffocated. And I don't think this is the same animal, I honestly don't, but what if I'm wrong? I want to help the kids, I swear I do, but if I get involved, and Emma gets hurt... I couldn't live with it. Or what if I get involved and the Animal does finally kill me? Emma has already lost you; she can't lose me too."

A tear fell from her face as she spoke. "And I know what you would say if you were here. You'd probably say something sickly optimistic, like living in fear isn't living at all, and that I need to get past the trauma and help whoever I can. But then again you went and got yourself killed, so what good is your advice?"

The words came out angry, harsher than she had meant them to, and so she rested her head in her hands, wiping off the tears. "I'm sorry. That wasn't fair. It's just hard, you know? As sad as it is, sometimes I miss how it was before I met you, when I was angry at everything and wouldn't let anyone in. I was depressed, lonely, but at least I didn't have to be afraid of losing anyone else."

Riley smiled, remembering everything that had happened. "And then you came along and ruined everything by making me happy." She lifted her head up, letting the sunlight cascade over it. "Emma reminds me of you so much. She has the same hopeless optimism that you had." Riley laughed. "Man, that used to annoy me, how you could just be so happy all the time. Why couldn't Emma have been a cynic, like me? It would make hating the world again so much easier.

"You probably think this is funny, don't you? That even after you're gone, your daughter is still forcing me to be happy, not letting me crawl back into that hole you worked so hard to get me out of." Riley sighed, remembering how lonely she had been before, how much she had fought back against him at first, his attempts to help her. "You always did know just what to say."

She sat there in silence for a few more minutes, lost in her memories, enjoying the peacefulness, until finally she forced herself to come back to reality as she felt the carved letters of her husband's name press gently against her back. Sighing, she suddenly knew exactly what he would say.

"I have to help them, don't I? You'd tell me that I have to help. If not for them, then for me. So that I can move on and not be afraid anymore. So that for the rest of my life, when I hug Emma, I won't be terrified of letting go, of never seeing her again. I have to help end this."

She tried to make her voice firm, unconsciously trying to convince him she wasn't scared. "Hank called and said that the kids were being put in a safe house, now that the one girl is stable. I'll go there tonight and see what I can do to help." Riley chuckled, realizing the change in her voice. She had never been able to hide it from him. "I hope you're happy with yourself. Even gone, you can still talk me into doing things I'm afraid of."

With those words spoken, Riley stood up, turning to look at the tombstone one last time, holding back another tear as she felt all of the pain and loss flooding back to her in an instant, standing there in the cemetery, all alone.

"Why'd you have to leave me too?"

CHAPTER TWELVE

Clyde couldn't sleep.

Everything he had seen just kept replaying in his head like a broken record, ingraining the brief glimpse of the monster his eyes had witnessed into his head forever. The black fur, the massive teeth, and what appeared to be bloodstains on its face.

It was a wolf. Of that Clyde was certain. However, it wasn't like any wolf he had ever seen. It was larger, darker, more monster than animal. But Clyde believed that at its core, if you looked past all the terrifying features, the haunting yellow eyes, the unnatural, distorted bones hiding within its black, withered, blood-covered fur, it was still just a wolf.

Which somehow made Clyde more uneasy.

Because if it was just a wolf, then its behavior made no sense. A wolf might stalk its prey from the woods, and it might even watch him without attacking at first, but there wasn't an animal on this earth that would chase its prey through the forest and then leave when it had the prey within its grasp. Something was wrong.

Something was different about this one.

Clyde turned over in the bed, trying to fall asleep, get his mind off this, but he couldn't. Not because he wasn't tired, for he hadn't really slept in days, but because nothing made sense, he felt anxious, and most of all, for a reason he couldn't explain, his bed felt too soft.

Where were the tracks? The question kept ringing in his thoughts. If it was really just a wolf, it would have left tracks, even more so than a normal wolf given its size. But he had found nothing, not a single trace that it existed other than what he had seen and the growling that still echoed in his ears. That wasn't possible.

And then there were these attacks he kept seeing on the news. Some creature was attacking kids, just like it evidently had twenty-five years ago, and yet Hank seemed convinced that the monster he had seen in the woods wasn't related.

How could he be so sure?

Confused and frustrated, Clyde felt like he

could scream. Maybe Linda was right. Maybe he was just getting paranoid, having dreams of a wolf that wasn't there, conjuring up some monster to run from because running felt more natural than standing still, because terror felt more comfortable than safety.

Outside, wolves howled at the moon, and in spite of all their brutal, predatory instincts, their howl still managed to sound majestic, echoing into the night sky for miles, filling the entire forest with the knowledge of their presence.

It also sent a chill down Clyde's spine. The howls sounded close, probably seven hundred feet at most. Clyde always did that by instinct, tried to determine how close the wolves were. They so rarely made a sound that their howls became one of the only ways to track them.

Clyde shifted to lying on his back, eyes still closed, and desperately tried to sleep. Tried to escape the thoughts, the fears, the horror he felt was closing in. Whatever was in town didn't have anything to do with him, and whatever was in the woods was just a wolf. Just a normal animal, like he'd seen a thousand times before.

Then he heard the glass break.

It was merely a crack at first, until it shattered fully, little pieces of broken glass falling to the wooden floor, the sound of them shattering revealing the truth of this dark night. Something

had broken through the window on the other side of the cabin.

Something was already inside.

In a burst of panic, Clyde tried to move, but before he could think, splinters of wood flew across the room as his bedroom door was broken.

Clyde froze as the broken door swung open, revealing the wolflike monster behind it. It stood on all fours, teeth bared, hungry yellow eyes piercing with the focus of a hunter. For a brief moment it stayed completely still, and they both watched each other, waiting for it to happen, for the attack to come, and as Clyde sat paralyzed, looking at the beast, he knew that he had been wrong. It wasn't just a wolf, it was a shadow, a dark reflection of a beast, something that existed outside of nature, outside of sanity, like the twisted reflection of a child's nightmare, a creature come to feast on his screams as well as his bones.

Finally, the attack did come, as the wolf opened its grotesque jaws and growled before leaping toward the bed, toward its prey. In a burst of pure adrenaline, Clyde shot off the bed, falling to the floor, watching as the massive animal missed its target and landed on the mattress, momentum causing its distorted body to impact the wall, cracking the wood as it did. Yet even that wouldn't deter it, for the monster turned in an instant to face him.

The rifle. He had to get the rifle.

He had left it at the foot of the bed, leaning against the frame. Terrified, Clyde went for it as the wolf stayed atop the bed, watching him from above as he scrambled for his life.

Desperate, he reached the gun and chambered a round, the wolf still studying him, motionless. For a brief second of hope, Clyde thought he could kill it as he lifted up the rifle and fired a shot.

The bullet passed through the wolf's neck, spraying blood over the cracks of the wall, a wound that would have been lethal to virtually anything breathing. But the animal didn't fall down, didn't whimper, didn't even flinch. It just stood there, watching him as he started to crawl backwards.

Clyde chambered another round and fired again, and once more, blood spattered on the wall behind it, but still the wolf didn't move, even as blood began dripping down from its black fur.

Have to run. Have to hide, Clyde thought in a panic as he crawled backwards, toward the closet door. It was just big enough to hide in. If he could get to it maybe he would be safe.

He was certain the wolf would pounce at any moment, but it didn't, allowing him time to crawl to the door and get inside, but not before firing a final round at the wolf. This time, the wolf growled, and as Clyde shut the door, he caught a fleeting glance of the beast midair, bloodstained teeth showing as it snarled.

Clyde's heart felt like it exploded in his chest when the wolf hit the door, almost breaking it. Panicking, Clyde dropped to the floor with his back against the wall and his rifle trained on the door.

Forced into a corner with no way out, he watched in horror as the door shook like a tornado was right outside, wood cracking, floor vibrating.

Crash.

But the growling was even worse. Vicious and frenzied, the animal didn't even sound like a wolf anymore, didn't sound like it was merely hunting or threatening its prey.

It sounded angry.

Crash.

Clyde stayed frozen in place, waiting for the animal to break through the door, his heart stopping with every impact, his lungs not willing to even breathe, fear having choked the life from them.

Crash.

As he waited for it to face him again, rip him apart and devour what was left, Clyde's hands began shaking as he realized he was waiting to die. Waiting for the next crash, when the door would be shattered and the beast would find him.

But the moment never came, and suddenly the growling stopped almost as fast as it had begun, leaving Clyde alone. Thin traces of moonlight

crept through the scattered cracks on the door, illuminating his cabin as he sat frozen in fear, terrified of being hunted, of being killed.

Afraid of becoming prey.

CHAPTER THIRTEEN

Betty felt like her lungs were lit on fire every time she breathed, which, considering how nervous she was, was quite a bit.

The safe house they were in hardly felt safe. It might have been on the edge of this cursed town, away from all the other houses, but even here you couldn't escape the forest. Betty could see it through the window: endless trees hiding who knows what, and the only way to escape it would be to leave the town entirely, something she herself had desperately wanted to do.

But her parents couldn't be convinced, and Betty would never understand it. After what had happened twenty-five years ago, she felt that any logical person would have left the town, gotten away as fast as they could, but for some reason, they hadn't. It was like everyone in this town was too fascinated with the stories, the legend of the Animal, and were simply staying in town in an attempt to one day experience the legend again, almost waiting for the Animal to return.

Now it had, and it was coming for her. For all of them.

Outside, it watched them from the forest.

"Are you okay?" Kelly suddenly asked her.

She nodded her head. "Yeah, I'm okay. Just nervous is all." As she spoke, her fingers crept up to the wounds embedded in her skin, and she noticed Kelly was doing the same, if unconsciously.

Betty and Kelly were both sitting on the couch, but Gabriella was across from them, sitting sideways on a chair.

"So, what's it like?" Gabriella asked.

"What?"

Gabriella rolled her eyes, seemingly put out that she had to clarify. "Getting stabbed? Does it hurt?"

Kelly looked at her like she was insane. "What do you mean, *does it hurt*? Obviously, it hurts."

"Sorry," Gabriella mocked, "didn't mean to touch a nerve."

"Didn't you get stabbed?" Kelly asked.

"Not really," Gabriella said, reaching behind her and tracing the wound on her back. "It just grazed me." She then turned to the deputy standing by the door, one of three that had been posted there to protect them. "What about you, have you ever been stabbed?"

"No," the man said, his tone implying that he wasn't in the mood to be questioned, but when had that ever stopped Gabriella?

"Have you been shot?"

"No."

"What about getting punched? Anyone ever hit you?"

"No."

"Well, then." Gabriella turned back to her friends. "Isn't he just the life of the party?"

Something moved in the woods. The deputy outside was sure of it. He'd been walking the perimeter of the house, bored out of his mind, when he'd seen it, the sudden movement of a shadow.

Raising his weapon up, he walked closer to the trees, searching for its origin. But he wasn't an idiot. He wasn't about to walk into the forest alone, so he stayed right at the edge, shining his flashlight into the woods, trying to find it from afar.

Wood cracked.

Heart suddenly racing, he moved the flashlight but saw nothing. How could there be nothing? He could have sworn it sounded right on top of him.

Something started growling.

It sounded so close, it had to be right next to him. Hands shaking, he frantically scanned the forest, desperate to find the creature before it could reach him, before its claws could take hold of his body and drag him back into the forest's depths. But then the growling got louder, and suddenly he couldn't breathe, as he realized where it was coming from. It was right in front of him, only it wasn't on the ground.

In slow, agonizing horror, he tilted the flashlight, its light slowly creeping up the trees until finally it revealed the animal waiting for him. Dark fur, sharp teeth, kneeling over a branch, watching its prey from above.

Before he could fire his weapon, the monster leapt down from the tree, crashing into him, bringing him down to the cold ground below. But he only felt the chill of the grass for a moment, because then he felt something stab into his chest and through his heart, causing so much pain that he couldn't even scream as the monster loomed over him, twisted features glowing in the moonlight.

Betty leaned her head back against the couch, staring at the ceiling. "So, who do you think the Animal really is?"

"I bet it's not even a real person," Gabriella said. "I think it's some kind of supernatural creature, like a werewolf or something."

Kelly shook her head. "You're saying you think it's an actual werewolf?"

"Yep."

"But," Betty started, "that makes no sense. Firstly, werewolves aren't real, and even if they were, why would one be in our town?"

Gabriella shrugged. "I don't know, maybe this town was built on a wolf graveyard or cursed by a witch. Isn't that how these stories normally go?"

Kelly rolled her eyes. "Welp, we've lost Gabriella."

"I don't see you two spitting out ideas."

Flashes of the animal stabbing her burst into her head as Betty spoke. "I used to think it was a wolf, like an actual wolf." The pain in her chest grew worse. "But then it walked on two legs, and stabbed me. So, I don't know anymore."

"Hmm," Gabriella said. "What about you, Kelly? You have any ideas?"

Kelly hesitated for a moment as Betty realized that she was the only one in the entire town to have seen the creature twice. She had even seen it more than the girl who'd survived all those years ago, assuming it was the same animal.

Betty herself had only seen it once, and she didn't know if she would ever be able to sleep again. She couldn't imagine what Kelly must be feeling. To have been hunted twice, to have made it out alive, knowing it was still out there, still hunting you.

Betty felt chills creep down her spine.

The second deputy was sitting on the back porch, trying to reach his partner over the police radio.

"Are you there? Please respond."

No response came, and he got nervous. It wasn't like his partner not to respond. Something had to be wrong. He stood up from beside the door and stepped over to the edge of the stained wood porch, using his flashlight to scan the trees, seeing bark, leaves, and...

The shock almost caused him to drop his flashlight. At the edge of the forest, his partner's corpse was leaned against a tree that had been out of his view just a moment ago, covered in blood and mouth still wide open: a sign that his last moments had been spent wailing in agony.

The deputy started walking down the steps in a desperate attempt to save a friend who was already dead. He reached for his radio, wanting to call for help, but fear and sudden terror stopped him in his tracks as he noticed what was on the ground in front of him. Traces of blood and grass pressed into the ground, creating a trail that led right underneath the stairs.

It was right under him.

Before he could scream, a fur-covered arm moved from underneath the creaky rotted stairs and shoved something into his right leg, through his ankle. The pain caused him to trip, and he fell off the stairs, landing on the ground below.

It was then that he peered into the opening beneath the steps and saw the animal hunched over, lurking within it, blood on its face, monstrous head tilted as it watched him. He reached for his gun, but it was far too late, and the creature took hold of his legs, grip tight as it dragged him underneath the stairs, before doing what all animals do when prey is in their lair.

It slaughtered him.

"I think it's a man."

"Really?" Betty questioned. "You think that the Animal is just a normal guy?"

"I didn't say normal," Kelly responded. "But given the choice between supernatural werewolf and insane costume-wearing psychopath, I think the latter is more reasonable."

"Don't listen to her," Gabriella told Betty. "She only thinks that because that's what her boyfriend keeps saying."

Kelly sighed, and Betty grew intrigued. "What? Who?"

"Please don't start this," Kelly said, sighing once more.

"Oliver," Gabriella said, clearly enjoying how much it annoyed her.

"Oliver?" Betty said, confused. She knew both of them but didn't usually hang out in their friend group, so it took her a second to place the name. But when she did, she almost laughed out loud. "The crazy kid obsessed with the Animal?"

"That's the one."

"No way," Betty said to Kelly, who looked both irritated and embarrassed at the same time.

"First off, he's not crazy. He's paranoid and obsessive, sure, but not crazy. And *secondly*," she said, attempting to murder Gabriella with her eyes, "we're just friends. Gabriella is just trying to irritate me for some reason."

"Don't get all worked up," Gabriella said, "I'm just trying to take our minds off the fact that there is an animal out there in the woods, probably coming for us as we speak."

The sentence made Betty's heart begin to race again as she wondered how Gabriella could even say it out loud.

"You've been hanging around Dylan too much," Kelly said, voice uneasy. "His annoying lack of empathy is rubbing off on you."

Gabriella just shrugged. "Calm down. We're in a safe house. It's not like the Animal is actually going to get to us."

The moment the words left her mouth, something crashed into the back door.

"What was that!" Betty tried to force her scream to become a whisper but failed miserably.

Kelly held her hand out, a signal to be quiet, and looked to the deputy still guarding the front door. He was already on his radio, trying to contact the deputies left outside, whose blood was being absorbed by the dirt at that very moment.

"Are you there?" he whispered. "What happened?"

No answer came, and the sound of something hitting the back door echoed through the house once more—and then again, continuing to haunt them with its sadistic knocking.

Gun drawn, the deputy slowly moved closer to the door, and Betty could see him flinch slightly every time the door shook. She felt herself suffocating, fear keeping her from breathing as she waited for the horror to arrive, waited for the horrific knocking to stop.

Crash.

Crash.

Crash.

The deputy was almost there now, and out of the corner of her eye, Betty saw Kelly shifting her weight, getting ready to run if she had to. She had always envied that, Kelly's ability to stay calm and know what the smartest move was. Betty got ready to run as well, still shaking as the deputy approached the door, and the knocking suddenly stopped.

The deputy planted his feet on the ground and leaned against the wall, gun still up as he unlocked the door and swung it open, ready for whatever was outside.

Betty felt a sense of dread she had never known existed as she waited for the animal to reveal itself, for the grisly reality to come into focus.

A dead body burst through the doorway, covered in blood. Behind it hid the monster, and the deputy attempted to fire at it, but his bullet hit the corpse's shoulder instead.

As the carcass's blood splattered on the wall, the creature let go of the corpse and grabbed the off-balance deputy, bringing him to the ground, stabbing him in the hand as he tried to fire his weapon.

Despite having readied herself, Betty stood paralyzed, eyes unable to look away from the carnage, until she felt Kelly dragging her by the arm, forcing her back toward the front door.

Betty almost fainted when they opened it, as the body of the third deputy, the one whose corpse had rested against a tree only a few minutes ago, fell onto them, drenching them in his blood, pale broken flesh brushing against their skin, lifeless eyes seeming to cry out for help. Screaming, Betty saw the animal covered in dark fur and blood once more as it quit stabbing the deputy, now running toward them, sharpened bone in hand.

Betty turned to run out the door, but her foot caught on the body of the corpse now lying on the floor, and she would have tripped completely had Kelly not grabbed her by the back of her shirt and kept her stable. The animal, however, had evidently expected her to trip and had lunged toward the door, narrowly missing her side with its blade of bone and crashing through the doorway.

The beast was now at the front door, its horrific features visible as an outlined shadow against the shimmering glow of moonlight. The back door led only to the forest and therefore wasn't an option, so with no other choice, Betty followed Kelly up the stairs, knowing all it could do was trap them in a corner and delay their deaths for just a moment longer.

It chased them up the stairs.

Betty swore she could feel its rancid breath on the back of her neck as they ran up the steps and down the hallway, practically diving into the room at the end.

Gabriella immediately ran to the other end of the room, getting as far away from the danger as possible. Fear finally overtook Betty and everything began to get blurry, her vision now a haze of distorted shadows, so thick she could barely make out Kelly shutting the door a second before the monster crashed into it.

Betty jumped back in shock, falling to the floor and crawling backwards away from the door. Within moments all three of them were together, crouching by the far wall, watching as the door continued to shake, wood continued to split, and finally, a bloodied bone broke through it.

They were going to die.

It was the only thought Betty could find inside her head. They had survived this long, but it hadn't mattered. They were backed into a corner, with no weapons, no savior, and no way of escape. It was over.

The Animal was going to kill them.

CHAPTER FOURTEEN

Riley had lied.

At the cemetery, she had told herself she was doing this to help the kids, to make sure no one else went through what she had. Part of that might have even been true, but it wasn't why she had called Hank and asked about the safe house. That wasn't why she found herself walking toward it, rifle in hand.

This wasn't about the kids. It wasn't even about the Animal.

It was about *her.*

She'd spent the last twenty-five years of her life hiding, afraid that the Animal would find her at any moment, afraid to move forward with her life. On some days, she even got scared of loving her own daughter for fear that one day the Animal would find her and take Emma away from her.

But she was done. Twenty-five years of rage and fear had suddenly erupted, and she was done wondering if this new creature was the same monster from her nightmares or a new predator. But most of all, she was done waiting for a monster to find her.

She would find it.

The sounds of the girls screaming almost drowned out the creature's growling, but they could still hear it on the other side of the door, clawing its way in. It would reach them soon, and then it would be over.

Riley approached the door cautiously, hearing screams as she walked up the creaking wooden steps and saw the bloodied body of a police officer lying in the doorway, stab wounds covering his entire chest.

Riley tightened her grip on the rifle.

The door broke, and Betty couldn't breathe.

She could see it now, standing across from them: dark grey fur consumed by the darkness of the house, monstrous head, pointed ears like a wolf, twisting the sharpened bone in its hand as it slowly moved closer to them.

Each footstep caused her to scream louder.

She could feel Kelly and Gabriella beside her, screaming just as she was, and she desperately wanted to run, but there was nowhere left to go as the realization finally took hold, bringing tears with it.

She was going to die.

Riley walked up the steps, hearing the screams, the horrific growling that should have sent chills down her spine. But all she could think about was what was waiting for her atop the stairs, only a few moments away. What if she'd made a mistake?

What if it was the real Animal?

The monster lifted up its weapon, now so close they could almost smell its rancid breath, almost feel its coarse fur on their skin as it prepared to strike, to finally kill its prey. Crying, Betty took one last look at its unnatural, distorted face.

Waiting for it to kill her.

But then horror turned to shock as she saw something move behind it. Outside of the room, across the hallway, now atop the stairs.

The creature must have seen her shocked expression, because it also turned, seeing the figure standing in the shadows, in front of a window at the end of the hallway. Betty's eyes desperately tried to adjust to the absence of light, and for a brief moment, she thought she could make it out.

It almost looked like a woman.

Riley saw it for the first time, standing less than twenty feet away, and it wasn't what she'd expected. Her hands didn't shake, her adrenaline didn't spike; her heart didn't even beat quicker. She just looked at it, the monster that had been terrorizing kids, haunting the town for days. White teeth, dark grey fur, unnatural movement; she could see why the kids were afraid of it.

In the darkness, it almost looked scary.

But she wasn't afraid. She didn't know what this creature was, but it didn't deserve fear.

The creature watched her for a moment, tilting its head and growling as they both faced each other. Shock turned to confusion as Betty desperately tried to understand why the woman wasn't running. Why she didn't seem scared.

Riley's grip tightened on the rifle, and she was about to lift it up, shoot the predator in the head, splattering its blood on the walls behind it, when something unexpected happened.

It took a hostage.

It grabbed one of the girls and held her in front, shielding itself. Riley recognized the girl. She was the one from the first crime scene: Kelly. The girl tried to fight back against the monster, but it moved its sharpened bone up to her neck, stopping her from struggling. Then, everything was perfectly still.

"Shoot it," one of the other girls screamed.

For a moment, Riley was confused, wondering what it was waiting for, until she realized it wasn't trying to kill the girl, at least not at that moment. It was threatening her, trying to get Riley to drop her weapon, like a rattlesnake warns its prey before attacking.

"Please," Kelly cried out desperately, begging Riley for help with tears streaming down her face and a knife pressed against her throat.

There was nothing that Riley wanted more in that moment than to put a bullet in the fake animal's skull, but she tempered her rage, knowing that right now all that mattered was the girl's life. So, after a few moments of hesitation, Riley reached out and dropped the rifle down the stairs, listening as it hit step after step until finally colliding with the floor.

Now that she was unarmed, the creature thought she was easy prey, and so it threw Kelly aside, charging Riley.

Ready to kill the girl who'd survived all those years ago.

The one the real Animal had missed.

⸎

No! Betty tried to scream, but her voice was gone. The woman had dropped her weapon, and now the animal was going to slaughter her, slaughter all of them. But then, through her tears, she realized the woman wasn't moving, wasn't even trying to run away.

What was wrong with her?

⸎

Wait, Riley told herself. It was less than fifteen feet away, running at her like a wild animal, arms outstretched, back hunched over, attempting to look imposing.

Wait.

It was ten feet away now, and Riley remembered the screams of her childhood, horrific bloodcurdling cries for help as her neighbors, her family, were charged by the Animal, unable to get away, unable to fight.

Wait.

Just a second longer, and it would be too close to stop, too close to run, and it would be too late. The creature wouldn't be able to get away from her.

Now.

The monster lunged, and Riley moved sideways, dodging its strike and watching as it stumbled forward. In an instant she grabbed the back of its head and used its own momentum to throw it forward against the wall, listening as it winced in pain.

Riley couldn't see its eyes, but she could feel its shock. It hadn't been expecting that.

The creature was back on its feet in an instant and charged her, swinging its blade wildly, almost frenzied as it growled.

Riley tried to move away, but she couldn't escape every swipe, and suddenly she felt something cut through her forearm, then her stomach.

Sharp pain made her hesitate for a moment as the creature shoved her back into the wall. Riley felt the wound; it wasn't deep but had drawn blood. Yet the pain was gone as quickly as it had come, replaced with hatred as she looked at the thing in front of her, wolflike features concealing what hid beneath. The monster's true face.

The creature swung again, but Riley caught its arm and forced it sideways, causing the blade to narrowly miss her stomach. Then she grabbed ahold of the monster itself, feeling its coarse fur as she shoved it backwards.

Before it could find its footing, Riley was on it again, drawing her own silver knife from her boot and swinging for its head. It moved out of the way just in time to save its life, but Riley still took its ear off.

Appearing to panic, it moved backwards away from her, but Riley lunged at it like a feral dog, swinging her knife at its throat over and over again, striking at its head, trying to kill it, forcing it backwards in the hallway, closer to the edge of the stairs, and the window above them.

Unrelenting, Riley swung her knife, once again going for the throat, but the creature managed to kick her leg, knocking her off-balance. Before she could steady herself, it was on her, shoving her to the wall, hands on her throat, choking the life out of her.

Its grip was tight, and she felt like her neck could snap at any moment as she struggled to breathe, to think. The monster was right in front of her now, and moonlight shone through the window, illuminating it clearly.

It wasn't real.

The darkness might have been able to hide it, but in the light, she saw what she had known she would. The fur that covered its body was dark grey, but it was fake. Its face looked like a wolf, but Riley could see the truth. It was also fake, an imitation. Hard plastic covered in faux fur, it was just a mask, and beneath it, hiding within the costume, was something human.

The grip around her neck tightened, and Riley knew what she had to do. She used what strength she had left to strike the monster in the face, shifting its mask over its eyes.

Blinded, it released its grip and tried to move the mask, regain its sight.

Before it could, Riley charged it again, screaming in anger as she shoved it backwards into the window, watching the glass shatter as the predator crashed through it and fell to the ground.

Ending the predator's attack.

Riley leaned out the window, watching it on the grass, dazed and struggling to get up. But it did, and it ran. Without a second thought, Riley was down the stairs, grabbing the rifle from the floor and running out the back door, passing a deputy's corpse as she did.

On the porch now, she looked out, seeing it run into the woods, limping but fast. She raised the rifle, but the scope was cracked from the impact of hitting the stairs.

Still, Riley tried to find the fleeing creature in the scope, even with the cracked glass and dark night making it next to impossible. But finally, she found it and fired a single round, which hit the tree next to it, less than four inches from its head. An instant later it was gone, running into the shadows, hiding within the heart of the forest.

Lowering the gun, Riley sighed as she looked into the woods. She heard the girls coming down the stairs, still quivering in fear, needing comfort, but all Riley could think about was the Animal. She had seen it when she was eight, and all these years later she still remembered it perfectly, every horrific detail.

What she had seen tonight wasn't it.

The Animal she remembered wasn't wearing a costume, wasn't covered in fake fur. Its wolf skin was real. It hadn't growled as a cheap attempt to scare her, hadn't used a blade to slaughter her parents; it had used its bare hands. Most of all, it hadn't run, even after the gunfire had started. It had just grown more frenzied, more vicious. She could still feel its presence to this day, watching her.

An animal that couldn't be human.

A monster that couldn't be killed.

What she had just seen was different. It might have been able to scare the kids, hide itself in the darkness, and fool those who'd never seen the real Animal. But now that she had faced it, she knew the truth. It might have been brutal, deadly even, but it was just a cheap imitation of a real monster, a stray dog pretending it was a wolf. It might have been scary, but Riley felt it in her bones.

It wasn't the Animal.

But the thought made Riley afraid once more. Because if this wasn't the horror she remembered, that meant the real Animal was still out there, hiding somewhere in the forest, waiting to return. A tear fell down her face as her thoughts went back to that night, when everything she'd loved had been stripped away from her by an unfeeling, inhuman monster and she had been left all alone, forever waiting for it to return, to finish what it had started and finally kill her.

Riley looked into the forest, examining the shadows within. It was out there somewhere, the monster from her past, the creature from her nightmares.

The Animal.

CHAPTER FIFTEEN

Something was in the room, and it was scared.

Covered in the blood of its victims, the Animal beat on the door, hearing the things inside scream at every impact. It could feel their terror, their presence, the blood coursing through still-breathing corpses, waiting to be spilled.

The door shattered.

The Animal stepped inside, facing the things hiding within. They were large, just like the rest had been, but they had no sharp teeth, no claws. Yet somewhere deep inside, the Animal sensed their savagery, the beatings they could inflict.

In an act of sheer bravery, the larger one charged, striking it. The Animal didn't flinch, only grabbing

the thing's throat and ripping it from him before shoving his head into the wall, crushing the thing's skull. The body writhed in shock as it hit the floor.

The smaller one screamed louder than it had ever heard, even louder than the wolves. For the briefest moment, the Animal hesitated, looking at the thing in front of it, before instinct took over once more.

The Animal struck the smaller thing in the face once, tearing its skin from its bone and leaving behind a mound of flesh unrecognizable, so little left on the bone that even vultures wouldn't touch it.

The corpse dropped to the floor.

Tilting its head slightly sideways, the Animal listened to more screams from afar. Living prey finding the bodies it had left behind, the trail of blood it had caused.

It would hunt them too.

But as it started to leave, it felt something. It heard no sound, saw no movement, but somehow it could feel the presence of prey, of terror.

Something else was here, and it was close.

Instinct revealing the truth, the Animal's eyes moved toward the bed. The thing it hunted was under there, hiding. This one must be smaller than the rest.

It took one step toward the bed, and then it heard it. The scream.

The voice sounded young; whatever it was, it was only a child. But that didn't matter. The Animal's hand twitched at the sound of the scream,

so terrified, so vulnerable, like a deer with a broken leg, moaning into the forest, hoping the wolves wouldn't come.

But they always did.

Because it was the pain that drew them, like sharks searching for blood in the water. Helpless prey that couldn't fight back, couldn't run, couldn't even hide.

It listened to the child's scream a moment longer before moving toward the bed to stop the screaming and end the prey's life. To rip it in two and silence it forever.

Suddenly, there was a loud crack and a flash of light, and the Animal felt something tear into its shoulder, spraying its blood over the room.

Gunfire.

Clyde woke up in a burst of terror, falling out of the bed and onto the floor beneath him. His hands were trembling as he thought of the dream. The bloodshed, the hunting. But something inside him knew the truth. It wasn't just a dream. It was a memory, scratching at the walls of his broken mind, trying to claw its way back into his head.

Shaking, he lay on the floor, body trembling, heart racing as he tried to escape the nightmare, escape the memories, the sudden sensation of hunting, killing. Most of all, trying to escape that uneasy feeling that the dream was the most natural he'd felt in years.

Tears streamed down his face as he tried to block it from his thoughts, but it wouldn't leave. Now that it had crawled its way back into his mind like a primal instinct fighting back against a new memory, it was never going away. All Clyde could do was lie on the floor in horror, haunted by the screams of his past.

"What's happening to me?"

PART TWO

THE
PREDATOR

CHAPTER SIXTEEN

They all seemed so scared.

The horror of the past night still lingered in her thoughts as Riley tried to figure out what to say to them. The girls who'd been attacked, the ones she'd most likely saved. What could she tell them? That it would be okay when she knew it probably wouldn't? That they were safe now, when that was only temporary? Ever since that night, Riley had become many things, but a liar was not one of them. Telling someone they were safe when they weren't was cruel, because then they couldn't prepare, couldn't brace themselves for what might happen.

What they might lose.

But that didn't make the truth any easier, especially looking at them now, still in the safe house, hiding from the police that were combing the entire area, looking for what had hunted them.

"So, you're Riley?" one of the girls said, startling her by speaking first. It was the blonde, the same kid she had seen at the first crime scene, the one this new predator was targeting. "The girl who survived?"

"Yeah," she said. "I'm Riley."

"I'm Kelly," the girl said, voice cracking slightly.

Riley nodded. She had known the girl's name; Hank had told her the names of both the girls and their immediate friends. But Riley had spent her entire life meeting people who knew her name before she told them, knew the stories before they knew her. She didn't want to do the same thing to these new victims. "So, what about you?"

The second girl looked athletic, but small. Extremely small, the kind who, if put in jail, could probably slip straight through the bars. But her size wasn't evident from her personality, because she said her name with confidence. "I'm Gabriella."

Riley nodded, then looked to the third. They were all scared, but this one was quivering more than the other two, her eyes still occasionally darting left or right, scared of something that wasn't there. All while she visibly clutched her midsection, protecting the wounds.

"My name is Betty."

"Well, it's nice to meet you all," Riley said, still trying to find the right words, the perfect thing to say to make them feel better. She considered what everyone else would tell them but couldn't bring herself to say the words. After a lifetime of people telling her everything was going to be okay, she'd grown tired of the lies, the false hope, and preferred truth no matter how twisted, because at least it was real. So, she gave up searching for the right words and instead just started talking; it was all she could do, and she hoped it would be enough.

"I know how it feels. The doctors will call it shock, but that's not it, not exactly. It's this strange feeling in the bottom of your stomach that tells you this isn't real. That you already died, and your body is just stuck in limbo, waiting to fall like your mind already has. You'll start seeing things in the corner of your eye and think that it's come back to kill you. You'll probably start having nightmares, and you'll wake up screaming. Eventually it might get so bad that you start to wish you had died. Not out of survivor's guilt, but out of fear. Wanting the pain to be over so badly that you will wish it had already taken you and ended your suffering.

"And I can't tell you that it's going to be okay, because I honestly don't know. But I can promise you this. As long as you're still breathing, you're still alive. No amount of fear can take that from you. So, savor every single breath you take, because if you don't, then what was the point of surviving?"

After that, the room grew quiet, and Riley wondered if she'd made it worse by telling them the truth. But to her surprise, a small hint of life came back into their faces. It wasn't much, but it was there. Betty even stopped shaking, if only for a moment.

"You're not what I expected," Kelly said.

Riley met her eyes, voice soft. "What did you expect?"

"I don't know," Kelly said. "But it wasn't you."

By her tone of voice, Riley knew the girl meant it as a compliment, but she didn't know how to respond. She'd heard the stories, knew what people said about her. That she was a crazy recluse who locked herself in her childhood home out of fear or insanity. In this town, she'd forever be known as the girl from the legend, the one who'd survived, almost a myth herself. She didn't care. This town could believe whatever they wanted to; it changed nothing.

"When your friends get here," Riley said, "they won't know what to say to you. So they'll most likely say something stupid, something that makes the pain worse, because they won't understand." As Riley spoke, her mind drifted back to how much she'd fought back against Hank and Linda's attempts to help. How much she'd resented them for thinking they could comfort her. But in the end, their help was all she had left. "Don't let it get to you. What matters is that they're there, trying to help. That's all that matters."

"Thank you," Betty said, voice shaky as she suddenly hugged Riley. "For saving me."

Riley gave her a sympathetic smile, even if she was visibly uncomfortable with the sudden show of gratitude. Aside from her daughter, she wasn't used to it, and so she was secretly grateful when the girl finally moved away.

"Why does it hate us?" Gabriella asked.

"It doesn't," Riley answered. "I don't know if this will make the pain easier or worse, but it doesn't hate you. Even though it's trying to kill you, it's not really you that it's after. Whoever this new thing is, to it, you're just another victim."

"New thing?" Kelly questioned. "I thought it was the Animal."

Riley shook her head, noticing a tear fall down Betty's face. "I don't know what or who this new predator is, and I don't know why it's targeted you, but I can promise you this. It's not the Animal."

It wasn't long before friends started to show up, some worried, some full-on crying. It felt strange to watch them, almost foreign. Even after everything Riley had gone through, this was still the one thing she couldn't relate to. Having family left, someone familiar to help you through it. Someone left alive.

A twinge of sadness cut through her as she looked over at Kelly, who was standing all alone in the backyard. The girl had no parents there to help her, alone just like she had been, and at first it broke her heart. But the sudden burst of sadness was somewhat dampened when another kid arrived and put his arms around Kelly, hugging her close. Riley recognized him, the same boy from the first crime scene. Must be the brother that Hank had told her about: Everett.

Riley held back, waiting for the parents to finish consoling their children. Riley didn't know what to say to them, but she wanted to meet the rest of the friends. So far it seemed like this new predator was targeting the kids, and therefore the close friends could be more potential victims. If Riley was going to help them, she wanted to help all of them.

Eventually, the police started questioning the parents, giving her an opportunity. Taking it, she walked over to meet Kelly's brother. If any of the other kids would be targets, he was by far the most likely.

"You must be Everett," she said, nodding.

To her surprise, he gave a slight laugh. "Who called me that?"

She raised an eyebrow. "The sheriff."

"Figures," the boy said. "It's just Rhett. No one calls me by my full name."

Riley nodded, examining the boy. Jet-black hair and piercing eyes, he seemed tough like his sister, but in a subtle way, an almost unnoticeable edge. But there was something else in his eyes too, something that Riley couldn't quite figure out. Almost like a darkness.

"You saved my sister," Rhett finally said, voice sincere. "Thank you."

Riley had never known how to respond to someone thanking her, so she just nodded, hoping it would be enough. She didn't have time to find out, because she heard another voice in the distance.

"Is that her?"

The voice was connected to a boy who had his arm around Gabriella's shoulder, walking toward them. "The one who survived the legends, lived through an Animal attack?"

Rhett glared at him. "Dude."

"It's okay," Riley said. "Believe me, he's not the first."

"And hopefully not the last," the kid said, pointing to himself. "I'm Dylan. It's an honor to meet a part of the legend, madam."

"Ignore him," Kelly said. "He's an idiot."

"Really, it's okay," Riley said, but she had to admit something was off about the kid. His girlfriend had just been attacked and he was acting like it was a party. His eyes were beaming and he had a borderline creepy smile. There was a trace of his body language that signaled he wasn't scared at all.

Maybe he was an idiot.

Thankfully the rest of the kids showed up before Dylan could say anything else. The first introduced himself as Russel and looked like he could tip over a truck without breaking a sweat.

The last one introduced himself as Luke, and Riley vaguely recognized him as Hank's kid, although they had never actually met before. "Nice to meet you," she said. "I know your father pretty well. He's a good man."

To her surprise, Luke just scoffed and refused to look her directly in the eye. It was like she had done something to offend him, but she wasn't sure what. Either way, they were all together now, standing in the grass, less than fifty feet from the forest.

Of all the horrifying things in this town, the forest had always been the worst. No matter where you went, how much you tried to hide, you'd never be more than a mile from it, even in the center of town. It surrounded everything, its twisted trees reaching out and infecting everything they touched, turning the whole town into part of its jungle, part of its food chain, and they were at the bottom.

"So," Rhett finally asked, "what do we do now?"

"Stay together," Riley said. "The more of you there are, the harder it will be for this new killer to get to you. So, everyone stay close. No walking home alone, not until this is over."

"What was it like?" Russel asked. "Going through it alone."

Riley shook her head. She wanted to help these kids, but she wasn't going to relive the past. "It doesn't matter. What matters is now." She looked to Kelly, who seemed to be holding up better than the rest of those attacked. "Tell us everything about the first attack. How it moved, where it attacked. Maybe there's a pattern."

"Okay," Kelly said. If she was terrified, she fought hard not to show it as she told them everything: how it had appeared in the woods, how it had gutted her friends, how it had chased her.

Most of all, how it growled.

As she described the sound, the same growl that Riley had heard herself the night before, everyone began shifting nervously, almost flinching at the mere description. The killing might have been brutal, but it was always the unnatural things that were the most haunting.

Except to Riley, who knew what the growl really was.

"It makes sense," Rhett finally said, not releasing the tension everyone felt. "Because that's what animals do. They growl when they hunt."

Riley sighed. "No, they don't."

All the kids looked at her in confusion, forcing her to explain.

"When an animal is hunting, it's silent. A wolf doesn't growl while stalking a deer any more than a lion growls before pouncing at a gazelle. To growl would be to give away their position and give their prey an opportunity to escape."

Kelly spoke up. "So then when does an animal growl, if not at its prey?"

"When it's challenged, or afraid. Growling is a form of intimidation, a way of making the animal seem terrifying to scare off potential threats. A wolf will only growl at another wolf, or something larger, to scare it off and avoid a fight it might lose. But a wolf would never growl at a sheep, because the sheep isn't a threat. It's nothing to the wolf other than its next meal."

"Is that all we are?" Kelly asked. "The next meal?"

"No," Riley said. "Because we aren't sheep, and it's not the Animal. The fact that it growls at us means it's trying to scare us into thinking it's something that it's not. If it was really the Animal, it wouldn't have growled, because it wouldn't have needed to."

"How can you be so sure?" Rhett asked.

"I just am," Riley said. "But that's good. Because that means it wants us scared, and we don't have to be. I looked it in the eyes; it's not some unstoppable killing machine. It's just a man in a mask, pretending to be something he isn't."

"What if you are wrong?" Betty asked. "What if it really is the Animal?"

"It's not."

"But what if the Animal is still out there? What if it comes back?"

Riley sighed again, not being able to lie to them.

"Then we're all dead already."

Riley didn't blame them for leaving. After what she had said, she would have judged them for staying. But they seemed like strong kids. Maybe there was a chance they could make it out of this okay. Not only survive but have enough left to move on with their lives.

Like she almost had, before all of this started up again.

In moments like this, she wished Emma was here, so she could hold on to her. She always tried to tell herself that she did it to make her daughter feel safe, but really, it was the other way around. But she'd left Emma with Linda, to keep her safe, away from all of this cruelty and death.

But as Riley stood there, alone once again, she noticed something else in the woods. Another kid was here, walking through the trees close to where the deputy had been killed. Before long, the kid knelt down, examining the dirt and looking further into the forest before writing something down in a small notebook.

Riley wasn't sure why, but something about the way the kid looked felt different. Everyone else on the scene was either a terrified victim, a worried parent, or an unsettled police officer. But here was this kid, standing in the forest where the animals hid and yet looking perfectly calm, almost focused.

Then, to her surprise, the boy looked straight at her. Not in the way that everyone else in the town did, staring at her like she was still the girl from the stories, but in a far different manner. Calm, almost understanding, like he was the only other person in this town who knew the secret of what she had really gone through and realized what it must've meant.

It was unsettling.

Who was this kid?

CHAPTER SEVENTEEN

Everyone in town thought Oliver was paranoid.

His hand felt the cold touch of steel as he reached down and unlocked his door, all three deadbolts.

Apparently, it was perfectly reasonable for everyone else in the town to obsess over the Animal as if it was some kind of folk hero, some legend they must never forget. Just so long as they never actually looked too hard at the myth, never peeked behind the curtain of the stories.

Oliver stepped into his house, walking through it without stopping until he reached his bedroom, checking the corners as he did, searching for anything that wasn't supposed to be there.

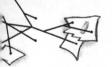

To be fair, Oliver was obsessed with the Animal, and he'd never denied that. But the only difference between his obsession and that of everyone else in this sick, corrupt town was the reason behind it. The motive behind the hunt.

Oliver reached back and locked his bedroom door: two deadbolts, a chain, and a metal bar that slid across it.

Okay, maybe he was a little paranoid.

But watch any true crime show on TV, any documentary on murders, and the victims will always say the same thing. *If only I'd known it was coming. If only I could have prepared for it. If only I'd been less trusting.*

Sitting down in his chair, he faced the papers taped up to the wall. Notes covered every inch of it, dozens upon dozens of pages ripped from his notebook, each and every one of them completely blank. Like so many times before, Oliver cracked a smile. If anything, them appearing blank only made him seem more crazy.

Pulling out his notebook, he set it on the desk in front of him. Then he turned and did another scan of the room, ensuring no one was hiding in a corner, waiting to stab him from behind.

When he was satisfied the room was empty, the locks ensuring it would stay that way, he reached over and turned off the lights, breathing quietly in the darkness. Then he let his hand inch under

the desk, finding the button hidden beneath it, turning on a different set of lights that he'd placed in secret.

Black light filled the space, not bright enough to give away the room's interior but enough to reveal everything written on the pages that covered the wall, and the notebook setting on the desk.

The letters appeared fluorescent blue, and the writing itself was fairly frenzied. It was hard to write in invisible ink, and it wasn't like Oliver was a calligrapher to begin with.

The words surrounded him, enveloping him in their twisted blue glow. Notes were etched everywhere, detailing blood patterns, local legends, corpses found. If insanity had a physical representation, this was probably it.

But Oliver wasn't insane. He was determined, focused like no one else in this town allowed themselves to be, out of unspoken respect for a monster. An entire town so desperate to catch a glimpse of the Animal's return that they hadn't even thought to cancel school after their students started being attacked, at least not until it had slaughtered them in their own gym.

Until the blood had already been spilled, and it was too late.

Now the town might care, might close down the schools, offer safe houses, and start a manhunt for

whoever was responsible, but Oliver's investigation had started a long time ago, even before this new killer had arrived.

Ripping the new pages out of the notebook, Oliver taped them to their place, right underneath two large words written on the wall itself.

New Suspects.

The police were probably looking at anyone in town with a record of violence, most likely repeat offenders, and to be fair, under any normal circumstances, Oliver would have agreed with that course of investigation. But this case was different. It wasn't just another killing spree. It was a killing spree inspired by something greater, and that changed everything.

There were seven constants. The party at Kelly's, the gym massacre, and the safe house slaughter all contained the same seven constants that Oliver couldn't ignore, even if he desperately wanted to overlook a few of them.

Once the pages were perfectly aligned, all the evidence he had collected about this new case, he examined them with a solemn sigh.

Seven constants, and six suspects.

Under normal circumstances, there would only be three suspects left. Four if Oliver himself was included, and he would judge anyone who didn't put him on the suspect list, given his history of obsessing over the legend.

But the legend of the Animal made everything different, which meant no suspect could be removed based on the typical evidence used to clear them. Most likely it would end up being nothing, and one of the three prime suspects would end up being the face behind this new mask. But to ignore the possibility of the others' guilt would be foolish, no matter how slight the chances.

No one was cleared, and no one was going to be until this was over.

That was the way it had to be.

But there was nothing new he could add to it now. The safe house killing hadn't revealed anything the gym attack hadn't, except that the new animal was willing to kill deputies in addition to kids, which wasn't really a bombshell.

So, Oliver turned his chair and faced the opposite wall, which contained notes that were far more important and far more vague. His investigation into the original attacks, the real Animal, not this new pretender.

The first section of notes detailed Riley. Not much was known about her, other than that she had a daughter and was both an orphan and a widow. Even that wasn't exactly common knowledge, but Oliver was good at digging.

Then, of course, there were the stories about her, the theories everyone liked to talk about. How

maybe she was the Animal, maybe she'd killed her parents and had been a psychopath even at the age of eight. Some even suggested she was an actual werewolf.

All of it was crap, and Oliver ground his teeth at the thought of it. The sad truth of it was the only reason people considered Riley a suspect was because it made her more interesting than if she was a victim. Because this town, just like everywhere else, didn't care about the victims left behind. Instead they were only captivated by the monster committing the atrocities.

If there was any justice in this town, Riley would have been the one the stories spoke of. The little girl who'd lost everything and managed to survive. But instead, they ostracized her so that they could focus on the Animal, their all-consuming fascination.

Then there was the Animal itself. Basically nothing was known about it, other than that, one night twenty-five years ago, it had killed seventeen people with its bare hands—or claws, according to some reports—and then vanished into thin air. No traces of its blood had been found at the crime scene, no DNA evidence, not even so much as a footprint had been found in the blood covering the houses.

Oliver could understand the lack of blood. If the Animal had gotten away unscathed, it made sense

it wouldn't have bled. And the DNA evidence, while harder to justify, was still possible. Whoever this psychopath was, he was apparently wearing some form of animal costume, which would have kept any particles of DNA, like hair, from falling onto the crime scene.

But the footprints made no sense. Oliver had seen the initial photos of the crime scene, and the amount of blood left behind. He'd walked into the houses himself, trying to avoid the blood patterns, and it was impossible. Somewhere, the Animal would have stepped in blood and left some form of footprint, and yet they'd found nothing.

Or at least, the sheriff claimed they'd found nothing.

But that was a conspiracy for another day, because these new killings meant the clock was ticking. Not many people in town knew what this new monster was really after, but Oliver did. It was written all over their attacks, their victims. They were after two things.

Firstly, to become part of the legends themselves.

Secondly, well, they'd most likely reveal their true intentions soon, especially given Riley's new involvement. Probably on the next attack, now that she was too close to the case to be scared off.

Which meant that every second that passed without the original Animal being found, the

danger grew, both for Riley and for everyone else in this town.

Oliver had spent years searching for the Animal. For the man behind the myths. Because once he found him, once the Animal's true face was revealed, it would change everything.

Then the legend could finally die.

Oliver glanced over at the stack of files left in the corner. The police wouldn't let him near the actual case files. He'd only been able to get evidence from the news, and it wasn't nearly enough to investigate a twenty-five-year-old case that had no suspects. So, Oliver had done the only thing he could think to do. Consider every single person in town a suspect, and then prove them innocent one by one.

It had taken an eternity, but he almost had. Of course, there were still a lot of names that didn't have perfect alibis, or at least wouldn't tell him, and there were a lot of people in town who had died since then.

But Oliver worked based on a single theory. That when the Animal had vanished, so had the man behind the mask. Every phone book, old newspaper, town ledger he combed through was for that purpose. To find out who had been in the town before, and vanished after that day twenty-five years ago.

Only one name fit that profile. A few brief records of his existence before that night, and then nothing. Not a single trace of him anywhere, even in some places where there should have been. All Oliver could find was a rough age based on a blurry old photograph, which portrayed the man as a little over fifty at the time of the attacks, making him ancient now. That and his name.

A single name that might finally put an end to this town's obsession, might finally reveal the Animal for what it truly was, not some mythical beast deserving reverence, or some unstoppable creature destined to become a legend.

Just a man who'd done horrific things, things he shouldn't be remembered for, things he should be forgotten for. Things the town should never speak of, unless it was to offer sympathy to the victims. A single man, within whom Oliver believed lay the truth about the Animal.

Arthur Conners.

CHAPTER EIGHTEEN

"Where are you!?"

Clyde screamed into the silence of the forest, searching for the wolf that had attacked him, unsure of whether it was to find answers, or out of the hope that it might finally kill him and end this descent into madness.

The dream had changed everything, because it wasn't a dream. It wasn't even a memory, at least not a complete one. His mind had been far too broken for memories of the past to still exist, much less crawl their way back into his consciousness. No, this was something else, almost like an instinct long buried that had now fought its way into his mind and would never depart again.

On his knees, hands in the dirt, Clyde screamed again.

"Where are you!"

Still, the wolf didn't reveal itself. If it was watching him, it was doing so by hiding in the shadows of the trees, which not even the morning sun could reveal.

There was something wrong with this forest. Clyde had always felt it. Even in the daylight, over half of it was still completely covered in darkness, shadows of branches choking out the light, keeping the living souls within shrouded in a cloud of nothingness.

But that wasn't what was wrong with it. The true terror was something far darker, something Clyde felt but still wouldn't admit to himself, even after the flashes of the past. Something he had always known in his heart but never been able to explain. Even now, the full answer eluded him.

The dream still haunted him. The bloodshed, the broken bodies, and most of all, the screams. Even now he could still hear it, ringing in his ears, horrific wailing cutting into the night as something had ripped the life from them.

The wolf wasn't coming, which meant answers weren't coming with it. Whatever the wolf truly was, whatever creature hid behind its coarse fur, it had come out of thin air to torment him and then

vanished back into the woods after the memories began to crawl their way back out.

Unless the wolf was a memory too.

For a while, Clyde stayed in the forest, lying in the dirt, twitching as the instincts he'd felt in the dream came back to him once more. Focus, terror, the need to hunt, to kill. An almost animalistic hunger for bloodshed.

What was wrong with him?

The Animal.

Clyde had watched any news he could find discussing the original attack twenty-five years ago and had compiled note after note of the victims, the killings, and most of all, the Animal.

There had been seventeen victims, and even the blurred-out photos shown on the news looked horrific, like abstract paintings of human bodies turned inside out and torn apart. Each one brought back something in Clyde's mind, not so much a memory but a quick flash of violence, of screams so loud he felt his ears would bleed from inside his skull.

But all the screams blended together, no single one important enough for his mind to recollect perfectly. Instead, it was just a frenzied combination of souls begging for mercy before

their skulls were crushed underneath their skin, tearing their flesh apart from within.

Still, Clyde flinched every time.

Then there was the Animal itself. A few hunters claimed to have spotted it in the forest near the game fence, but none of them could describe any more than a fleeting shadow. The only actual witness had never spoken of it, at least not to the press, or the police for that matter.

However, a few details remained constant. Black fur, animalistic, almost wolflike, and vicious. Time of death for most of the seventeen victims was within minutes of each other. Whatever the Animal had been, it had killed them fast, like a wolf that found a herd of defenseless sheep waiting to be slaughtered.

The most disturbing fact, though, wasn't the corpses left behind, or the details of the monster that had massacred them. It was the time. Twenty-five years ago. The one thing Clyde couldn't rationalize, couldn't claim was a fear-induced fantasy, was that his first clear memory was exactly twenty-five years ago. Before that, there was nothing except a mixture of fear and survival.

That was too specific to ignore.

Despite that, Clyde still tried to explain everything away, because accepting it meant something far darker than he could have ever imagined.

The dream wasn't a memory; it was just a nightmare, brought about by both his damaged mind and the fresh attacks of the wolf from the forest. The flashes of blood still stained in his mind were nothing more than delusions. Even the screams could be explained away. It wasn't the sound of specific victims, but one large mixture of years of terrified creatures, some human, some not. That meant it could just be his mind playing tricks on him. There was no way to prove it was the actual screams of the Animal's victims.

Until he saw Riley.

She was different. She had survived.

Somehow, he'd known that even before reporters had said it. Known that she had gotten away, that she was still breathing. His entire body flinched suddenly when he saw the picture of her when she was eight, right after the attack, nothing more than a defenseless child.

Fear coursed through him as he heard it, ringing in his head as if it was right behind him. This one wasn't a collection of sounds but a single terrified cry, full of sorrow and pain, a cry that had never been silenced.

Clyde remembered her scream.

CHAPTER NINETEEN

This was the kill that changed everything.

Riley walked up to the crime scene, sorrow in her heart because she already knew what would be there. What it would lead to. A single message inscribed as a revelation of the new predator's true purpose. But first, she walked the crime scene, looking at the grisly clues left behind, which told the tragic story of what had happened just a few hours earlier.

The old man walked through his house, singing with the birds of the morning. It was a beautiful day, and it would be a shame not to enjoy it, so he poured himself a cup of warm coffee in his favorite porcelain cup and stepped out to the back porch to sit and enjoy the sunrise coming up over the trees.

Riley knelt down on the front porch, picking up a piece of the shattered white porcelain that covered it. It still felt warm in her hands, as her fingers crept around the sharp edges where it had been broken. The first sign of the danger that was to come.

As he sat there, his mind drifted back to the girl he had found on the road, bleeding and scared out of her mind. He'd seen more reports about her on the news. Evidently, she'd been attacked several times. He couldn't imagine what kind of person would want to kill a young, innocent girl like that.

In the light of the rising sun, his quiet thoughts were interrupted by the sound of something breathing. Slow, deep breaths, in and out, so close he could almost feel it on the back of his neck.

Cold, putrid breath crawling up his skin.

In sudden terror, his old bony hands began to shake, spilling coffee as he turned around slowly, not wanting to imagine what was behind him but doing so all the same. When he finally saw the monster, the grave terror set in, and the coffee cup fell, shattering on the porch.

Riley sighed, knowing what the old man must've felt: the first realization that your next breath could be your last, that someone or something might take it from you.

She moved over, walking down the creaking wooden stairs, noticing the slight indention on the top step, where something had suddenly slipped, as well as the lump of pressed grass at the bottom, where something had fallen.

It was covered in fur, and its face wasn't human. Neither was the sound coming from its throat, as it growled at him, a deep, throaty snarl that almost made his heart stop.

The old man stepped back in shock, not realizing what was behind him, only what was in front. The monster attacking the town, which had now come to slaughter him as well. He had to get away.

But in his fear, he moved back too far and slipped, falling down the stairs, his fragile back colliding with the grass that lay beneath.

"No, please," he begged, helpless on the ground as he saw the monster take a step toward him. It tilted its head and held up some kind of bone that was in its hand, moving it across its own throat like some kind of demented threat.

Then the old man knew the truth. It could have killed him already if it had wanted to. Whatever this animal was, it was crueler than that. It wanted to scare him, hunt him, and he had no choice but to run.

Footsteps lined up together in the grass, forming a trail that led straight from the house toward the car parked in the garage to the left. Riley walked the trail herself, her own footsteps mirroring those that came before, trying to form a picture in her mind of exactly what had happened, what had led to the bloodshed.

Limping, the old man ran as fast as he could.

He had to get away. Tears fell down his face as he thought of dying, of the hollowness that would be left, the empty place in the world that would linger after his passing, just as it had when cancer had taken his wife. An empty place on the bed where something had once thrived, now only a dark *reminder of the death that comes to all. Now, as the reaper came to knock on his door and the memories of pain flashed in his eyes, he found himself afraid. Afraid of the nothingness.*

Afraid of dying.

His left foot dragged in the grass as he moved, trying to get to the car, to safety. If he could get there, he could leave. Maybe then he could survive, escape death's cold grip for a moment longer.

Even now, his bones ached from the fall as bruises formed on his skin, causing more pain with every step, but he was so close. Just a few more feet and he would reach the back door of the garage. But as he did, he looked back to the porch and almost had a heart attack as he witnessed what remained, what was still coming for him.

Nothing.

The creature hadn't followed him, hadn't chased. It had vanished. Confused, he hesitated. Where would it have gone if it wasn't to chase him? Unless...

'Oh no! Please, no!'

The garage door slammed open, revealing the monster standing behind it. It appeared massive in the doorway. Somehow the old man hadn't noticed it before, but the creature was huge, looking like it could kill him with a single blow, using only its grey hands that appeared rotten and covered in claws.

As it stepped toward him, the old man started gasping for air but received none in return.

A broken lock, an open door, and a car that hadn't moved.

The old man hadn't made it in time. The predator had been waiting.

Riley bent down and inspected the door handle. It was bent down, and pieces of wood were chipped off the frame. The killer hadn't picked the lock; he had kicked the entire door, forcing it open, which explained the black markings left in the center.

The frame was cheap, but it still would have taken a good amount of force to bust it open like that. Whoever this new killer was, he was strong.

Very strong.

Sighing, Riley stepped back over to the grass, noticing how it was torn up at first, as if fingers had been buried in the dirt, scraping away roots and grass in a frenzied panic.

Someone must've been crawling.

He crawled backwards, gasping for air, screaming in desperation.

"Help! Please help me!"

No one answered, and the monster moved closer, growling viciously. But it didn't attack him immediately, instead moving toward him slowly, savoring every moment of its prey's struggle, forcing him to crawl further back before finally he tried to stand once more.

Footprints led backwards.

The old man ran as fast as he could, sweat pouring from his face, vision becoming blurry as he tried to focus on running. "Help!" he screamed again, but no one came. He was too far outside of town for anyone to hear. Yet still he screamed, begging anyone to help him, save him before the darkness could claim him forever. Before his eyes glassed over and only a hollow corpse remained, frozen in an expression of death, the same one he'd seen on countless friends as they'd lain in a casket, waiting to be buried, never to speak again.

"Please! Help me!"

Following the trail of footsteps he'd created, Riley was led into the forest, and she held back a tear of sorrow for a stranger she'd never known. He'd had no choice but to run into the forest, knowing what it would mean, knowing he'd never escape.

"Help me!" he screamed as he reached the trees, heart pounding inside his chest. He couldn't take a breath, for his fear-stricken lungs wouldn't allow it, and the lack of oxygen was causing his body to tremble so badly that he could barely stand.

Vision blurry, all he saw as he ran was a mixture of tall shadows that looked like ghosts, when in reality it was only the distorted fragments of trees that surrounded him as he ran further into the forest, trying to escape the predator chasing him.

Just when he thought he had, just when he allowed himself to hope for a mere moment that he'd escaped the reaper's cold grip, he heard the growling once more, and something fell down in front of him.

Something dark.

Riley knelt down in the dirt, next to a large track left behind. Something must've fallen from the trees above. Glancing up, she searched the branches, finding a few that could have held someone.

But even though the man was most likely limping, and far beyond his running years, the killer would have had to be fast to pass him in the forest and climb the tree before him. Difficult but not impossible.

Reaching over, she placed her hand on the nearest tree, feeling the rough bark touch her skin, just below the bloodied handprint left behind.

The creature growled, twisting its skeleton unnaturally as it moved closer to him, holding up what looked like a bone.

"Please, no," he begged, but it didn't stop the creature from digging the bone into his side, twisting its hand as it did, tearing the skin around the wound.

The old man gagged, trying to both breathe and vomit at the same time, but his body did neither as the monster removed the bone from his side and watched him move away.

Dying, having felt the bloodied wound in his side, he reached up to steady himself, leaving a stain of crimson on the tree beside him. Then, as tears streamed down his face, he tried to run once more, praying for his life as he did.

A final attempt at escape.

Drops of red led Riley to the right, and she followed the trail, wincing slightly when she saw what it led to. The larger pool of blood resting in the now-wet dirt.

So much blood. Too much.

The creature came from the side, stabbing him in the stomach once more, right into the slit of his rib cage. In pain, he fell to the ground and desperately crawled away, trying to scream.

Another stab, this time on his left shoulder.

The old man cried out, completely collapsing onto the dirt, no longer able to even move. As his body went into shock, he lay paralyzed on his back, forced to bear witness to the monster standing over him, surrounded by looming trees. The creature that would take his life.

"Please," the man tried to beg, but the words wouldn't come out as he began coughing up blood, watching the beast covered in fur step closer, growling as it did.

'Was this punishment for saving the girl? Why was...?'

The old man never got to finish the thought as the predator slit his throat, spilling what was left of his blood into the heart of the forest.

The first true sacrifice.

The body was propped up on a tree, throat slit, arms forcibly outstretched.

Riley didn't know whether she wanted to weep or scream in anger. It was so pointless to kill an old man just because he had saved Kelly from the predator's grasp. Just because he was probably one of the few people in this town that cared more about the victims rather than the Animal.

Now he was dead, his lifeless corpse propped up against a tree like it was a sacrifice to something greater: a meaningless victim who only existed to be used as a message to reach a monster long hidden.

Riley had known what would be there, but it still sent a chill down her spine. The letters written in crimson blood, scattered across the trees. She saw the B first, then her eyes traced back and forth over the rest of them. Scattered like this, they spelled nothing, but when she stepped back and stood at just the right spot, then the trees aligned perfectly, and the message could be seen. The letters written on the bark spelled out two words, inscribed in the old man's blood. A request that finally revealed this new predator's true purpose. The horrifying truth behind their murders, the longing, the search for what had come before, the obsession with the local legend.

Two words that changed everything.

Come Back.

CHAPTER TWENTY

Dodging the blade, Riley knelt down and swept her legs, knocking Betty off her feet. As she fell, Riley grabbed her wrist and twisted, taking the knife from her hand just before she hit the ground below.

"Now you're on the ground, and I have your knife," Riley said, winking at her. "Do you want to try it again?"

Betty groaned as she stood back up, wind knocked out of her. "No, thanks. I think twenty times is enough."

Riley nodded. "Fair enough. Who's next?"

None of them answered immediately. They were all standing in the backyard of Kelly's house.

Apparently, her parents weren't home often, which meant they could do this without fear of one of the other kids' parents objecting to it, although Riley couldn't imagine why any of them would. Their kids were being targeted. It only made sense to learn some self-defense, but it was probably safer to ask forgiveness than permission in this town.

There were eight kids here in total. She had met seven of them before, at the safe house the morning after she'd fought the new predator: Kelly, Betty, Rhett, Luke, Russel, Dylan, and Gabriella, who was currently petting a massive German shepherd. However, it was the other kid that she kept a closer eye on. The kid who had looked over at her from the forest and now kept writing something in his notebook every time she made a move while training Betty. Kelly had told her his name was Oliver and that he was a good kid, just a little too obsessed with the legend. Yet something about him seemed different than the rest.

She just couldn't figure out what.

Finally, her original question was answered as Gabriella shrugged. "I'll go."

Riley nodded, and Gabriella stepped closer, catching the dulled blade that Riley tossed her and not waiting for someone to say go before she lunged.

Riley grinned, moving out of the way and using the girl's own momentum to push her forward. "When the killer attacks, he'll have a knife, and there are two main ways he'll try to hurt you." She spoke loudly, so that all of them could hear. "The killer could swipe wildly with the knife, like Gabriella is doing." As she spoke, she began stepping back, each time out of the blade's reach. "If he does, then just keep moving back, until he gives you an opening, like this."

Reaching her hand up, Riley caught the girl's wrist and twisted it, stealing the knife and shoving her backwards in the process.

Seeing its master injured, the German shepherd leapt forward, massive claws pawing the air as it struggled to attack her. The only thing holding it back was Russel's tight grip on its collar, but even he struggled to control it.

"Mean dog," Riley commented.

"He can be a little grumpy." Gabriella steadied herself, looking agitated that Riley had gotten the best of her.

"Grumpy," Rhett scoffed. "It killed your neighbor's cat."

"It's a dog," she defended, "it's in their blood."

"Well," Riley added, "it's probably not a bad idea for the rest of you to get guard dogs too. Something else to help protect yourself."

"Do you have a guard dog?" Kelly asked.

"No, but I'm old enough to own firearms."

"Ahh."

"What's the second way he could stab?" Dylan asked from the crowd, less of a serious question than it was an attempt to provoke Gabriella into fighting back harder.

Evidently it worked, because the second Riley handed the knife back to her, the girl lunged forward again.

"The killer could stab straight at you. But then," she said, moving out of the knife's path and grabbing the girl's arm, "all you have to do is grab the arm, bend, and—"

Her words were cut short as the girl twisted her wrist in a way it wasn't meant to bend, causing Riley to lose her grip. Then Riley heard the click of two bones grazing against each other as the girl shifted her hand back into place and attacked again.

It looked almost unnatural.

Taken by surprise, Riley almost didn't block the next swipe, aimed at her side. But she did, just in time, blocking the blade and grabbing onto Gabriella's entire body, tackling her, and bringing them both to the ground.

She had to give it to the girl, she had gotten pretty close, especially considering how small she was. "What did you do to your hand?"

Still lying in the grass, Gabriella smiled and pulled on her thumb, appearing to break it. "I'm double-jointed. I can dislocate most of the bones in my arm."

"That's good," Riley said. "Use that if the killer grabs you."

"Already did," Gabriella responded. "If you don't mind me asking, why do you keep calling him the killer instead of the Animal?"

"Because he's not the Animal."

"Yeah, but"—Gabriella stood back up—"even if he isn't the same animal as before, shouldn't he still be called an animal?"

Riley didn't know how she could explain it. How the thought of even calling this new predator anything resembling the name given to the monster she had seen would have made her physically sick. Because this new killer wasn't the Animal. Didn't deserve the name, or anything like it. It was just a pretender. But she couldn't tell them that, because they were scared enough already.

"You ready to go again?" Riley asked, deflecting the question.

"Until it's perfect."

The girl hadn't been kidding.

She had sparred with Riley for what felt like an hour, getting put on the ground over and over. But each time, she got back up, attempting to get better, to be perfect to the point that it concerned Riley. She didn't even seem to be doing it to learn to defend herself. Instead it seemed as if her only reason for doing it was to perfect it, and only then could she move on, only after she was better than everyone else.

Riley felt a twinge of sadness. Kids didn't develop that trait by themselves. It was learned from someone, forced perfection at any cost.

Finally, though, exhaustion kicked in, and Gabriella began panting for air, having trouble even standing up straight without her face turning red.

"That's enough for now," Riley said, knowing the girl wouldn't stop on her own. "Who else wants to try?"

"I don't get why we all have to do this," Dylan said. "I mean, only the three girls have been attacked. Why do the rest of us have to learn self-defense too?"

Riley shrugged. "None of you have to do anything. But the girls are confirmed targets, and Russel made himself a target when he stopped the killer at the gym. Rhett is Kelly's brother, you're dating Gabriella, and it might target Luke because his father is the sheriff running the investigation. All of you are connected to this somehow."

"It's nice to be included," Oliver chimed in, leaning back on the wooden chair he was sitting in, still writing in his notebook, occasionally looking back at the forest.

Riley laughed it off. "Do you want to train, then?"

Oliver shook his head. "No, thanks. I'm just observing."

"Why are you even here, Oliver?" Rhett asked, his sternness surprising Riley. "You don't have any stake in this at all. Except, oh yeah, that's right. You're an insane freak who's obsessed with the Animal."

Oliver grinned but didn't look up from his notebook. "One of those statements is true."

Apparently not liking that Oliver practically ignored him, Rhett pushed it further. "You know, everyone knows why you're so obsessed with the Animal. Why you can't let it go."

"Enlighten me," Oliver said, but there was something about the calmness with which he responded that unnerved Riley. Because it didn't sound like he was actually calm; it sounded like he was in a perpetual state of fear and used the calmness to cover it up.

Just like she did.

"You're obsessed with it because you think if you can find out who it is, it will make you special. That if you can connect yourself to the Animal's story, it will make you matter. That it will make your life worth something, something people won't ignore like they do now."

"Sounds like a good motive." Oliver grinned. "Is it yours?"

"What?" Rhett asked.

Oliver smirked but didn't explain further, even as Riley stared at him with a curious expression growing on her face.

What had he meant by that?

For a moment everyone was silent, before Riley finally motioned over to Luke. "Do you want to try?"

"No," he scoffed, arms folded, glaring at her. He seemed just as upset as he had back at the safe house and hadn't spoken at all since she'd gotten there.

What was it about her that he disliked so much?

She then motioned toward Russel, but he shook his head. "Do I look like I need self-defense training?"

So instead, she attempted to train Dylan, but it didn't last long. Evidently, he thought this whole thing was a joke.

"Shouldn't we be learning something from this?" he said as he swiped at her with the knife.

"Like what?" she asked, slowing down her movements so the kids could see how she moved away from the knife more plainly.

"I don't know," Dylan said, still swinging at her. "I just always thought that whenever big killing sprees happened, everyone involved was supposed to go on some kind of emotional journey. Y'know, learn something worthwhile from the experience, change for the better, and all that good stuff."

Riley visibly twitched when she heard him say it, not out of shock but anger. What made her more upset was the fact that most of the other kids nodded, almost in agreement. Except for Oliver, who only rolled his eyes.

"Do you think this is a game?" she asked all of them, suddenly shifting right and ripping the knife from his hands, trying to keep her adrenaline from rising. "Do you think this is some kind of joke?"

"C'mon, that's not what he meant," Gabriella said.

Riley ignored her, kicking Dylan's legs and dropping him to the ground. Before he could move, she had her knee on his back, pinning him to the grass and driving the knife down into the dirt, almost grazing his left eye. Beside her stood the rest of the kids, staring in shock like deer in headlights.

"There is nothing to learn from this. This isn't an emotional journey. It's not some form of self-discovery. There is no hidden truth to uncover, no light at the end of the tunnel. There is survival, and there is death. If you think for a moment that learning something or being a good person will keep the predator from ripping your heart out at the slightest opportunity, you're wrong."

Riley hesitated for a moment, voice cracking as her thoughts drifted back to everyone she'd lost: all good, all innocent, all dead. "At the end of this, each of us will either be alive or rotting in the ground. Nothing else matters except survival."

Not a single kid said a word. Instead they just stared at her in silence, the grave reality of their situation appearing to finally have taken hold.

Except for Dylan, who still laughed despite the knife an inch from his eye. Riley just rolled her eyes in frustration. Something was wrong with that kid.

Next up to train was Rhett, and he was probably the most competent fighter so far, but it was clear he was holding back. Riley had no idea why.

"What did it look like?" he eventually asked. "The real Animal?"

She never answered him.

The only one left to train was Kelly. Riley hadn't known what to expect, but the girl still surprised her. Riley barely had to hold back to keep pace with her as they both swung and dodged each other's attacks.

As they did, she smiled. The girl was strong, stronger than she had originally given her credit for, and smart too, knowing when to advance and when not to. That was probably why she'd managed to survive three attacks and save two friends with her. Riley had heard the breakdowns of what had happened, and it was clear that Kelly had been the one deciding where to move and how to hide. That was probably why Betty and Gabriella were still alive.

But even though she was tough, the girl still seemed to be at her breaking point as she started to swing more wildly. "What's the point of this? It's not like we can defend ourselves against the actual killer."

"Why not?" Riley asked.

Kelly moved to the left, trying to protect the wound in her stomach, even though Riley would have never gone for it. "Because we can't."

"Why?" she asked again, taking the knife from the girl's hands.

"Because we're just prey," Kelly sighed, giving up entirely, voice sorrowful and defeated. "You said it yourself. Even if it's not the Animal, it's still a predator, still stronger than us. I tried to fight it, and it almost killed me. It did kill my friends. We can't fight back; we can't kill it. All we can do is run, just like all prey do."

Riley sighed and offered the girl a consoling smile. She had lost friends and was scared. Riley couldn't blame her; she'd felt the same way for so long. It was natural to feel helpless, even when you weren't.

"Deer are prey too," Riley finally said, voice soft. "They don't have sharp teeth or long claws. They're constantly hiding, terrified of a wolf or a hunter finding them, always having to run away from the danger, not wanting to fight it head-on. But if it gets desperate enough, if the moment comes when it can no longer run, no longer hide, it will fight back with every ounce of strength it has left, because…" She flipped the knife in her hands and presented it to Kelly.

"Even deer have horns."

Riley watched as Kelly took the knife, part of the fear leaving her eyes, a hint of fight returning. If nothing else, Riley wanted the kids to know that they could at least fight back against this new killer. That survival was possible.

As long as the Animal didn't return.

Riley had trained with them for another hour before finally leaving for home. It had been too long since she'd seen her daughter, and she was getting anxious not being right beside her at all times. But she had left her in good hands.

She knocked on her own door, just to let her know she was home. Then she stepped inside and came face-to-face with an old woman wearing thick glasses and an old white coat.

"Hey, Linda."

Linda smiled. "Hi, sweetheart."

"Where's Emma?"

"She's upstairs, sleeping."

"She been good?"

"An angel, just like you were."

Riley laughed. "Now I know you're lying."

Gradually they moved their conversation into the living room. "How have you been?" the old doctor asked. "I know this new case can't be easy on you."

"It's not the Animal," Riley said, still clinging on to that single fact: that the Animal hadn't returned.

"I know, but still, I imagine it's dredging old memories back up."

Riley shook her head. "The memories never went away to begin with."

Linda nodded in that motherly way she always had, as if taking care of Riley was her responsibility, her job.

"I don't like what Hank has you doing for the kids," she said abruptly, surprising Riley. "It's not safe. He shouldn't have involved you."

"It's okay,"

"No, it's not, you shouldn't have to—"

"Really," Riley said, leaning her head sideways, smiling at her. "It's okay. Honestly it was wrong of me not to help the kids sooner. If someone could have helped my parents before they died, I would have wanted them to. Besides, it's no different than how you and Hank took care of me after it happened."

"No," Linda said, shaking her head. "No, what we did was different. You shouldn't have to put yourself in danger ever again. You should be allowed to move on."

Riley shrugged. "Have you moved on?"

"What do you mean?"

"I mean, you still look at me like I'm an eight-year-old girl you have to save."

Linda chuckled, and her smile returned. "To me you still are that eight-year-old girl." Then she turned and looked at a photograph of Emma hanging on the wall. "She looks just like you did. So full of life."

Riley nodded, staring at the old doctor, remembering everything she had done for her. A lifetime's worth of friendship and help. "I don't know if I've ever thanked you for everything you and Hank did for me. Not just that night, but everything after. I don't know what I would have done if you hadn't been there for me, trying to help."

As she heard the words, Linda's smile changed, growing more solemn as a tear dropped down her face. But there was always that small hint of guilt behind her voice that Riley had never truly understood, like what had happened that night had ripped her heart as well. "You don't have to thank me."

"Yes, I do."

Soon, midnight had covered the town in its ghostly shadow, and Riley was in Emma's room, silently watching her sleep. She looked so perfect lying there, not afraid of anything, completely at peace. Riley remembered how Emma's father always used to do this, watch her sleep, completely fascinated by their daughter's very existence.

Now, Riley did the same thing, not because she was fascinated, but because watching Emma made the world feel smaller. Like it was just the two of them, safe in this room, together. Made her feel like she wasn't alone.

Riley stepped closer to the bed and knelt down, eye level with her daughter, reaching over and adjusting the strand of hair that was almost in her mouth. A smile grew on her face as she did, and she could have stayed in this moment forever.

Then Emma woke up, and seeing someone less than a foot away from her, she screamed in shock.

"It's okay," Riley said quickly, reaching over to her shoulder to calm her down. "It's just me."

Emma struggled to calm down, still shaking. "What were you doing?"

"I was just watching you sleep," Riley said, holding back a guilty grin. "I'm sorry I startled you."

Emma saw her grin and, to Riley's surprise, began to laugh, nervously at first, until Riley laughed with her.

Riley couldn't fathom why scaring her daughter was so funny, but it was, and for a brief moment all the death that surrounded her didn't matter as she laughed with her daughter.

"Come here," she finally said, pulling her daughter close, feeling her embrace. She felt so warm, so perfect. Riley had lied earlier, about surviving being the only thing that mattered.

To her, the only thing that mattered was in this room, in her arms.

CHAPTER TWENTY-ONE

The lack of security at the hospital was concerning. Under different circumstances, Oliver would've been tempted to alert them to how easy it was to break in, but at the moment it worked to his advantage.

So, he figured he'd let it slide.

Getting inside the hospital was the easiest part. All he'd had to do was walk inside. Moving past the two receptionists was also easy to the point of boredom, considering one of them was ninety-eight years old, legally blind, and asleep, and the other was evidently far too young to actually care about the job.

It was moving through the hallways that finally gave him a little trouble. Multiple doctors and

nurses were walking through them at almost all times, and Oliver kept having to step inside rooms to avoid getting caught, but even that wasn't too overwhelmingly difficult.

Oliver had come for a simple reason, the same reason for which he did pretty much everything. To find out who the Animal really was, and expose the face behind the legend.

Admittedly, his obsession with the legend probably wasn't healthy, especially since it had now evolved into breaking and entering. But no one else in this town was going to do it. They were all far too in love with the Animal, or at least the myth it had created.

It wasn't just this town either. It was everywhere, people obsessing over the monsters this world creates, giving them each time in the spotlight for everyone to obsess over and fascinate themselves with. It was disgusting, and they knew it, but they did it anyway, because why not?

Who did it hurt?

A doctor turned the corner in front of him, and Oliver quickly stepped into a room, out of sight.

Hiding inside, he turned around to see an elderly man lying back in a hospital bed, who raised an eyebrow as he saw Oliver seeking refuge behind the door. But to Oliver's surprise, he didn't say anything, instead winking.

Oliver nodded his thanks and waited for the doctor to pass by the doorway. When he had, Oliver started to leave but was momentarily stopped by the words of the older man.

"They say it's come back."

"What's that?"

"The Animal," the man said. "They say it returned."

Even the elders of the town, those who'd supposedly grown wise with age, couldn't help but join in on the insanity.

Oliver's response was simple. "Don't believe everything you hear."

As he left, walking further into the hospital, he couldn't help but roll his eyes. Even though he tried to ignore them, comments like that bothered him. Because the old man hadn't said it out of fear. Oh sure, if the Animal attacked him, the man would probably have a heart attack on the spot, but it was hard to be afraid of something you'd only ever heard of. Something you'd never seen for yourself. No, the man wasn't afraid; he was reverent. Even the way he'd pronounced the words, the Animal, almost quiet, as if saying it too loudly would tarnish its reputation.

In the years Oliver had been in this town, he'd barely been able to go a week at a time without hearing some mention of the Animal: a whispered word, a secret note, sketched images

of the creature hidden everywhere from lockers to hospitals. And yet not once was Riley mentioned, unless it was to suggest that she was the Animal herself. And never the other victims. Not once was another victim named. Instead they were all lumped together as the seventeen victims the Animal had killed, as if being its prey was all their lives amounted to.

Never mind that one of them had a kid, who'd eaten a bullet a few months later when he could no longer stand the constant retellings of the story. Or another victim who'd had a wife, who'd drunk herself to death within two years.

Because no one cared about them, not really. Sure, if they were mentioned on the news, people might pretend to care for a brief moment, but the truth was that every single person in this town recited the story of the Animal religiously, and yet not one of them could have named a single victim other than Riley. Because unless it was about the monster, the beast of mythical proportions who'd massacred an entire street of people without being stopped, then it wasn't interesting enough. Unless it was about the Animal, no one cared.

Focus, Oliver told himself as he slipped past another nurse and made it to the far end of the hospital, where he knew an office would be.

A very specific office.

Contrary to popular belief, Oliver didn't put much stock in conspiracies. They were typically the useless fantasies of someone with far too much time on their hands. But every once in a while, when the stars aligned perfectly and you least expected it, a conspiracy might turn out to be true. And in this case, if that happened, ignoring it would mean a death sentence.

Oliver had a theory, and at the moment it was all he had. No physical evidence at the crime scene, no arrests, no witnesses. Nothing at all to suggest the Animal had ever even existed, except for the seventeen victims, and the legends that had come after.

Something like that didn't happen by chance. If the Animal was human, and Oliver believed beyond a shadow of a doubt it was, then no matter how careful it was, some form of evidence would have been left: a footprint, hair, something. Because you don't kill that many people with your bare hands without leaving something by accident.

And if it wasn't human, if it truly was a monster capable of defying nature, then what would it have cared if it had left tracks?

Someone had to help cover it up. Oliver wasn't sure why, but it was the only answer that made sense. And honestly, the why wasn't important. Everyone always seemed to think it was, as if a singular motive explained away all the atrocities

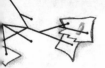

a killer had committed. But in the end, it didn't matter. It could only explain the dark deeds already committed, not those yet to occur.

Whatever the motive, someone had covered it up.

So, then, the only question was, who?

To Oliver, there were only two choices that made sense. The first was the sheriff. He would have been able to cover up the tracks, and by all reports he'd been first on the scene that night. Plus, Luke had strongly hinted that his father was still in contact with Riley, and had been ever since he could remember. But Oliver hadn't yet figured out a way to break into the sheriff's office, so for now he was concerning himself with option two: the good doctor.

Linda Parker.

Eyewitness reports had her at the scene that night, helping Riley into the ambulance. But she was a surgeon, not an EMT, so why would she have been there that night? More curious was her continued relationship with Riley.

Both the doctor and the sheriff had remained in contact with Riley over the years. For the sheriff, it was easier to dismiss the suspicions because while it was uncommon, it wasn't unheard of for a police officer to stay in contact with the victims of a case. However, the doctor was harder to explain away.

Dr. Parker had been seen with her in town numerous times. Not only that, but at one point, albeit briefly, Riley had actually stayed at her house when she was a child, almost like an adopted daughter.

While Oliver desperately wanted to believe people did good things only because they were good people, it simply didn't work that way, at least not in his experience. More often than not, good deeds were a result of guilt, an attempt to atone for mistakes made in the past.

Which begged the question: what was the doctor trying to atone for by helping Riley?

Oliver reached her office and encountered the first real obstacle to his break-in so far. The door was locked.

Well, you've come this far, Oliver thought as he wrapped his jacket around his elbow and then used it to break the window in the center of the door before reaching down and unlocking it from inside.

The office was empty, just like he'd known it would be. Riley had been training the rest of the kids all day, which meant someone must have been watching her daughter. The obvious choice for a babysitter was the doctor, especially given that she was probably one of the few people Riley trusted after that night.

Which meant she must be off for the day.

It was a large office, probably the result of years' worth of work and promotions. There was a wooden desk in the center of it that held a computer, filing cabinets that rested in the corner, and papers that were clipped up on the right wall, next to a few paintings.

Putting on black latex gloves to hide his fingerprints, Oliver got started. He checked her desk first, not really knowing what he was looking for, only that it would be from that night. The drawers were filled with papers and forms, but none of them were dated beyond the last year. The top of the desk was even less interesting, containing only a few pens, a stapler, and a picture of some blonde woman Oliver didn't recognize, probably family or something.

The computer was a bust too. It was password-protected, and he wasn't exactly a hacker. Besides, if the doctor was hiding a file from twenty-five years ago, it wouldn't have made sense for her to make a digital copy for the hospital's system.

The filing cabinets were the next obvious choice, but they were locked, and Oliver couldn't find the key. So he sighed, reaching behind his back and grabbing the screwdriver he had hidden in his pocket.

It paid to be prepared.

He had them open within a few seconds, but the bending of the metal made a loud screeching

noise as it unlocked, and Oliver grew nervous that someone was going to catch him soon. The glass on the door was shattered; all someone would have to do was look this way and it would be over.

With that in mind, he raced over the files, not taking the time to do it cleanly, letting papers fall to the floor around him.

It had to be here somewhere.

The filing cabinets now empty, Oliver turned to the board on the wall with papers pinned up to it, desperately scanning over them, looking for something, anything to help him solve this mystery.

Nothing. There was nothing!

Angry and confused, surrounded by hospital records scattered over the floor, Oliver wanted to scream, but he knew he couldn't. So instead, he moved his attention to the paintings, checking behind them for a secret safe hidden in the wall.

When he found none, he tore off the back paper of the paintings, looking for files hidden inside. Still, he didn't find anything. Not one shred of evidence that the doctor had anything to hide.

Defeated, Oliver stood amidst the chaos he had created. The desk drawers had been raided, the file cabinets emptied; even the paintings now rested on the floor, backs torn open. Breaking into a hospital had gained him the same amount of information that years of research had. Nothing.

How could there be nothing?

He sat on the floor for a moment, too disappointed to even care about getting away before someone found him. He had been so sure something would be here, some single shred of evidence the doctor hadn't been able to bring herself to dispose of, but now it was hopeless. There was nothing left to check.

Except for the photograph.

It caught his eyes, still propped up in a picture frame on the desk. A single photo of a woman who looked to be in her thirties, with blond hair and a warm smile. Instinct had told Oliver it was probably family, but now that he focused on it, he couldn't remember ever hearing that Dr. Parker had family: no brothers, no sisters, and certainly no children.

So why this single photograph?

Reaching for it, he took a brief moment to observe the details of the picture before breaking the glass and peering behind it, finding what he'd spent years of his life searching for.

Unfolding it, he raised it up to the light, laughing quietly in victory as he examined it: a single X-ray, taken of a human skull. The skull was covered in small cracks, and a larger fracture was present on the left side, caving the skull in slightly. This amount of head trauma would have done something to a person, something he couldn't imagine.

There were no dates attached to it, nor any name. But Oliver knew in his gut this was it. The clue left behind. The single piece of evidence that hadn't been destroyed.

The Animal's skull.

CHAPTER TWENTY-TWO

The scream was still ringing in his ears, and in that moment, Clyde knew it would never go away. The child's cry of sorrow and fear, pleading for her life with an Animal who couldn't hear the emotion in her cry and mourning her parents, who could no longer hear anything at all.

But the scream wasn't what disturbed Clyde, not really. If it had merely been a memory of a girl screaming, he could have easily dismissed it, no matter how loud it played in his head. It wasn't even the feeling that the thing the girl had been screaming at was him, that he was the monster who had slaughtered her parents without a moment's hesitation and would have

killed her just as easily. That was haunting, but his fractured memories meant even that feeling couldn't be trusted, at least not completely.

What he couldn't escape, though, was how the child's scream made him feel now, in this moment of clarity. Every time the shriek echoed in his mind, he felt it, like a caged animal looking over at its prey from behind a glass barrier. Desperate to shatter the glass and rip its prey to shreds, not even for food or survival, but for the hunt itself. Because that was what it was, in its bones.

A hunter.

His fingers began to twitch as he desperately denied the feeling. He wasn't thinking clearly; something must still be wrong with his head.

But the scream wouldn't go away.

So, he screamed himself, crying out into the forest where he now stood. The sudden cry sent birds from their nests, scattering widely in the sky, streaks of black and blue feathers high in the clouds, trying to escape the sound, escape the danger.

Clyde shuddered at the sight of it. At the implication it could carry, but the moment he thought it, he removed it from his mind. It wasn't him. It was the sound that had startled them.

But whatever reason the birds had for fleeing, the end result was that Clyde was left alone in the forest, surrounded by living trees that couldn't see

him. That couldn't watch what he had become, either now or before. Trees that couldn't run, like everything else had.

Why did he think that?

The thought was so sudden it sent chills down his spine. In his mind it hadn't even sounded like him saying it; instead it was almost like his body itself, some form of instinct that had no thoughts, no conscience, only the will to survive.

Just like that, more started coming back as Clyde began to run through the forest in the false hope of escaping what he feared he was.

The sound of screaming, and the flash of blood.

Clyde ran faster, moving through the trees like a shadow, making no noise at all as he ran.

Bones cracking, flesh ripping off.

Silence echoed into the forest as he moved, nothing at all to alert the creatures of the forest to his presence. Yet they seemed to move away from him all the same.

Howling of wolves, sharp teeth clicking in the silence as wolves bit into their prey, into him.

Something about this felt eerily familiar, the path he was running. The paralyzed trees he was passing. The sound of gunfire clicked into his head as he felt a buried instinct to move his hand up, and a hidden rage to slaughter what had once stood there.

What if the wolves find me, Mom?

Terror stopped him dead in his tracks as he collapsed onto the dirt beneath him. The buried instinct almost consumed him as he fought the sudden urge to find the nearest living thing, the cause of the gunfire that rang in his mind, and tear its lungs from its chest.

But this instinct that he now felt, it hadn't existed as long as the others in his mind. Not near as long as the instincts about the wolves. No, this instinct hadn't always been present, hadn't been learned gradually.

This place, these trees... it felt familiar. This was the spot where it had started, when the new instinct had taken hold. It was a sudden burst, an unimaginable rage that overtook everything else. An instinct learned twenty-five years ago.

Suddenly, his eyes caught something resting in the dirt a few feet away. It was almost entirely hidden within the ground, but a small piece of it had broken through after years of erosion.

Unable to focus on anything else—on the girl's screams or the monstrous wolf that still hadn't revealed itself—Clyde reached over and picked it up, examining the single object left. Something that had once been a piece of an entire body but was now only a broken fragment.

It was small and hard like a bone, stained in dirt and partially rotten, but there was still no mistaking what it was. A piece of someone forcibly

removed from them, torn from its original location. A human tooth ripped from its jaw, causing a scream that Clyde now remembered as well.

CHAPTER TWENTY-THREE

"Why would someone do this?" Linda asked, looking in tragic disbelief at the shattered glass on the floor of her office.

"I don't know," Hank said, kneeling down and picking up papers from the floor, trying to help sort them. A kind gesture to an old friend.

Riley just sighed. The place had been dusted for prints, specifically the paintings torn down and the broken window, but they'd found none, and there was no other physical evidence to tie anyone to it. What bothered her more was motive, mostly the lack of one.

What reason could anyone possibly have for breaking into Linda's office and ransacking the place? It didn't make any sense. They hadn't taken anything of value, so it wasn't a robbery, and Linda didn't have any enemies in town that would have been after revenge. She was probably the sweetest person Riley had ever met.

So why would anyone do this to her?

"Did they take anything at all?" Riley asked, helping Hank pick up the papers and then sweeping up the shattered glass.

"We had the hospital records keeper run over everything that was in this room, and it was all accounted for," Hank said, before looking to Linda, "provided nothing was in here that you hadn't logged."

Riley noticed a slight inflection in his voice as he said it, not quite accusatory, but it also wasn't just an empty question.

"Of course not," Linda answered, but there was a second of hesitation before she got the words out. It was like they were having a different conversation. One that didn't include Riley, despite her being in the same room.

"Any personal items?" Riley asked, desperate to find an answer to this madness. A reason for the break-in. Things like this had always eaten at Riley—things that didn't make sense, couldn't be explained.

There was one thing she couldn't explain, one thing in her life that defied all natural reason.

The Animal. Nothing could ever be said to explain its existence, its monstrous form. The feeling that still lingered in her bones. The fear she'd known before she'd even caught the first glimpse of the beast, when she'd merely felt its presence. That alone had been enough to shroud her life in fear, even without the bloodshed she had witnessed.

Riley had been forced to let that one thing go, one single tragedy in her life that had no explanation, that only existed in spite of nature. She wasn't willing to allow a second.

"Any personal items?" she asked again, startling the old doctor, who had become lost in thought, staring at her desk in sudden anxiety.

Hank moved closer to her, growing concerned. "What is it? What did they take?"

Still no answer came, and Riley watched in increasing confusion at Hank's sudden aura of nervousness over something as simple as a stolen desk item.

"Linda, what did they take?"

A tear fell down Linda's face as she turned to face him, her expression both sorrowful and full of dread.

"A photograph."

A few minutes later, outside in the warm glow of sunlight, Riley was leaning on the old, faded white bricks of the hospital wall, thinking quietly to herself.

She still couldn't get the new attacks out of her mind. The new killer inspired by the Animal of her past. It almost made sense; if all you'd ever heard was the legend told in this town, then it might be conceivable for some sick, twisted madman to idolize the legend, to want to bring it back out into the light.

The words found on the trees, written in crimson blood, came into the forefront of her mind.

Come Back.

Whoever this new killer was, they didn't know what they were doing. The legends might have told the story of a creature born of pure darkness that sought out the defenseless souls in this town to devour for itself: a behemoth, a beast that couldn't be seen, couldn't be killed.

But the truth was so much worse.

If this new killer had seen it, or even felt its presence, they wouldn't have written those words. No matter how sick this killer was, how much of its humanity was lost, fear was still present in everyone's bones, and the fear the Animal instilled would have destroyed their very being just as it once had hers.

"Come here often?"

The voice interrupted her thoughts, and she turned to see a kid with short hair, wearing a brown jacket and holding a small notebook in his hands.

"Hey, Oliver," she said, surprised at his appearance. "Why aren't you with your friends?"

He shrugged. "Suppose I could ask you the same question."

She glanced into his eyes, trying to find the purpose behind them. Of all the kids, he seemed to be the least connected to the group, the least likely to be attacked based on his relationships with the victims. Yet he also seemed to be the most involved, the most concerned, even if he tried to hide it.

"What do you want, kid?" she finally asked.

Oliver smiled and raised an eyebrow. "Aren't you a little young to be calling people kid?"

"Not when they are one." She returned his sarcastic smile. "Seriously, though, what's up? Did something happen? Are the kids okay?"

"As far as I know," he said, joining her in leaning back against the wall.

"So, what? Have you just been following me?"

"Yeah," he said, surprising her with his honesty. "But don't get too flattered. I follow a lot of people."

"So I've heard."

"Let me guess, people have told you I'm paranoid, strange, and far too obsessed with the Animal."

"Among other things." She wasn't lying. After she'd seen him in the woods, she'd asked some of the other kids about him, and after the training session, she'd asked Hank if he'd seen the kid before. Apparently paranoid and obsessive didn't quite cut it.

"Lucky for me," he began, tone completely serious, "you probably don't put much faith in the stories this town makes up about people."

Clever kid. Just like that, now she had to give him a chance to explain himself, because he was right. The stories this town told were never fair, and she knew that better than most.

"Fair point. So what is it you want from me?"

"I want to show you something." He looked back over his shoulder, not the first time he'd done so. "But not here."

"Where, then?"

He hesitated before saying it, apparently knowing how suspicious it would sound. "My house. At the edge of town."

"So let me get this straight," Riley said, moving off the wall and standing directly in front of him. "This town is in the middle of a new wave of attacks. A masked killer is out there mimicking murders that I was involved in. And you want me to follow a kid obsessed with the legend back to his place, at the edge of town, alone?"

Oliver nodded. "That pretty much sums it up."

"What's there that's so important?"

"If I told you now, you'd think I was crazy."

"Already do."

"Fair enough. But I do have a peace offering. Something to prove I'm not just a crazy conspiracist who doesn't actually know anything."

"What's that?"

A sly smile spread across his face. "I know who broke into the doctor's office."

"How could you possibly know that?" Riley said, trying to call him on it. There was no way he could have known who did it. Whatever name he was about to say would be a guess at best.

"Because I did it."

That single sentence changed the entire tone of the conversation, as her emotions suddenly flipped between disbelief and anger.

"You're lying."

"No, I'm not. And I can prove it." He wasn't smiling anymore, but something about his tone of voice made Riley listen as he reached into his pocket. "The only thing that was missing was a photograph, wasn't it?"

As he spoke the words, he pulled out a single photo and held it up so she could see. It was a picture of a blonde woman with a warm smile, which looked to have been taken a long time ago.

Before he could react, lightning flashed in Riley's eyes, and she shoved him back to the wall, pressing against his throat with her forearm. Her voice was sharp, hostile. "Why would you do that? Why would you break into Linda's office?"

Oliver struggled to get the answers out with the pressure on his throat, but eventually he managed a few words. "Because... hiding... something..."

Riley ground her teeth but released her grip on his throat and waited a moment for him to catch his breath. His next words had better be chosen carefully, because she was one second away from calling the cops, who at the moment weren't very far away.

"When she noticed the picture was missing, she acted strange, didn't she?" Oliver said, coughing as he did. "Almost nervous, like it was more than just a family photo. And I'm guessing she wouldn't tell you who it was."

Riley's right eye twitched slightly, as she suddenly grew unnerved by the kid's statements. Not only because he knew what had happened, but because every question he asked was one she was already asking herself. Linda had looked scared, and neither she nor Hank would tell Riley why.

"Behind the photograph," he continued, "I found something. Something she was trying to hide. I think it might help find the real Animal."

Despite knowing how foolish it probably was, Riley let curiosity get the better of her. She knew Linda hadn't told her everything, and if this kid was right, she'd rather know the horrible truth than live in blissful ignorance. But still, trust wasn't something she gave out easily.

"Okay, I'll bite. But first, answer me this. Why are you so obsessed with the Animal? It has nothing to do with you."

To her surprise, his voice grew solemn. "I know. But despite what you may think of me, I'm not obsessed with the Animal. I'm obsessed with the flesh and blood behind the legend, the man behind the mask."

"It's not a man," Riley said, a hint of terror in her voice.

For a moment, Oliver looked as though he didn't know how to respond, but finally he did. "Whatever it is, I don't care. All I care about is finding the truth about what the Animal truly is, so that the legend can finally die. So that the victims left behind become the ones the town remembers, not the monster who killed them."

"So, you care more about the victims than you do the Animal?" Riley questioned, trying to find his true motives, trying to decide whether she could trust him even a little.

Oliver nodded.

"Then what were their names?"

For a moment, he said nothing, just as Riley had expected. No one in this town actually cared about anything other than the legend. They'd say they did, offer their condolences, but then spend all of their time wondering about the monster rather than those left behind.

This kid was no different.

But then, to her surprise, it happened.

"Mia Stevens. Ericka Bateman. Susan, Richie, and Francis Harvey. Bruce and Amber Collins. Dave Rogan. Elijah Summers. Harry and Betsy Norman, along with Betsy Junior, who was eleven. Sebastian Rodgers. Ellie and Avery Bradley. And Donald and Evelyn Grayson, your parents. Seventeen victims.

"Unless you also count Camilla Rodgers, who drank herself to death after her husband's passing, or James Stevens, who was out of town that night and committed suicide a few months later, after hearing one too many stories about how the Animal killed his mom. If you count all the walking ghosts the Animal's victims left behind, the number just keeps growing."

Hearing all their names out loud almost brought a tear, but she didn't dare allow it. Still, Oliver knowing each and every name wasn't something that she had expected. If she hadn't known better, she'd say he had lost someone that night. But he hadn't even been born yet, and according to his friends he'd only moved to town a few years ago.

"Why do you know that?" she asked, trying to understand him. She'd gotten so used to no one caring about the victims that it almost felt wrong to hear someone say their names. "Why do you care so much about who the Animal killed?"

Oliver just shrugged and started walking off. If there was a secret in his past, he wasn't going to reveal it. "You coming?"

Eventually, Riley nodded.

If there was ever a place to kill someone without being seen, it was here.

The wood on the side of the house was chipping off, and the paint was so faded it might as well not have been there at all. However, the most distinguishing thing she noticed about the house was that it was one of the few places in town that was more than half a mile away from the forest.

Curiosity was the only thing that kept her from listening to her better judgment and getting out of here. Instead, she followed Oliver up to his front door and watched curiously as he unlocked three separate deadbolts.

When he was done, they both stepped inside and into the living room, dimly lit by flickering lightbulbs, appearing almost abandoned.

"Where are your parents?"

"Dad comes around every once in a while, but never for very long. He kind of has a drinking problem, which doesn't help."

"And your mom?"

Oliver ignored the question, occasionally glancing behind himself, as if he expected something to kill him at any moment.

Within seconds they had reached another door, and he began to unlock it, making Riley even more uneasy.

How many locks did this house have?

Once opened, they stepped inside, and Oliver turned to lock it again before hesitating. "Would you feel more comfortable if I left it unlocked?"

"Yeah," Riley said without a second thought. Most likely she could take this kid if he attacked her, especially with the knife in her boot and the pistol hidden under her jacket. But she still didn't want to be locked in a room with someone, regardless of who they were.

"Okay," he said, leaving it unlocked, even if doing so made him visibly uncomfortable. Still, he didn't mention it again, instead turning right to the evidence he had promised to show her.

A stack of books and papers lay in the corner of the small room, piling up halfway to the ceiling: phone books, newspapers, even some history books from the library, most likely well past their return date. But more curious were the sheets of notebook paper taped to the walls, all of which were blank.

"So far, I've only been able to find three pieces of evidence for the original Animal," Oliver explained as he began showing her everything he had. "The first is a name: Arthur Conners. I've checked every single piece of history in this town, and he's the only person who I can verify lived here before that night but was never once seen after it."

Riley ran her hand over the stack of papers, in awe. What kind of dedication did it take to search an entire town's population, spanning decades, for a single man? That had to be thousands upon thousands of names. "How long did this take you?"

"A while," he said but didn't stop to dwell on it. "But I couldn't find another trace of Conners anywhere. Then this new animal showed up, and I started to get desperate. I've always suspected that either the sheriff or the doctor knew more than they let on, so last night I broke into your doctor friend's office and found this." He clipped the photograph to the wall that was covered in blank notebook paper. "A photograph of a woman, which looks like it was taken quite a long time ago."

"So," Riley asked, growing impatient, "what's the connection to the Animal?"

"This," Oliver revealed, holding an X-ray up to the light. It was of a human skull, badly fractured.

"This was hidden behind the photograph in the doctor's office. There's no date written on it, nor any name, so I can't prove it has anything to do with the Animal. But if it didn't, then why wouldn't she have told you about it?"

It had always amazed Riley how a single idea could make someone question everything they had ever held to be true. How the mere hint of darkness behind the curtain made even its beautiful patterns fade to grey in someone's eyes, out of blind fear for what could be hiding within.

"Keep going," she told him.

Oliver smiled. It was clear he had been worried that she'd think he was insane. "Okay. I knew that the X-ray and the photograph were related, and the woman looked familiar to me. So this morning, I went back over all my old notes, and I found this." He laid an old newspaper down on the desk in front of them. On it was a photograph of the same woman from the picture, standing in front of a tall grey fence with a hunting rifle in her hand. The headline read:

Game Ranch Officially Open.

Riley studied the photograph. "Is that the old game ranch at the edge of town?"

"Yeah," Oliver said. "I went to the library this morning and managed to find some old property records about it, although most of what should have been there was missing. It closed down several years before even you were born, and from what I can tell it's been abandoned ever since. But guess whose name I found on the property info."

"Arthur Conners?"

"Bingo," Oliver said. "Which gives us a connection we can use."

"Okay." Riley considered the evidence he had presented. "Where are you going with this?"

"I don't know," Oliver admitted. "I do know that the injuries on the skull indicate serious brain damage. Maybe even permanent memory loss, but I'll need to research it more to be sure. I don't even know how Conners and this woman are connected yet, but at least we have somewhere to start. But I do know this—I can feel it in my gut." He pointed to the X-ray. "That is the Animal's skull."

"No, it's not," Riley said, shaking her head. "It can't be."

"Why?"

"Because that skull is human."

Oliver gave her a genuinely curious expression. "You don't really believe the Animal is actually some type of inhuman monster, do you?"

Riley sighed, not knowing how to answer him without sounding like a mental patient telling stories of an imagined nightmare. But in the end, all she could tell him was the truth.

"I know how this sounds, but if you could have seen it, felt its presence, then... then you'd know what I know. Whatever that thing was, it wasn't human."

Oliver didn't look convinced, but he nodded, not pushing her on the subject.

"Now," Riley continued, "I hope you didn't bring me here just to show me an old X-ray and a name."

"No," Oliver said, reaching over and turning off the lights before hitting the switch underneath his desk. "No, I didn't."

The sight of it took Riley's breath away. Invisible ink illuminated by the black light, the blue fluorescent colors almost dancing around her, spelling clues and notes about the Animal. Then, however, she saw the names, and her surprise turned to dread.

"Why do you have those names written down?"

Oliver said nothing, instead gesturing at the words written above the names.

New Suspects.

Riley turned to him in disbelief. "You don't really think—"

"Yeah, I do."

"But these are your friends."

"I know."

The identities listed weren't what made her skin crawl. It was why they were listed. What they were suspected of. It wasn't possible.

There were six names written in total, inscribed in fluorescent blue ink, glowing in the darkness.

Below each was a rundown of locations, motives, and anything else that tied them to the new attacks. Riley shook her head as she read them again, unable to believe it—the new suspects he'd been looking into.

Kelly. Rhett. Dylan. Gabriella. Russel. Luke.

"You really are crazy," she said in complete shock. Not trusting Hank and Linda was one thing, but these were the kid's own friends. This wasn't just paranoia; it was something else. She turned in an instant, about to walk away when he stopped her with conviction in his voice.

"There were only eight people who knew about the location of the safe house, aside from you and the police. Betty, me, and the six names listed on that wall."

"That doesn't prove anything."

Oliver continued without hesitation. "Those are also the only six people who could have known Kelly was throwing a party that night. Or that Kelly was going to be at the gym to pick up Gabriella. The only constant in every attack is those six names."

That got her to stop walking away, and she turned her attention to him once again. "Do you really think that the person killing these people is a kid?"

"Why not?" he asked. "You know, at the safe house, I saw the piece of the new animal's mask that you cut off. The ear. Only a few places in town sell costumes with ears like that, so I went to check it out and see if they had sold one to anyone recently. And do you know what the clerk told me? He said it would be quicker to tell me the people in town that he hasn't sold one to. Said that he's sold even more after the new attacks started."

Oliver sighed, trying to bring his point home. "I think this town is sick. It's obsessed with the Animal in a way that can't be explained, and I think every single person here is to blame. So, yes. I think anyone old enough to hold a knife is old enough to be fascinated with the legends to the point of murdering innocent people."

Riley considered it, not wanting it to be true but unable to deny the possibility. "Still, they're your friends."

"You keep saying that. Every serial killer ever caught has had friends, people that cared about them. Why should this case be any different?"

"Typically, the friends aren't the ones who investigate them."

"Typically, the friends are the ones who wind up dead."

Riley groaned but didn't know what else to say. He wasn't letting it go, and to be fair he had been right about Linda hiding something in her office, even if she wasn't quite sure what it meant.

"Okay," she finally said, surprised at herself that she was actually considering it. "What evidence do you have on them?"

"Not much," he admitted. "But if we assume it has to be one of them, then we can use a process of elimination. Kelly, Gabriella, and Russel have all been seen being attacked by the new animal, so they're most likely cleared."

"Most likely?"

"I'll get to that," Oliver promised. "But for now, that leaves Rhett, Dylan, and Luke. All of them could have known about Kelly's party and the safe house, and none of them have alibis. It's like they just vanished those nights. So, if I'm right that it's one of these six, and there's only one killer, then it has to be one of the three."

Riley held back a shudder. "What do you mean only one killer?"

"That's the thing," Oliver said. "Typically, serial killers work alone. It's not unheard of for two to work together, but it's very rare. However, this isn't a serial killer. This is someone who puts on a mask and kills in the hope of bringing a long-hidden animal back into the spotlight. Someone who's obsessed with the legend and has to see the Animal for themselves. Which means it could very easily be more than one killer—both obsessed with the Animal, working together like a cult to bring it back to them.

"That's why you still have all the names up there," Riley said, beginning to understand.

"If it does happen to be two, then even those attacked can't be ruled out. Besides, Kelly has some stab wounds, Gabriella a small cut on the back, and Russel was sliced in the chest, but none of the wounds were near fatal. Kelly's stitches were the worst of it, and she was out of the hospital before school even started. Considering how violently everyone else was injured, it seems strange."

"Maybe it's because they fought back."

"Maybe," Oliver admitted. "Or maybe they wanted to clear their names but didn't want to get hurt too bad."

"What about Betty? She would have known about the safe house too."

"Yes, she is the seventh constant, but honestly she should have died at the hospital. I may not think as highly of Dr. Parker as you do, but even I'll admit that she's the best surgeon within a thousand miles. Whoever this killer is, they meant for Betty to die. So, she's clear."

Riley kept silent for a moment, going back over everything that was said. It should have sounded crazy. It did sound crazy. But what if it wasn't? Finally, she made up her mind. "Assuming I believe a word you've said, who do you really think it could be?"

Oliver seemed to breathe a sigh of relief, apparently shocked that she was taking him seriously. Most people in town must not.

"If it's just one killer, then I would lean toward Rhett. It would have been the easiest for him to have attacked at the party and cut the lights, since it was his own house. Plus, Kelly surviving three separate attacks could mean that he doesn't want to kill his own sister. It also makes no sense that he wasn't at the party that night or by his sister's side at the next two attacks.

"However, Dylan makes sense too. He's a little... well, you've met him. But he also doesn't have an alibi, and his complete lack of empathy matches pretty well with the killer's MO."

"What about Luke?" Riley asked. "He's Hank's son. There's no way he could be the one behind this. He'd have no motive."

Oliver hesitated for a moment, a curious expression growing in his eyes. "You know he hates you, right?"

"What? Why?"

"Why wouldn't he? He blames his father for his mom leaving when he was younger, and dear old dad judges every move he makes like he's constantly on trial for murder. Obviously, he's going to hate the girl his dad never shuts up about. *The girl that he saved that night. The girl who was strong enough to get over it.* It might not sound like much to us, but for Luke, it's pretty rough. Maybe even rough enough to try and kill you himself."

So that was why he'd stared at her like that, with venom in his eyes.

She didn't know what to say.

"If there are two killers," Oliver continued, not missing a beat, "then certain groups make sense. Rhett and Kelly for obvious reasons: both upset that their parents are never around, trying to get attention somehow, which could be why they both came back to school so quickly. Then there's Dylan and Gabriella, the classic psychotic couple. It could also be Rhett and Dylan, which would explain why Rhett was so upset with Dylan the day after Kelly hit her head at the gym. Dylan might've gone too far, hurt his sister, and Rhett didn't like it. Russel and Luke are harder to pair up, but not impossible."

"Still," Riley said, shaking her head, "I just can't picture kids doing this. I know they're almost in college, but still."

"Youth doesn't dull cruelty. Did you know that Russel has broken the legs of two players in practice? His own teammates. Sure, he says it's an accident, but it's really just revenge for being picked on when he was smaller. And you know Gabriella's dog, the one that they said killed the neighbor's cat?"

Riley nodded.

"It didn't. She did. Broke its legs and then buried it alive behind her house. I heard it squeal, and when I got there, she was dropping it in the hole. Then she *watched* as it tried to crawl out before covering it with dirt one shovelful at a time. I would have stopped it, but at that point that cat was already dying."

"Why?" Riley asked, horrified.

"I don't know. Her parents are perfectionists, critique everything she does and make her train her fingers to the bone at the gym. Maybe she needed to release tension. Maybe she'd hung around Dylan for too long. Who cares? What matters is that she did it."

"Why are you telling me this?"

"Because you need to understand that just because they're kids, it doesn't mean they're saints. If Gabriella can torture a cat, then any of them are capable of anything."

"Why me?" Riley asked, not quite sure what all of this meant. "You apparently don't trust the cops, the doctors, or even your own friends. So why are you trusting me with this?"

"Because the legend of the Animal has corrupted every single person in this town, bloodied all of them with the memories of its victims. Except for the eight-year-old girl who lived through the worst pain imaginable. I trust you because you can't be this new killer, any more than you could have been the killer twenty-five years ago. And maybe I am too paranoid. Maybe this really is insane, and the killer is going to turn out to be someone we've never heard of. But if I'm right, then I thought you should know that one of the kids you're trying to save could be the monster trying to kill you."

To even her own surprise, Riley smiled. She wasn't used to people trying to help her, but even the few times they had, it had been with sympathy, condolences, and understanding. This time it was with suspects, facts, and a hunt for the new animal. Something Riley appreciated far more.

However, the obvious still had to be stated. "What about you? You say all your friends could potentially be killers, so why not you? You're obsessed with the legend and don't have any alibis for the attacks. Why should I trust you?"

"You shouldn't," he said plainly. "If anything, I should be your number one suspect. But I don't care"—he pointed to the names glowing in the dark light—"just as long as you know that they are all suspects too."

Riley nodded and began to walk away. The suspect list had surprised her, as had the information about the kids. But at the end of the day, all of it was related to the new predator, and it didn't scare her very much. She'd seen it at the safe house. Nothing more than someone wearing a fake wolf costume and swinging a sharpened bone.

It had even run from her.

What bothered her was the information about the old attacks, the real Animal. The game ranch, the hidden X-ray, the mysterious woman, and the name Oliver had found that connected them all.

But it wasn't possible. The beast she'd seen couldn't have a name; it couldn't be a man. It wasn't even a monster; it was something far more terrifying.

An Animal.

"One more thing," Oliver called out to her as she approached the front door of the house. "That game ranch, there isn't much known about it before it shut down, but I was able to find one thing."

"I know," Riley said, walking away. She'd heard people talk about the game ranch before, about what it had been like before it was abandoned. It used to have elk, deer, bobcats, anything at all that someone would hunt. But it had also held something else, something darker.

Wolves.

CHAPTER TWENTY-FOUR

It was cold, even with the sun shining down on them. It never really seemed to warm the town enough, always leaving just enough light for a tree to grow but not so much that it could thrive.

Rhett felt the chill on the back of his neck, almost like the sun itself was the source of it and had chosen this cursed place as the piece of land to envelop in its cold touch of an icy breeze, even though winter was months away.

In moments like this, surrounded by the trees, Rhett felt small, unimportant, like he was just another wanderer in this town who'd be forgotten before he even died. Even his parents had seemed to forget he existed, visiting him and Kelly once every few months to say hello and then disappearing back into the world, spending their time on more important things. Things that mattered.

"It's quicker. I swear," Dylan's voice said, bringing Rhett's focus back to the conversation.

"That makes no sense," Kelly responded.

"I'm telling you, cutting through the forest is a shortcut."

Kelly looked at him as if examining a babbling madman. "Our houses are on this side of the forest. Just because it isn't on the road doesn't make it a shortcut."

"I disagree," Dylan said. Rhett couldn't tell if he legitimately believed it or was just messing with all of them. "Let's prove it." He then gestured to himself, Gabriella, Luke, and Russel. "We'll cut through the forest, and the rest of you cowards can take the road. We'll see who gets there first."

Betty shook her head immediately. "No, Riley said we should all stick together."

Luke rolled his eyes. "By all means let's obey whatever *Riley* says."

Sometimes his constant annoyance at the mention of her name even got under Rhett's skin, which wasn't an easy thing to do. Unless, of course, your name was Oliver, but thankfully, he wasn't here.

"Dude, can you please shut up about your grudge against her?" Rhett told him. "We get it. You don't like her. You don't have to keep reminding us."

Luke winced like an insulted child but didn't say anything further.

"Betty is right, though," Kelly said. "We shouldn't split up. That'd be stupid."

Dylan looked to Rhett to back him up, but he shook his head no. Dylan couldn't have really expected him not to back up his own sister.

"Okay, fine," Dylan said, putting his arm around Gabriella. "We'll be intelligent prey. Because whatever is hiding in the woods definitely wouldn't take the effort to walk ten more feet to reach us here."

"He does have a point," Russel said, standing tall behind them. Rhett swore he was almost blocking out the sun. "Just because we're a few feet from the trees doesn't make us any safer."

"Of course you're not scared," Gabriella said. "Some of us don't bench-press cars."

Russel tried to hide the slight smile, but Rhett saw it. He always liked to be reminded that he was the strongest among them.

A few moments of silence passed before Betty spoke again. "Why did Riley call us prey?"

"Because an animal is hunting us."

"So," Betty said, visibly contemplating it, "does that make the animal that attacked us a predator?"

"Sure does," Luke said.

"And they're the animals that kill other animals. The bad ones."

"Not necessarily," Rhett said, surprising most of them.

"What do you mean?" Dylan asked. "Of course the predators are the bad guys of the animal kingdom. Killing is like their whole thing."

"Please don't get him started," Kelly muttered under her breath, having heard her brother's speech more times than she could count.

Rhett simply ignored her. "The food chain isn't just good or bad, just like it's not simply predator and prey."

"Go on," Russel goaded.

Rhett smiled. "Well, an animal can be both bad and good, depending on which perspective you look through. To a snake, a hawk is a monster that hunts them from the sky like a horrific shadow, waiting for the right moment to lift them from the ground and rip them in two with their massive talons. But to the rat, the snake is the monster, crawling without legs to swallow it whole and suffocate it.

"So, when a rat sees a hawk, it doesn't see a monster lurking in the clouds above. It sees its savior, an angel who swoops down and saves it from its predator's grasp, killing the snake that thirsted for its blood."

Rhett looked over to the forest, searching the trees for the legend that hid within. "If you look at animals long enough, eventually you'll find that all of them are both prey and predator. It's just a matter of which they are at any given moment."

"Except for the apex," Russel said. "The predator who has no rivals."

"Even an apex has rivals," Rhett said, looking back to the group. "A lion has nothing to fear, except another lion. Another apex."

Everyone was quiet for a moment, taking in what was said. Normally it would have just been a simple, if somewhat boring, conversation about animals. But at the moment, nothing seemed normal to them.

"Hey," Gabriella suddenly said, pointing in front of them. "Is that the old abandoned game ranch?"

"I think it is," Kelly said.

The fence looked massive, stretching up farther than even Russel could reach, even if he jumped. Interlocking grey steel blocked it off, separating it from the rest of the forest, keeping it walled off. Nothing could get in, and more importantly, nothing could get out.

Rhett walked up to the fence, followed closely by Kelly, Dylan, and Gabriella. Feeling the cold metal touch his hands, he wondered about the old stories he'd heard told about the game ranch.

About how it contained more than just deer.

Then he heard the growl, and his skeleton almost leapt out of his skin. Within seconds he saw it running toward them, a streak of grey, four paws colliding with the dirt as it charged them.

Suddenly, even the fence didn't feel like it could protect them.

Rhett grabbed Kelly in a panic and jumped back from it, falling to the ground on his back and crawling away as the wolf leapt in the air. A second later it collided with the steel, pushing its bloodstained teeth through the openings, trying to reach them.

It seemed enormous.

For some reason, Rhett had always expected a wolf to be the size of a dog, but it dwarfed them in size as its teeth snapped, and it raised its sharp claws up, trying to cut through the fence to reach them. It appeared old, grizzled, a long jagged scar covering its eye, but that made it no less terrifying.

Gabriella had fallen back from the fence too, and everyone else was already back on the road, watching from a distance, not daring to venture closer as they heard its primal growling, bore witness to its attempt to break through the fence and kill them.

Everyone except Dylan, who began laughing. Then, to the rest of their alarm, he actually moved closer to the frenzied canine.

"Dylan, get back," Gabriella warned.

"Why?" he asked, tilting his head to match the wolf's crooked stance. "It's behind a fence."

To be fair, Rhett wasn't very scared himself, at least now that the initial shock was gone. It was behind a fence, and it couldn't get to them. Still, he held Kelly, making sure she was safe. But then Dylan did something even Rhett thought went too far, raising his hand up and stepping even closer to the fence.

"Are you crazy!" Gabriella screamed. "It's going to take your hand off."

"Maybe," Dylan said, hand now less than an inch away from the animal's teeth, which snapped together every second in a desperate attempt to take even a small piece of him. "But I want to see what it feels like."

Rhett thought about telling him he was crazy, but if anything, that would have only encouraged him. So instead, they were all forced to watch in suspense as Dylan showcased why he was known as the insane one.

Growling still echoing within the trees, the wolf's eyes still overtaken with hunger, Dylan took a deep breath and pressed his hand against its head, attempting to pet it.

Quicker than a flash of lightning, the wolf adjusted its bite and caught his hand.

Dylan let out a wince of pain as he took his hand back and shook it, little drops of blood falling to the ground. The wolf's teeth had grazed his skin, taking off a piece of flesh on the left side of his hand, but not quite enough to cause a major injury. It would probably heal in time.

Still, it bled a lot, and it had to have been painful.

"Are you okay?" Kelly said, running over to inspect the hand.

Dylan didn't answer her, instead choosing to look back into the wolf's eyes. "It felt soft." His smile turned into laughter. "The big bad wolf felt soft."

Russel walked up and slapped his back. "Something's very wrong with you, man."

Dylan just shrugged as they all began to walk away, waving his bloodied hand at the wolf as he did. Almost as though he was waving goodbye to a friend, rather than to an animal who'd just ripped into his flesh in an attempt to eat him.

But Rhett didn't leave, at least not at first. Instead, he stayed there, a few feet away from the fence, watching as the wolf paced back and forth, Dylan's blood still on its teeth.

If the fence wasn't there, Rhett knew the wolf would attack him, probably go for his throat immediately. But it was caged, locked inside a barrier that kept it from advancing, forcing it to pace in hunger.

That meant it wasn't a threat. Wasn't even a predator. As long as it was trapped inside the fence, then it was nothing to him. If he wanted, he could grab a gun and shoot it in the head, dropping it to the dirt right then, soaked in its own blood.

Which meant that right now, the wolf wasn't the most dangerous predator, the apex of the moment.

They were. He was.

"Are you coming or not?" Kelly's voice called out to him.

"Yeah," Rhett answered, taking one last look into the wolf's hungry eyes, "I'm coming."

CHAPTER TWENTY-FIVE

It had to be here somewhere.

The answer to all of this. The monster hiding behind the yellow eyes that had watched him from the forest.

Crumpled paper lay scattered across his room as Clyde desperately searched through his notes, everything the news had mentioned about the attacks twenty-five years ago, scouring them for anything that would explain the tooth he'd found hidden in the dirt.

It would have been easy to ignore it, just like he'd ignored everything else. To chalk it up to coincidence, to something that couldn't be explained, and therefore wasn't worth the investigation. But too many buried thoughts had

come to light, and too many hidden feelings were revealing themselves once again. He couldn't dismiss the signs any longer. Something was wrong with him. Even if it wasn't the Animal, something deep down in his bones was corrupted, hungry.

Clyde had to find out what it was before it consumed him from within.

But just as he'd feared, his notes revealed nothing. There were no reports of any of the original seventeen victims missing a tooth, at least not a single one; several were missing their entire jaw. In desperation, Clyde even checked his own mouth, running his fingers over his teeth, searching for a missing piece that he knew he wouldn't find.

Sighing in defeat, he bent down over the floor, trying to remember. For his entire life he'd only known what they'd told him: Hank and Linda. How they explained away his broken mind, and the mystery of his past. But what if they'd lied? What if he wasn't a good man? What if he wasn't even a man at all, at least not at his core, in his bones?

What if something else had been hiding inside of him all these years, waiting to reemerge and feast once again?

Clyde could feel every one of them now. Every scar that littered his body. Every sign of the life that he'd known before. The life he couldn't remember, before he'd become whatever he was now.

But what if they lied about the scars too?

In an instant he was in the bathroom, looking at his reflection in the full-length mirror, examining the scars that covered him.

They'd told him they were cuts inflicted by a human monster, someone cruel and heartless, and Clyde had never questioned it. Never had any reason to. But now he saw them for what they were. Not cuts inflicted by a human, but scars formed by claws digging against his flesh. He even recognized the patterns carved into him.

The scar on his chest looked canine. So did the eight on his side. The one on his ribs looked strange, a few thick circular scars formed inches from one another, in a wild pattern.

Antlers.

More scars littered his arms, but they were nothing compared to the ones on his neck. Small cuts, but dozens of them: scars formed on top of one another, creating distorted skin and broken tissue. Something had gone for his neck more than once but had always been stopped right before its teeth could puncture his throat and spill his blood onto the ground.

Then, with rising dread, Clyde saw the three larger scars, massive patches of discolored flesh

that had grown over the wounds: one on his shoulder, one on his rib cage, the last directly on his chest.

The only three scars they hadn't lied about. The only three scars that could have been inflicted by a human, by a weapon: a shotgun most likely.

But what if they'd lied about who had shot him? *What if they'd lied about why?*

The sound of gunfire rang in his head, mixing with the sound of the girl's screams. Flashes of yellow light cascaded over his eyes as he remembered pain. Excruciating pain.

Suddenly, his head felt as though it would explode as more memories began crawling their way back inside his head, viciously gnawing in his skull, trying to resurface.

Clyde's mind felt as though it would break once again from the strain, and as he saw the monstrous wounds that distorted his flesh, he knew only one thing for certain. He shouldn't be alive. Whatever had done this to him should have killed him a long time ago. Any one of these wounds should have been lethal.

How was he still alive?

Suddenly, he noticed something. The flash of gunfire in his eyes had been shared by his reflection. Only it hadn't gone away. The light was still there, eyes reflecting light from them, glowing yellow in the dark room.

Clyde's hand trembled as he recognized them. The same eyes that had watched him from the forest. The same ones that had belonged to the wolf that had chased him, that was now resting in his own reflection.

Low, vicious growling filled the room as his reflection began to change. Its head twisted and its bones cracked as it moaned in pain and growled in hatred.

In horror Clyde watched it, unable to even tremble as the face distorted, cheekbones shifting, tearing his own skin as they did, blood dripping from the wounds.

All the while, the yellow eyes still watched him.

The monstrous reflection howled in pain as black fur began to cover any trace of his once-human skin, soaking up the blood and covering the revealed bones in its shadow, replacing him with its inhuman form.

The teeth came last, forming themselves from the creature's own jaw. The broken fragments of bone jutting out, stained in its own blood.

At last, the animal in front of him, born from his own reflection, finished its grisly transformation, howls of pain becoming growls of hunger as its yellow eyes focused on him, as if it was eating him from within.

As though it already had...

Fear tried to drag Clyde back, away from the monster, and every bone in his body agreed, almost forcing themselves to move. But instinct didn't allow them to. It was something that had always been wrong with his head; if he felt his instinct kick in, there was nothing he could do to fight it, to stop it.

So, he was forced to stare back into the monster's eyes and come to a horrifying realization. The scars on his own body were mirrored in his reflection, wounds cutting through the black fur, drawing blood from the animal's flesh.

But the monster wasn't Clyde. It might have been created from his own flesh, ripping itself free from his own skin, but the creature he saw in his reflection wasn't him, at least not entirely.

Yet it also wasn't the wolf from the forest, the one that had stalked him, hunted him. It was something else, something in between both of them.

An Animal born of a human but created by wolves.

Suddenly, he could feel the wolf behind him, staring at the same reflection he was, both of their shadows joining together to create the shadow of the Animal.

Clyde screamed in pain and shoved his fist into the mirror, shattering his twisted reflection along with it. Then he fell to the floor, trying not to

hear their screams, trying not to remember their blood.

Another memory flashed in his head, overshadowing the rest. Soft words echoing in his mind, a voice he'd never forgotten, contrasting sharply with the screams of pain still filling his ears.

"Wolves aren't monsters. They're just animals."

CHAPTER TWENTY-SIX

"Do you mind if I take notes?"

The old man shrugged, looking out into the forest as if he was searching for past lives, for the days of his youth long since passed.

I'll take that as a no, Oliver thought as he pulled out his notebook and began writing. He was sitting in a chair on the old man's porch, raised up off the ground, overlooking the forest. He'd shifted the chair so that it was against the outer wall of the house to ensure nothing could sneak up and slit his throat from behind.

The old man was sitting in an ancient wooden rocking chair, slowly rocking back and forth in the gentle breeze of the evening. His eyes were

tired, and his skin was wrinkled, signs of age and experience.

But Oliver hadn't come for wisdom. He'd come for information.

After he'd found the connection between Conners and the game ranch, he'd spent hours researching it, visiting every place in town that kept records, but had found nothing else. The newspaper, the old deed, and the stories told were the only records that the ranch had ever existed, other than the fence that still stood tall. Almost like someone had tracked down and burned every shred of evidence, every track left behind.

But Oliver was nothing if not determined, and he'd set out to walk the length of the game ranch in search of answers.

Most of the fence cut through the forest itself, and it didn't reveal anything he hadn't already known. Neither had the stretch by the road. However, on the far end, after countless miles of walking, Oliver had finally found it. A house near the fence, close enough that you could see the steel links from the porch where he now sat.

The owner had seen him coming and at first had drawn a rifle on him, thinking he was a trespasser, which technically he was. But after he'd explained himself, the old man had set the rifle down and offered to speak to him about the ranch. About its history.

"So," Oliver started, "what can you tell me about the game ranch?"

"It used to have good deer," the old man said. "I hunted there for a couple of seasons, way back when I was still young enough to see straight. Saw a whitetail once. Antlers as big as a tree branch. Missed it, though. Blasted scope ruined my aim."

Oliver grinned but didn't comment. "Did you ever see any other animals in there?"

"You mean did I see the wolves that everyone says are in there?"

Oliver nodded.

"No, I didn't. At least not when I was hunting. You see, I hunted there the first couple of seasons after it opened. The wolves didn't come until later."

"But you have seen the wolves?"

There was a slight hesitation in his voice as his eyes moved to focus on a single spot in the fence. Suddenly it appeared as though he became lost in a memory, flinching slightly. But finally, he spoke again. "I've seen 'em. But mostly I've just heard them. They howl at all hours of the night. Makes sleeping a challenge."

"I bet," Oliver said, wanting to ask about the sudden nervous twitch, but knowing it wasn't the right time. So instead, he shifted his questioning. "The man who used to own the place, Arthur Conners, did you know him?"

"*Know* is a strong word," the man said. "I saw him a couple of times when I hunted. Tanned a few hides for me, checked me into the ranch and all that. I guess you could say I knew him, but..." The man's voice changed, becoming forceful. "I was *not* his friend. Once I realized what kind of man he was, I stopped hunting on his ranch. It wasn't long after that the wolves came."

What kind of man he was. The words stuck out like a leper, holding corrupted secrets and buried trauma. Exactly what Oliver was looking for.

"You said you realized what kind of man he was. What do you mean by that?"

The aging hunter held up his hand, dismissing the question. "Doesn't matter. Just the memories of an old man."

"It does matter."

"Why do you care so much about Arthur?"

"Because," Oliver said, hesitating for a moment as he decided to tell the truth, "I've been trying to find the man behind the attacks twenty-five years ago, and so far, Arthur Conners is the only name I've found."

To his surprise, the man scoffed. "You think that bum is the Animal?" He laughed to himself for a moment. "Son, Arthur Conners is no more the Animal than the mosquito flying above your head."

"But you said–"

301

"I said I found out what kind of man he was. A coward who beat his wife, because he was a cruel little piece of trash who beat and threatened anything he could find so long as it was smaller than him. But that's all he was, a coward. Just like this new killer the news talks about, going around and killing kids. Cowards, both of them. Think they're scary because they're bigger, stronger. But put them in front of a real monster, they'd cry like babies scared of the dark."

"On that, I agree," Oliver said. "But what makes you think the Animal isn't a murderous coward, just like them?"

The old man grew deathly silent as Oliver spoke the words, as if afraid it would anger some spirit that lived in the woods, unleashing its vengeance upon them. He began to breathe heavier, and for a moment, Oliver thought the old man might actually collapse, before finally he calmed back down.

"I've seen the thing that haunts those woods." His eyes focused again on the fence, staring as if some haunting nightmare was unfolding right before his eyes. "I've seen what it's done to monsters."

Leaning further forward, Oliver persisted. This was it. Someone other than Riley had seen it. "Tell me."

"It was years before the attacks. I woke up one night, hearing the wolves howling louder

than usual. And that's what I thought it was at first, howling. It sounded like it was right outside, so I stepped out onto this porch to see what was happening. Then I realized... the wolf wasn't howling."

Fear filled the old man's eyes as he spoke, hands trembling, voice cracking.

"I didn't know a wolf could scream. I didn't think they had it in them to be terrified, but there it was, clawing at the fence until its paws bled. It was trying to get through it, not to kill me, but to escape, screaming into the night. I... I still hear it sometimes, the horrible wailing."

The old man's face lost its color.

"Then I saw a shadow move behind it. Some dark figure in the woods, moving closer. The wolf fought harder, dragging its bloodied paws against the metal. But it couldn't escape. The shadow behind it took hold, and it was dragged backwards, claws digging into the dirt, trying to avoid its fate."

Struggling to speak, the old man almost looked like a ghost, terrified beyond comprehension. "I still remember the look in the wolf's eyes as it was dragged back into the forest. The fear."

For a few moments, it felt as though the world was frozen, as Oliver felt the fear himself. It was the same exaggerated story everyone told, and Oliver had gotten used to dismissing them. But he also remembered what Riley had said, about

the monster not being human. Now there was this man who'd seen the terrified expression of a timber wolf, something that wasn't created to be afraid but to instill fear, reduced to wailing prey all the same.

Maybe the Animal was something worse than he'd imagined.

"After the attacks happened twenty-five years ago, why didn't you tell the police what you'd seen?"

The old man sighed. "I did. But they thought it was just a crazy story from a senile recluse. Said not to spread any more rumors about it, to just keep to my own business."

Oliver raised an eyebrow, paranoid thoughts immediately going back to his little conspiracy. "Who was it that told you that? Who exactly?"

The old man scoffed. "The sheriff."

CHAPTER TWENTY-SEVEN

Riley had never liked walking into the police department.

Something about it always sent a chill down her spine. It didn't even have anything to do with it being one of the first places she'd been to after that night. No, she didn't like it for a much less psychologically complex reason.

It was creepy.

The paint was old and pale, the interior lights were always flickering, and the small interior jail was kept in the far corner, in plain view. Although the lights surrounding it were even worse, barely illuminating the few people trapped inside.

This was a small town without much crime—most likely those jailed were simply drunk and disorderly—but in the low light and behind the thick black bars, they looked as threatening as any deranged serial killer off the street.

Granted, it wasn't like they could escape even if they were dangerous. The cells were always locked, and Hank kept the only set of keys with him at all times.

But it was still creepy.

However, she ignored it as she walked past several deputies and toward Hank's office. After her conversation with Oliver, she couldn't stop thinking about it. The kid was right, something did feel off, and if anyone could have covered something up, it would have been Hank. So, after twenty-five years, it was long past time she had a real discussion with him about the Animal.

But as she reached the outside of his office, she heard the voices and realized someone had beaten her to it.

"Why didn't you follow up on the old man's story?" Oliver said.

"For your information," Hank said, voice bordering on screaming, "that old man has a history of making up stories to the cops to try and get attention. So, your key witness, *kid*, is a liar."

"That a fact?" Oliver protested. "Or just another lie to cover something up?"

"I do not have to explain myself to a child who thinks he can play detective!"

Riley stayed outside of the room, listening in, waiting for Oliver's response. To her surprise, it was laughter.

"You can't see it, can you? What your lies are doing to everyone. You've spent your whole life covering something up. It cost you your wife, and now it's costing you your son. I hope whatever it is you're protecting is worth it."

"Watch how you speak about my son," Hank threatened.

"You can't be that naive. You've spent your whole life protecting the Animal, protecting Riley, all the while projecting your guilt onto Luke, and then you expect he won't resent them for it? You think that kind of childhood won't do something to a kid?"

The sound of wood raking against the floor abruptly screeched through the door. Even Riley could feel the sudden tension as Hank stood up from his chair. "What are you implying?"

"You know good and well what I'm implying, *Sheriff.*"

"Get out!" Hank screamed. "Or I'll have you arrested."

"You know, if you are really as committed to finding the Animal as you say you are, why haven't you investigated your son for the new attacks?

Can you honestly say he has an alibi for any of them? Isn't that a conflict of interest?"

The abrupt silence seemed to last an eternity before Riley finally heard the deep breath and knew Hank was calming himself, trying to avoid doing something he'd regret. She had to admit that Oliver might have a point. But at the same time, if he'd accused Emma of something, she probably would have killed him.

"You want to talk about conflict of interest?" Hank's voice had become deadly serious, and eerily calm. "You think I don't know who you are? What happened to your mom? Inventing a conspiracy won't bring her back, son. Let it go. This case has nothing to do with you."

For a moment, Riley felt her heart break. That was why Oliver had ignored her question, why he seemed so sad underneath all his anger. Something unspeakable had happened to his mom.

Just like something had happened to hers.

"You know, it's funny," Oliver said, his light tone surprising Riley. "It used to be that when I came in here talking about the Animal, you'd dismiss me offhand, acting casual and friendly. Now you threaten me and bring up my dead mother. I'm getting closer, aren't I?"

If a response was coming, Oliver didn't wait for it, stepping out the door and letting it close on its own. Then he noticed Riley.

"Was all that really necessary?" she asked him.

"Probably not," Oliver said, tone still light, expression calm. "But now he's got the idea in his head."

Suddenly the truth of the conversation hit Riley, and her eyes widened with shock. "You wanted to get him upset. That's why you brought up Luke."

"Of course." Oliver nodded. "He was never going to listen to me anyway. Now the thought is in his mind. The corrupt little idea that Luke could be the killer, and it won't let him rest. He'll watch Luke twenty-four seven until he knows for sure. So, either no more attacks happen, and we'll know Luke is the new killer, or another attack comes, and we'll be able to cross Luke off the suspect list."

Riley smirked. "Provided there is only one new killer."

"That's the spirit." Oliver winked as he turned to walk away.

"About your mom—" she started, before Oliver cut her off.

"Goodbye, Riley."

She nodded in return and glanced at the door to Hank's office, seeing the etched inscription of his name on the glass window, preparing herself as she did. It felt strange, knowing that she had to confront Hank. It wasn't like accusing a stranger of something; Hank was a friend, one of the few people who had been there for her. Still, resolve coursed through her veins; she had to do this, she had to find out the truth.

She readied herself and opened the door.

Inside, Hank was sitting down at his desk, wiping his eyes with frustration. At first, he didn't even look up to see who had entered.

"Hey," Riley said, alerting him to her presence.

"Now's not really the best time."

"I know," she said, "I overheard."

Finally, he looked up from his desk, sighing as he tried to compose himself. "That kid is going to make an exceptional detective one day, but for the sake of my health, I pray that it's in another city."

"He's not so bad," Riley said, her gaze moving to the plaques that hung on the wall. Awards for a lifetime of service. Hank's tired voice echoed softly behind her, showing just how much that service had cost him.

"I've gotten too old for this. All this madness. These new attacks. I should have quit a long time ago."

"What about that need you're always telling me about? The need to help others and make up for the crimes of the guilty."

"It was the foolish dream of a younger man. You can never do enough; once something is broken it can't be fixed. Trying to atone ends up causing so much damage, it would have been better to just leave it alone."

Riley cut her eyes at him, but her voice remained soft. "What did you do, Hank?"

He didn't answer, only stared off into the distance, eyes remorseful.

She didn't allow that, walking over to his desk and leaning down over him, forcing him to focus on her question. "What did you do? What are you hiding from me?"

For a second it looked as though he might reveal something, take some guilty weight off his soul, whisper some dark secret. But the moment the expression came, it vanished, and his eyes grew indifferent once again. "You've been talking to Oliver too much."

"Okay, then, if you have nothing to hide, tell me who was in the photograph at Linda's office."

"An old family friend," he said, shaking his head.

"You're lying," she whispered, voice growing more forceful. "If that's all it was, Linda would have told me. Who was she?"

He waved his hand, dismissing her question. "What does it matter?"

Riley's eyes twitched slightly as she held back the anger. "You know why it matters. I watched my parents get slaughtered in front of me, and for my entire life I've had to live with not knowing what killed them. Then you get me involved in this new case. You tell me to help the kids, putting me and Emma back in danger, and then you *hide* something from me? Something about what happened? So, I'm asking you again"—her voice almost became a growl—"who was she?"

"Okay, fine," Hank said, voice frustrated. "You want to know who she was? She was one of Linda's patients at the hospital. Was always coming in covered in bruises, face messed up. Before long, Linda realized her husband was beating her, so she called me, and we tried to help her. Then she wound up dead because of it!" Hank slammed his fist on the desk, appearing to shock even himself. Soon, however, regret overcame his rage. "That's why her photo was on Linda's desk, and that's why we don't like to talk about it. So please, Riley, just leave it be."

Silence filled the room in an instant, cruel and almost overbearing. Everything was different now, and they both felt it. After so many years, the trust was now broken, even if the friendship remained.

Finally, Riley backed up, nodding gently as she did. "Okay, Hank. I'll leave it be."

Not another word was spoken.

The cold breeze blew through the field, taking leaves with it, brittle remnants of dying trees dancing in the air as if in celebration of those that lay in the ground below.

"It's me again," Riley said, leaning back on the tombstone. "I brought a friend this time, just like I promised."

Emma ran across the field to catch up with her, playing in the grass as she did.

"I know it's not our anniversary or anything," Riley whispered, "but everyone else in my life seems to be hiding something, and I needed to come see you. Remind myself that there was one person I could trust."

After a few moments of silence, she continued. "I think Hank and Linda know something about the Animal that they're not telling me. And I know you'd say that they're friends, and I should trust them, but I can't. Not anymore, not after these new attacks. The Animal not being found created a legend, and something else has decided to try and bring the legend back. It killed an old man in the forest behind his house, strung him up like a sacrifice. Wrote *Come Back* on the trees in his blood.

"I wish I could say that I don't recognize what the town has become, but it's what I've always seen. The cruelty, the fascination. Do you know that you're the only person who never asked me what it looked like? I don't think I ever told you what that meant to me."

Wiping a tear from her cheek, she changed the subject. "Met a kid the other day who wants to help. Thinks he knows who the new animal could be. He's blunt, but smart. You'd probably like him." She sighed. "I wish I could trust him."

She looked over to Emma, who was stepping on a leaf in the field, listening to the crunch, laughing happily as she did it. "She knows what's happening, and she's still so calm. Just like you used to be. Before the war."

Her voice trembled slightly. "I understand it now, why you had to go back for another tour, go back to the war. I can't take it either. The waiting, the feeling that something is coming. Unable to see it from where you sit, but knowing it's there all the same. Is that what I should do, then? Go to war?

"If so, and it ends how it did for you, who will protect her?"

Across the field, Emma waved, and Riley waved back, smiling as she did, before leaning her head down and running her fingers against the stone. "Do you remember when we met? When you shot that bear? When you saved me? I was so angry, and I remember screaming." Riley chuckled softly. "I think I even hit you. But you let me. You never asked why I was doing it, or what had happened in my life to make me this way. You just waited until I started crying, and then you held me. I'll never forget that." Tears streaked down her face. "I wish I could have been there for you when it happened. Made you think everything was going to be okay, that you'd get to see your daughter again."

Suddenly, she felt her daughter's embrace and for a brief moment felt that this world wasn't broken.

She kissed her daughter's forehead and hugged her before finally whispering in her ear. "We've got to go now."

Emma nodded and then ran up to the tombstone, hugging it tight. "Bye, Dad." Then she took off back down the field, running through the grass without a care in the world.

Riley turned back to the grave for one final moment. "I've got to go. But I'll come back." She pressed her hand against the stone. "One way or the other, I'll see you again. I promise."

CHAPTER TWENTY-EIGHT

Clyde ran through the forest, trying to escape the monster that chased him, the beast that had crawled out of the shadows once again.

The black wolf.

Its massive paws collided with the ground, parting the dirt with every step, the impact thundering upward into the setting sun.

Clyde ran as though he was possessed, cutting between trees as if it was habit, instinct, not knowing where he was and yet knowing exactly where to go, how to escape.

But the wolf couldn't be outrun. It caught up to him in mere seconds, but rather than striking, it ran through the trees beside him, moving past them in a blur of darkness, its position highlighted

only by the two yellow eyes that tracked him, forcing him to turn. It was almost as if it wasn't chasing but rather leading him somewhere.

With no other option, Clyde was forced to jump over a dried-up creek, the same one as before. He barely made the jump, body colliding hard with the mud below. But still he ran, trying to escape.

Clyde didn't know who he was anymore. He could feel the monster inside of him, clawing into his skin, tearing itself free inch by inch, but that was all it was. A feeling. Something he could deny, something he could run from.

Then the wolf had revealed itself once more, and forced him to run from it instead.

Clyde heard the crash of the wolf's paws colliding with the dirt behind him, having leapt the creek in a second. Within moments, growling began to echo louder into the forest, drowning out everything else, consuming everything in its path, until it suddenly stopped, and nothing could be heard at all.

Which was all the more terrifying.

Where did it go?

A new memory suddenly came back to him: a fresh one, made only a few days ago, causing him to realize where he was. When the wolf had chased him before, it had led him to this exact same spot.

Above him, there was a small opening within the branches of the trees, revealing a glimpse of the night sky, and the moon that now rested in it: glowing in the darkness, covering the forest in its presence.

In front of him stood a large jagged rock, unnatural in the forest, a single piece of it that wasn't living, wasn't growing, merely stuck in the dirt, marking the same position forever.

Behind it, in the shadows of the trees, the eyes appeared once more: bright yellow, reflecting the traces of moonlight that reached them, moving slowly through the forest, circling Clyde.

One moment they would be watching him, the next, they'd pass behind a tree, allowing one brief moment of uncertainty before they revealed themselves again. Always steady, always watching him as if it expected him to do something, rather than the other way around.

"What do you what from me!?" Clyde screamed, begging for an answer that would never come. Animals didn't answer questions. They just hunted, just killed, and yet here this wolf was, stalking him like an unnatural creature of the night.

Clyde knew it wasn't real. That the wolf hunting him was in his head. That was why it left no tracks, and why it acted unnaturally. Yet the fear didn't go away as Clyde dropped to his knees, begging it to kill him, to end his suffering.

But even that plea went unanswered as the eyes faded from view, and the animal disappeared.

Clyde felt the night air surrounding him, felt the chill of the forest, and the shadows it contained. Something was wrong with this place. Something he'd always known but never admitted, the true terror lurking within the trees.

The cabin always felt safe, and yet it was wrong. So wrong. Anxiety crippled him as he waited constantly for the attack to come, for the illusion of safety to be pulled away.

Now, here in the forest, there was no illusion of safety. At any moment, a wolf could come and rip his throat out, tear his bones to pieces, bite into his flesh, and rip his limbs from his body.

Clyde collapsed completely, lying in the dirt, surrounded by predators.

In that moment, as he started to sleep, the horrific truth of the forest was finally revealed to him. It was a monstrous place, full of death, full of terror. He'd never be safe from the wolves, never be calm, always running, always hunted. It was a cruel, dark land, filled with nightmares and the screaming of devoured prey.

It was home.

CHAPTER TWENTY-NINE

Hidden outside the police station, breathing quietly, adrenaline racing, the stalking predator watched the deputies going about their jobs, unaware of its looming presence as it waited for the right time to strike.

"You seem uncomfortable," Kelly said.

"Just anxious, that's all," Rhett replied. "I don't like just waiting around."

"You poor baby," she said, rolling her eyes. "Imagine how I feel all the time."

Rhett waved his hand at her, dismissing the complaint.

She just sighed. He had a point; all the waiting around was annoying, but it wasn't like they had anything else to do. The sheriff said school was off-limits until they caught the new killer, and Riley had made it very clear not to be seen walking around town. So unless they wanted to outright ignore them, this was all they could do. Sit and wait.

"Where is Luke?" Gabriella asked, petting her German shepherd, its head rising above the armrest of her chair even as it lay down, appearing bigger than she was. "I thought he was headed over here too?"

"His psycho dad has him locked up in the house," Rhett answered.

"Why?"

"I have no idea."

Luke stormed down the stairs, flashes of anger sparking in his eyes. He wasn't going to sit here in this little prison just to make his dad feel more comfortable. Besides, it wasn't like the doors were actually locked from the inside. His dad wasn't completely insane, just overbearing.

Reaching the front door, he opened it in a rage but was stopped in an instant by his father's strong voice. "Don't."

"You can't just force me to stay in here. I haven't even done anything wrong!"

"Just..." Hank sighed, sitting at the table across the room, solemnly looking at old family photographs. "Just sit down, please. I need to talk to you."

The predator knelt silently beside the back door, waiting, eager for blood and ready for bloodshed, until finally an unsuspecting deputy stepped out, unaware of the monster lurking.

The sharpened bone was in the man's throat before he could think. Seconds later his blood spilled down on the concrete steps as his body contorted unnaturally with shock. Then, he was pushed backwards onto the ground, his dying carcass stopping the door from shutting and becoming locked once more.

Giving the predator a way inside.

"You're wrong," Kelly said, lying comfortably on her couch, shaking her head in disappointment. "It's a dolphin."

"No, it's not," Gabriella said, now pacing the floor out of boredom, stepping over her dog as she moved back and forth. "I'm telling you. The smartest animal is a gorilla. Every nature show that I've ever seen always says that monkeys are the smartest animals."

"Technically," Betty added, leaning back in a chair, lightly holding on to her stomach and wincing as the wound acted up, "monkeys are the smartest mammal, but they're not the smartest animal overall."

"What's the difference?" Gabriella said, not really wanting an answer. Kelly heard her mock Betty under her breath, calling her something that sounded like nerd. Kelly just rolled her eyes. Why was Gabriella always like this?

"You're all wrong anyway," Rhett said, sitting on the floor, back against the wall.

"Enlighten us, then," Kelly mocked. "What's the smartest animal?"

Rhett smiled. "A shark."

Luke sat in the chair opposite Hank, slightly unsettled by the look in his father's eyes. It was almost like he was afraid of something—an emotion Luke hadn't known he was capable of.

"I know you blame me for a lot of things," Hank began. "I know you blame me for your mother leaving and for judging you too harshly. Honestly, you're probably right. I've been a poor father, and I've done things I'm not proud of."

Speechless, Luke stared at him. He'd never spoken to him like this before. His tone was always demanding or emotionless. Never like this.

"I've done things in my life that I can't forgive myself for. Your mother knew it, and that's why she left. Because of what I did. And if I've taken my guilt out on you, I'm truly sorry."

Suddenly, Hank's voice changed from apologetic to terrified. "But you need to listen to me now, son. Please."

"Dad," Luke said, his father's deathly tone causing him to grow uncomfortable, even afraid himself. "What's this about?"

Hank's voice cracked as he said the words out loud, fear crawling into the air, as if the words themselves would bring it back into the light.

"The Animal."

⫸

The deputy had heard something walking alone in the hallway, the slight creaking of wood from someone hiding in the room next to the exit. Laughing, he walked up to the door, thinking his friend must have snuck off for a smoke. "You know, those are gonna kill you one day."

As he poked his head inside the door, something sharp was shoved into his eye, and a monstrous hand covered in fur held his mouth, keeping his screams from echoing into the main room and alerting the rest of the deputies to the creature's presence.

The man was dead in seconds, and as his corpse hit the floor, the predator found the switch box it had been looking for, exactly where it had known it would be. Then, the monster simply turned the lights off, cracking its neck as it did.

This was going to be a massacre.

"You're insane if you think a shark is smarter than a dolphin," Kelly said, tilting her head as if talking to a first grader.

"As much as I hate to admit it," Gabriella said, "I have to agree with your sister on this one. Everyone knows dolphins are smarter than sharks."

"Well, everyone is wrong, and I can prove it," Rhett said, voice excited, as if he was about to explain his genius. "You see, there's a type of fish in the ocean that both sharks and dolphins eat, but the fish are too quick and far too small to make chasing them down one at a time worth the effort.

"Now, sharks are nowhere near capable of coordinating an attack with each other. All they really know how to do is swim and hunt. But dolphins are smart enough to know they need to work together and smart enough to know how."

Kelly raised an eyebrow, confused by her brother's ramblings. "I feel like you're proving our point."

"Hold on," he said. "Now, the dolphins coordinate together and attack groups of the fish at once, surrounding them and slowly herding them together as if they were cattle, until finally the dolphins have created a giant buffet of fish, unable to escape without the dolphins attacking. And all the dolphins have to do is keep pushing forward, keep making the captured group of prey smaller until finally the fish have nowhere to run, and the dolphins can feast."

Rhett flashed an evil smile. "But that's when the sharks come. They know they can't group the fish themselves, so they wait in the background, letting the dolphins do it. Then, once it's done, the sharks attack, scaring away the dolphins and taking the prey for themselves.

"So, I ask you," Rhett finally said, holding his hands up to exaggerate the question, as if he was talking about so much more than fish, "which is smarter? The dolphins who can coordinate an attack? Or the sharks who sit back and let their prey do the work for them?"

"I know you're involved in these new killings, and I can't stop you."

Luke felt his heart stop for a moment. His own father accusing him. "Are you serious? How could you think–"

"That's not what I meant," Hank said, trying to calm him down. "I meant your friends have been targeted, and so you're involved in the case too. That's all I meant."

Luke forced himself to stay calm. "Okay... so why are you telling me all this now? About you, about Mom, apologizing. After all these years, why now?"

"Because you've never listened to me. Whether that's my own fault or not, it doesn't matter anymore. But you have to listen to me now, son, please. You have to listen."

Luke wasn't used to seeing his dad like this, truly terrified. It was unnerving, causing a chill to slowly creep down his own spine, even as he stayed silent, listening to Hank's shaky voice.

"At first, I thought these new killings were just a copycat, someone trying to imitate the legend. But then they left a sacrifice in the woods for the Animal, and wrote a message in blood, begging it to come back. And I can't get it out of my head. I can't stop thinking about what if, somehow, they actually do it? What if they bring it back?"

The masked predator moved into the main room, seeing the outlines of the deputies that stood there confused, bright blue uniforms revealing them in the dark, breathing victims waiting to be slaughtered.

But the darkness shrouded the predator's dark grey fur from view, allowing it to move closer to them, carved bone in hand, adrenaline rising as it prepared to kill them all.

"For animals like sharks, survival's not about intelligence. It's about instincts."

"What does that mean?" Betty asked.

"It's when a predator can block everything else out: emotions, fear, pain. Not even think, only focus on the hunt, on killing its prey."

"If it does come back..." Hank said as the color began to slip away from his face, and his hands trembled. "If the real Animal comes back, you have to promise me you'll run."

The predator found its first target in the darkness and slit his throat before he even knew it was there.

"Instinct is how a wolf can take down an elk five times its size. It's how animals unlock something within themselves that we'll never understand. The power. The rage. Killing things in unnatural ways that shouldn't be possible."

The man screamed, clutching his throat as his blood spilled out of him, alerting the rest of the deputies to his location. But the monster was already gone, vanished back into the darkness.

"How will I know if it's the real Animal?" Luke asked.

Hank's entire body began shaking, and he closed his eyes, as if the horror he'd once known was right in front of him. "You'll know."

The predator moved behind another man, monstrous grey fur still melting into the shadows as he carved into the man's chest with his bone, puncturing the heart, causing the man to cry out in agony.

"When instinct takes over, the animal is no longer what it was," Rhett continued. "It becomes something more, something darker. It can't hear its prey's cries of pain, can't feel empathy, can't feel anything. Only knows how to kill."

Two more deputies were butchered before one finally fired a round into the darkness, aiming for a shadow. He missed, but the flash briefly illuminated the monster in front of him: bloodstained fur, massive teeth, animalistic head.

It slaughtered him within seconds.

"If it comes back, don't try to fight it," Hank said, voice desperate. "Don't try to save your friends. Don't try to kill it. You can't."

Another deputy screamed as 5the predator struck his face, knocking him to the floor. Before he could stand back up, the monster began beating him, viciously attempting to crack his skull.

"Don't try to hide. It will find you."

The predator stood up, running toward the final deputy left standing, who saw the shadow coming but couldn't stop it.

It tackled him into the wall, shoving the man's head into the brick over and over again, drawing blood with each strike, until finally the man's cheekbone caved in slightly, and he took his last breath.

"Just run."

The predator howled into the room, a cry of victory as it loomed over its fallen prey. Blood was scattered everywhere, lifeless bodies resting on

331

the floor like rag dolls, deputies slaughtered like lambs.

When its howl was concluded, it looked over to the cells in the corner of the room, seeing the prisoners cowering behind the bars, balled up on the floor, trying to hide from it.

The rush of killing was still in its bones, and it wanted so badly to kill them, but it couldn't reach them through the bars. So instead, it walked past the cells, growling as it did, watching them cry in fear.

Finally, the predator crept slowly through the darkness once more, blood still dripping from its hands, approaching what it had come for. Its true target.

The sheriff's office.

<hr />

"Promise me," Hank begged. "Promise me you'll run."

"Dad, I—"

"No, you don't know what it is! I've seen it, Luke." Hank's skin went ghostly pale. "I've seen its eyes. If it comes back, it won't stop until everyone is dead. Promise me that you won't fight, you won't hide, you'll just run. Please!"

"Okay," Luke finally said, trembling himself. His dad had never seemed afraid of anything, hardly ever displayed emotion at all. But right now it looked like the single memory would kill him from within, choke the life out of his very bones. As if the Animal really was the creature the stories made it out to be.

"I'll run. I promise."

"But how can instinct just take over like that?" Betty asked.

"It just can," Rhett answered. "Once instinct is ingrained in an animal's head, it can never be forgotten. You can take a tiger from a jungle, cage it, domesticate it until it's as friendly as any dog from a pet store. But the instincts will still be there, buried deep inside. All it takes is a single sign of its old life: one scent of blood, or one painful scream of its prey, and instinct will take over once again. The animal that would never have hurt another living thing will tear through flesh in an instant, without hesitation. All it takes is one scream."

No one said anything for several moments, taking in the weight of all that was spoken. It was strange to think something like that could be real. That animals could have something inside them that took away fear, took away emotion, and left only bloodshed, only survival.

Kelly almost shuddered.

Suddenly, the eerie sound of a broken branch echoed outside, and she saw a shadow hiding in the forest outside her window.

It was gone the moment she saw it, but the sudden crack of wood had alerted all of them. Usually it was only Betty who grew deathly afraid, but this time, nerve-racking dread filled every single one of their eyes.

Even Rhett looked concerned.

"Someone was out there," Kelly said, pointing in shock. "I saw it."

Not waiting for any of them to protest, Rhett grabbed a knife and ran outside into the woods, followed closely by Kelly.

Once within the forest's cold grasp, they saw it: a single broken branch, barely an inch thick, lying on the ground. Beside it were footprints, breaking up the dirt, leading back further into the forest's heart.

Confused, Kelly stared down at it, not knowing what to say, not knowing if it was real. Even after everything that had happened, this single event felt wrong, almost unnatural, but the truth couldn't be denied. Because the shadow didn't look like the new predator, or the stories told of the original. It looked different, the fleeting glimpse of something appearing almost human, revealing the grisly truth.

It might not have been an animal, but someone was watching them.

The only question was, who?

CHAPTER THIRTY

There was so much blood.

It stained the walls, the desk, dried blackened pools of it soaking into the carpet below, outlining where the bodies had been.

Where Riley now stood.

Hank had screamed, cursed the new animal, cursed himself, before finally breaking down completely and removing himself from the scene. Almost all of the deputies in this town, slaughtered in their own police station.

It was a horror show, and the dread it caused almost crept into Riley as well. This was different. It wasn't attacking kids, wasn't killing a defenseless old man. It was attacking armed deputies, risking getting shot in order to do it.

Riley couldn't imagine the predator she'd faced at the safe house being capable of something like this, this level of violence, but maybe she'd misjudged it. Maybe it was more of a threat than she'd realized, even if these bodies were still recognizable.

But it hadn't come for the deputies. Not really. No, the predator had come in search of answers, in search of a way to find the Animal and bring it back to life. That was why the door to Hank's office was broken, and that was why the place had been ransacked.

It had been looking for something.

Riley felt a sudden chill. The broken door, the frenzied search for answers—it reminded her of something, of someone. But she didn't dare contemplate the idea. It was similar, yes, but this time people had been murdered, which changed everything.

It couldn't have been him.

Could it?

Before long, some of the kids arrived, visibly unnerved about something.

"Someone was watching you from the woods?" Riley asked.

"Yes," Kelly said. "I saw it run, and we found footprints right outside our house."

"Did it look like this new killer? With the wolf mask?"

"No. I just saw a brief glimpse, but it looked human."

"Okay." Riley nodded, playing over scenarios in her head, trying to find the right one. It was strange that the killer would watch them without its mask. "It might have just been a trespasser, but don't assume that. Treat it like it was the killer watching you."

"What do we do?" Betty asked.

"Well, for one thing, stop hanging out at Kelly's house. It's already attacked there once, so there's nothing stopping it from doing it again."

Betty was shaking, far more nervous than the rest of them, occasionally twitching at every little sound that echoed in the distance.

Of course, being surrounded by the blood of slaughtered deputies didn't help.

"Whoa," Russel's shocked voice sounded from across the room as he entered the crime scene. "What happened here?"

"New animal attacked," Rhett answered.

"Looks like it," Russel replied, looking around at the blood, almost fascinated by it.

"Killing armed deputies like that," Gabriella said, "this new animal must be tough as–"

Riley cut her off with a glare.

"Sorry," Gabriella said, almost mocking in tone.

It was moments like this, making light of dead bodies, that made Riley want to hit that girl. But she restrained herself, sighing instead and focusing back on the larger issue at hand.

The kids said something that looked human had been watching them from the forest, and this crime scene proved the new predator had attacked again and stolen something from Hank's office, hoping to bring the Animal back.

This was more than a simple message written in blood. This was direct action, hunting down information about the Animal. Riley could feel her heart rate quickening as the dreaded truth came into focus.

This new predator could actually do it. If it was given enough victims, enough time, it could actually create a trail of bodies long enough to bring the Animal back out, back into her life, or what little of it she would have left if it truly returned.

She had to stop this now, before it could go any further. Waiting might feel safe, but every second that passed, the opportunity for the Animal's return grew closer.

The thought caused her to shudder.

If it did happen, if somehow this new predator did bring it back, then nothing she did, nothing any of them did, would matter. They couldn't hide, couldn't fight. Even if they tried, it would all be for nothing, like throwing a knife into a hurricane, thinking it could stop the waters from destroying everything in sight. But forces of nature couldn't be stopped, couldn't be contained, even more so forces outside of nature.

This had to end now, before the monster was awoken.

Before the Animal started hunting.

"So, what else do you have?" Riley asked, standing inside Oliver's room, once again surrounded by the blue glow of fluorescent ink.

"Not much," he replied. "There is the story the old man told me about the thing in the forest that hunted wolves, but even if he's not lying, it doesn't tell us anything we didn't already know. Did you find out anything from Hank?"

She shrugged. "Only that the woman in the photo was an old patient of Linda's, who always came in with bruises. But when they tried to help her, she died."

"Hmm," he said, eyes cutting to the side, thinking over something.

"What is it?"

"Probably nothing, but the old man told me that Arthur Conners used to beat his wife, and that it was only after the abuse started that the wolves came into the game ranch."

"You think she was Arthur's wife?"

"It's possible. Are you sure Hank said she died, not went missing?"

"Positive. Why?"

"Because I looked over the obituaries from the time of the original newspaper that detailed the game ranch's opening, up until the Animal attack, and she was nowhere to be found."

Riley raised an eyebrow. "Maybe she was listed, but without a photograph. We still don't know her name."

"True, but there was no mention of anyone with the last name of Conners either."

"Maybe they used her maiden name."

"Possible. But do you really think someone who beats his wife is going to list her maiden name in the obituary? More likely Hank is lying to you about what really happened."

Riley sighed and rubbed her eyes. Every road they went down led back to either Hank or Linda.

"Tell me," Oliver said, seeming to sense her hesitation, "that night, when the Animal attacked, how'd you escape? How'd you survive?"

Heart racing, Riley relived the past once more. "I don't know. I was hiding under the bed–"

A flash of blood entered her mind.

"Then I saw it coming for me."

She remembered screaming.

"And then gunfire. I remember the flash of gunfire, the sound of it echoing through the house. I covered my eyes and hid under the bed until the gunfire stopped. I... I never saw the Animal again."

Oliver waited a moment and then asked his question. "It was Hank, wasn't it? He was the one who fired the gun, who shot the Animal."

"Yes."

"How long was it after the gunfire stopped before Hank found you under the bed? Before he told you it was safe?"

"I don't know," she said, shaking her head. "A few minutes, at least. Probably more."

"Enough time to cover something up?"

Her voice had grown tired. "What are you saying?"

"I'm saying I think Hank fired on the Animal, and when he did, he realized something. I don't know what, but whatever it was, it made him panic, and he covered it up. That's why there was no evidence at the scene, and why it took him so long to go to you after it happened."

Riley didn't know what to say. Deep down, she'd always known something was wrong, but she had never been able to admit it to herself: that there was just one more person lying to her, focused on the Animal rather than its victims.

"Think about it," he continued. "If Hank shot it, then there would have been blood in the room. Its blood. All the police would have had to do was one lab test and they would have known the Animal's identity, but Hank never allowed that."

"Maybe they did test it," she said, tone deathly serious. "And maybe the result that came back wasn't human."

That shocked him, if only for a moment. "You can't really think that it's not human."

"You didn't see it," she said, trembling as the sight of it came back. "You didn't feel its presence, the chill on your skin."

"Riley, I promise you. Whatever you think it is, it's not. At the end of this, if we finally find him, the real Animal, it's not going to be some dark evil or an ancient werewolf. It's just going to be a man."

She shook her head, a tear falling from it as she held on to the thoughts of a child. *Animal.*

"It's not going to be what you need it to be, some mysterious force that can't be explained, can't be stopped. Whoever killed all those people is no different from any other killer, no different than this new predator. It's not a monster. It's just a human, someone in a mask, who has a face."

Years of fear exploded in her heart, and she forced herself to stop trembling, to stop remembering, even if just for a moment. Finally, with a broken voice that still managed to sound firm, she admitted the horrible truth: the only truth she'd accept. The only truth that could be possible.

"It might be a mask. And it might have a face. But it's not human. In its bones it's not human. It can't be."

Nothing could be said after that. So, after a period of silence, Oliver changed the subject to the new predator.

"Well, the good news is that Hank was with Luke the entire day yesterday, so the killer at the police station couldn't have been him."

"But that still doesn't clear him, does it?" Riley asked, voice sorrowful and tired. "Because there could be two of them, so we still have nothing. The killer breaks into the police station, kills everyone, finds something in Hank's office to help it find the Animal, and we still have *nothing*."

"Well, about that," Oliver said, voice cautious. "The killer didn't find anything in Hank's office."

"How do you know that?"

"Because I broke into it an hour earlier."

Her eyes widened in an instant, unease creeping into her voice as she remembered how similar Hank's office was to Linda's. The ransacking, the broken door. "What?"

"I found this." He picked up a folder from his desk. "The file on the attacks twenty-five years ago. Everything the police have on the Animal." He opened it, revealing what was left inside.

Nothing.

"It was next to a lighter."

She knew what he was implying, that Hank had burned the files, but that wasn't what caused the chill creeping over her skin. "You broke into the police department? The same one that now has blood soaking into the ground?"

"Yeah," he said, tone not changing. "After I met with Hank, I never left. I just hid in a storage room until you two finished arguing, and he rushed home to find Luke."

She was almost speechless, and within her voice there were hints of mistrust, hints of betrayal. "Are you lying to me, Oliver?"

"What?" he asked, only then realizing what she was implying. "You can't really think−"

"Why not?" she said, mirroring his own words in horror. "Why can't it be you? You're obsessed with the Animal. You're trying to find it, just like the new killer is. And now you have a file from the one place we know it just attacked. Same motive. Same location."

"No," Oliver said, tone now low and forceful. "That's not what this is."

"But what if it is? What if this whole ruse about the other suspects is just your way of getting closer, finding out more about what happened, so that you can bring it back? How do I know that you've not just been using me?"

"Why would I have shown it to you?" Oliver asked, raising his voice for the first time, seemingly noticing just how nervous she was. "Why would I have told you I have the file if I was the new killer?"

"Because you had to. You needed to show me that Hank was burning the evidence, so that I wouldn't trust him, and so you had to show me the file."

"That's not—" Oliver stopped himself, running his hands down across his face as if realizing how his story sounded. How everything about his actions screamed *guilty.* Finally, he spoke once again, pleading with her. "It's the same goal, not the same motive. This new killer wants to find the Animal just like I do, but for very different reasons."

"Does the motive matter?" she asked, voice almost sorrowful, already knowing where this was going. Another brief friendship broken. Another trust shattered.

"I don't know. Honestly, it might not. But it's all I have."

"Then what is it?" Riley begged. "Tell me why you're doing this, why you've spent the last few years chasing a monster that has nothing to do with you."

A little bit of color went out of his eyes, and she almost regretted what she'd said, what she'd asked of him. She knew what it felt like to be expected to relive the past, relive the tragedies.

But she had to know.

Taking a deep breath, Oliver began. "Have you ever heard of the hitchhiker murders? Happened up north?"

Riley shook her head.

"Well, about six years ago, this hitchhiker would walk on the side of the road, trying to find anyone who would give him a ride. Take him home to see his sick kid, or to attend his wife's funeral; doesn't matter, they were all lies. He just waited until someone gave him a ride, and then he'd pull out his knife.

"Ended up killing five women before the cops caught him. The fifth victim, who didn't have it in her to be distrustful, who couldn't assume the worst of someone, was my mother. Her body was left bleeding out in a ditch, all because she trusted the kind words of a stranger."

Oliver stopped for a moment, eye twitching in irritation. "It was a big story. Nothing like that ever happened in my town. Media was all over it, the trial was a spectacle, and everyone wanted to know why. Why he did it, what made him snap. I saw his *face* on the news every day for two years, smiling as he was on trial, eating up the attention like a pig. I heard the stories, people whispering in school. *I wonder why he killed those women. I wonder how he did it.*

"Even after he was incarcerated it didn't stop. They did a documentary about it on TV, even got him for an interview. They had him talk about his childhood, what drove him to madness, the secret behind his eyes, as if he was the architect of some great tragedy. Someone that we all needed to understand, to feel sorry for.

"You know they mentioned her name once in that entire documentary. Every other time it was just, 'victim number five.' As if that's all she was. But the murderer who killed her gets to tell his story, gets an entire town fascinated by his every movement. And I can't do anything about it! I can't make them see how wrong it is. I can't kill the legend he created."

A single tear streamed down Oliver's cheek as he tried to hold it together. "But then we moved here, and I heard it. The stories of the Animal. How it was some kind of mythical creature that slaughtered seventeen victims with its bare hands. How it didn't have a face, didn't have a name.

"Then I knew what I had to do. I had to find it and reveal it for what it really was. Not some great monster... just another killer, dressed up in a mask in a desperate attempt to be remembered."

For a few moments, there was total silence. Oliver rubbing the tears from his eyes. Riley not knowing the words to say.

"And I'm not naive," he continued, voice cracking. "I know that finding the Animal won't change anything: it won't bring her back, it won't stop the stories about her murder. But maybe I can change this town. The stories it tells. Maybe just once, I can get people to see the killers for what they are. Something to be forgotten. It's not much, but it's all I have."

Riley wanted to console him, to say something, anything to make the pain in his voice go away. But she couldn't. Because as much as she wanted to, she still couldn't trust him, not after the police station. The pain stung in her heart, knowing it was over. She had gotten used to being alone, but that didn't make the despair of losing trust any easier.

"I'm sorry," she said, walking away. "But I can't trust you."

"I know," he answered, voice sorrowful as he looked down. "You shouldn't. Trusting someone"— another tear fell from his face—"is how you wind up in a ditch, bleeding to death."

There was nothing she could say that would change anything, no kind words that could be offered, because she knew from experience it wouldn't help. So instead, she gave a soft smile and offered a final piece of advice.

"Be careful, Oliver."

Then, she left, not daring to look back at him, left alone in the dark room, surrounded by years' worth of notes and evidence, searching for a monster he didn't know in a desperate attempt to move on.

But it wouldn't work.

It would never make the pain go away, never make his life whole again, any more than it had hers. She closed her eyes for a moment, remembering all the years she had wasted, avoiding the truth. Holding on to the suffering.

Hunting the wrong animals.

CHAPTER THIRTY-ONE

This is where it happened. This is where he killed them.

Clyde stepped into the first house, escaping the night air, his breathing steady as he lifted up his hand and felt the back door: the rough shattered wood, the faint traces of blood still visible even after all these years.

Something screamed as its head was broken, skull shoved into the door, caving in on itself.

Wincing as the memory came back, Clyde pushed on what was left of the splintered wood and stepped inside.

Another one screamed, smaller than the last, voice shrill as it dropped to the floor and tried to crawl away.

A tear fell down Clyde's face as he walked the same path that was frozen in his mind, not thinking, just letting the instinct move him.

"No, please!" the thing screamed, desperately crawling away on the floor, wailing in terror and agony as it tried to escape.

Every muscle in his body twitched at once as the memory of the woman's broken bones and bleeding flesh flashed before his eyes. Clyde could feel the woman's blood on him even now, warm and dripping. Fresh.

Clyde shut his eyes, trying to fight the memories. He had been wrong to come here, wrong to remember. *What had he done?*

But they wouldn't leave him. A voice rang in his head, worried and tense.

"I heard screaming. Is everything okay?"

The thing stood there, in the shadow of the front door, shining a flashlight inside. It sounded concerned at first, until the flashlight revealed the monster, and the thing tried to scream. "What in—"

The thing's jaw was ripped from its body, and a moment later its eyes rolled back in its head. Dead.

Clyde could feel his heart beating faster as the feeling came back to him. The feeling of hunting,

killing. "No," he said, shaking his head, trying to make it go away, trying to deny how it felt. Natural.

Two more things appeared in the distance outside, screaming as they saw the blood spilling out from the lifeless carcass left on the door frame. One of them held the other as they ran away screaming back toward their own den, seeking protection that wouldn't come.

Closing his eyes, Clyde tried to forget the memory he'd just seen, deny the massacre that was coming.

The thing being held, the one screaming the loudest. It was small. Very small.

"No," Clyde begged, not wanting to remember what he'd done. Not wanting to remember the child.

It chased them across the street.

Instinct forcing him to move, Clyde walked the path taken twenty-five years earlier into the neighbor's house, moonlight shining down from the sky.

At the far end of the street, someone looked out of Riley's window, watching Clyde walk down the street in disbelief and horror, unable to breathe, unable to move.

The wailing prey ran inside and slammed the door, but it didn't save them.

More tears streamed down Clyde's face.

"No, please," the larger one screamed as the door was shattered, holding the child in its arms, scrambling to run, but not near fast enough to escape the hunting predator.

Clyde remembered the woman's blood as she died first. Remembered how it felt to crack her skull and end her screaming forever.

The child screamed.

"No," Clyde whispered, falling to his knees, surrounded by the house where they died, by the blood that still stained the floor.

The Animal attacked.

"Please, no," Clyde begged, crying in pain.

The screaming stopped.

Trembling, Clyde wept on the floor. "What did I do?" Everything in his head was still blurry, still broken fragments, but he remembered enough. He remembered their blood, their cries of pain, their fear. All of them.

"I'm sorry," he cried, words cracking through the tears. "I'm so sorry."

Across the room, a cautious voice whispered, "You shouldn't be here."

Uncovering his twitching eyes, he turned to see Linda, outlined in the doorway by the glow of the moonlight behind her.

"What did I do?" he asked, tears falling from his face, trapped in the memories, trapped in the nightmare, the blood seemingly still warm on his skin.

"Nothing," she said simply, walking over to him and placing a hand on his shoulder.

He jumped at her touch, crawling away from her, afraid of what he might do. "Tell me what I did, please."

"You didn't do anything," she said, voice calm. "You didn't hurt anyone."

"I remember them," he whispered as his face started to lose its color, and his eyes felt as though they were hollow. "All of them."

"No, you don't," she said softly, walking closer and kneeling down beside him. "You think you remember, but it's just your mind playing tricks on you. Like it did with the eyes you saw in the forest, and the wolf you told Hank about."

"No, this is different. I can hear their screams."

"Clyde, listen to me," she begged, staring into his eyes. "What you're feeling, what you're remembering: it's just a symptom of the head trauma that was inflicted."

"It feels too real."

"I know it does, but it's not. Clyde, you suffered more head trauma than anyone I've ever seen.

Your skull was fractured, splintering inside, causing catastrophic brain damage. I did what I could, but I couldn't fix all of it. The wounds are still there, causing you to see and feel things that aren't real. Anyone with that amount of head trauma has hallucinations, almost like dreams that creep into reality, mirroring things you've seen.

"You saw the story of the Animal on the news, the new killings, and it crept into your mind, making you think things that aren't real. You're not the Animal, Clyde, or some other monster your mind might make you out to be. You are just someone who has lived through more cruelty than most and still suffers from the scars left behind.

"That's all you are, I promise. Nothing can change that unless you let it."

Clyde wanted desperately to believe her, to trust her. To believe that he couldn't be this monster, that their blood wasn't stained on him.

"What if you're wrong?" he finally said, staring at his hands, afraid, twitching as he remembered the ripping of flesh in two.

"What if I'm something else?"

CHAPTER THIRTY-TWO

Moonlight cascaded down from the sky, slipping through the cracks on the roof, little beams of light dancing around Riley as she waited.

The note she found was simple enough. Come to the warehouse on the far side of town on the edge of the forest. Evidence had been found there that she needed to see. It was signed: from Oliver.

She took a deep breath, walking underneath one of the streams of light, letting the moonlight shimmer in her eyes, enjoying the quiet moment before the storm.

Even if this town hadn't contained the monsters, and even if she hadn't known she was a target, this warehouse still would have been unsettling. The rusted metal on the side, one piece so torn it caused a small opening in the corner, the broken chains hanging from the ceiling next to strips of plastic, clear enough to see through, but not so much that they didn't distort what lay beyond them, twisting the images into fragmented versions of themselves.

She wondered where it was hiding.

The note was a trap. Obviously. It stopped just short of telling her to come alone and unarmed. It also seemed to implicate Oliver. But then again, if it was him, why would he have signed his own name? Just like everything else about this new predator, nothing could be taken at face value.

But Riley was long past caring.

The night was quiet. No animals howling in the distance, no wind to shake the trees and rattle the leaves, just silence, peace, as if the whole world had stopped for a moment, waiting to see what would happen, just as she was.

She cracked a slight grin and popped her neck before loosening her shoulders and basking in the silence. She now stood in the middle of the warehouse, surrounded by little strips of light and far more darkness.

The truth was she was tired. Tired of the killings, tired of the legends. But mostly just tired. Twenty-five years of waiting, of fear, with nothing to show for it. The Animal hadn't come back, which meant all the feelings she'd been bottling up inside herself all these years had never been released. She'd tried hunting real animals, but it hadn't worked. She'd tried letting them hunt her, but it wasn't the same.

But now, this new predator presented an opportunity. She'd felt it at the safe house: the opportunity to take out twenty-five years of aggression on something that deserved it, something that looked like the Animal, but would scream like prey.

"I know you're out there," she said, slowly spinning in the dark, looking for a trace of movement, of life.

"This is a good location: creepy, gives you a lot of places to hide, without giving me many ways to escape. Plus, if you kill me here, they probably wouldn't find the body for a while, which adds to the creep factor, I guess.

"But that's all this killing spree of yours is, isn't it? A series of attacks trying so hard to be scary. And sure, you've checked all the boxes. You have the wolf mask, the sharpened bone, which is unique, I'll give you that. Then you have the victims, a few high school kids, mostly girls, and of course a few cops trying to protect them. Mix in a few creepy locations: a girl's home, a gym, and a safe house. I will say the attack on the police station was clever. You don't see something like that every day, but it was still just another surprise attack on victims who couldn't fight back. Everything you need to start a killing spree, to create a terrifying monster that gets inside people's heads, to make them remember you as something else. Something horrifying.

"Only I'm not scared."

Riley stopped for a moment, hearing something breathe behind her, hidden in the shadows. It was listening.

"Because that's all you are. Someone who wants to be scary, wants to be taken seriously. A dog who wants to be a wolf. But you're not. You're not the Animal, not even close. You may have the mask, but that's all it is: a mask hiding the face underneath. A pathetic attempt to capture the fear of something you don't understand."

Something moved in the shadows, stalking her, waiting to strike, growling as it did.

"Oh, that's original," she said, sighing as she saw the movement. "You don't get it, do you? All this, this stalking, this manufactured growling, it's not what an animal is."

The shadow moved closer.

"An animal is terrifying because it doesn't try to scare something, doesn't care if its prey is afraid. It doesn't care what goes through its prey's head before it rips out its throat. It just does, because that's what it is. Everything you're not."

The growling got louder.

She saw its mask illuminated behind a sliver of moonlight: grey fur and hollow holes where its eyes should have been, allowing the human eyes hiding within to watch her. Below the mask was more fur, a makeshift wolf costume, which in the dark might have been enough to frighten those who hadn't seen a real monster.

"So come on, attack me," Riley said, slipping a knife out of her boot, twisting it in her hands. "See if I scream."

It lunged at her with its sharpened bone, swiping the blade at her in a flash of rage before hiding back in the darkness, behind the broken chains.

Grinding her teeth, she searched for it, listening for its breathing, for its footsteps. They were faint, but she could hear it, coming toward her again.

Wait, she thought, watching for movement, listening to the footsteps. It was close, moving fast. It would reach her in a few seconds, maybe less.

Now.

She moved, dodging the bone meant for her face, feeling the wind from it as it passed by her. Then her eyes turned to the monster holding it.

"Hey," she said, striking it in the face, causing it to stumble backwards. "Not so easy when it's not kids, is it? Or when they know you're coming?"

Growling, it attacked again, grey animalistic features almost glowing white in the darkness, revealing it as it swung its blade at her stomach. Once. Twice. Three times, missing all of them as she moved effortlessly, anger rising as she did.

This thing thought it could kill her.

Thought she was its prey.

Lashing out, the masked killer took one more swing at her chest. She blocked the strike, but doing so caused the blade to graze her arm, drawing blood—a small red line that streamed down her arm, reaching her fingers before falling onto the floor.

She held her hand up for a moment, letting the blood fall from it, still facing the killer waiting to strike again. Finally, Riley spoke. "Let's see what your blood looks like."

Swinging her own knife, she attacked it, going for its neck but barely missing as it moved out of the way, shocked and desperate.

Not letting up, she attacked again, swinging the knife at its throat once more, and when she missed, she then went for its stomach. She almost grinned as she saw how it moved away, like it was shocked that something would attack it, almost scared.

Her next attack cut its costume, the knife passing through its side, not cutting skin, but opening up the fake grey fur, revealing a small glimpse of flesh underneath. A wound that revealed the truth she had always known of this new predator.

It was human.

The predator ran. Whatever it had been planning, it was now afraid for its own life. Trying to escape, it moved toward the door, pushing against it as Riley stayed where she was, watching it with a grin on her face.

The door wouldn't open, and the predator turned in a panic.

"I locked it from the outside," Riley said, her arm warm as blood continued to flow down it. "There's no escape."

In a rage, it attacked her again, swinging its sharpened bone aggressively, aiming at her head, her throat, anything that would bleed.

She did the same but still held back, waiting for a true opening. Eventually it came when the monster shoved its blade into her stomach, taking her breath.

For a moment, everything was quiet as she felt the bone grazing against her ribs, cutting into her flesh, spilling her blood onto the ground. Even the killer's breathing changed, going from quick bursts to calmer, slower breaths.

Until it looked in her eyes.

Wincing in pain, she grabbed its hand, tight grip keeping it from removing the blade in her side, forcing the killer to stay close, within range.

Where she could hurt it.

"You think you're a monster?" she said, growling herself as she lashed out, striking it in the eye, maintaining her grip, keeping it close as she began beating it.

"You think you're the Animal?"

Her knuckles grew bloody as she struck its face again, wanting to cry out from the pain in her stomach, but her rage wouldn't allow it.

"I've seen the Animal, and you're not it!" she screamed, finally allowing its hand to move before tackling it to the ground.

It tried to move away, but she stayed on top of it, bringing her knee down on its chest and striking it in the head, listening to the sound of her hand impacting its skull.

She struck it again, over and over until she could hear it coughing up blood from underneath the mask. Still, she didn't stop, screaming as she did, anger and rage taking over. It thought she was its to kill, thought it was something other than prey. It was wrong. Something was hiding underneath its mask, and it could be broken, bloodied.

"Show me your face," she whispered, growling as she reached for its mask, striking it again as it struggled, trying to force its mask off, trying to reveal the monster hiding within. "Show me your face!"

She'd almost ripped the mask off when the cornered monster grew desperate and tried to strike her in retaliation. She blocked it but in doing so gave it just enough room to reach over and grab its sharpened bone—its weapon used for carving flesh, like the horns of a deer or the claws of a wolf.

It shoved the blade into her thigh, tearing flesh and drawing blood, forcing her to wince just enough so that her knee released its pressure on the killer's chest.

In an instant, the predator moved from under her weight and began desperately crawling away, still dazed from the impact to its head, distorted moans of agony escaping from within the confines of the mask.

Bleeding and angry, bone still sticking out of her thigh, Riley reached over and grabbed its foot, tripping it back down as it tried to stand. It looked back in confusion and then appalled surprise as it saw her smile.

It tried to run. The monster covered in her blood, dwarfing her in size and covered in inhuman fur, unnatural mask now partially cracked, actually ran away from her.

She chased it.

But the bone in her leg caused her to limp slowly as she followed the killer, who was no longer growling.

It reached the side door first, slamming its entire body against it, but it didn't open.

She'd locked it too.

"Where are you going?" Riley whispered, wincing as she ripped the bone from her leg and spun it in her hand.

Panicked, it turned from the door, the terror of its hidden eyes illuminated by traces of moonlight as Riley brought the blade down into its shoulder.

Crying out in pain, it struck her, landing the blow and sending her to the floor. She was too dazed to chase it as it limped away from her, but she watched it nonetheless—pathetic and crying out, as it applied pressure to its shoulder, seeing the bone that stuck through the front and reached out the back.

She could tell it wanted to scream, but it couldn't without revealing its voice. So instead it stood there silently, shifting in anger as it looked at her.

"C'mon," she pleaded, picking up her dropped knife, knowing how badly the monster wanted to charge, she herself feeling so desperately the urge to kill it. "C'mon!"

It ran.

Away from her, away from its death, and toward the corner of the warehouse, scrambling to get through the small opening in the metal, almost cutting itself as it did, leaving her alone with no corpse to show for her efforts.

But it didn't matter. She'd done what she'd had to. She'd cut it, marked it like a wild animal being studied, being tracked.

That was enough.

CHAPTER THIRTY-THREE

Covered in blood, Riley beat on the door.

She'd walked over two miles to get here through the forest, limping the whole way, left foot dragging on the ground as the blood streaming down her leg left a trail in the dirt.

But she had to come. She had to know.

She continued to knock violently, until finally, she thought she heard movement behind the door.

"It's me," she said, whispered words not revealing her true intentions.

The sound of three deadbolts being unlocked cut through the silence of the night, and the door finally opened, revealing Oliver standing behind it, eyes widening with concern as he saw the blood.

"Oh my... what happened? Are you—"

His question was cut off as she pulled out her knife and pointed it to his throat.

"Whoa!" he said, expression suddenly nervous, backing up and raising both hands into the air. "What are you doing?"

Leaning on the door frame for support, she didn't lower the knife as her eyes pierced through him, a tired expression covering her bruised face.

"Show me your shoulder, Oliver."

"What?"

"Show me your shoulder!"

"Why would you...?" He stopped for a moment as a look of realization crossed over his face, his nervous shaking turning into quiet chuckling, then full-on laughter. "Oh, you beautiful genius. You stabbed it, didn't you?"

"Oliver!" she growled.

"Right," he said, nodding as he took off his jacket and raised up his shirt's sleeve, revealing the shoulder underneath. Unbloodied. Unharmed. Riley breathed a sigh of relief.

It wasn't him.

After a few moments passed, Oliver spoke again, smiling as he did. "You mind lowering the knife?"

"Oh yeah," she said, grinning herself as she lowered it. It felt good not to be nervous, not to be worried the person across from her was hiding something, if only for a moment.

"Told you it wasn't me," he said, stepping closer. "Although, to be fair—"

"I know," she said, finishing his thought, "If there are two of them, you could technically still be in on it."

But she knew that he wasn't. If she was sure of only one thing about Oliver, it was that he did things alone. If he was going to go on a citywide killing spree in search of the Animal, he would have been smart enough not to involve anyone else who'd just get him caught.

So, without the wound on his shoulder, as far as Riley was concerned, she could trust him. That was rare in her life, something to be held on to.

"You're bleeding pretty bad," he said, looking to both her side and her thigh.

"I noticed," she said, pain creeping into her voice as she slid down the door frame and rested on the floor, taking the pressure off her leg.

"Call an ambulance?"

"Eventually." First, she just wanted to rest there for a moment, calm down and take in the quiet night before the nightmare inevitably started again.

"Well, we have to at least wrap those wounds," Oliver said, pulling out an extremely professional first aid kit from a hidden spot behind the door.

"Why do you have—" she started to ask before remembering who it was. "Never mind."

A few seconds later, he began wrapping her leg very tightly, causing pain to suddenly surge through her body. She grunted as her hands turned into fists and she punched the floor, releasing some of the agony.

"So," Oliver said, "how'd this happen?"

"I attacked it in a warehouse about two miles from here."

"You attacked it?" he questioned. "How'd you know where it was?"

Wincing in pain from her leg, she pulled the crumpled note from her pocket, letting him take it.

"I found evidence," he read in a mocking tone. "Meet me, blah blah blah, signed, Oliver." The last word caused him to laugh. "Subtle. It was a trap?"

"Obviously."

"How'd you know it wasn't me who wrote it?"

"I didn't know for sure, but when's the last time you wrote something in normal ink?"

"Good catch." He dropped the note and tied the bandage. "So, if you knew it was a trap, why'd you still go?"

She thought for a moment, calm despite the bleeding, almost on the verge of peace, even in this nightmare.

"When I was younger, a little over ten years ago, I guess, I used to go hunting. At first, I told myself it was normal, that I was just doing it for the same reason as everyone else, but eventually I realized that I was just lying to myself. I didn't really want to hunt, I wanted to be hunted. I wanted to find something that could give me the same feeling of dread and horror that the Animal did, so that I could kill it and move on.

"So, when the hunting didn't work, I started letting them charge me. At first it was just deer. They didn't always do it, but every once in a while, one would feel trapped, I guess, and it would run straight at me, antlers forward, ready to impale my chest.

"The last deer I shot was a whitetail with huge sharp antlers. It ran at me like it was possessed. I let it get within two feet of me before I shot it; the momentum caused the antlers to still graze me. Bled for a week. But it wasn't the same.

"So, I moved on to predators. Bobcats, coyotes, a few wolves. I'd track them, make noise, and then let them come, test how close they could get, praying one of them would make me feel terror like it had. But nothing did.

"Eventually, I found a grizzly bear. It was massive, could have ripped me in two with one swing. And I let it charge. It screamed, running at me through the trees, dead eyes, monstrous roar, teeth that could crack my skull like glass."

A tear fell down Riley's face. "I started crying as I saw it, felt it coming for me. It wasn't the same. It never would be. I knew then that I could spend my life tracking every monster on earth and nothing would ever shake my bones the way the Animal had. The horror of the single glimpse would never go away.

"So, I dropped my rifle and let the bear come. I wanted it to kill me. I wanted it so badly, to die, to finally be safe from the memories of the Animal. The ones it slaughtered.

"It was close enough that I could feel its breath when suddenly I heard the gunshot and turned to see someone holding a rifle. I cried, screamed, hit him, but eventually I stopped, and he held me. I didn't feel alone after that." She sighed, closing her eyes for a moment. "But then he died, and every day since then I've thought about the bear, wondering if somewhere out there existed an animal I could hunt that would make the nightmares go away."

"Did it?" Oliver asked. "Did hunting this new animal make the real one less terrifying?"

"No," Riley said simply, voice somber at first, before she calmed down once more and remembered how the new predator had bled, how it had run. "But it felt *great*."

Oliver laughed. "You're kind of a psycho, aren't you?"

"Maybe," she laughed before grunting in sudden pain as Oliver finished the wrap around her stomach, forcing her to punch the floor again.

"Warn me next time."

"Next time don't let it stab you in the stomach."

"I'll try," she said, voice calming down as the pain went away. Now done with the bandaging, Oliver sat on the floor next to her, staring off into the distance.

"It's about to be over," he said. "It's marked now. You did it."

"Yeah, well, I guess we're going to see if your suspect list is accurate."

"I guess so."

"Any final predictions?"

"I don't know," he said. "I guess at the moment I'd lean toward Dylan, but anything's possible, I suppose."

"I thought Rhett was your number one suspect."

"Things change."

"Like what?"

Oliver just shrugged.

"Well, either way..." Riley groaned in discomfort once more as she applied pressure to her wounds and stood up. Moonlight shone brightly beyond the clouds of the night: her bloodied side shimmering in its light, resolve flashing in her eyes.

"Let's hunt it down."

///

The morning sun was almost warm, shining bright in the sky, causing the clouds around it to glow, basking in its light. Riley was leaning back against a tree, one of the few in town that was disconnected from the forest, standing tall in the middle of the small park. Oliver knelt down a few feet away, writing something in his notebook, using invisible ink as always.

The plan was simple. They had contacted each of the kids, every suspect Oliver had, and instructed them to meet up here: the park in front of the hospital where Riley had been stitched up.

Hank was in a squad car just a few blocks away, along with the few deputies who hadn't been killed at the police station.

When the kids arrived, whoever had a bloodied face, and more importantly a stab wound on their shoulder, would be caught and arrested on the spot. If it was one of the kids, then they couldn't hide any longer. If it wasn't, then they would start tracking down the rest of the town, one by one if they had to.

It was a simple plan. Until they saw Betty, and it all fell apart.

She had tears in her eyes and was crying as she walked up to them, jumping at everything, even the gust of wind that suddenly blew through the air.

But it wasn't the crying that alarmed them. It was the blood.

Her face was beaten. It had been bandaged, but strips of blood stained the once-white bandages crimson. Even her nose looked broken.

Worse than that, her shoulder was bleeding.

"Oliver?" Riley whispered, reaching for the knife behind her back as Betty grew closer.

"No," he whispered to himself, suddenly looking back and forth in every direction, eyes covered in dread. "It can't be her."

"Oliver?" Riley whispered again, voice growing nervous. She'd been ready for anything, but not this. Her body felt paralyzed in confusion, unable to process it, unable to move.

"It doesn't make sense," Oliver continued, still talking more to himself than to her, voice shaky. "It can't... there's no way. It's wrong."

"Stop," Riley finally said, drawing her knife and aiming it toward Betty.

"What?" Betty asked, still crying, rubbing her shoulder in pain, taking another step forward.

"Stop!" Riley screamed so suddenly that it caused Betty to jump backwards, falling to the ground and almost huddling up in confused fear.

"What is it!" Betty asked, voice terrified.

This was wrong. It didn't make sense. "Why are you bleeding?" Riley asked, tone deathly serious.

"I... I..." Betty stuttered, seemingly too shocked to speak.

"Why?" Riley screamed again.

"It attacked me," Betty said, crying as she finally got the words out. "Last night it came into my room and held me down. It beat me." Her weeping grew worse. "I thought it was going to kill me, but it just kept hitting me over and over as it held me there, growling as it hurt me..."

Her words after that weren't understandable, as the fear and weeping took over completely.

Riley stood horrified, not sure whether to comfort the girl or attack her. It was wrong. All of this was wrong.

She turned to face Oliver, seeing the same expression in his eyes. Fear, confusion, the dying of hope.

"Hey, guys," a voice said from behind a tree, weak and pained.

Startled, Riley spun the knife around, almost jumping out of her skin as she saw the kid standing behind it. Broken nose. Bleeding shoulder.

Dylan.

Grip tightening on the knife, Riley stood speechless.

Oliver, however, found the words, speaking quietly. "What happened to you?"

"It broke into my house," Dylan said, in the same casual way he said everything. "Tied me down, beat the crap out of me, stabbed my shoulder. Then just left. It's a freaking lunatic."

Riley couldn't think, couldn't move. She just kept holding on to the knife, slowly realizing the unthinkable horror.

"Did you hurt Betty?" Oliver asked. "To hide what you did?"

"What?" Dylan asked, seemingly confused until

he saw Betty in the grass behind them, bleeding even worse than he was. "Why would you—"

His question was cut short when someone else approached, again causing Riley to turn defensively, now back-to-back with Oliver, each watching in a nervous panic as more kids arrived, growing increasingly uneasy with each one.

"What's happening?" Hank pleaded over the coms in Riley's ear.

She didn't answer, couldn't speak.

Gabriella was first, with a beaten face and bloodied shoulder. Then Russel, then Kelly and Rhett, and finally Luke.

All held down. All beaten. All bloodied.

Riley and Oliver stood in the middle of them, still back-to-back, Riley gripping the knife so tight that it felt as though it was a part of her own flesh.

This was insane. It was horrific, terrifying, unthinkable. This wasn't just anger or rage. This was different, calculated, cruel. A monster covering his tracks, beating and torturing children to do so.

In that moment, surrounded by beaten kids she couldn't trust, she felt helpless, afraid.

Standing amidst a wolf she couldn't see.

CHAPTER THIRTY-FOUR

Not making a sound, barely even breathing, Clyde tracked it. The doe he had seen in the forest, no antlers, faded white spots from its youth still present on its fur.

Clyde had to find it. It was the last hope of denying the sins of his past.

Animals didn't lie, didn't keep secrets. It wasn't in their nature. Humans could lie, could hide the truth and twist it until it became something unrecognizable. He could even lie to himself, his fractured mind playing tricks, making him see and feel things that weren't real.

But the deer wouldn't.

Kneeling down, Clyde found more tracks in the dirt, leading him closer to the animal he was after.

When he'd last seen the doe, it had been startled by his presence but not afraid. Hadn't jumped, hadn't panicked, merely moving away slowly, gracefully, as if it could sense he wasn't a predator.

But that was before the instincts had crawled their way back out. That was before he'd learned what he was, what he'd done. If it was true, if he was the monster his instincts revealed, the deer would know, and it would run.

It was the last hope he had. The last remnant of peace that he might not be the monster who had slaughtered everyone, and in his mind he found himself begging that the deer would see him and merely watch, just as it had done before.

The truth, however, was far worse.

The tracks in the ground began growing farther apart. Something had spooked it. Clyde continued on the trail, weaving between trees, desperately searching as the tracks grew even more frenzied.

It wasn't just spooked, it was terrified. Something must've been hunting it.

He moved faster, running as he searched for it, afraid that he was what it was running from. That it had sensed him and, feeling the presence of a predator, had run for its life.

But then the tracks stopped, and Clyde discovered the truth.

The deer was lying in the dirt, between two massive trees, shaded by their twisting, hideous branches. Its head was limp on the ground, and its eyes rolled back in its head, now appearing white and hollow. Its throat was ripped, almost missing entirely, and three wolves stood over it, ripping its flesh from its body, spilling its blood as they devoured it.

They looked like monsters from behind, bloodstained fur and horrific features, jaws clicking together every few seconds as they bit into their fallen prey piece by piece. The two wolves on either side seemed younger, sleek fur and broad shoulders, but the one in the center appeared old, matted fur and weaker bones, far more ancient than any he'd ever seen.

This was it, Clyde realized. The deer couldn't tell what he was anymore, but the wolves could. If they saw him, they would attack to defend their kill, and his instinct would either kick in or it wouldn't. Either way, he'd finally know what he truly was.

Breathing slowly, just loud enough to alert them to his presence, he stood there motionless as they began growling. At first it was just a low rumbling, signaling a threat to whatever was behind them, but then it grew into something far more vicious

Finally, the wolf in the center turned, and Clyde saw its face. A scar ran down its left eye, and its reaction revealed its true age. It was old. Old enough to remember the monster. Old enough to recognize it.

As their eyes met, the moment froze, a single second becoming an eternity as Clyde saw it. The wolf's expression. Trembling jaw, pupils dilated in fear, its vicious growling turning into a quiet whimper of unspeakable dread.

The other wolves turned as well, but the fear had reached them too. They were young, not near old enough to remember, but they felt it all the same.

For a moment they just stood there, too frightened to even move, until finally the older wolf backed up, tripping over himself as he did, lowering his head and whimpering in agony and fear, almost begging to be spared.

Then they ran faster than he'd ever seen, stumbling as they did, legs buckling in shock and desperation.

They left him alone, standing over the carcass of the deer, bloodied and eaten.

If nothing else had happened, if no memories had come back, the look in the wolf's eyes would have been enough. The sheer unimaginable horror that had erupted in its eyes like a flash of lightning as a monster from its past returned. Scared of being ripped apart. Scared of death.

Scared of the Animal.

CHAPTER THIRTY-FIVE

She should have seen it coming.

Kneeling down in a small wooden deer blind in the center of the woods, holding a bloodied corpse in her arms, Riley cried.

She should have seen it coming. The signs were there, unnatural occurrences signifying tragedy and giving warnings of what was to come. Warnings that she had ignored, in her mind still treating this new predator as an imitation, something to be wary of but not take seriously.

She'd been wrong. So wrong.

The first sign of horror was the silence.

It had been two days since she had seen the faces of the kids, beaten and tortured in order to cover the monster's tracks. Hurt, but not killed.

She'd taken it for granted that they'd been allowed to live, but that was foolish. The predator's rage was still there: the wish to inflict the same violence on someone else as Riley had inflicted on it. She'd tried to kill it, tried to slit its throat and rip off its mask. It hungered to do the same.

Riley was sitting in her house, enjoying a peaceful moment with Emma, when she got the call. The old phone shook the table gently as it rang, waiting to be answered, itching to reveal the dark truth.

For a second, she almost didn't answer it. Quiet moments like this spent with Emma had grown rarer in the past few weeks, and she didn't want something to ruin it. Besides, it probably wasn't important anyway.

Yet something forced her to answer.

"Hello?"

"Riley!" Hank's voice said, scared and desperate. "The kids..."

"Slow down."

"I got calls from the kids' parents. They haven't come home. Neither has Luke."

"How long?"

"They should have been back hours ago."

She rubbed her eyes, feeling the dread creeping into the air. "Where are they?"

"They were walking back from Russel's house on the edge of the forest. Less than two miles away from your street."

"Hank?" she started, realizing what he was asking her.

"Riley, please, you're closer than I am. Please."

It was strange hearing Hank this scared. He was old, experienced in the world. But everything changed when your own kid was in danger. Even animals feared for their young; if she heard her pup in danger, a mother coyote would chew off her own leg to escape a trap and reach them.

"Okay," she said without hesitation. "I'm there."

She reached over and grabbed her rifle, loading it as she spoke to Emma. "I have to go help the kids. Hide in the safe room upstairs, and don't come out until I get back."

"Okay," the girl said, running over and hugging Riley for a moment before rushing up the stairs.

Riley sighed and chambered a round.

The second sign was the rain.

It never rained in this town. There was snow, hail, wind, mist, fog, but it rarely rained. When it did, it was only a sprinkle, just enough to prolong the suffering of dying plants, keeping them alive in this twisted nightmare just a moment longer.

But right now, it was pouring.

Water was gathering in the ditches around her, dark gritty clouds blotting out the sun, rain so thick that she could barely see the end of her rifle; so loud all she could hear was the crash of thousands of drops hitting the ground at every moment, drowning out all other signs of life.

She should have known something was wrong when the rain started. Anywhere else it would have meant nothing, but here, in this place corrupted by legends of a monster, even the town itself seemed to grow around the legend, just as the forest had grown into it.

A warning, as if the very weather was trying to tell her to protect them, to help them before it was too late. But she'd ignored it, thinking it was nothing, only a coincidence.

But the truth was, there was only one night in her life that this town had suffered a worse storm. A night where she remembered thunder, lightning, and the earth itself crying out in horror, weeping for the slaughtered victims.

She ran through it, down the road and beside the forest, desperately searching through the rain for any traces of the kids. Any sign that they were still alive.

Then she heard it. Screaming.

"Help! It's here!"

She saw the kid across the road, barely making out his features through the rain. As he ran, he screamed for help, like Paul Revere warning of an invasion. A horrified messenger.

It was Luke.

Finally, he saw her as well and ran to her, stammering. "It... it attacked us. I ran."

"Where?"

His body trembled.

"Where!?"

Shaking, he lifted up a finger and pointed, straight into the heart of the forest.

The forest was the next sign.
   The warning she should have seen.

The killer had attacked its victims in a warehouse, a police station, and the kids' own homes. But, except for the old man who'd fled, it hadn't attacked in the forest yet. In the home of animals. The den of monsters.

Feet caving in the mud, she ran through it, rifle ready. Somewhere in here was the killer she'd hurt, and the kids who'd pay the price if she couldn't reach them in time.

Rain streamed down her face, soaking her completely in its cold embrace, freezing her to the bone. But still she ran, hunting. Soon, she found a few tracks in the mud, frenzied, multiple sets. Running prey. Following them, she ran faster, desperate to save them.

Suddenly, she saw it. A hint of red mixed in with the flowing water on the dirt in front of her, circling around from the other side of the tree.

Gun ready, she steadied her aim and moved around it, slow, sliding her feet in the mud, moving between trees until the source of the blood was finally revealed.

Russel, lying back against a tree, clutching his bleeding side, face twitching in pain. Gabriella was beside him, blood on her own head, trying to wrap his wound and stop the bleeding.

They both saw Riley at the same moment, rifle in hand, finger on the trigger.

"Is he okay?" Riley asked.

As Russel grunted in pain, Gabriella answered. "I think so. The wound doesn't look too deep, but it's bleeding a lot."

"What happened?"

"It attacked us on the road," the girl said, voice hollowed out with terror. "Came out of nowhere, chased us down. We ran in here, tried to escape. But it caught us. It threw me against a tree." She reached up to her wound, her hand temporarily stained in blood before the rain washed it off. "I must've blacked out. When I woke up, I was here and saw Russel bleeding."

"I tried to fight it," Russel said, voice cracking in pain. "But I couldn't stop it." Suddenly, his body twitched in concern. "They're still out there. It's after them."

"Who?"

"The girls. I think Dylan got away, but it chased Kelly and Betty. It's going to kill them!"

"Where did they run?"

"To the right," he said, groaning in agony as the wound started bleeding again.

"Wrap it fast and stay quiet," Riley said. "I'll come back for you."

"Find them," Russel pleaded. "Please."

Riley nodded and moved further into the nightmare.

It didn't take her long to find their trail. Tracks in the mud, leading through the trees. Faint traces of red mixed with the water that filled in the holes.

How had she let it get this far? Why hadn't she been able to kill it at the warehouse and end this murderous spree?

She weaved between trees, each time keeping the rifle up, searching for anything that moved, any sound beyond the rain.

Mud crept up to her ankles, as though the forest itself was attempting to consume her as she ran, searching for the girls. But a disturbing thought entered her mind.

Was she desperate to save them, or to kill their hunter?

Finally, she saw it, a faint glimpse of something unnatural within the rain, within the trees. It was wooden, painted green and black, and positioned in a small clearing.

As she approached it, she saw the windows circling it, small rectangles designed for hunting, for killing deer from a hidden location.

It was a hunting blind, and the tracks led up to it.

Moving slowly, fighting against her heart as it tried to raise her adrenaline, she forced herself to be still, forced her hands to be steady as she held the rifle and approached the door.

She put her ears to the wood, trying to listen for signs of life. The rain almost drowned it out, but finally she heard it. Heavy breathing, whimpers of fear, bodies shaking the wood as they trembled.

Cautious, she opened the door, slowly removing the camouflaged wood and revealing the victims hiding within.

Still breathing. Still alive.

A rush of relief flooded over her as she saw them, Kelly and Betty, huddled closely together on the far side. They were safe, alive, not even bleeding.

The final sign.

She should have felt it, the ominous warning, the uninjured prey, the brief moment of hope. It should have felt wrong. She should have kept her guard up, but for a singular moment she allowed herself to hope. A moment later the sky fell out, the winds shook the trees, and it was too late.

Betty saw her. A glimmer of survival flickered in her eyes as she stood up from the wall, about to run toward Riley, run toward safety. All while the outline of her neck shone from the light of the rectangular window behind her.

"Betty, no!" Kelly screamed, reaching to pull her back down but not making it in time.

The moment the cry of fear happened, the monster appeared in the window behind her, grey fur dripping wet as it reached its arm through and grabbed Betty by her hair, pulling her back against the window, displaying the body as a message to Riley.

Forcing her to watch as it slit Betty's throat.

A second later the rifle fired, but it was far too late. The monster had retreated to the forest, and Betty's eyes had already lost their color. The girl was dead before her body even collapsed onto the floor, blood spilling from her throat.

The predator's target.

The world seemed to stop for a moment as Riley fell to the ground and held the girl in her arms. It was her job to protect them, prepare them for the monster. Instead, she'd attacked it, gone for its throat, provoking it to do the same.

Rain crashed down onto the wooden blind, covering it completely and almost removing it from the world for a moment, drowning out Riley's weeping. Another girl dead, another terrified victim she couldn't save from an animal.

This was her fault.

CHAPTER THIRTY-SIX

None of it felt real. It was like she was trapped in her own nightmare: unable to escape, unable to stop the monster lurking in the shadows of her thoughts, forced to watch as everyone around her was slaughtered.

But it wasn't a distorted dream, wasn't something she could wait out in hopes that it would end soon. It was something she could never escape, never wake up from.

Her own life.

The cries of Betty's parents could be heard from the other side of the morgue as they identified their daughter's body. Horrible weeping ensued as they no doubt saw her slit throat and lifeless eyes.

Betty had told Riley that she had always wanted to move, get away from this town, and away from the stories of the Animal. But her parents had stayed, thinking that was all it would ever be. Stories.

They would be like her now, would feel shame, guilt, regret for not being able to save the ones they loved. Like all the other victims the Animal claimed without having to kill, they became ghosts who existed only to further the memory of the dead.

Riley could still see it. The glimpse of the monster behind the window, slashing the girl's throat. Even though it was a wolf mask, frozen in place, Riley could swear she saw it smiling, as if it enjoyed the cruelty.

The room outside the morgue was quiet. Every kid was there, faces frozen in mourning, not wanting to accept that Betty was gone. They'd lost other friends, but this one was different. They'd known she was a target, just like all of them were. But they couldn't save her either.

Russel's side was still bleeding slightly, but the cut wasn't deep. It should heal up within a few days. The rest of them were bruised but alive, most of them still feeling the wounds in their shoulders.

The mark the monster had given them.

Kelly was the worst of all. She'd knelt down in the corner, holding on to Betty's jacket, covering her face and crying into it.

Closing her eyes for a moment, Riley felt suffocated. This was her fault. She'd underestimated the killer, thinking that just because it wasn't the Animal, it wasn't a threat. Thinking it was just a pretender, that she could kill it at the warehouse and be done with it forever.

She was wrong. It might not be the same monster she knew, but after the forest, seeing the kids scattered in fear, the viciousness with which it had attacked Betty and the cruelty in its actions as it had taken revenge for the beating she'd inflicted on it, maybe it was an animal.

Not the same one from before, but a new breed, more violent, more sadistic. Not a wolf, but also not the dog she'd assumed it to be. Something in between. Clever, focused, threatening. A fox stained with the blood of the henhouse, waiting to strike again.

Riley's fists balled in anger, but she held her rage back. Everyone was here, the kids and their parents, all terrified of what could happen to their children. Except for Rhett and Kelly, who were still all alone.

The rage returned, and suddenly her eyes focused, narrowing in on the one thing gained from this last attack. The only kid who wasn't there.

Rhett.

With a piercing glance, she motioned for him to follow her outside. He looked confused, but eventually he did, unaware of what would soon follow.

The second they were outside the door, she grabbed his throat and shoved him against the wall as hints of the previous rain still trickled down from the sky.

"Where were you?"

"What?" he asked, possibly faking the confusion.

"The attack. Everyone else was there, but not you. Why?"

"I was across town when they left," he said, voice cracking slightly from the pressure she had on his throat. "I was going to meet them later. Why?"

"Every time your sister has been attacked, you weren't there." Riley spoke harshly, letting her anger take over her words. She was tired of waiting for the killer to slip up, tired of waiting for the reveal, ready to force a confession if necessary. "Why?"

"It's not like I know when she's going to be attacked," Rhett growled, seemingly annoyed at the implication.

"Why aren't you with her every second?" she growled back. "Do you not care?"

His eyes revealed anger for a moment as he scoffed. "Screw you." He then pushed her hand off his throat and started to move away.

At that, Riley gave a light nervous laugh. He thought this was a joke, that she wasn't serious.

She then reached out and slammed him back against the wall, drawing her knife and putting it to his throat before whispering into his ear, tone deathly serious. "You were the only one not there in the forest when Betty was attacked. You haven't been at any of the attacks. The only reason I don't slit your throat right here is the small chance that I'm wrong, that maybe the anger and loss are clouding my judgment. But make no mistake"—she moved the knife closer, pressing it against his neck—"if there is another attack, and you're not there... I will kill you myself, whether you're the killer or not."

Silence echoed, the harsh threats lingering in the air between them, until finally he shoved her off him and walked away. But before he did, Riley almost thought she saw something in his face. Not anger, not sadness, but something else: a small hint of a grin, almost joy at being accused.

But maybe she was just seeing things.

It felt as though the town itself was closing in on her, suffocating her with its rain and wind, forcing her to remain helpless forever. It was the same feeling she'd had when she was eight years old, trapped under the bed, unable to stop the death.

In frustration, she hit the brick wall, drawing blood from her knuckles. Sometimes the pain, the blood, helped. Made her remember she was still alive, still able to hurt, to fight.

"This isn't your fault," a voice said from behind her.

"She's dead, Oliver. It doesn't matter whose fault it is."

"It does when you blame yourself." He moved closer, leaning on the wall next to her. "You've done more to help her than her own parents did. You taught her to fight and hunted the animal that was after her."

"It wasn't enough."

"Sometimes it's not," he said, light rain hitting his face and almost hiding the tear that went down it. "Sometimes people just die, and there's nothing you can do to change it. No monster to hunt. No mystery to solve. Nothing that will ever bring them back."

After a few seconds, as the sun started to set in the sky, barely visible through the massive grey clouds, he finally continued. "You should go home, try and move on from this. You survived one horror; you shouldn't let this new one be your grave."

Riley sighed, and her eyes met his. "What about you? If you keep going after this, one way or the other, something is going to happen to you too. This case shouldn't be your grave either."

"You know, it's a funny thing about graves," Oliver said, beginning to walk backwards, leaving her alone in the rain. "Sometimes we dig them ourselves."

Oliver stepped into Hank's office, determined.

The sheriff was sitting in a chair behind his desk, eyes red with grief. Luke was across from him, shaking in fear.

"Give me the files, the evidence you have," Oliver said simply.

"Please," Hank said. "Not now, Oliver. My son almost died."

"Exactly. Your son almost died because you're still protecting something."

"Oliver..." the sheriff started.

"No!" Oliver screamed. "No more hiding it. Betty's dead. It slit her throat in the forest as some kind of sick message to Riley, some sort of sacrifice to the Animal that you're protecting. And you just let it happen!"

"Not now!" Hank screamed.

For a moment, Oliver quieted down. Even this felt wrong, to yell at the sheriff and demand the files, all without knowing if he'd even be able to find the Animal and stop this. But Betty was dead. Even if they hadn't really been friends, it bothered him. Another girl who'd be chalked up to a victim number. A forgotten life, but a remembered death, just like his own mother. Because everyone was too obsessed with the monster to care about the victims.

Oliver couldn't take the madness anymore.

"I know that I'm just a kid, and that this won't bring my mother back. Won't change what happened to the victims. But if you care at all about this, the kids that died, your own deputies, what it's doing to Riley, then please, let go of the legend. Let me reveal the face behind the Animal and end this twenty-five-year nightmare you created by hiding the truth."

Hank's answer was simple. "Get out."

Oliver nodded, moving toward the door, but not before one final word. "Their blood is on your hands now," he said before pointing at Luke.

"His will be too."

Neither of them said anything for a moment as they took in all that Oliver had said.

Something about it had unsettled Hank. It was strange seeing Oliver like this, desperate. Maybe the kid did care more than he'd given him credit for. But it didn't matter. There was nothing that could be done. It had come too far.

He shook it off. "I don't know how you're friends with that kid."

Luke responded, tone shocked and almost sorrowful. "Why won't you give him the evidence, Dad?"

"What?"

"Why won't you give him what you have on the Animal? Oliver's smart, maybe he can find it. Maybe he can save us."

"I don't have anything on the Animal."

"Really?" Luke asked, almost hurt at the lie. "Dad, you talk about the case like it happened yesterday. You hid something, and it made Mom leave, made you different all these years. Even now, even after it attacked me, you still won't admit it?"

"There is nothing. I promise," Hank lied.

A tear streamed down Luke's bloodied face, and his words pierced Hank's heart.

"Is protecting it worth more to you than my life?"

After that, looking at his wounded son, beaten and tortured, stabbed in the shoulder and hunted, Hank finally forced himself to see the truth of what his sins had caused. The legend it had borne in the town.

The new monster it had created.

Riley stepped into her home covered in rain, hiding the defeated, solemn tears as she walked in. She'd done what she'd sworn she would never do again. She'd gotten close to the kids. Cared about what happened to them.

Only to be reminded of what happened to those she cared about.

But the truth was that Betty's death wasn't why she was upset, wasn't why she felt tears on her face. It was what it meant: that she couldn't protect anyone, least of all the one she cared about the most.

For what felt like a lifetime, all she felt was dread, until she saw Emma running to her, and somehow the sadness left her in an instant.

"Hey," Riley said with relief, kneeling down to hug her daughter.

It was moments like this that scared her the most. Happy moments. Moments when she was reminded of the single blessing still in her life, terrified by how much it meant to her and afraid that one day the Animal would take it from her too.

But she forced it out of her mind and enjoyed the time she had, savoring every second of the embrace, reminded again how quickly everything can change.

She remembered the cries of Betty's parents, seeing their daughter's lifeless face, knowing they could never hold her again, never feel her warmth. The thought made her realize something. Even after everything that had happened, all the monsters she'd seen, she still had Emma. She could still hold her daughter and see her smile.

Maybe she wasn't cursed. Maybe she was lucky.

CHAPTER THIRTY-SEVEN

Clyde could still see the look in the wolf's eyes. Terror.

What kind of monster must he be for even wolves to be afraid?

The impulse was stronger than ever, long-dormant instincts coming back to the light, almost forcing their way out. Clyde could feel it within his own skin, ripping him apart.

Something was inside him. He had always felt it, buried deep down in his bones, but now it fought for control. Fought to escape, to take over, and slaughter everything that moved. Deer. Wolves. Humans. Children.

In the forest, surrounded by the setting sun, Clyde struck a tree with his fist, feeling the pain as his knuckles collided with the bark, drawing blood. But he didn't do it out of frustration. There was a much darker reason behind the impulse. He needed to draw blood, because he felt it too.

The hunger. The violence.

It wasn't just the monster inside him that craved it; he could feel it within himself as well. All the years he'd spent suffering without knowing why, anxious within safety, restlessness within walls; this was why. Because the monster he felt inside him wasn't something else. Wasn't some other being separate from him.

It was him.

It was instinct, survival, longing, rage. He felt the desire the same as it did. To hunt. To draw blood. It was wrong, but he wanted it, needed it, like a caged predator desperately searching for something to chase. Something to allow it to be its true self.

Clyde needed blood. So, he struck the tree again, drawing his own. Again he hit it, blood now pouring from his knuckles as he screamed, trying to hold back the monster, trying to fight the urge to find any deer who'd left tracks in the dirt and rip out their throats, fighting the need to hunt the wolves he'd seen and break their teeth from their bodies.

As his fist struck the tree again, a memory flashed in his head.

The wolf screamed as he hunted it.

Another strike. More blood drawn.

It reached the fence, begging for something to save it. Cutting its own paws as it tried to crawl its way out of the wire, wailing in agony and fear.

Clyde began to scream.

The wolf cried out as he dragged it back from the fence and ripped its skin from its body.

Clyde cried out louder, drawing blood one final time before collapsing on the ground and looking at his hands, now stained in red. He remembered how it felt to kill the wolf. How it felt to kill all of them.

Natural.

Suddenly, a voice rang out in his head.

"What if the wolves find me, Mom?"

The voice was his own, and with it came a new memory. One from before the wolves, before everything went dark. The only clear memory he'd ever had from before it happened.

He was young. Very young.

He'd seen the wolves in the forest and heard them growl as they'd run behind the trees like monstrous shadows, attacking a deer in the field. He'd seen

their teeth as they'd chased it down and torn out its throat. He'd seen the blood and heard the cries of prey.

It horrified him.

Running as fast as he could, he left the forest, running into the cabin and into his mother's arms, crying as he did.

"What's wrong?"

"I saw... I saw..." he stammered, unable to use the words; even they seemed terrifying.

"It's okay," his mother said, not forcing him to speak, only holding him. He listened to her breathing, calm and deep, and he tried to replicate it. Tried not to be afraid.

But the monsters were still out there.

"Wolves," he finally said, voice cracking, eyes watering. "They killed a deer. I saw... I saw blood."

"Oh, baby," she said softly, holding him closer. "I'm so sorry."

"How could they do that?" he asked. "Why would they hurt it?"

She sighed, giving him a warm smile before leading him to the couch and sitting down beside him. She could have told him anything, lied to make him feel better, but instead she told the truth.

"Because they're wolves. Hunting is what they do, who they are."

"Monsters," Clyde whispered, remembering how the teeth had dug into the throat.

She wiped the tears from his face and smiled once more. "They are not monsters, Clyde. They may look scary, but they're just animals, same as the deer."

"But why did they kill it?" he asked, stammering, hands shaking.

She hesitated for a moment before holding him closer and taking his hand in hers. "Every animal that exists was created for a purpose. Sometimes it's clear and beautiful. Bees pollinate the flowers. Beavers build dams. Even elephants will use their tusks to dig for water in a drought, providing a source of water for the rest of the animals.

"But other times, the purpose is different. Wolves are like all predators in nature. They exist to hunt. It's what they do. And it may look scary and evil, but it's not. Because if the deer were never hunted, eventually the population would grow too large, and they would eat all the grass. Then everything in the forest would die.

"So, wolves aren't like people; they aren't evil or cruel." She held him tighter. "They're just hunting like they were designed to do. It's what they are. It's their purpose. They exist for a reason, even if it's scary."

The tears had stopped, but he was still shaking. "What if the wolves find me, Mom?"

She smiled once again, winking at him. "I'll never let that happen."

Clyde screamed, beating his bloodied hands into the dirt, wailing in pain as he fought the urge to hunt. The memory was a beautiful lie. An innocent moment from before the horror had started, before the hunger.

Something new crawled into his mind, a mixture of instinct and recollection, and it pushed him to run.

So he did.

He couldn't explain it, but as the sun began to set, he chased a ghost. Something he'd hunted twenty-five years ago. Something cruel. Something that had screamed louder than the rest.

Running as if possessed, he tore through the trees, hearing the screeching of birds and the flapping of wings as they desperately flew away, as if the forest itself was trying to escape.

Leaving tracks in the dirt, he kept going, remembering the flash of gunfire. How it had alerted him to its presence—the prey he'd slaughtered.

Suddenly, he reached the spot where it had happened and remembered a cry of desperation. The prey in front of him.

Clyde couldn't remember what it looked like, only its screams, and its heartbeat. He could still

feel it pounding inside the man's chest as he crushed it. He could still see it, the look in the prey's eyes as it screamed without a voice.

In an instant Clyde realized where he was.

Where he'd found the tooth.

Knees hitting the dirt, Clyde reached his hands over the cold soil, parting it with his fingers right where the tooth had been. The sign of the broken pieces that lay beneath. The mark of the grave.

Clyde dug.

Before long he was covered in dirt, but he kept digging, searching for answers buried in the mud. Finally, he found them.

It was four feet down and stacked in a pile, white bones still stained black with dirt. Clyde reached down and pulled the pieces out of the hole one by one.

A skull broken in half. A twisted spine. A shattered jawbone missing all of its teeth. Dozens of other pieces broken and distorted, barely recognizable. Finally, a rib cage impaled in the chest where the heart would go, bones caving inward, still stained red.

All of it was human.

CHAPTER THIRTY-EIGHT

With only a flickering light in the corner to light her path, Riley walked through the police station, stepping over the carpet still stained in blood, moving past the handful of prisoners still locked behind the bars at the far end of the room.

This place didn't scare her anymore. It wasn't the reason her heart was racing, the reason she felt her skin crawling and every instinct in her body telling her to run away and leave this town forever, like she should have done long ago.

She'd come for answers. Her friendship with Hank had denied them for far too long. Now that Betty was dead, there was no choice left. She couldn't let it go, not even for Hank or Linda.

If they were hiding a monster, she had to know.

She stepped into Hank's office, finding him behind his desk, crying as he stared at an old photograph. From where she was she couldn't see it clearly, but it looked like it was a photo of the same woman from Linda's desk.

"This has to end, Hank," Riley said, kind but firm.

"I know it does," he said, nodding with regret.

"Where is the evidence? I know you. You would've kept something."

"I gave it to Oliver."

"Good," she said, stepping closer. "Now tell me. What is it? What have you and Linda been hiding all these years?"

For a moment, Hank's eyes glassed over, and he almost spoke the words without thinking. "A monster." Then, he snapped back to reality. "You should go. Take Emma, get out of this town. Forget the kids, forget the Animal." He looked over at her, eyes begging. "Please, this town is sick, always has been. Please just get out now." His eyes cut toward the photograph again. "Before it's too late."

Riley noticed how his eyes glanced at the woman as he spoke the warning, and a question entered her thoughts.

"Who else was it too late for?"

Oliver rushed into his house, not stopping to lock the outside door as he moved into his room, which he locked quickly.

This was it; he could feel it. All the years of searching for the face behind the mask were coming to an end. The Animal was about to be revealed for what it was. Not some supernatural beast or inescapable monster, just a man with a twisted mind and a need for bloodshed. A psychopath, like all the rest.

Monsters didn't exist. Only men who wanted desperately to be one.

Oliver set the file on his desk and opened it, almost afraid of what he would find. Afraid it wouldn't be enough to find the Animal he'd hunted.

But then he saw it. Only two small pieces of evidence, unconnected, unexplained, and yet it was enough.

The first was a bag containing the only physical evidence found at the scene: a few pitch-black hairs, long and jagged. On the bag was written the origin of the hair, the fur, but Oliver wouldn't have needed it to know what they were, the beast they originated from.

Timber Wolf.

But even more haunting was the second piece of evidence: a single photograph, the image old and faded, but visible enough to reveal the secret, reveal a glimpse of the cruelty it was spawned from.

The photograph was of a family, standing in front of the game ranch at the edge of town. In the photo, the ranch seemed alive with green trees reaching up into a blue sky, nothing like the monstrous forest he now recognized.

The man in the picture didn't surprise Oliver. It was exactly who he'd expected: Arthur Conners. In the photo he stood tall, chest puffed out, attempting to give himself a look of power, of dominance, holding an old rifle in his left hand.

His right hand reached around the shoulders of a woman and held tight to her neck, as if to claim ownership. On the woman's face was a smile, but Oliver saw the slight hint of pain behind it. The man was hurting her, even as the photo was taken.

The woman was the same one from Linda's photo, still smiling through the discomfort, seeming to glow in front of the tall silver fence of the ranch.

Even though this confirmed what Oliver had thought, that Arthur Conners had married the woman in Linda's photo and beaten her, it wasn't the thing that caused the chill slowly crawling up Oliver's spine. It wasn't the sign of the monster, the Animal hiding within.

Suddenly, Oliver found it hard to stay calm. Everything was becoming clear, but his eyes wouldn't leave the photo, looking in shock and horror at the third person there. The source of the monster. The Animal itself.

It was a child.

With the moonlight shining brightly behind him, Clyde stepped into his cabin, body covered in dirt and mud from digging up the buried secrets.

As he stepped inside, he saw the woman sitting on his couch, watching him with eyes that were both kind and terrified.

Linda.

Somehow, he'd known that she'd be here to check on him, to tell him he wasn't a monster, convince him that the Animal didn't exist outside of his mind.

He was tired of the lies.

Clyde knew what he was now: a killer, an animal that only existed to survive, to hunt its prey and spill their blood. He just didn't know why, didn't know what had happened to make him this way, chipping away at his humanity until only the monster was left.

Before she could speak, before she could lie, Clyde threw what was in his hands down in front of her. The broken, shattered bones made a crack as they impacted the floor, spilling out over each other. The skull landed closest to Linda, both pieces of it twisting on the floor to face her, as if even the dead were crying out in pain, agony, and fear of the Animal.

"Who is that?" Clyde asked, tone almost a growl.

A haunted expression grew across Linda's face, knowing it was over the moment she saw the skeleton. Unable to lie anymore, she finally spoke the truth in a whisper, as if she was afraid the earth itself would strike her down at the mention of it, out of fear she would bring the monster back.

"Your father."

"Her name was Alyvia," Hank began. "The day I met her was the day Linda came to my home, crying, begging me to help save the woman. I still remember what she looked like when I first saw her."

Riley saw Hank's mouth quiver as he spoke, guilt and regret pouring over his face.

"Her whole face was bruised, black eyes, purple cheeks, and she held her shoulder in pain. It had been dislocated when her husband had thrown her across the room and into the wall. I've been a police officer all my life, and not once before or after have I seen a woman beaten like she was. The cruelty in her scars."

"Her husband?" Riley asked.

"Arthur Conners," he answered, rage in his voice. "I wanted to go and kill him on the spot. Beat him till he bled like she did, but I held back. Tried to do it the right way.

"I told her that Linda and I could protect her. That she had to leave him and get away from that monster." Another tear fell from his face. "But she wouldn't go. Not for her sake, but for her son's. She was afraid if they ran, he would find them and hurt the boy too. But then he did anyway.

"A few months later, she brought the boy up to see Linda. His father had struck him multiple times and shoved his head into the ground. The trauma was so bad," Hank stuttered, voice full of pain. "His words were slurred, and his memory was shaky. The boy could barely tell us his own name."

Hank closed his eyes, shaking his head. "We told her to run, to get out of this town, escape while her boy could still breathe. At first, she was still too afraid, but then a few days later, when her boy could finally speak again, she decided to try. I set up a safe house for her out of state. All she had to do was get the kid out of the house and drive."

Another tear fell. "We thought she had. We thought she'd escaped. Until the safe house called. They'd never shown up."

Then the wolves came.

Oliver saw it now. The grisly picture. The tormented truth. The woman had tried to run, tried to save her child, but she hadn't escaped. Hadn't gotten away.

There was no obituary that mentioned her death, no signs of escape. She had merely vanished from the earth that night, along with her child.

The old man had said that the wolves had come into the game ranch after the beatings had started. Monsters brought in for a reason: to feast on prey.

A chill crept up his neck as he put the information into a single thought, visualizing what had happened. What the wolves had done.

Arthur had been planning it. He'd known she was going to leave, so he'd brought wolves in. Then, when she'd tried it, he'd beaten her for the last time, as well as their son, ensuring they wouldn't be able to get away once he threw them both into the forest, bleeding and wailing in agony.

Food for the wolves within.

Oliver's fingers ran over his notes, illuminated in the darkness.

No evidence had been found. No traces of their bodies. The wolves had eaten them—everything that could be found, devoured by monsters.

With haunted eyes, Oliver looked at the original newspaper, detailing the slaughter twenty-five years ago. The Animal who'd killed them all.

Or at least, they thought the wolves had eaten everything.

"We promised to protect her," Linda cried. "We promised we'd protect you."

Clyde stood still, not saying a word. After all these years, he'd finally learned what his life had been before the memory loss. Only to learn his father had been a cruel fiend who had beaten his wife and tried to murder his own son. A tear fell from Clyde's eye as he realized the reality behind his true nature. His father was a monster.

Monsters breed monsters.

"I'm so sorry," Linda continued to cry. "By the time we came, it was too late. You were both already lost to the wolves. Hank beat your father within an inch of his life, but we couldn't do anything. We couldn't prove it, and we couldn't save you. We... we thought you were dead."

In a moment of sorrow, she moved closer to him, but the movement made his instincts flare, and he jumped back, not scared of her, but ready if she attacked. He remembered this feeling, the feeling of assuming everything that breathed would attack him, taking every movement as a threat of bloodshed, and desperately seeking survival.

Linda wept as she saw him move away, horrified at what he had become. "If we had known... if I had known you were alive..." Her cries got louder. "I'm so sorry, Clyde. I'm sorry we left you here... in this place."

She cried more, almost wailing, and Clyde felt something buried within himself tensing up. The monster inside himself had heard it: the cries of prey.

"I thought he was dead," Hank said, eyes glassy, mind somewhere else. "Even if the wolves didn't kill him immediately, he wouldn't have survived long. I swear I thought he was dead."

Riley could feel the dread in his voice as he began to relive the same night that had been forever burned into her own mind.

"Then I got the call twenty-five years ago. The neighbors heard screaming. By the time I got there, everyone was dead. Except you. I saw it in your room, covered in your parents' blood, about to kill you too, and I fired.

"The first round hit its shoulder, buckshot, point-blank. Should've taken any man off his feet, but the monster just turned to me, looking right in my eyes for a moment." His eyes almost went white in front of her. "Then it charged.

"I shot again, in the ribs and finally the chest, but even then, it barely went down. It lost enough blood to kill three men, but it wouldn't stop breathing. Wouldn't die.

"Finally, I took the mask off, ready to shoot it again when I saw it." Hank started to cry. "The face of the boy I'd left to die for over ten years, grown up and in pain. But different, violent, hungry. Not a boy, not even a man. Something else. Something we'd left him to become. Something his father broke, and the wolves created."

Oliver couldn't breathe.

A child, in the forest alone. Surrounded by predators, by hunting wolves. And yet it hadn't died, been eaten, or turned into prey. Somehow it had survived the wolves' teeth, survived even their claws.

The silence in the room could be felt as Oliver realized what the timber wolf fur meant, why it had been found at the scene. It hadn't been a costume. Hadn't been fake fur. The Animal had ripped the skin from wolves' bodies, torn it from their flesh, and worn it as its own.

Unable to stop his hands from shaking, Oliver felt it now. What Riley had always felt. That the Animal wasn't human. That it really was the monster the legend told it to be.

She'd been right all along. It couldn't have been human, not in its bones. A grown man thrown into the midst of wolves would be slaughtered in an instant. A child's throat would be ripped out before it could even squeal, even if it had an intact mind.

Oliver's eyes crept over to the X-ray. The fractured skull, the broken mind. He saw the truth now, the horror he'd never expected.

The skull was human. But the mind wasn't.

Not anymore.

"It wasn't your fault, Clyde," Linda pleaded with him. "It was never your fault."

Clyde held back the Animal inside him, forcing the instincts to stop listening to her cries, to stop wanting to silence them.

Another tear fell from his face. "I killed them," Clyde said, voice broken.

"You don't understand. Please listen to me," she sobbed, voice begging him to stay with her, trying to calm him, as she had probably tried to calm his mother.

"Clyde, I operated on you that night, twenty-five years ago. I x-rayed your skull and saw what your father had done to you. The brain damage was unlike anything I've ever seen. Bone chips resting in your head, causing increased aggression, constant fear, forcing you into an eternal state of fight or flight.

"The fracture had also caused memory loss, but it wasn't just the memories you already had. You'd completely lost the ability to form memories at all. You were a child thrown to wolves, without the ability to think. You couldn't form emotions or think rationally. You couldn't remember what or who you were. Unable to retain any thought for more than a single moment. Except for..." she stuttered.

"Except for instincts."

Wolves howled in the distance.

"Somehow you survived," she continued. "Somehow instincts took over, forcing themselves to be learned inch by inch, ingraining it in your very being. That's all you had become. Instinct. No emotion, no thoughts, no soul. Just the need for survival, the need to hunt.

"For over a decade, that's all you were. An Animal."

Clyde felt it now more than ever, instincts taking over. He couldn't remember the years in the forest, but he could feel them, echoes of the instincts learned.

Hunt what runs.

Kill everything that breathes.

Even now he felt it, screaming inside him each time Linda cried, desperately wanting to slaughter her, rip her throat from her body and let the blood pour from it.

"Then, twenty-five years ago, your father went hunting. When you saw him in the woods, somehow a memory of pain broke through. You remembered cruelty. You remembered what humans did.

"So, you killed him. Then you broke through the fence and went hunting for more. When you found the street, you killed everyone, everything that was the same species as your father. But it wasn't you, Clyde. It was instinct. To you they weren't people, they were just prey. Your mind was too broken to know the difference. A wolf can't be blamed for hunting sheep. It's who you were, what you had been forced to become, until that night when I finally repaired what I could of your mind; fixed what was done to you. But what you'd become wasn't your fault."

For a moment, he said nothing. He felt it, the memory of instincts, how it had felt to kill them. To him, to whatever had taken over inside of him, slaughtering them that night had been no different from killing the wolves or hunting the deer. They were all animals, all prey.

But that didn't make him innocent.

"I still did it," Clyde said, voice hollow. "I still killed them."

Suddenly, his eyes cut toward her.

"Why didn't you kill me?"

"I couldn't kill him," Hank cried. "I couldn't let the other cops find him. I had to protect him. Like I had promised I would."

"What did you do?" Riley asked, skin crawling, memories of fear returning.

"I called Linda. She came with an ambulance and operated on him that night."

"You saved it?" Her voice was horrified, full of betrayal. "You saved the monster that killed seventeen people, killed my parents?"

"I... *we* had to try. But he still should have died." Hank's face went white with fear. "He'd lost so much blood... nothing should have lived through that. He should have died that night."

"What else did you do?"

"I got rid of as much evidence as I could before the rest of the police arrived. What I couldn't get rid of that night, I burned later, including the wolf skin he wore, removing any traces of the man behind the monster. Then a few days later we searched the game ranch and found Arthur's body. There was barely enough left to bury, but we did."

"This thing you saved, the monster you've been protecting..." Riley's voice was a whisper, terrified of the Animal who'd attacked her, who'd haunted her thoughts every waking moment of her life since that night, even more scared of the question she was about to ask.

"Is it still alive?"

How could it have lived?

Even with a perfect memory, most still would die in a forest surrounded by wolves, by predators. Yet it had lived ten years: hiding, running, and finally killing.

When had it become a monster? When had its instincts stopped forcing it to hide and allowed it to hunt, to draw blood from its predators?

In that moment, Oliver knew he had been wrong all this time, thinking that the Animal was like the new predators, thinking it was like the serial killer who'd murdered his mom.

Thinking that revealing the Animal's identity would take away the horror.

It might have a face, but Riley had been right. Whatever had survived this, over a decade of being hunted, knowing only instinct, only survival— if it had once been human, it wasn't anymore.

It never would be again.

"You let me live," Clyde said in confusion. "You let it live? The monster inside me?" He could feel it under his skin, trying to burst through, trying to escape and cut down Linda where she stood.

"You're innocent, Clyde. You deserved a life. We had promised your mother that you'd have one."

"A life?" Clyde asked, struggling to hold the instincts back, shaking as he did. This feeling, this instinct, it was his life, who he was inside. For the past twenty-five years he'd stood still, unable to live, unable to sleep, knowing something was wrong. And it wasn't the forest or the monster. It was this... this cruel lie. Clyde looked over the cabin, seeing its true nature for the first time. The makeshift cage they'd kept him in, hoping he'd never remember the forest. But it hadn't worked. He had never forgotten the instinct.

It had just lain dormant, waiting.

It was his life. The monster was all he was. All that had been left from the forest, every other memory and piece of him, chipped away, leaving nothing else. It had never gone away, never would, because there was nothing left of him to replace it.

He was still the Animal.

As the thought flashed into his mind, the wolf inside him cried out, almost forcing itself out of his skin, baring its teeth to slaughter Linda.

Clyde fell to the floor, fighting it, fighting his instincts. "Get out."

"Clyde, no," she said, stepping closer, tears falling from her face.

"Run!" he growled.

He saw it in her eyes then. The look of sheer terror. She'd seen it in his face, even if just for a moment. Felt its presence fill the room. The Animal that had never died.

She stumbled backwards, face drained of color and eyes drained of hope. Then she ran, as fast as she could. Away from him, away from the monster he'd become.

Clyde stayed on the floor, fighting against it: the instincts buried deep within.

The Animal was still inside him, and it wanted out.

"This whole time," Riley said, voice broken as a tear fell from her face. "It's been alive all these years, and you knew? You knew!"

"I'm sorry," Hank cried, "but I had to protect him. I promised."

"It murdered innocent people. It killed my parents."

"That wasn't him. He was sick. He's not a monster, he's just broken. Clyde–"

"No!" Riley screamed, holding her hand out to stop him. The Animal didn't have a name. It couldn't. She couldn't take it if it did.

Hank opened his mouth to continue but then hesitated. He had to have known he was defending a monster, pleading that an Animal was still human.

"Where is it?" Riley growled.

Hank said nothing.

"Where is it!"

"Riley—" Hank said, pleading with her.

Suddenly, the realization hit her. "The game ranch. You've hidden it out there all these years."

In a burst of anger, she turned for the door, thinking that maybe if Hank was right, maybe if even a piece of it was still human, she could kill it now and end this twenty-five-year nightmare once and for all.

But the moment she took a step, Hank leapt from his chair and grabbed her arm, voice terrified and eyes bloodshot.

"No!" he screamed. "You can't! It's still inside him! I've seen it behind his eyes! This new case is bringing it back. Linda is there now, trying to talk to him, but if he sees you..." For a moment, Hank looked as though he might die on the spot, struck dead from terror at the mere idea of the monster's return. "If he sees you, it'll come back. Back for its prey. Riley," he begged, "if you go there, it'll come back and kill us all!"

Cold, haunting thoughts of death surrounded her, almost suffocating her from within. It had never died; she'd never escaped it. It was just waiting for her, stalking from afar. Still hungry for blood, for *her* blood.

It wasn't human. It might have been once, but whatever the forest had done to it had made it the monster she remembered. The Animal that she'd witnessed.

It didn't have a name. It couldn't.

Her mind went back to the thoughts of a child hiding under her bed, covered in the blood of her parents, too scared to say anything else but the horrifying truth.

Animal.

CHAPTER THIRTY-NINE

He'd done it.

After years of searching, beginning to think it was in vain, Oliver had finally found the monster, or at least the man behind it. The child of Arthur Conners thrown to the wolves and left to be devoured, only it wouldn't die.

The only place that made sense for the now-grown child to be was the game ranch. It was old, abandoned—the only logical place to hide an Animal.

Oliver was still in his room, frantically writing everything down. A record of his discoveries, a ledger that only Riley could find, a backup so the information didn't solely rest with him.

Just in case he was right about what might happen.

Part of him wanted to leave right then. He'd found the Animal, and even though it was a far worse monster than he'd expected, knowing the truth of the Animal would still hurt the legends. If it was human, if it had a name, then it bled. If it bled, then it wasn't a monster. At least not to those who'd believed in the stories all these years, the legends told of death itself.

If the Animal was truly gone, if the man was all that remained, then maybe the legend could die. Maybe if he stopped it before the new predator brought the Animal back out, then all of this madness could finally end.

But that was why he couldn't leave yet. The new predator.

In his grief, Hank hadn't just given Oliver the evidence of the Animal; he'd given him everything. Files upon files of evidence on the new predator, who was evidently much worse at covering his tracks.

Oliver spilled out the files on his desk, quickly arranging the evidence below his suspect list, looking over each piece carefully, trying to see the full, grisly picture come into focus.

There were photos from the crime scenes, some from places the cops had kept Oliver from going. Others were from the camera at the police

station. There were also blood patterns, and the single piece of the predator's costume that Riley had cut off: an ear removed at the safe house.

The more Oliver looked at it, at the twisted puzzle created from the insanity of a murderer, the more he understood why the police hadn't caught the killer. Why they couldn't.

None of the evidence made sense. Blood patterns were wildly different and frenzied, and the predator's footprints were all over the place, in no discernible pattern. Nothing about it followed logic or gave any insight into who would do something like this.

Unless, of course, you already had a suspect list and knew where to look.

The evidence bag listed the victims' times of death, confirming Oliver's rough guesses and the alibis of most of his suspects.

All Oliver had to do was find the true nature of the killings, a method to this madness, and he would find the man hiding behind the new mask, the spider hiding within its web of darkness, hoping its prey becomes entangled before it sees the monster lurking.

First, Oliver examined two photographs that had been taken of two different crime scenes. The first was from the safe house, when the killer had evidently dropped from a tree to attack a deputy.

The photo showed marks on the grass, two for the feet, two for the knees, and one abrasion in the dirt that almost looked like a handprint.

The second photo was from the forest, where it had killed the old man. A single set of two footprints, no other abrasions around it, too deep to have merely stepped there. It had fallen from the tree again and left another yet different track in the dirt, falling smoother than before.

Tracks Oliver recognized.

Which left four more suspects.

Next, he saw another singular photograph taken from the footage of the police station's camera. A still shot of the monster surrounded by its bleeding prey. Its arms were stretched out, and it looked to be howling to the sky, a cry of victory.

Oliver recognized it too, and he stepped back in disbelief.

Three suspects left.

Another insidious thought crept into his mind as he remembered why Hank had given him the files. What had convinced him to let go of the secret.

Two suspects left.

Dread creeping under his skin, heart racing, he remembered what Riley had told him. That when Betty had died in the woods, every kid had been there, except for one.

One suspect left.

Betty had stood up, and Kelly had tried to save her, screaming for her to get down, but it was too late. The monster had already slit her throat. A cry that had gone unheard, except by the victims left behind and the animals in the forest.

No more suspects.

Backing up in horror, Oliver saw it now. The full picture. The secret behind the new predator. The only identity that made sense, made all of this madness work.

Have to warn Riley! Oliver thought in a moment of panic, and for that single second he let fear take over his caution, turning off the black light and opening the door to his room, prepared to run through the entire town if he had to.

Anything to warn her of the monster he'd found.

But the predator was waiting outside his door, cloaked in the dark image of a wolf, grey mask and faux fur covering its body, and without hesitation it stabbed Oliver in the chest.

As he felt the blade cut through his skin and bury itself in the flesh beneath, he remembered his mistake. When he'd rushed in, in his hurry to find the Animal, he'd left the outside door unlocked.

Careless.

The predator pulled the sharpened bone from Oliver's chest and then shoved it back in, underneath his ribs, ripping his stomach open, before it threw him down to the floor.

433

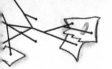

Oliver didn't feel the impact of his body hitting the hard wooden floor. The cuts had already caused him to go into shock. All he felt was warmth as his hands touched his chest, and he felt the blood pouring out from it.

For a brief moment, the shock took over, and Oliver's mind drifted away from reality and into the hallucinations of a dying soul, where truth often lay. Deep down inside, there was something he had never admitted to himself. A secret he'd buried in his mind, too ashamed to even confess the thought.

He'd always blamed his mom for dying.

Even if he'd never said it, it had never been the hitchhiker he'd truly hated. Instead, it had been his mother he resented, for letting that monster into her car, for trusting someone, and leaving him.

For being so careless.

But now, mind coming back to him, seeing the killer above him, cloaked in the monstrous features of a wolf, Oliver realized he'd been wrong.

It had never been her fault. No amount of paranoia or distrust would ever save you from a fate destined to happen. She'd never been wrong, never meant to leave him. She'd just made a mistake, just as he had.

Sometimes you dig your own grave.

The words of the monster standing over him broke through his thoughts, bringing him fully back to reality, to the moment of his own death.

"Do you know how long I've waited to do that?" the voice behind the cracked mask said, looking over the files on Oliver's desk, the ones of the new animal. "Just had to wait long enough for you to find the Animal for me."

The voice didn't surprise Oliver. But he didn't give it the satisfaction of a response.

"You found it, didn't you?" the predator said, moving closer to the light switch, ready to illuminate the room. "You found the Animal."

The light flipped on, taking away the dark and revealing every note, every paper, that Oliver had left on his desk or attached to the wall. Dozens, even hundreds of them, all containing the secrets he'd found, the most recent containing the identity and location of the Animal.

But it was blank. Like all the rest.

For a moment the killer stood in shock, almost frozen in place as it realized its answer wasn't there; inches away and yet hidden from view.

Oliver started to laugh. Quietly at first, but then it grew, until he was hysterically laughing at the killer in front of him. The monster who'd killed countless victims, stabbed Oliver in the chest to find its target, and was now kept from it by a single black light switch, hidden underneath his desk.

"What is this?" the monster asked in confusion before turning its head, wolflike features following

the movement as it stared at Oliver in complete disbelief, unable to make sense of the blank pages.

Finally, its anger took over, and it knelt down, ripping its mask off to show Oliver its face and putting a knife to his throat. "Where is the Animal?"

Oliver's answer was to spit blood in its face.

"Where is it!" the killer growled, pushing the knife further against his throat. "I'll kill you!"

Coughing up more blood, Oliver laughed at the threat. "You already did. You should have waited." More blood came out, and he felt his heart slowing down. "Idiot."

The monster holding the knife screamed in primal anger, dropping Oliver back down and searching the room for whatever else it could find. Anything there to answer the question it had come to seek.

Finally, it saw the X-ray.

"The doctor knows..." the predator whispered in shock. Then, with a twisted grin, it turned back to Oliver and spun the bone in its hand.

For a moment, it bent back down beside him and pressed the blade against his throat. But then, in a moment of cruelty that only humans are capable of, it didn't kill him, instead leaving him to bleed out in pain. A slow death.

As it walked away, Oliver's vision started to fade, but he spoke to the new predator one final time.

"You don't know what it is. You don't know what you're bringing back." More blood filled his lungs and dripped from his mouth as he issued the final warning.

"It's going to kill you too."

The predator said nothing as it walked away, putting its mask back on and leaving Oliver alone in a pool of his own blood.

Within a few seconds, Oliver could no longer breathe. Within a few more, he felt everything around him grow blurry, a haze of images that looked real and yet were translucent at the same time, as if they were merely the ghosts of what they had once been. This was it. He'd lost too much blood. Even with an ambulance he'd still be dead within seconds.

The first wound had grazed his heart.

It was over now. They'd lost. The killer would find Linda, and it wouldn't make the same mistake it had with him. It would keep her alive long enough to torture her and get the information it needed.

Enough to find the Animal and bring it back.

It wasn't death that scared Oliver; it was knowing the face behind the new predator and dying without warning Riley. Dying without helping to save the victims, without revealing the truth behind the new monster, and taking away its legacy.

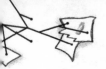
In his last moments, Oliver realized he had never been meant to find the Animal, never been meant to reveal its face. Because it was the monster the legends told of. The Animal that would never die. But the new predator, it was just another mortal coward, like all the rest, like the man who'd murdered his mother. That was the monster he could stop, the killer whose face would remove the fear and leave no story to tell.

But there was no way to warn Riley, no way to inscribe the monster's identity. In the end his death would mean nothing more than his mother's had. Just another corpse that would be forgotten with the rest.

Unless...

CHAPTER FORTY

It was Riley who found the body.

At first, she'd screamed, cursing the new predator, cursing herself for not being there. Then she'd sat beside him, allowed herself to think it wasn't real. That Oliver wasn't really dead. That he was just unconscious, and when the ambulance got here, they'd patch him up. Then he'd wake up, hurt but alive.

And then everything would be okay.

Riley knew it was a fantasy. You couldn't lose that amount of blood and wake up from it, but that didn't stop her from hoping, begging for him not to be dead. Just as she'd done when she was a child, begging for her parents to come back to

439

her. Or as she'd done only a few years ago, when the soldiers had shown up on her doorstep, and she'd prayed they were lying—pretending it wasn't real, that it was just a bad dream.

But eventually, the fantasy ended, and Riley cried.

Soon, the ambulance arrived, but the moment they saw the blood, they knew it was too late. They didn't even have to check for a pulse.

To Riley's surprise, Hank showed up a moment later, not as a cop investigating a murder, but as a friend mourning with her. He sat beside her and said something about Oliver being clever, being a good person, but Riley wasn't listening.

All she could hear was Oliver's voice in her head, telling her no one ever remembered the victims. At the end of the day, they ended up being just another corpse left behind by a monster.

Now, that was him. Everything he'd done had been in vain. He'd found the Animal, she'd seen the notes on his wall illuminated in the black light, but it wouldn't matter, at least not to him. Even if it did end the Animal's legend, Oliver would never get to see it.

His final words to her rang in her ears.

"Sometimes we dig them ourselves."

It was like he'd known. As if deep down, he had always seen his story ending this way, in blood, the same as his mother's.

A final tear streamed down Riley's cheek before her sadness transformed back into rage, and in that moment she wanted nothing more than to go hunting for the new monster.

But a hunter needed tracks. Something to follow.

Police sirens echoed in the distance, deputies coming to set up a crime scene as Riley stood up and looked over the room, searching for signs. Oliver was smart; he would have found a way to leave something, some clue behind for her to follow.

All she needed was a single name.

Instead, she found a location.

Her eyes cut toward the X-ray on the wall. Everything else written about the original Animal was transcribed in hidden ink the killer wouldn't have found, and the picture of the family at the game ranch was meaningless without the story behind it. But the X-ray...

The X-ray would give it a target.

"It's going after Linda," Riley said in shock.

In an instant, Hank saw the X-ray as well and fear flashed in his eyes. Without hesitation, they both moved for the door, desperate to get to Linda before the monster did.

But then, all at once, Riley's eyes caught something else. Something unnatural that she hadn't realized before, sorrow having clouded her mind.

The way Oliver's body was positioned on his stomach, chest resting on his own hand, it wasn't right. That wouldn't have been the position he'd died in. His face should have been staring up, as he would have looked at the killer above him.

So why was he looking down?

As she leaned down over the body and rested her hand on its cold shoulder, she hesitated. It was strange to feel the chill, the body left behind. It felt wrong to move it, but if she was right, then it was what Oliver would have wanted. What he would have counted on.

Breathing deeply, she rolled him over, eyes wide as she saw the message he'd written below, in his own blood. It was a name, but incomplete. He'd died before he could finish the message.

The letters written in blood spelled E V E.

Her mind raced, trying to decipher the name he had written, trying to connect it to a face. But no one she knew, none of the kids Oliver suspected, were named Eve, or anything that contained those letters; neither their first or last names.

Riley's eyes went to the last letter his bloodied hand still rested on. It was incomplete, but it almost looked like a B. No, it was an R.

E V E R

"Ever," she said to herself, going over the possibilities. Maybe Oliver was speaking in code. Maybe it was an anagram. "Ever, Ever."

Then, in a single instant, her skin went pale as she remembered the name. She'd only heard it once, had forgotten it until now, until this very moment when she whispered it quietly to herself.

Rhett's full name.

"Everett."

CHAPTER FORTY-ONE

Riley ran desperately out of the house, away from the bloody message Oliver had left, followed closely by Hank. Dread flashed in both of their eyes like lightning in the night sky, filling their mind with a single spine-chilling thought. They had to get to the hospital before the killer did.

Before Rhett did.

Spinning the sharpened bone in its hand, the predator hiding within the costume of a wolf entered the hallway leading to Linda's office. Its unnatural grey fur was offset by the backdrop of cold white hospital walls as it cracked its neck.

It would find her and make her talk, make her reveal the Animal.

The eyes hiding behind its mask met with the doctors and nurses littering the hallway, blocking its path.

But first, it would make them scream.

They were in the sheriff's car in an instant, sirens blaring in a beacon of panic as they tried frantically to radio the hospital, but no one answered.

Riley felt her hands shaking, terrified they'd be too late. Terrified of losing another friend.

The predator slashed a nurse's throat, her blood spattering on the wolflike mask it wore, blood dripping down in front of its eyes, turning its vision to a haze of red.

Through the blood, it saw more prey in front of it.

A doctor tried to rush at it, but it pushed its blade into his eye. Another nurse tried to run, but it grabbed her hair and violently shoved her face into the wall, again and again, until her expression no longer contained traces of life.

445

Growling echoed into the hallway, once-white walls now stained red.

As it stepped further toward the doctor's office, it saw glimpses of itself in the windows lining the door, little square reflections of the monster it was. Grey fur now painted with crimson, tilted head, canine features.

It was a monster. It was an Animal.

Riley felt it inside her, not just the desperate need to save Linda but the longing to find it. Hurt it for what it had done to Oliver, before it could escape back into the shadows of this sick town.

Every moment that passed felt like an eternity.

Two more nurses fell, hearts bleeding.

An elderly doctor tried to run at it with a scalpel and actually came close, but the predator was faster and took the scalpel from him, taking the weapon just as Riley had taught and then stabbing it into the man's stomach. It looked into his eyes as he fell to the floor, savoring the carnage.

That was who it was. Who he was.

Who he was meant to be.

Only one more thing stood between the monster and the door: a single security guard, holding a black baton in his hands, shaking as he looked at the predator coming for him. Under normal circumstances, it might have lost, but the stories told had changed everything.

It was the mask, the monstrous features, and the legend they represented. The victims were all too afraid to really fight back, to stop it, too afraid it was the real Animal standing before them.

Growling, the predator attacked, and the man fought back. It was a struggle, but finally the monster managed to cut the man's hands, allowing it to rip the baton from him and beat him to death with it. It struck him over and over, blood spattering with every swing, until finally the man's face was broken. When it was done, the killer stood up, its victim's blood dripping down from its fur.

But it didn't howl in victory, didn't scream. It merely took in the moment, appreciating the bloodshed, reveling in the carnage, before finally it moved toward the doctor's office.

Dark clouds blotted out the sun and dread fell over her as Riley realized the truth. They were never going to make it in time.

The predator stepped inside, seeing the doctor cowering in the corner, afraid at first of the monster that had come for her.

But then, the eyes resting behind her glasses saw it: the grey fur, the mask, and immediately her fear went away, her voice calm, merely stating the fact.

"You're not the Animal."

Growling in anger, the predator lashed out, rushing toward her and shoving the knife against her throat. "Where is it!?"

She didn't answer, instead staring in disgust, as if it wasn't a threat.

Hatred almost caused it to slit her throat right then, but it held back. It had to know where the Animal was, had to see the legend for itself.

"Animals aren't cruel," the monster said, running its blade down her face, cutting skin as it did, ready to do whatever it had to. "I am."

Finally, Riley saw the hospital in the distance.

When they reached it, she ran from the car before it could even stop, barely thinking, barely breathing. Maybe it wasn't too late.

But then she reached the hallway and saw the bloodied corpses left behind, the white walls drenched in crimson. It was too late. They were already dead, bodies broken, screams silenced.

Suddenly, a cry of agony erupted from the office at the end of the hall.

Riley ran as fast as her feet would take her, bursting through the door, bearing witness to the horrific scene waiting inside.

Linda was tied to a chair, bleeding, entire body covered in lacerations, barely conscious, eyes hollow and in pain. But somehow, through it all, she saw Riley, the girl they'd found at the house twenty-five years ago, and the old doctor spoke to her one final time.

"Forgive me."

The monster behind her slashed her throat.

"No!" Riley cried, watching the life go out of her friend's eyes, watching the monster standing in the background, tilting its head in satisfaction.

Her fist tightened, and she felt rage in her bones. She wanted to kill it, hurt it, make it suffer just as its victims had. She wanted to hear it scream.

But before she could, Hank reached the door and saw Linda's limp body. The sight of it was enough to freeze even the experienced sheriff for a few seconds, until finally he drew his weapon on the monster who had killed her. "Drop the knife!"

To Riley's shock, the killer listened.

It cursed in frustration at first, but then it dropped the knife, surrendering, taking away her chance to make it suffer. As much as she wanted to, she couldn't kill it like this, not if it wasn't fighting back, and the predator knew it, having dropped the knife to take away her chance for vengeance.

"I know who you are," Riley snarled, words harsh with anger. "Rhett."

For a moment the killer didn't move, until finally it slowly moved its fur-covered hands up to its mask and took it off, revealing the kid underneath: jet-black hair, something off behind his eyes, grinning as he saw her.

"You said if there was another attack, I had to be there," Rhett said as he dropped the animal mask to the floor.

"Here I am."

CHAPTER FORTY-TWO

They locked him up in the holding facility at the police station. From where he now stood, the stains of blood from the murdered deputies could still be seen.

After the arrest, the police had stripped him of his costume. The cracked wolf mask and the fur were thrown into the evidence lockup three rooms down, sealed up tight just in case any other fanatics in this town decided to steal the new animal's fur and keep it for their own.

The other kids had watched as he was brought in, eyes wide with betrayal, but none more so than Kelly. She screamed, cried, cursed his name, fought through two deputies in an attempt to hit him. All the while he only watched her, not saying a word, just solemnly staring into the distance, as if he didn't see any of them. As if he didn't care at all.

Until finally, the kids left, and it was just him and Riley, alone in the police station, dimly lit by the flickering light above them. Through the brief flashes of light, she stared in at the new inmate, no expression in her eyes.

Rhett stared back at her, dressed in a white prison jumpsuit, smiling as she watched him. Basking in the attention.

For a while, she said nothing, not sure if there was even anything to say. She didn't care why he'd done it, didn't care how. He was the one behind the mask, and now he was caught. End of story.

Yet something kept her there. The feeling this wasn't over. The feeling that something much darker had been awoken.

The real Animal.

It wanted out.

Clyde screamed, beating his hands against the floor, cracking the wood and drawing blood.

It had stayed dormant for so long that it had almost been forgotten, its instincts reduced to fleeting emotions and sudden irrational thoughts.

But it had survived.

All it had taken was the mention of its name, of the victims it had claimed that night, and it had awoken from its hibernation, crawling back out of his bones and into his mind.

His neck twisted sideways, an impulse he couldn't stop. He struck the ground again and pain dug into his knuckles, but the blood it had drawn wasn't enough. It would never be enough. Because at their core, it wasn't the blood that animals craved. It was the hunt.

The prey.

"At the hospital, before I took the mask off," Rhett questioned from inside his cell, reduced to nothing more than a common prisoner, "how did you know it was me?"

For a moment, she considered not telling him. After all, he deserved no answers after what he'd done. Eventually, however, she decided that he should have to live with the fact that, in the end, Oliver had gotten the last laugh.

"Oliver wrote your name in his own blood."

Rhett scoffed, both impressed and mortified. "You're telling me I stabbed his heart, and that freak had enough time to write Rhett?"

"No," she said, shaking her head. "Your full name. Everett. He died before he could finish more than the R, but it was enough."

For a moment, Rhett looked genuinely confused as he mouthed the letters to himself before suddenly erupting in laugher, loud and crazed, as if it was the funniest thing he had ever heard.

Finally, when the laughter stopped, he merely stared into the distance and mumbled to himself, shock in his voice. "That crazy freak. He actually did it."

But soon, his attention turned back to Riley. "Aren't you going to ask me why?"

"Don't care."

"Then tell me," Rhett said, moving closer to the edge of the cell, closer to her. "Why are you still here?"

Riley moved closer as well, not shrinking away from his attempt at intimidation. "Because before Linda died, I think she told you something. I think she told you where the Animal is. Who it was."

Rhett nodded, clearly intrigued by her tone.

Riley continued, focusing on what she felt she had to say, her voice low and full of dread. "Whatever she told you about the Animal, whatever name she gave it... she's wrong."

⁂

The screams returned to Clyde's thoughts.

The screams of a deer, legs broken from falling in the creek, a desperate attempt to escape him.

Screams of wolves who had attacked him, only to find their own throats torn from their bodies and their flesh ripped off. Human screams of fear, and the squealing of smaller prey.

Every cry of agony erupted into his mind: hundreds of cries from over a decade of horror all melding together to create an unnatural wail of agony and fear.

It wouldn't let him go.

Soon, Clyde's own scream of fear was added to it as he saw his reflection in the window before shattering it a moment later. But the broken glass on the floor still reflected the image of himself, but different: vicious, unfeeling, wearing the coarse black fur that had been ripped from wolves, from prey.

But even now, he was lying to himself.

There was nothing inside of him, no monster that wanted out that he was fighting against. It was just him, what he'd always been. The reflection he'd seen was his true face, was what he'd become in the forest all those years ago.

It was him who felt the instinct coming back, him who needed to hunt, who felt at home in the forest, among the monsters. Not just a piece of him, but everything he was, every aspect of his being.

Whatever Linda had done that night had fixed his head, giving him back memories, emotions, a conscience, but the instincts still remained. A wolf still stained in the blood of sheep, who now realized the atrocities it had committed yet was still unable to deny its true nature.

"It's not a man. It's not someone like you, hiding behind a costume. It doesn't have a name. It doesn't have a face." Riley's tone was forceful, trying to get him to understand. For some reason she couldn't explain, she couldn't take the thought of Rhett locked up, still thinking he'd won. That he was the new Animal. The continuation of the legend.

"It's just an Animal," she said. "You're not. It's over."

With that, she turned, trying to deny how scared she was. Not of Rhett, but of how close he must've come to bringing the real monster back.

In his office, Hank had been terrified, pleading with her not to go to the game ranch, afraid the Animal would come back. Afraid it still existed. If they hadn't caught Rhett, if they'd let him get away with the Animal's location, he might have really done it.

Brought the Animal back, and killed them all.

Suddenly, Rhett spoke behind her, his words forcing her to stop.

"It's not over."

Clyde heard footsteps behind him. Something was on his front porch.

Stopping himself from breathing, not making a sound, he listened to the pattern. The slight clicks of claws hitting the wood, four sets. The steps were slow, deliberate, anxious. It was scared.

The urge to hunt it flashed into his veins like fire, but he fought the instinct, listening to the prey's breath. It was slow, heavy, old. Clyde recognized it.

Somehow, for a moment, the instinct to kill subsided.

Clyde moved to the door, its wood creaking as he pushed it open, slowly revealing the animal outside. The grey wolf marked with a scar on its face. Old beyond reason, withering body representing a lifetime of hunting. Its eyes were weary, and its bones shook. By every right it should have died long ago, been allowed to rest, but here it was, staring back at him.

In its eyes was fear, just as before, but the fear was different. It was no longer terrified, no longer shocked at the monster's return. The terror was strange, something Clyde didn't understand, at least not at first. For his thoughts were focused on what the wolf had brought, the small animal crushed by its teeth, hanging down from its mouth.

Dead, but uneaten.

"It'll never be over," Rhett said, beating his hands against the bars, voice focused. "Not until the legend comes back. Because you're right. At its core, it's not a man. It's an animal. And no matter how long an animal is caged, no matter how long they're domesticated, all it takes is one drop of blood, one squeal of prey, and the predator will show its true colors once again. It'll come back to finish what it started. It'll come back to kill you all."

"If it does come back," Riley asked, tone still sharp, "it'll kill Kelly too. You realize that, right? The Animal you want so badly to come back will kill your sister."

Rhett smiled. "I guess you better protect her, then. You better protect all of them. Because it will come back. It will hear you scream, and it'll come for blood."

The scarred wolf opened its mouth, allowing its fallen prey to drop from its teeth and onto the wooden porch in front of Clyde. It was a rabbit: hollow eyes, snow white fur ripped in two.

Food from the last hunt.

Then, the wolf backed up, head lowered, tail steady, not daring to take its eyes off Clyde, its grey fur illuminated by the setting sun. Finally, it turned and ran. A hunter going back to the forest. A wolf going back to its pack.

Leaving its prey for Clyde.

Leaving its kill for the Animal.

"You're wrong," Riley said, staring into his eyes, not giving an inch. Rhett wasn't the monster that he thought he was; he was just a kid who was sick. A kid who'd been caught. "It won't come back. It won't remember my cry. Because I won't scream."

With that said, Riley walked away, leaving him in his cell. The new predator, caged like the animal he so desperately wanted to be.

But his words echoed behind her.

"We'll see."

PART THREE

THE PACK

CHAPTER FORTY-THREE

A tear fell from Riley's face.

The air was cold. She could feel the chill on her skin, could see her breath as it floated away from her body, bright and visible for only a moment until it vanished into nothing.

The morgue was as cold as she remembered. Not just the temperature, but the feeling it gave her. A room of death, of decay, surrounded by those who belonged in the cold, for they could no longer feel it. No longer feel anything, the warmth of the sun or the steady pulse of their own heartbeat.

Sometimes she dreamt about it: the moment from her past. In the nightmares, she was still eight years old, trapped in this morgue with the frozen bodies of her parents, unable to escape, unable to save them as they stared back at her, begging her for help. Begging her to do something to save them from the hunting monster. In their eyes she saw fear, as if even in death the memory of the Animal still haunted them, lurking in the shadows their broken bodies created.

She had always told herself it was only scary because she was a child. That as an adult, the chill of the morgue wouldn't scare her. That its chipping white paint didn't really look like an asylum, and that its utter silence wasn't a sign of the dead trying to scream, trying to cry out to the living, but without voices left to do so.

But now, if anything, she was more scared than before.

Because as a child, none of it felt real. The shock had set it, and for weeks she had still expected, deep down, that her parents would walk through the door at any moment and hold her once again. That the nightmares had been all the morgue was. A dream.

Now, she knew better.

She knew that the body lying in front of her was real. Knew the bloodstained neck and the open skin weren't just a hallucination. This wasn't a crazed dream; it was a carcass, the corpse of a friend now gone.

Dr. Linda Parker.

For so many years, Linda had been all Riley had. Even if she was hiding the Animal, nothing could change what she had done for her. How Linda had cared for her, cared *about* her when no one else had.

If it hadn't been for her, Riley didn't know what she might have become. The person she would have turned out to be. She was still damaged, still broken inside from the suffering, but had it not been for Linda, she might not be here at all. Might not have lived long enough to meet the man she loved or to have her daughter.

Both things Linda deserved, yet life had never allowed her to have them. As if punishment for the things she had done, for the Animal she had saved.

As Riley looked down into her friend's eyes, she wished she could have told her it was okay. That she didn't have to feel guilty for protecting the Animal, didn't have to use her dying breath to ask for forgiveness. It would have been given anyway.

Footsteps broke the silence, but Riley didn't turn from the body. She knew who was behind her.

"I know she never told you this," Hank softly whispered, "but she thought of you as her daughter."

Another tear fell down her cheek.

"I know how you feel. I know what it's doing to you inside, the loss, the survivor's guilt. But if she was still here, if she had known her story would end with her dead but you still alive, still fighting, she would have smiled.

"You were her second chance. All she ever wanted was to save you, give you a life. Free you from the pain the monsters caused." Hank sighed, voice full of sorrow.

"That's all she wanted for *both* of you."

Her eyes flinched at the mention of it. She wanted to scream, to fight the implication that they were even remotely connected. Wanted to remind Hank what the Animal was, and what it had done.

But looking down into Linda's eyes, she couldn't. Not here, not now.

"Rhett didn't do this just to be cruel," Riley said, voice low, still almost whispering to respect the dead. "He did it because she told him what the Animal was, and he knew she was the only one who could stop it, who could reach out to the monster and talk it down."

Hank sighed but didn't disagree.

"He knew he was caught, but he still killed her," Riley said, trying to make sense of it. "He still made sure that she couldn't interfere."

"What are you saying?" Hank asked.

"What if this isn't over? What if he killed Linda

because he believes he's already done enough to bring the Animal back? What if he knew putting him in jail wouldn't stop it?" Silence echoed in their bones like thunder, bringing with it fear of what was still to come.

"What if the Animal has already returned?"

Clouds covered the sky, blocking out the setting sun as Riley knelt beside the single tree in the middle of the park.

This was where she had stood with Oliver when they'd realized what Rhett had done. Mutilated his friends, his own sister, just to cover his tracks. Now, it was where she had come to think, and contemplate her options.

Even behind bars, Rhett was so confident about what he'd done. About bringing the Animal back.

Maybe he was bluffing, maybe he was just insane, but if there was even the slightest chance, then she couldn't ignore it. Had to assume it was true. That the monster the legends spoke of had finally returned and was coming for her.

But it wasn't just her it would come for. If it had heard about the new attacks, it would have seen the victims Rhett tried to take. The prey that got away.

The kids.

The Animal would come for her, and when her blood was spilled and cries of pain silenced, it would hunt them next. One by one, killing everyone who survived, ending their lives without thought, without hesitation.

They would scream, but it wouldn't stop. They would beg, and it would rip them apart. They would bleed, and it would tear their hearts out.

Riley thought to leave town. Take Emma. Get as far away as possible. It was the same thought she'd had every day of her life, the same instinct.

Run.

But she had never been able to. Because deep down, she knew that if she ran, it would chase. Like a deer who runs from wolves, it only prolongs the hunt. Eventually monsters find their prey, one way or another.

It might have been foolish, but she couldn't do it. Her parents hadn't run. The flag on her mantel was a reminder of the love of her life, who, when his time had come, hadn't run. She couldn't run either. It wasn't who she was, not who she wanted her daughter to be.

Which left her with only one option. It was risky, and she didn't like it, but she wasn't sure she had another choice.

In the light of the setting sun, glowing like an ember beyond the clouds, Riley saw Kelly walking toward her: tears staining her face, eyes filled with betrayal.

"How could he?" Kelly asked, more to herself than Riley. "I can still see their faces. How... how could he kill them? How could he hurt me?"

Riley considered trying to console her. She could tell her everything was going to be okay, that Rhett was just sick and would never have hurt her. But all of it was crap, and even if it wasn't, she knew how Kelly felt. It wouldn't have made a difference: pain was pain. All you could do was wait for it to go away.

Even though it never did. Never would.

"How dangerous is your brother?" Riley asked.

"What?"

"I know what he's done," she clarified. "I know how dangerous he is as the masked killer, but how dangerous is he outside the mask? What is he capable of?"

"What are you asking me?"

"When I talked to him in the jail, he said he was going to bring the Animal back. Said it wasn't over, that the Animal was coming back to kill us all. I want to know if he's bluffing."

In an instant, the look in the girl's eyes turned from sorrow to fear. "Rhett doesn't bluff." Her hands began shaking. "If he says it's going to kill us, then..." Her voice trailed off, and in her eyes Riley saw the memories of friends, bloodied and beaten. Kelly's hand even crept up to her shoulder, the wound her brother had given her, the scar that marked her as prey for the beast.

Finally, the girl spoke again, voice defeated as hers once had been. "We're still going to die." Tears mixed with the words. "Rhett's going to let it kill me."

It hurt Riley to see Kelly like this. The girl had been so strong this whole time, so brave, but the final reveal of her brother's secret had destroyed her.

"If the Animal comes back, it will hunt us," Riley said, a last-ditch effort to help remind the girl who she was. What they both were. "It might kill us. But we won't die without fighting."

"How can we?" Kelly asked. "I couldn't even stop Rhett from killing my friends. We're just prey."

It was crazy. Riley knew it. Even if she had been able to fully trust the kids who remained, what she was contemplating would still be dangerous—herding up the potential victims in one location.

But she couldn't even trust the kids left. Oliver had been right. There could very well be two killers. While she personally wasn't sure if she believed there were, she couldn't deny the possibility. What she was going to do might invite wolves into the den, hidden among the sheep.

But there was no other choice.

If they were going to fight, if they were going to have any chance at all, they had to stay together.

Not only that, but they had to do so in their own habitat, a place built for security, for fighting against monsters. Her home.

She looked to Kelly, offering one final chance of hope.

"Prey is strongest in a pack."

Within an hour, the kids were ready to go. Dylan and Russel were arguing about dolphins or something equally random, and Gabriella was rolling her eyes, probably at how long it was taking to leave.

To what looked like Hank's genuine surprise, Luke actually hugged him before they left, a move that came out of nowhere, and yet it looked as though it meant the world to Hank. A single moment that might signal healing. Then Luke walked over to Kelly and gently patted her shoulder, supporting her before she took a deep breath and walked back inside the police station to see her brother once more.

Riley wondered what she'd say to him, if she'd cry or scream again, but it didn't really matter. Within minutes Kelly was back, and whatever scornful words she'd said to her brother were left behind her as she joined her friends, ready to head for safety.

But Riley had one thing left to do.

"Goodbye, Hank," she said, hugging him. She was still angry about the secrets he'd kept, but that didn't matter right now. After seeing Linda and not being able to say goodbye, Riley couldn't let the anger get in the way of saying what she felt.

"Good luck," he said, hugging her back before putting his hand on her shoulder. The look in his eyes said more than his words ever could. He felt the same as Linda had, eyes beaming with sadness and pride. The broken look of a man who'd messed up every single aspect of his life: his job, his marriage, his family. Except for protecting her. The single bright spot in his life.

The only thing he hadn't failed at.

In his eyes she saw all of it but knew he would never say the words. It wasn't who he was, any more than it was who she was. So instead of speaking, they merely stood there in each other's embrace, feeling the gravity of the situation.

This would be the last night of the horror. If the Animal didn't return now, it never would. If it did return to hunt them, then they would make a final stand in her home and pray it was enough.

Twenty-five years of terror, dread, and pain ending in a single night. Even if they both lived, they wouldn't be the same after this, and for a moment, Riley allowed herself to enjoy the quiet. The calm before the storm.

But eventually it had to end, and Riley pulled away.

"After I lock up," Hank said, "I'll go to the game ranch. I'll see if the Animal is back. I'll contact you when I know something."

Riley nodded.

"Tell Emma I said hello."

"I always do." She winked. After a second of hesitation, she was about to walk away when she saw a sudden look of sorrow in Hank's eyes once more.

"Riley..."

"Yeah?" she asked, hearing the pain in his voice as he spoke about the monster from the past, the Animal from the legends.

"He's not what you think he is."

She didn't know what to say, didn't know what to think. So she merely walked away, looking into the tired face of her oldest friend. She'd always known what the Animal had taken from her, but looking at Hank now, she realized that it had stolen his life too. Yet still, he protected it.

Just as he had always protected her.

In the distance, Riley saw her home.

It stood out from the rest: old wooden siding, roof so dark it didn't reveal itself in the light, haunting windows lining the top, two wooden pillars in front of the doorway, and surrounded by a metal fence with spikes at the top, circling the house closely. The house where she had watched her parents get slaughtered. Where she had learned what loneliness truly felt like. The house that hadn't kept her family safe twenty-five years ago.

But it was also the house where she had grown up. The house where she'd first danced with the love of her life. The house where she'd watched Emma take her first steps. The house that had kept her family safe ever since that night.

As they passed the other homes on the street, they were unrecognizable. Broken down, hollowed out, nightmarish reflections of the savagery they had once witnessed.

But her home had survived. It had witnessed the gruesome sights of that night, and all the loss she had endured after, and still it stood tall in front of the vast forest behind it, the last sign of life for miles.

She prayed it would survive one more night.

When they finally reached it, she watched as the kids walked up to it, not understanding what it meant, the last lifeline it offered. Russel ducked underneath the doorway, Dylan picked at the wooden siding, and the rest, Gabriella, Luke and Kelly, just stepped in, as if that was all it was. A house.

But Riley waited, staring at her home for a moment longer, until she saw Emma appear in the doorway, moving past the kids, and running to her.

"Hey," Riley said softly, embracing her daughter, feeling her warmth cutting through the frigid air. She'd hated leaving her alone, but she didn't want her daughter to see the morgue like she had. Besides, she could take care of herself for a few hours.

"Are those the kids you're helping?" Emma asked.

Riley nodded. "They're going to stay with us tonight."

Emma's expression changed from light to concerned. "Is the Animal coming back?"

"I don't know, sweetie," she said, brushing her daughter's hair across her face.

To her shock, Emma hugged her once again. "It's going to be okay."

Despite everything that was happening, comfort filled her heart as Riley heard her daughter's words. Even though she never said it, somehow Emma knew how scared she was of the Animal, and rather than be afraid herself, she tried to console Riley. Tried to make *her* feel safe.

Riley kissed her forehead. "I don't deserve you."

Her daughter smiled again before running back toward the house, evidently excited to meet the kids.

"Hey," Riley called after her, voice cautious. She was still wary of who to trust, of the wolves who hid among sheep. "Stay with me tonight, alright? Don't leave my side."

"Okay." Emma nodded.

For a few more moments, Riley waited outside, staring up at her house and the forest behind it. The setting sun was just barely visible now, a crack of light over the horizon, but in an instant it was gone completely, and the night arrived.

The darkness began to slowly creep into the sky, brought to life by the sun's absence. But there was still light in the sky, something brighter than the stars, revealed behind the clouds. A light that should have given hope but instead caused more horror than the darkness.

The light of a full moon.

CHAPTER FORTY-FOUR

Night had come.

Massive clouds crept over the moon, hiding its bright glow, letting the darkness grow like a parasite, slowly taking over everything in sight as if it was feasting on the light itself.

But the house only allowed it to creep in so far. So long as the row of fluorescent lights above their heads still glowed, the darkness couldn't reach them, couldn't bring with it the monsters that hid in the shadows of this town.

The kids sat in the living room. Dylan was on the couch with his arm around Gabriella. Kelly was sitting in a chair, seemingly isolated from the group. Russel stood tall over them, and Luke lay on the floor, staring into the lights above.

Two dogs joined them, Gabriella's behemoth of a German shepherd as well as a Siberian husky that Rhett had bought Kelly for protection. Since, in her own words, they weren't old enough to own firearms.

Across from them, Riley sat on the layer of stone in front of her fireplace, letting the warm flames softly heat her back as she held Emma in her arms. The flames felt good, approaching painful but not quite reaching it, merely keeping her focused, alert. A single fire battling the cold, frozen air.

At first, everyone was quiet, silenced by the gravity of the night itself, but before long the kids began to speak and ask the same questions everyone always did.

"What will it look like if it comes?" Dylan asked.

"What is it, really?" Russel continued. "I know Rhett figured something out. Did you learn anything?"

"What was it like that night?" Gabriella chimed in, voice genuinely interested for once. "What did the Animal really do?"

On and on it went, questions that might have been well intentioned but were no less misguided.

Even if she had wanted to answer the questions, what could she have said? She could have lied, and then they wouldn't be ready if the true monster came for them. Or she could have told the truth about what she'd felt twenty-five years ago, in which case they wouldn't remain calm. More likely, if they knew what it truly was, as Riley did, they would run screaming for their lives, too terrified to protect themselves.

So, she said nothing, merely keeping Emma close, hands shaking as she waited. Waited for the inevitable to come. For the Animal to return.

Having received no answers, the kids decided to debate amongst themselves and provide their own theories.

Dylan went first. "I think it's a real werewolf."

"Werewolves aren't real," Kelly countered, rolling her eyes.

"That's exactly what the werewolves want you to think," he said, nodding his head slowly as if what he'd just said wasn't insane.

"It's just some normal dude," Russel countered. "Everyone in this town probably treated him like crap, and one day he had enough. So he put on a wolf costume and got his revenge."

"I agree," Gabriella said. "I used to think that it was a werewolf, but looking back, knowing what we know now... the Animal being a normal person who was forced too far to the edge and finally snapped to release tension sounds more reasonable."

"I feel betrayed," Dylan scoffed.

"You're all wrong," Luke said, still staring up at the ceiling. "Whoever the Animal was, he had to have known one of the victims personally. They must've ruined his life, so he decided he'd take theirs. Then he killed the rest just to cover it up."

Riley listened to them go on like this for what felt like an eternity, telling stories of a monster they didn't understand, of an Animal that might very well be hunting them as they spoke. Yet their tones suggested not fear but reverence, just like everyone else in this town.

Because the legends only told the stories of the aftermath, of the specifics of the wretched night. It could never capture the feeling of being trapped underneath a bed, watching a bloodstained beast slaughter everything you loved.

It was why legends like the Animal grew. It was why even now, the kids weren't really afraid, not as they should have been. Deep down, even though it would stop the stories, Riley hoped they'd never see the Animal. Never feel the fear. No one should have to.

As they continued to speak of monsters they didn't understand, Riley looked down to Emma, smiling and holding her daughter, scared of what would happen if the Animal came for her. Terrified she wouldn't be able to protect the only thing that still mattered in her life.

It was then that she noticed something. A small piece of wrinkled paper sticking out of Emma's pocket.

"What do you got there?" she asked, assuming it was a drawing or something else her daughter had made.

She assumed wrong.

"Oh," Emma said, a look of recollection flashing in her eyes. "I forgot. This was in the mailbox earlier. But I didn't know what it was."

Riley took the piece of paper from her, ready to dismiss it until in an instant everything changed, and she realized not only what it was but who it was from.

It was small, bent in the middle and slightly textured on the edges. A simple note.

But it wasn't the note that sent shivers down her skin. It was what was written on it. The words left behind. The message revealed.

Nothing.

The light above Hank flickered gently as he stared at the plaques on the wall. Monuments supposed to crown his achievements, which instead only echoed his failures. A lifetime of police work he desperately wished he could take back.

This town had always needed a sheriff. It had always been broken, long before the Animal had come. But it had needed someone else, someone better.

If he hadn't let fear of punishment weigh on his mind, he would have beaten Arthur Conners before he'd ever had the chance to murder his wife and leave his son for the wolves. If he had, an innocent woman would still be alive, Riley would be happy, and the Animal would have never been created.

Then, after the attacks, in a desperate attempt to make up for his own sins, he'd protected the monster, allowing a legend to grow in its wake and a new killer to form. Something crueler that had taken even more victims, all in reverence to the monster.

However, in a moment of selfishness, he knew that wasn't the reason for his regret, at least not entirely. It was what the legend had cost him; his own mistakes. A wife that had left him when he couldn't handle the guilt the Animal caused. A son who was basically a stranger, who hated both the Animal and Riley for stealing his father's focus.

At his core, Hank still believed he was a good person, trying his best to set things right, but that didn't remove the blood from his hands.

If there was any justice in this world, it would have been him lying on the silver table in the morgue, not Linda. It was what he deserved, and later this same night, when he would go to the game ranch to check on Clyde, if the Animal was really back, it might be what he got.

Because he wasn't going there to talk reason to Clyde. He knew he couldn't. Not even Linda could, not really. If the instinct had come back, the need for bloodshed, the true Animal, then nothing he said would matter.

Because you can't talk a wolf out of hunting.

But maybe, if the Animal had come back, Hank would be enough. He sighed as he allowed himself to admit his true intentions. He was going there to die, to offer himself as prey, as bait. Because maybe if it took his blood, its need would be quenched, and it would spare Riley. Spare his son.

Maybe his death would make it right.

In solemn silence, he took one last look at his office before turning the flickering light off and shutting the door behind him.

Under normal circumstances, a deputy would have stayed overnight with the prisoners kept inside, but not enough were left. So the only option left was to merely lock down the entire station and leave the prisoners caged inside.

But as he reached for the keys that hung around his belt, his hands felt the empty space and the grisly truth set in.

His keys were gone.

For a moment, Riley smiled as she looked over the note. It felt so out of place, and yet somehow she felt that she should have expected it. That Oliver would leave a note, a final message, hidden behind invisible ink.

But there was no way to read it. Without a black light, the message was invisible, and it wasn't like she kept a stock of them in the basement. So close to the message, yet with no way to decipher it.

She shook her head and tried to think. Oliver wouldn't have left a message unless it was important, and he would have known that she wouldn't have the correct lighting to read it.

Unless... maybe she did. Maybe this message was different.

She turned to face the fireplace behind her, holding the small white note in front of the flames. A grin spread across her face as the message was revealed by the fire, letter by letter.

Then, the sadness came. She remembered how he looked lying on the ground in a pool of his own blood, killed because of the legend, killed by the new predator he was trying to stop. Whatever was written here would be the last words he ever spoke to her. The final warning he made before his life was taken from him.

Riley stood up and walked out of the room. Not too far, she had to stay close to Emma, but enough to get away from the noise. To have a brief moment of quiet, of peace, as she closed her eyes.

A second later she unfolded the paper once again and read the words revealed by the flames.

Dear Riley,

I haven't been able to shake the feeling that I'm the predator's next target. I can't explain why, but it's this feeling in my gut that is telling me that the moment I find the real Animal, the new killer will attack me just as it has all the rest. That it's been keeping me alive just to find the Animal for it. Otherwise, it would have killed me by now.

A tear hit the note as Riley read the words. He'd known it was coming. All this time, he'd known what it would cost him to stop the legend. And he'd chosen it.

But then, she kept reading, and her sadness turned to dread once more.

If you're reading this, I was right, in which case I'm glad I reached back out to the old man I spoke to and asked him to leave this in your mailbox if he saw my name in the obituaries or on the news as a victim. Didn't figure I could trust anyone else, and I needed to make sure I could warn you about this new killer.

When you asked me what changed my mind about Rhett, and I said I didn't know, I was lying. It wasn't that I didn't trust you. I was just afraid that if you knew the truth, you wouldn't trust me.

The footprints the kids found outside of Kelly and Rhett's house a few days ago. The person they saw watching them. It was me.

I still think it's Rhett. I've always thought it was him, which is why I followed him back to their house that day. I thought he was going to kill Betty or Gabriella right then and there. But then the police station was attacked across town at the same time that I was watching Rhett. That attack, it couldn't have been him.

So, I know one thing for certain. If the killer is Rhett, if at the end of this he's the one behind the mask, then he's not the only one.

Someone else is guilty too.

Stay alive,
Oliver
P.S. Thanks for not thinking I was insane.

The note fell from her hands, and she stood there in shock, unable to move, unable to calm herself. She'd known it was possible, but it's a very different thing to know you might be in danger than to know the killer is right in front of you, invited into your home.

Suddenly, every twisted detail began to make sense. Why Rhett had been so confident, even behind bars. Why the killings had been so effective.

He wasn't the only predator.

In that first horrifying moment, Hank did what anyone would do. What every victim he'd ever interviewed did in the first moment that they felt the shadow of death creep into their bones.

He denied it.

Someone hadn't taken his keys; he had merely left them somewhere by mistake. But then he stepped back into his office and found they weren't inside.

Drawing his weapon, an old black revolver, he stepped back out into the main room, suddenly aware of how dark it was. He switched on the lights, but they did nothing.

In truth, he knew someone had turned off the breaker, just as they had when the killer had attacked the deputies, but once again he fought the truth, telling himself it was just a power outage.

But what he couldn't deny was the cell door.

He heard it first, the banging of metal, the creaking of hinges. Gun drawn, he approached the doors slowly, until finally he saw it. Every cell was open, but every prisoner hadn't escaped.

They were all left inside their own cells, lying on their small white cots now stained with pools of red, throats slit before they could even wake up to scream.

All except one.

Rhett.

<hr />

It could be any of them, Riley thought, suddenly rushing to get back to Emma, heart racing until finally she had her daughter in her arms again, and she breathed a sigh of relief.

Relief that would never last.

"Are you okay?" Russel asked as all the kids stared at her, sensing her discomfort.

She stared back at them, surrounded, trying to find the secret behind their eyes.

The wolf hidden among the sheep.

Cautiously, Hank moved to the edge of the wall, looking down the hallway, seeing what he feared. The door to the evidence room, left open as a sign of the slaughter to come. Rhett had found his wolf skin.

Suddenly, a shadow moved in front of him.

The kids started talking again: light, friendly conversations, but Riley couldn't hear any of it. All she could see was the way their eyes moved, the way their fingers twitched, any sign whatsoever of the horror they could be hiding.

She saw Kelly, still isolated on the couch, tears in her eyes from her brother's betrayal. It could be an act. She could have been faking this whole time. The betrayal of her brother, mourning for the death of her friends.

Red herrings meant to lead Riley away from the truth.

Hank jumped, aiming his gun at the shadow, but it was gone in an instant, replaced by the sound of footsteps echoing all around him. One second he heard them in front of him, the next behind.

The killer was circling.

Or it could be Dylan. That would explain why Rhett had been upset when Kelly had gotten hurt, and why Dylan found all of this so amusing. Why, even now, he was smiling at the mention of the Animal's legend.

It could even be Gabriella. She might have been small, seemingly unthreatening, but Oliver had revealed her darker side.

Her torturous side.

The footsteps moved in closer, and Hank felt his old heart pounding inside of his chest.

Riley looked to Russel, standing tall over the rest of them, always imposing, always making himself a threat. Oliver had said he used to be picked on. Maybe this was his revenge.

Or maybe it was Luke who wanted revenge. Revenge on Riley for what he thought she had done to his life. Revenge on his father for focusing on the legend rather than him.

For the first time, Hank heard growling. The sign of the predator. A warning of death. He clenched his fist and desperately searched the shadows before him. He had known he might die tonight. But not like this. Not to this monster.

But time had stolen his vision, and his eyes struggled to adjust to the absence of light.

Finally, he heard a footstep behind him, and he fired his weapon. But when the muzzle flashed, and the flash of light revealed the predator, it was far too late.

Holding her daughter in the midst of five kids, Riley felt alone. Trapped. It wasn't even the fear of them but the fear of the idea. The paranoia. The distrust.

This was a mistake, inviting them here. But deep down she had truly thought it was over. That the only threat left was the real Animal.

Now that she knew the truth, she couldn't stop thinking about it, staring at them, expecting an attack at any moment, unable to breathe. Waiting for someone to shed their sheep skin and reveal the wolf beneath.

It felt cold, cutting through the skin below his rib cage, the blade crawling its way up his chest until finally it pierced his heart.

In his final moment before death took him, he saw the killer in front of him, clothed in a wolf mask, hiding the face of a child beneath it. But then, in the child's eyes, Hank saw his true intentions: what Rhett planned to do with his body, the reason he had attacked him rather than escaping.

The last act Hank would ever commit in this life.

A final sacrifice.

CHAPTER FORTY-FIVE

It could be any of them.

It had been over an hour since she'd found Oliver's note, but the thought wouldn't leave her mind. The paranoia, the adrenaline coursing through her body, paralyzing her as she waited for any sign of aggression, any attack.

But so far, it hadn't come.

Russel is too close to Kelly, Riley thought in a panic. *If he goes to kill her, I couldn't stop him in time.*

She shifted how she sat on the fireplace, ready to move at any moment, wishing she'd kept the pistol hidden behind her back, wishing she had more than the knife in her boot to protect her, protect her daughter.

Dylan just looked at Emma. What if he's planning on killing her first?

Riley held her tighter, not sure what else to do. It wasn't the threat itself she was scared of. She'd fought the new predator before, whether it was Rhett or his partner. She'd seen a real monster once, and this new killer wasn't it.

It was the waiting that scared her, knowing a killer was within inches of her, close enough to reach her daughter in a few steps, and not being able to fight back. Not knowing who to fight against.

Luke is on the ground. What if he laid there so he could drag Emma away by her feet? So that he could hide a knife in his back pocket?

On and on it went, the nervousness, the anxiety.

They brought backpacks. What if the killer's mask is inside one of them?

Her breathing quickened, struggling to get oxygen as her heart pounded inside her chest, over and over again, waiting for a sign of the monster. Anything to break up the silence she heard in her mind. Finally, a sign was revealed.

But it didn't come from inside the house.

Footsteps echoed, almost imperceptible, but she heard them all the same. The creaking of an old wooden porch as something dark walked upon it, right outside the house. Only five feet away, maybe less.

Suddenly, the footsteps moved again, growing closer to the door, passing by a window on its way, suddenly revealing the monster that lurked just outside, waiting to strike.

It was only a brief glimpse, no more than a second, but Riley saw it. The grey fur, the bloodstained mask peering in at her, stalking them from a distance.

Rhett had escaped.

The other kids saw it too, and in an instant, they were back against the opposite wall, staring at the door, at the monster who'd come for their blood. Their own friend ready to kill them without a second thought.

She could hear the panicking once the glimpse disappeared, frightened kids afraid of where the killer might be. She could see their hands shaking and eyes glassing over in disbelief.

But Riley wasn't afraid. Her breathing didn't quicken, it slowed. Her hands were perfectly still, and her heart calmed down, finding its rhythm once again.

Because this wasn't a monster hiding among sheep. It wasn't an attack she wouldn't know was coming. It was just Rhett, playing pretend that he was the Animal.

That, she knew how to prepare for. How to fight.

Once he passed out of sight, she moved slowly to the door, as silently as possible. She knew what

Rhett was thinking, how his sick mind worked. Before he killed them, he wanted to scare them.

He'd move to the door, beat against the wood like it was a horror movie, trying to build tension with every strike. There was a window in the center, but he wouldn't reveal himself in front of it. He'd keep the monster hidden. It was clever, probably would've worked on most people.

Riley wasn't most people.

Beside the door, she nodded at the kids to stay quiet, watching their nervous faces as she pulled the silver knife from her boot, gripping it tightly.

Then she waited, planning her attack. The moment Rhett beat on the door, she'd swing it open and bring her knife down into his shoulder, causing enough pain to debilitate him. Then, as he writhed in agony, it would allow her to bring him inside and do to him what he had done to Linda, until he confessed the identity of his partner.

Seconds passed, feeling like hours as she waited in silence, focusing on the knife in her hands, on where the target would be.

More footsteps, right outside the door.

She planted her feet, getting ready.

The footsteps stopped.

She moved her hand, ready to unlock the latch.

The monster struck the door, beating against the wood, wild and frenzied, as if an animal was trying to break its way in.

Gotcha, Riley thought as she raised the knife up and got ready to strike. But then, something unexpected happened. Someone cried out.

"No!" Kelly screamed. "He'll kill you!"

It was said through nervous tears, as a cry of warning. A girl trying to protect her, concerned that Riley was making a wrong move. A mistake that would claim her life.

But that wasn't what Riley heard.

Riley stood frozen for a moment, a second away from unlocking the door, as she turned to face the girl, distrust in her voice. "Why did you say that?"

Kelly's expression slowly turned into confusion. "What?"

"Just now," Riley said, moving away from the locked door and closer to Kelly, suddenly anxious. If she had been a second later, if she had already unlocked the door, Rhett would have heard his sister's cry and known what was coming. Known to attack first.

"I was trying to warn you," Kelly stammered, almost convincing.

Almost.

"Like you warned Betty in the forest?" Riley asked with an accusing tone, as suddenly everything became clear. How Rhett always knew the perfect moment to strike. How he'd known to kill Betty just as she'd stood up.

Riley's head shifted slightly at the betrayal. "You've been calling out targets this whole time."

In an instant, the gravity of what she was saying set in, and the other kids moved away from Kelly, isolating her once again. Once they had, they stared at both of them in shock, seemingly not knowing who to trust: their friend or a stranger.

"Riley, no," Kelly stammered, shaking in what looked like fear. "I was trying to warn you. I swear."

Riley said nothing, merely gripping her knife tighter and reaching her spare hand behind her back, closer to the door. Closer to the lock.

"Please, believe me," Kelly cried, moving closer to Riley, pleading with her. "Please..."

Riley looked into the girl's eyes for a moment longer. "I'm sorry. But I don't."

In a sudden flash of movement, she dropped the knife, grabbing Kelly tight by the arm and unlocking the door behind her. Then, without hesitation she threw the defenseless girl outside, into the grasp of the monster lurking there.

She had the door locked once again before either of them could react.

Now that it was done, she stepped back from it, watching them through the small glass window resting in the center. Kelly had collided into Rhett but jumped away in a panic, backing up against the wooden pillar, too scared to run but too scared to stay.

Or at least, that was what she wanted it to look like.

Through the window, Riley heard Rhett chuckle as he took off his wolf mask, revealing his face once more, the unsettled look in his eyes. "Oliver's gotten you too paranoid, hasn't he?"

Riley didn't answer.

"You throw a victim to me just because you get a little frightened. Are you really sure she's the one helping me?"

Riley's silence was answer enough.

Suddenly, Rhett reached over and grabbed Kelly by the throat, holding her back against the wood and drawing a knife. "How sure are you?"

Riley didn't move.

Rhett moved the knife up to his sister's face, inches away from her eye.

"Please," Kelly begged, crying again, trying to fight against Rhett's choking grip.

The knife moved closer, grazing her skin.

Kelly screamed. "Help me!" Tears ran down her face. "Please, Riley, help me!"

A look of insanity flickered in Rhett's eyes, and even the kids behind Riley started to scream, begging her to help their friend, to save her, scared she was innocent. Scared Rhett would kill her as she cried.

"I'll do it," Rhett exclaimed.

Still, Riley didn't move. She wanted to, more than they could have ever known. She wanted to help the girl, save her. Wanted to believe that she really was innocent, that Kelly wouldn't do something like this, that the girl wasn't just another monster. But she couldn't. Not this time.

Not too long ago, in that safe house, Kelly had begged Riley to save her while the new predator held a knife against her throat. Now it was happening again, only this time Riley was calling their bluff.

Praying it wasn't a mistake.

"Okay, then," Rhett said, pushing the knife forward, causing the kids to jump in horror, and for a brief moment Riley felt her heart stop.

Until she saw the blade's path. Into the wooden pillar, missing Kelly's face, not even drawing blood.

Then Kelly turned, part of her face hidden by the silver knife still stuck in the wood, warping her appearance. Her eyes glared at Riley, but her scared expression turned into a psychotic grin.

"You heartless witch."

Riley took a step back as she watched Kelly move from the pillar, her once-scared eyes beaming with enjoyment and thrill. In that single moment, she had become another person. The real Kelly, standing beside her brother, equally mad.

"She did a good job, didn't she?" Rhett chuckled, tilting his head as he watched Riley with an evil smile. "For a moment there, even I almost bought it."

Kelly piped in, voice light. "I guess I saw Betty cry so much I knew how to fake it."

The more they spoke, the more Riley wanted to open the door and shut them up. She didn't feel betrayed, not really at least. She'd never trusted Rhett and had only tentatively trusted Kelly. No, the betrayal wasn't the source of her anger, or her shock.

It was the idea of them. What the legend had done to this town. Two kids who'd murder their friends and laugh about it. Kids who thought it was funny to see the blood spatter and to hear the cries of pain.

This town, this legend, it corrupted people. It didn't change them, but it brought out their true selves. The stories of the Animal crept into their minds until they idolized it, thought it *was* the escape, the way out.

Riley's hand balled into a fist.

"Easy there," Rhett said. "You don't want to do something you'll regret."

"I won't regret it."

"True," Kelly said. "But you still haven't seen the whole picture."

"Oliver saw it," Rhett said, holding up his knife and tapping on the window. "I don't know how, but the little freak actually figured it out. And he even tried to warn you, but you just couldn't see it."

Suddenly, Riley heard movement behind her and listened as the nervous breathing of the kids stopped as suddenly as it had begun.

Something was wrong.

"You see, you're clever," Rhett continued, still holding her attention. "And you were so close. But you forgot two things."

Emma's nervous voice called out beside her. "Mom?"

Riley looked down and saw Emma, staring with terrified eyes at whatever was behind her.

"First, you forgot how alone you really are."

Riley began to turn, realizing the truth, realizing her mistake.

"Second," Rhett growled, "not once in his life did Oliver ever call me Everett."

Riley saw it now. The horror, the full grisly picture, the secret that had been right in front of her. The monsters the legend had created.

The kids were watching her now, each one having covered themselves in grey fur and the mask of a wolf, four of them standing in silence right in front of her, slowly tilting their heads in unison with the two that stood behind, now beating on the door, wanting in.

In that moment, staring at the pack of wolves that surrounded her, Riley realized what Oliver

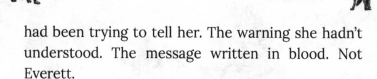

had been trying to tell her. The warning she hadn't understood. The message written in blood. Not Everett.

Everyone.

CHAPTER FORTY-SIX

They surrounded her.

Six killers, dressed as the Animal from her past, heads tilting as they watched her silently, trying to scare her, trying to scare her daughter.

It was working.

Riley couldn't breathe, suffocating as she tried to think of a way to escape.

Rhett and Kelly were behind her, both wearing the wolf masks and holding sharpened bones fashioned into knives, slowly raking them across the wooden door, the scratching echoing into the night.

The monsters in front of her began to spread out, circling her, growling as they did. Even the dogs seemed to join them, both following their masters as they stalked her.

As they moved closer, she heard Emma start to cry, shaking beside her, not understanding why they were holding knives. Why they were going to kill them.

Have to protect her. It's all that matters.

Slowly, Riley knelt down to pick up the knife that she had dropped to the floor, never taking her eyes off the pack of killers who were closing in, fake grey fur illuminated by the light of the house, plastic masks frozen in an expressionless, emotionless face.

It had to be now.

In a flash of movement, Riley threw the knife at the beast in the center, larger, more monstrous than the rest. Russel.

When the knife dug into his leg, drawing blood, the rest of the kids hesitated in shock.

Riley didn't.

She had to make it to the kitchen door. Had to make it outside.

She attacked the killer to her right, shoving whoever was behind the mask into the wall before taking Emma's hand and pulling her through the room, away from the monsters.

But they followed her.

Something pulled on her arm, and Riley turned to see a masked predator, hand on Emma's other arm, dragging her backwards.

Emma cried in pain, but Riley had no choice. She pulled harder, ripping Emma away from the predator's grip and causing them to become unbalanced. Then, Riley kicked them in the stomach, forcing them back, giving her a second to run.

But before she could, she watched as the monster she'd kicked, groaning in pain, twisted its body, moving unnaturally like a monster possessed, bones shifting, shoulders almost breaking. Another scare tactic.

Must be Gabriella.

Riley didn't stay to find out, desperately running through the hallway, dragging Emma behind her and heading to the kitchen. There was a side door there. The only chance at escape.

They were a step from it when she heard the growl and turned to see the German shepherd: massive, teeth bared, leaping through the air straight for her.

Riley pushed Emma out of the way when the dog crashed into her, bringing her to the floor and going for her throat. She managed to block it with her arm, but the animal's teeth dug into her wrist, drawing blood.

Unable to stop it, Riley cried out from the pain as the teeth left her skin, only for the dog to bite her again, this time on her forearm, ripping away a piece of flesh.

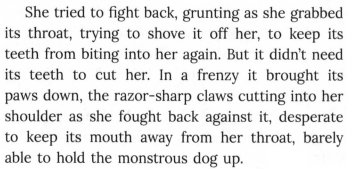

She tried to fight back, grunting as she grabbed its throat, trying to shove it off her, to keep its teeth from biting into her again. But it didn't need its teeth to cut her. In a frenzy it brought its paws down, the razor-sharp claws cutting into her shoulder as she fought back against it, desperate to keep its mouth away from her throat, barely able to hold the monstrous dog up.

Finally, one of its paws found her face, ripping into her skin, carving four cuts into her face, drawing four lines of blood with them.

One for each of its claws.

Emma was screaming. Riley was trying not to scream, just trying to survive, when she heard the whistle. A command.

A moment later, the dog stopped attacking and ran back out of the kitchen, toward the psychopath standing at the edge of the hallway, blade in hand.

"Good boy," Gabriella's voice said.

Another predator moved beside her, and Dylan's voice came from it. "But she's ours."

As they moved closer to her, Riley struggled to her feet, the four lines of blood warm as it cascaded down her cheek, out of breath and wincing in pain.

But still, her eyes glared at them, watching as the dog moved away. "That..." She coughed. "Was a mistake."

They rushed her.

507

Gabriella leapt onto the kitchen counter, graceful as she swiped the knife toward her throat. Riley barely moved out of the way in time before Dylan tackled her, shoving her back against the wall behind them.

She tried to move, but he held her there as Gabriella laughed, slowly moving closer with the knife.

Fur-covered hands on her throat, crazed monster pinning her to the wall, she gasped in pain as Gabriella charged, swinging the knife at her chest.

But something hit the girl, causing her to hesitate just enough for Riley to kick Dylan's legs and give herself enough room to dodge the knife as it passed into the wall.

In an instant, she grabbed Dylan's mask, ripping it from his face before shoving her elbow into his mouth, knocking teeth out and forcing him back in pain.

Then Riley looked to Gabriella and saw what had hit her. Emma.

She had tried to tackle the killer and force her away from Riley. Now she was backing up in fear as Gabriella moved toward her, backhanding her across the face, not yet aware of what Riley had done to Dylan.

"Hey," Riley snarled, causing Gabriella to face her, eyes growing wide as Riley backhanded her in return before shoving her against the wall. With her pinned there, Riley grabbed the girl's wrist and pulled her arm violently, dislocating her shoulder. Finally, in a fury, she struck her again, this time in the eye.

Once the girl's dazed body hit the floor, Riley turned to her daughter, seeing the mark that had already appeared on her face.

"Thanks," Riley said, making Emma smile slightly before they both rushed for the door. Behind them, two more monsters walked into the room, stepping over Dylan, who was still on the floor, mouth bleeding.

Russel and Luke.

Riley was out of the house before they could get to her, but she heard Dylan's crazed laughter echoing through the wood. "We'll get you," he laughed as though he didn't feel the pain from the broken teeth. "You can't run forever!"

Something was very wrong with that kid.

Locking the door behind her, Riley ran with Emma beside her, through the night air, through the grass, and toward the edge of the spiked fence that surrounded the house. Toward the gate within it, the key to safety

But standing in front of it were two more predators. The two alphas, leading the rest, more dangerous than the remainder of their pack.

Both cloaked in the guise of a wolf, Rhett stood tall beside Kelly: larger, more imposing. But they both moved together, focused, hunting as a single pack, gripping their blades and growling at Riley.

Deep, vicious growls that couldn't have come from a human or even a dog.

Then, like the animals they so desperately wanted to be, they attacked, only they didn't go for her. They went for Emma.

Riley moved in front of their strikes, taking a blade to her side as she pushed Emma away and tried to rip the sharpened bone from Kelly's hands. But she couldn't find an opportunity.

Instead, when she tried it, Kelly moved out of the way flawlessly, having remembered the move from when Riley had trained them.

But Riley hadn't shown her how to dodge a kick to the knee, and so she shoved her heel into Kelly's joint until she could hear it crack.

Kelly fell back in pain, leg not broken but badly hurt, dropping her to the ground as she clutched her knee. Hearing his sister's cries of pain, Rhett attacked Riley in anger, tackling her to the ground.

She struck his face, but it didn't stop him. Adrenaline and rage wouldn't let him stop. She'd hurt his sister, and he was angry, defensive, cruel. But he didn't stab her. Instead, he stood up, looming over her as she realized in horror what he was doing.

She'd kicked his sister's leg. He was going to return the favor.

Before she could move, his heel crashed into her knee, snapping the bone.

Riley grunted in pain, biting her tongue so as not to give Rhett the satisfaction of hearing her scream.

But then, as he stepped away from her, he did what all killers did when they thought their prey was defeated. He got careless.

Her hand moved over the grass, finding a rock left there. It wasn't much, but it would have to be enough. So, gripping it tight, she used it to strike his ankle. As he knelt forward in sudden pain, she struck his eyes, drawing blood and bringing him to the ground.

In unspeakable agony, Riley stood up, falling over as she did, her knee giving way. But she didn't have time to crawl.

So she stood up again, tears streaming down her face from the overwhelming strain on her leg as she moved toward the gate, joined by her daughter once again.

She didn't know what she would do when they escaped. She could try the car, but Rhett would have slashed the tires when he'd arrived. Now, with a broken leg and Emma beside her, she wasn't even sure they could get to the forest in time to hide.

But still she moved, limping to the gate, wincing in pain every time her foot hit the ground, until finally she reached it and pushed hard against the metal. Only then did she realize what else Rhett had done.

A chain wrapped around it, held together by a thick metal lock. The same kind she had used at the warehouse.

She couldn't escape. She'd led Emma out here to die.

"Not so funny now, is it?" Rhett growled, standing up, his wolf mask hiding the bleeding eye underneath.

Riley tried to think, holding Emma close, backed against the metal fence, into a corner with no way out, as the pack of monsters began closing in.

Rhett and Kelly stood up first, rising up from the grass like ghosts, costumes dimly lit by the moonlight that escaped through the clouds, making them appear horrifying in the night sky.

Then the kitchen door crashed open, and a monstrous form stepped out from it, having kicked the door down. Russel. Soon, he was followed by the rest of the pack: one masked killer moving unnaturally, their bones clicking as they effortlessly relocated their shoulder, one laughing like a psychopath, and one just staring at her, full of hatred.

Seeing her backed against the fence, Russel howled into the sky, a cry of victory. The dogs joined in, all of them screaming at the moon, having found their prey.

Tears of anguish streamed down Riley's face, mixing with the blood flowing down from the cuts. Her leg was broken, and they surrounded her. She couldn't escape this, couldn't fight them all.

But she couldn't let them take Emma.

As they began to growl, Riley knelt down and whispered into her daughter's ears, afraid it was the last words she'd ever say to her.

"When I attack, run."

Then, Riley reached into her left boot and grabbed the second knife she kept hidden.

She wasn't going to escape. But maybe if she gave Emma enough time, she could make it to the safe room. Maybe she could hide until Hank came to check on them.

Maybe.

Riley attacked, going straight for Kelly. Her splintered knee almost brought her to the ground as she did, but she managed to reach the girl and swiped the silver knife at her throat.

The monster beside her moved to push Kelly out of the way, but it created a slight opening in the middle of the pack.

"Run!" Riley screamed.

Emma did, darting through the opening, rolling on the ground as she had so many times before, trying to escape. She almost made it before a predator caught her hand, staring as it did, body frozen in hatred.

Luke.

Riley tackled him, giving Emma time to escape.

A tear fell down Riley's face as she watched her daughter running for her life, away from the monsters she'd wanted to protect her from.

The laughing predator moved toward the house, but Rhett's voice stopped him.

"We'll find her later." Then he tilted his head to the giant, who in turn grabbed Riley and threw her against the metal fence as if she was a rag doll.

As she lay bleeding on the grass, they all moved in on her like a pack of rabid dogs, hungry for her blood.

Knife still gripped in her hand, every one of her senses dizzy, she fought back, desperately trying to take them with her.

In the end, she had stabbed three of them and struck two more before finally the largest monster struck her face, knocking her to the ground and ending the fight.

As her vision faded, she saw all of them, six predators looming over her in the darkness, wolf masks staring down at her, monsters standing over their prey.

The last thing she saw before she passed out was their faces, animalistic and covered in her blood, shimmering in the light of the full moon watching over them from above as the horror unfolded below, revealing itself for only a moment before vanishing within the clouds once more.

Leaving her in the dark, alone.

Always alone.

CHAPTER FORTY-SEVEN

It was the water that woke her up.

Cold, freezing water hitting her face, shocking her system into action, opening her eyes in an instant. For a moment, it almost suffocated her, numbing her body even more than the cold of the night had. But then the pain of shattered bones broke through the chill, forcing her to gasp for air, body going into shock.

"She's up!" Dylan's voice called out.

Body shivering violently, her vision came back, and Riley looked around, seeing where she was. The upstairs bedroom, her parents' room.

Where the first attack had happened.

Cords cut into her wrists, forcing them to stay behind her back, forcing her to remain tethered to the chair where she now sat. Slowly, instinctively, she tried to force her hands out of them, but they dug into her skin so far that they almost reached the bone.

In front of her stood Dylan, still wearing the wolf outfit, only without the mask, allowing his face to be revealed. As always, he had that insane grin, tongue moving over his bloodied teeth. In his hands was an empty bucket.

Surrounding him were the rest, all five of them, dressed up as the animals they wanted to be but allowing their faces to show, as if gloating about the secret finally being revealed.

She hadn't noticed before, but now, as her senses started to come back to her, she saw the clues in their costumes that revealed the secrets of their attacks. Dylan's mask was missing an ear, the same one that she had cut off at the safe house. Gabriella's was scraped from bark, having climbed the tree in the forest when they'd killed the old man, and Russel's fur was stained in far more crimson than the rest, the blood of all the deputies, where the pack had sent their strongest member. Kelly and Luke's costumes were mostly untouched, one having been watched too closely by his father, the other controlling the situations as a victim, but they still bore a few marks of blood. Finally, there was the cracked mask that Rhett held in his hands, the one she'd broken at the warehouse, when the leader of the pack had attacked her.

Six suspects, six killers, six wolves.

The dogs were even there: the Siberian husky watching her closely, the German shepherd baring its teeth still stained with her blood.

As the grogginess left completely, Riley was forced to sit there, immobile, holding back the cries of pain that desperately wanted to escape. The water was cold, but even it couldn't numb it all.

"I told you the water would work," Kelly said.

"Stabbing her again would have worked too," Gabriella added.

Rhett chuckled. "That will come later."

It was said as an ominous threat, but honestly, Riley didn't care. Emma wasn't with them. They hadn't found her. Which meant she was safe, hiding in one of the locations they couldn't get to. Beyond that, she didn't care what they did to her.

They could torture her with the sharpened bones that each of them held, slit her throat with the knife they carried, or Rhett could even put a bullet through her skull with the pistol in his hand, which she recognized as her own, stolen while she was knocked out. None of it made a difference.

Not so long as Emma was safe.

"I bet you're wondering how we did it," Rhett said, smirking as he knelt down to face her at eye level.

She didn't answer.

"It wasn't hard," he said, continuing anyway. They were clearly proud of what they had done and evidently wanted Riley to know the full scope of their plan. "Aside from Hank, we knew the rest of the deputies, like everyone else in this town, would immediately assume the Animal was back. So, anyone young like us wouldn't even be a suspect. And as far as Hank went"—he pointed to Luke—"we had a blind spot."

Kelly continued the story. "But I knew Oliver would know better, so I came up with the plan to switch out and give each other alibis. Figured by the time Oliver caught on that it was all of us, he would have already found the Animal for us. All we had to do was give the town a new monster to be afraid of, and it all started with that party. Britney, Eric, all the rest, they never even stopped to wonder why I was throwing a party on the twenty-fifth anniversary, or why I only invited a couple of people; practice for all of us to perfect the killings, the switching out between kills, calling out the targets. It wasn't even hard to lure them there; this town is so obsessed with the legend all I had to do was mention the forest, and those idiots willingly walked out to it. Lambs to the slaughter. Our first victims."

"It all worked out so well," Rhett said. "We had Russel, who gave us the imposing size, Gabriella with her freaky double-jointed movements, and Kelly to call out the targets. Dylan thought of the growling." He held up a tape recorder hidden in his mask, letting it play, snarling of wolves echoing into the room. "And then of course we had Luke. All he had to do was go crying to his dad about the Animal, and we knew that old fool would give Oliver the files.

"The escape was easy too. First, Luke gave his father a big hug, probably meant a lot to the old man. As he's doing it, he takes his keys before handing them off to Kelly. Who in turn"—Rhett held up the sheriff's keys—"handed them off to me."

Riley just sat there, listening to their speech, uncaring. Almost amused, even.

"Of course," Kelly added, "it would have gone a lot smoother if Betty had died when she was supposed to. But your doctor friend saved her, which meant we had to keep pretending we were innocent little victims, even when we weren't around you."

"We got her good in the end, though," Gabriella smirked.

"We really did," Kelly added. "Had to cover up my face at the morgue to hide the grin when I saw her parents. They looked so sad."

"I will say," Rhett continued, "stabbing my shoulder was brilliant. You almost ruined everything right then and there. But then Dylan kindly offered to stab all of us."

"What can I say?" Dylan said, grinning like a madman. "When my friends need help, I'm there."

"I have to admit it, though." Rhett nodded to Riley. "You put up a heck of a fight. I mean, c'mon." He motioned to their black eyes and bruises. "Well done. Really made us work for it. Certainly more than Oliver did."

Riley smiled to herself. He said it hoping for a reaction, hoping that she'd get upset, scream at him, do something to justify his speech. Instead, she just ignored it. He didn't deserve her fear. None of them did.

"Now the whole town is scared of us. They think the Animal is back," Luke boasted. "And here you are. The survivor my dad never stopped talking about, tied to a chair."

"And here we are," Kelly said, "the helpless victims you thought you needed to save. Too bad no one is here to save you."

Finally, Rhett stepped away and pulled out his sharpened bone, spinning it in his hands. "The news was right about one thing, though." He held out his arms, motioning to his entire pack of friends, of killers. "The Animal's legacy has returned. We are the new Animal. When this is over, it will be our legend the town remembers."

Riley wanted to ignore them, but she couldn't help herself, and she began to laugh, not out of humor but pity.

"No one is going to remember you," Riley scoffed. "You've killed all these people for nothing. You're still not the Animal. You never will be."

Rhett laughed at first, shrugging her comments off. "We've had this town scared for weeks, not just a single night. We've killed more people than the Animal ever did."

Riley tilted her head back, looking at them in shock, almost disappointment. "You don't get it, do you?" Her voice was quiet, almost pleading. "You never have. This new killing spree. The town's obsession. No matter what you do, how many people you kill, it won't matter. You'll *never* be the Animal. Kill a thousand people, heck, cut their heads off if you want to, it wouldn't change anything. Wear that costume, that mask, like a religion, like a symbol, and it still won't make you scary, because what's underneath it is just so disappointing."

Riley looked over the kids with a sickened expression, first at Dylan and Gabriella. "The psycho couple, killing because it's fun." She turned to Russel and Luke. "The athlete with a chip on his shoulder. The scorned kid out for revenge." Her eyes cut from Kelly to Rhett. "And the two trust fund brats mad that Mommy and Daddy didn't love them and willing to do anything to make themselves feel special."

Rhett slapped her in anger.

Riley brushed it off, a crazed look in her own eyes. "Maybe for a moment this town thought you were. Maybe for a second someone thought it was scary: the bodies, the killing spree, the mask. But the moment they see your faces, it's gone. Because they've seen you before. The infantile motives. The pathetic need to be remembered. Hide behind the masks all you want, pretend to be the real Animal, but it won't change what you are. Six kids who thought they were special, just like all the rest."

Riley sighed, staring at the kids in front of her, seeing what she always had.

"The Animal killed seventeen people twenty-five years ago, and its legend is still spoken in whispers by the people of this town. You could kill a hundred, and they'll still forget you in a week."

None of them said a word as sorrow filled their eyes, like hurt dogs scolded by their master. But a moment later, it was gone, replaced by a flash of lightning as they denied the truth to themselves once again and grew filled with rage.

They might have killed her right there had Rhett not stopped them.

"I wonder," he said, "if we aren't scary, then how come Hank seemed so afraid of me?"

Dread filled Riley's bones in an instant as shock erupted in her expression. She'd assumed Rhett had just escaped after Hank had left. She hadn't thought...

For a moment, sorrow echoed within her hazel eyes. Rhett could be lying, but deep down she knew he wasn't, knew that he didn't bluff, not about things like this. Realizing she'd lost her final friend, Riley looked to the floor for a moment of mourning as her eyes began to water.

Hank hadn't deserved this. None of them had.

"It's not funny now, is it?" Rhett said, voice harsh. "Because I wasn't lying when I said we were going to bring back the Animal. I just needed Hank's help to do it."

The mention of the monster's name stopped her heart, and she looked at Rhett in sudden distress.

"What did you do?"

The forest surrounded him, endless trees appearing to move closer, to suffocate him, force him to become something else.

Force the Animal out.

Clyde heard it now. Everything. The breathing of deer twenty feet to his left, unaware of his presence. He could reach them in seconds, break off an antler, and use it to slit their throats.

Even in the darkness, he could see. Feel the movement around him, the animals of the forest, years of instinct back in full force. He remembered what it felt like to run when the monsters had chased him, attacked him, bitten into his skin. He remembered what it felt like to hide, unable to think, unable to process where he was, and yet letting instinct take over, forcing him to survive.

Most of all, he remembered hunting. Not the thrill of it, no emotions, no cruelty. He remembered it because it was what he had become. What the forest and the wolves had carved him into.

It wasn't a choice. It wasn't thought. It was instinct, forcing its way out. The Animal was what he was, and it wanted blood, wanted to hunt, like a caged animal returned to the forest, itching for the bloodshed of its prey.

But one instinct stood out among the rest, one memory. The child who had escaped. The girl who had screamed. It filled his head, every memory of the cry forcing the animal within him out piece by piece.

It wanted her blood. Her scream.

Clyde wanted it too.

Alone in the dark forest, Clyde screamed, crying out as he beat the ground, trying to hold on to his thoughts, his consciousness. But the instincts were too strong. They'd spent half of his life in total control, blocking out all thoughts and emotions.

Hunt her.

"No," Clyde pleaded with himself, trying to fight it. He didn't want to hurt her; he couldn't let himself.

Kill her.

"No!" Clyde screamed, desperately reaching for the deer rifle he'd left on the ground, knowing what he had to do. He shouldn't have survived. He should have died in that house, twenty-five years ago. Linda had even said it; he'd lost so much blood that night, he should have died.

Clyde chambered a round.

It was getting stronger: the instinct, the urge to be the Animal he once was. To find the girl who'd escaped and kill her. Kill them all. He had to stop it. He couldn't let himself become the monster again.

But just as he was about to do it, do what should have been done twenty-five years ago and kill the Animal forever, he heard something. Something far away, blaring into the night.

Police sirens.

"I stopped by the game ranch," Rhett said, eyes filling with madness. "And I left something for the Animal. Blood, to bring it back out."

Clyde ran toward the sound, seeing the tracks of wolves as he did, until finally he approached the edge of the ranch and saw the source of the noise. The police car stuck in the ditch, breaking the fence, allowing the wolves' tracks to flow through it, escaping its grasp, escaping into the forest.

The sirens were blaring, giving color to the night, marking the horror in the darkness. Clyde dropped the rifle, approaching the car in terror, unable to deny the urge to see what was inside.

Hank's dead body, covered in blood.

Clyde's head twitched as he saw it. He felt his hands shaking, the Animal coming back out, crawling out of his skin, drawn to the blood, hungry for more.

The Animal remembered the smell of the blood, the feel of its warmth as it spilled from the prey's bodies, from their throats.

Clyde backed away, screaming, fighting back against it. He couldn't give in, couldn't become what he once was.

Couldn't let the Animal take over.

*

"But if what the doctor said is true," Rhett continued, "then it won't be enough. He'll fight it, try to bury the Animal within himself, try to lock it away again. Which is why you're still alive."

Clyde's body shook violently, fighting itself, screaming in pain, until finally he heard it. The static from the police radio.

It stopped.

"You're going to scream," Rhett said. "And like a shark to blood, or a wolf to a lamb, the Animal will hear the cry of prey, and it will come for you. It won't be able to stop itself, not if it hears you scream like you did all those years ago."

A moment later, Rhett set a police coms unit on the floor in front of them and turned it on, revealing three sounds. The police car's siren. The rustling of leaves from the forest. And finally, breathing.

Rhett smirked. "He's there."

"Please," Riley pleaded as she realized what Rhett was going to do. The Animal he was about to unleash. "Don't do this."

Rhett moved the knife closer to her.

"Please, just kill me," she begged, thinking of the Animal from her past, knowing what it would do to them, to her, to her daughter. "Don't bring it back, just kill me!" She began to cry from fear. "Please!"

Rhett lifted the microphone up to Riley's mouth. "Now," he said before clicking it on and shoving the blade into her stomach. "Scream."

Clyde stood frozen, hearing the breathing on the other end of the line. The desperate gasps for air, groans of excruciating pain.

It sounded familiar.

Tears fell from her eyes, her body jumped in pain, but she didn't scream. She held it in, knowing what would happen if she did.

She couldn't let it come back.

Rhett stabbed her again, this time in her leg. It took everything she had, but still, she cried in silence.

Finally, Rhett clicked the speaker off for a moment before leaning in close and whispering to her. "We will find your daughter. It may take us a little while, but eventually we'll find her. And if you don't scream"–his eyes flashed a look of cruelty she'd never seen before–"I will torture her before she dies. Make it last for hours."

His head tilted slightly to reinforce his point. "I'm going to stab you again. This time, don't hold back."

The radio clicked back on, and Rhett shoved the knife into her side once more, cutting flesh and drawing blood, and this time she had no choice.

Riley screamed.

Clyde heard it. The scream.

Riley crying out over the radio and into the forest.

It rang in his head just as it had twenty-five years ago, the cry of pain, bringing out the monster. Taking away everything else, leaving only instinct.

Unable to stop it, he fell to the ground, body shaking, trying to fight who he was one last time. But the scream was too much, echoing in his head.

Hunt.

The Animal wanted out.

Kill.

Clyde wanted it too. But it was wrong. He couldn't let it happen. He had to get the rifle, had to kill himself. It was the only way to save her. The girl he remembered, crying out underneath the bed as the Animal inside him slaughtered her parents.

But then the screams stopped, and another voice echoed into the forest. Something mad, something cruel.

"We'll save her for you."

The radio clicked off.

"No," Clyde cried, alone in the dark forest. She was still going to die because of him, even if the Animal didn't slaughter her itself. Even if he didn't rip her flesh. The one he had heard scream.

Riley.

Suddenly, Clyde heard footsteps echoing from behind and turned to see yellow eyes staring back at him, eyes that were attached to a monstrous wolf, black fur stained in blood. It might not have been real, but it was to him. The Animal inside his head.

In that moment, as they stared at each other in silence, neither one attacking, neither one fighting the other, Clyde saw what it wanted. Why it had chased him, why it had come back now, after all these years.

Why the Animal had survived.

CHAPTER FORTY-EIGHT

The wolf ran through the forest, darting between trees like a shadow, pursued by the Animal. Pursued by Clyde.

The moon was hidden behind the clouds, stealing the light from the night sky, but it didn't stop him. Like a wolf hunting its prey, he moved without thinking where he was, passing trails he didn't remember yet had never forgotten.

He shouldn't have survived.

Clyde chased the wolf, stalking it from behind, following its shadow through utter darkness, moving between trees he couldn't see, running on the dirt beneath him.

He should have died that night. The legend should have died that night.

The wolf leapt over the dried-up creek. Clyde did as well, not letting it escape, knowing it wasn't trying to.

The wolf had brought him prey.

As Clyde ran, he remembered more of what he had become. What the Animal was. It hadn't killed everything. It might have hunted, might have longed for bloodshed, but just as all animals did, it hadn't killed unless threatened, hadn't slaughtered without purpose.

It hadn't slaughtered all of the wolves.

Maybe that meant a piece of Clyde was still inside it. Buried deep within the Animal's instinct, something keeping it from slaughtering everything. Something that had been lost when he'd seen his father. Something that caused the Animal to turn into something else. Something cruel.

Clyde could feel it inside of him as he ran, instinct already taking over, crawling over his skin, embedding itself into his bones, taking away the fear, the thoughts, the emotion.

Finally, the wolf stopped, and Clyde saw where it had led him once again, hitting the ground as he did. In a vast forest, the wolf had brought him to a single rock, a marker of something hidden. Above, there was a small opening within the twisting branches of the trees, allowing a glimpse

into the night sky—the moon, once hidden behind clouds, now slowly revealing itself.

As Clyde felt the dirt, the wolf vanished for the last time, and Clyde remembered what was buried here. What the wolf in his mind was trying to show him. They had burned it, but he'd buried another.

Below the soil lay his true face.

Hunt.

Clyde dug, pushing his hands into the dirt, desperately searching for what was hidden, feeling his thoughts slipping away. Feeling the Animal taking over.

Kill.

Finally, he felt it, hidden within the trees of the forest, buried within its dirt, waiting to be found once again.

Clyde lifted it up, looking into its hollow eyes, its black fur, its monstrous features, all kept together by the wolf's skull that still lay hidden underneath.

The wolves' skin. The wolves' flesh.

The Animal's mask.

Clouds vanished in the sky, allowing its glow to reach down into the forest, attracting the howls of predators.

In that moment, twenty-five years after the attacks, screams of victims ringing in his head, staring into the hollow eyes of the mask, the face of what he had become, what he still was, Clyde

stopped fighting and let instinct take over once more.

In the light of the full moon, as the howling of wolves echoed throughout the forest, the Animal returned.

PART FOUR

THE
ANIMAL

CHAPTER FORTY-NINE

The sky opened up and rain poured down from it, scattered in the wind, drenching everything within its grasp, covering the entire town.

But it wasn't just the sky that cried, reacting in fear, knowing what had been brought back. The monster unleashed once again.

Riley could see them. Even tied to the chair, she could see them in the forest. Birds, frantically scattering in the sky, escaping the branches, escaping the trees. Hundreds of them all at once, desperately fighting against the rain, against the wind, pulling their bodies through the layer of jagged branches that held them contained.

But they didn't just escape the forest. Once out, they fought even harder, some giving way to the downpour and falling to the ground, but those strong enough to fight its grasp tore through the sky, darts of black and blue passing over the stars, struggling to get as far away as possible.

Some of them flew straight up. Some scattered to the north. The rest flew south, heading directly over the house where Riley was now trapped. As they passed over it, the flapping of wings filled the night, overtaking the rainfall for just a moment, flocks of birds screeching in unison, trying to escape the monster.

Those who couldn't fight the rain fell, impacting her home, some crashing into its wood, others hitting the windows, cracking the glass. But even then they still cried louder and flew again with broken wings, flying from something.

Riley felt her hands trembling. She knew what they were running from.

It was coming.

She began to fight against her restraints, willing to break her hand if she had to. Anything to get away, anything to escape before it came. Before the Animal reached her again.

But Rhett noticed her struggle and pointed the pistol to her temple, shaking his head, a final warning.

In desperation, she almost didn't stop, more willing to be shot through the skull by him than witness the monster again. But if she died, then no one would be there for Emma. So she stopped fighting the restraints but couldn't stop the trembling, her bones rattling in fear.

Suddenly, Rhett motioned to Dylan. "Go find the girl."

"Aye-aye, Captain," Dylan remarked, blood still dripping down his mouth from where Riley had struck him, yet still he smiled as though he didn't feel it. It was with that twisted grin that he put his mask on, missing an ear, ready to hunt for more prey. Soon, he was gone, and an insidious thought crept into Riley's mind, a fear she prayed was irrational.

What if Emma had gotten too scared? What if she hadn't hidden in the safe room but had done what all children did when they were afraid, when they panicked? What she herself had done all those years ago.

What if she had merely hidden underneath her bed?

A moment later, the house went dark.

"I cut the power, just like you said," Luke exclaimed, walking into the room.

"Good." Kelly grinned before turning to Riley, noticing even in the darkness how much she was shivering. How terrified she was.

"If it makes you feel better," Kelly said, "this isn't personal. We don't care about you. We just want to make sure it comes back. Want to see it for ourselves, before we let it take the fall."

For only a second, Riley stopped shaking and looked at them in confusion.

"You didn't think we were bringing it back just because we're insane, did you?" Kelly asked, devilish grin growing on her face.

Riley couldn't respond.

Rhett laughed. "I think she did."

Kelly laughed with him before moving closer to Riley, their eyes mere inches apart. "You were right about one thing. This town had given all of us a reason to hate it. To feel insignificant, unwanted. Luke's dad ignores him, nothing is good enough for Gabriella's parents, Russel had been treated like crap his whole life, and us..." She paused, eyes losing their glow for a split second, replaced by sadness, her true face kept hidden behind the madness. "Our parents wouldn't even come back to see us when they thought we were attacked." She laughed, but her smile was a pained expression, hiding the hurt that momentarily slipped through.

Rhett continued for her. "But the one thing no one in this town overlooks is the Animal. The one thing that matters to everyone. So, we decided to become it. To make ourselves into the thing this town fears and hurt them. Watch them become the insignificant prey. It was fun... man, it was fun," Rhett laughed. "But we also don't want to spend the rest of our lives in jail. So we have to give the town another suspect: the true Animal."

Kelly spoke again. "Once the Animal comes back, once it kills you, everyone will assume it's been the killer all along. They won't even question it, because deep down they want it to return. They want to see the face behind the mask. Then, without you or Hank, no one can prove anything on Rhett. No one else actually saw him at that hospital. All they know is that Hank arrested him. But now Hank is dead, along with all the other criminals who saw Rhett escape. And when they find your body in the morning, and Rhett back in his cell, they'll assume they arrested the wrong suspect. So he'll be let go, and we'll be free, knowing that we were the killers the town feared, and the prey who survived."

Riley listened to their words, hollow and empty, the words of the dead, still unaware of what was coming.

Suddenly, lightning crashed in the sky, echoed by thunder, the earth itself screaming out. A cry of warning. A cry of fear.

The thunder shook the house, and the lightning struck again, over and over, shaking their bones, trying to warn them, trying to share its terror.

Of all the years Riley had lived in this town, she'd only seen a thunderstorm like this once before. The night it happened.

Suddenly, the sound of cracking wood echoed beneath their feet, and the dogs started barking.

Dylan moved through the dark house, trying to find the girl, humming as he did. "Where are you?" he whispered, spoken as an eerie poem, something to frighten the child.

It was so dark that he almost couldn't see, but flashes of lightning shone through the windows, accompanied by moonlight, their combined glow just enough that he could make his way down the hallway and into the room beside it.

Grinning, he noticed the door was slightly ajar.

Someone was inside.

Crazed barking filled the room as the dogs felt it. The same thing Riley felt in her bones, in her heart. Its presence.

At first, they had merely growled, but soon their throats erupted with frenzied cries, eyes twitching everywhere, calling out the darkness that was now within the house. The horror they felt but couldn't see.

On and on they went, drowning out the rainfall, even drowning out the thunder. The kids tried, but they couldn't shut them up. Instead they just kept barking, massive dogs baring their teeth and digging their claws into the ground, ready to attack a monster they couldn't see, couldn't even hear.

But then it happened. All at once, as quickly as it had begun, the barking stopped.

Stalking slowly, Dylan entered the room, looking for his prey. Looking for the girl. It was fun, hunting her, trying to find her in the darkness.

He hadn't even noticed the dogs' cries.

As he stepped further into the room, he scanned it for signs of life, hearing something coming from below him. Something breathing under the bed.

Wolf mask still on, he slowly bent down beside it until he was face-to-face with the girl hiding underneath.

"Boo!"

Once the barking stopped, even the kids felt it. Something was wrong. Something was close.

"No..." Riley stammered, knocking her chair over, trying to break it, trying to escape.

It was here.

The kids looked at her as if she was crazy, but then the dogs joined her in the fear.

Once vicious and crazed, the dogs slowly backed up, tripping over themselves as they did, softly whimpering, now hiding their teeth, hiding their claws.

The girl jumped, escaping the bed and backing up to the wall, pressing her body against it as if she could escape through it. Escape him.

Dylan smiled as he held up his blade and ran it across his mouth, letting his blood stain it, an attempt to frighten the child.

But she didn't scream, too strong for that, instead darting her eyes back and forth across the room, seemingly trying to find a way to escape.

Dylan sighed, gripping the knife tighter. She was going to scream before he dragged her through the house, one way or another.

But then, as he stepped closer, her eyes caught something moving in the darkness.

The dogs cried out again, not a threat, but a cry, whimpering as they backed up to the wall, bodies shivering as they dug their claws into it, scraping the wood, trying to claw their way out of the house.

Trying to escape the Animal they felt.

The kids tried to stop them, but it was no use. They just kept squealing, eyes widening, bodies trembling as they dug into the wall, hoping for an escape that wouldn't come.

Finally, they cried out again, one last sign of the horror that had returned.

The girl's face lost its color, and at first Emma was unable to even scream, staring at the horrific figure that loomed in the darkness.

"Now you're scared," Dylan laughed from underneath his mask, unaware that she wasn't looking at him but the monster lurking behind him.

As she saw it, her body froze, unable to believe that something like that could even exist, something darker than any nightmare she'd ever known. Then the fear took hold, and she screamed at the top of her lungs, crying out in fear of the monster that had found them.

Riley felt her heart stop as she heard Emma's screams echo through the house.

The kids around her smiled, almost laughing as they heard the girl scream, assuming Dylan had found her.

But then they heard Dylan scream too.

His cry rang in the night, almost shaking the house itself. A cry of pure fear, of pain, bones being broken and flesh being ripped apart, terrified wailing so filled with agony that it almost didn't sound human.

A moment later, it stopped.

Then everything stopped.

The dogs stood frozen. The cries of pain were silenced. Even the rain grew soft for a moment, not daring to make a sound, afraid to interrupt the quiet terror growing in its midst.

But then, footsteps began to echo. Quick, heavy footsteps that were headed straight for them.

Riley tried to fight against the restraints, cracking her own bones as she did, desperate for escape.

The kids heard it coming and got ready. Ready to throw Riley to the monster, to let it consume her. But they had also heard Dylan scream, and so now they were scared, scared of what they had done.

They dragged her chair out into the hallway, Kelly holding a knife to her throat, Rhett pointing the pistol down the hall, waiting for the footsteps to reach them, waiting for the beast to arrive.

The footsteps grew closer, bones and skin crashing into the wooden floor as something ran. *Thump. Thump. Thump.*

The kids held their breath.

Thump.

Riley cried.

Thump.

Suddenly, something passed in front of the window at the end of the hall, distorted features, groaning in agony as it continued to limp closer.

Thump. Thump.

Finally, it reached them, and to the kid's shock and Riley's relief, it wasn't the Animal.

It was Dylan.

His jaw was broken, hanging limp from his mouth. His leg was shifted sideways, fractured in on itself, and half of his face was caved in.

He collapsed into the wall as he reached them, mumbling in fear, distorted whispers escaping from his broken jaw. "Mistake..."

"What happened?" Rhett asked, moving to him.

Dylan leapt in his skin, grabbing Rhett by the fur of his costume, pleading in fear. "Animal... found... found me..."

"Calm down," Rhett said.

"Kill... me..."

"What?"

Suddenly, a door creaked in the distance, soft and low, but the sound caused Dylan to cry, jumping in terror, turning as if a monster was right behind him. "Find me..." He spoke with a broken voice. "Can't let it..." He turned, seeing the gun Rhett was holding, ripping it from his hands in desperation. "Can't let it find me..."

Crying in horror, Dylan shot himself in the head.

CHAPTER FIFTY

Blood spattered everywhere.

It didn't just stain the walls, it scattered over the kids, drenching their costumes with the blood of their own.

Dylan's blood.

He was dead before his body fell, eyes rolled back before his corpse crashed into the wood. When it did, the haunting look was still visible on what was left of his face, frozen forever in that expression: mouth open, eyes white and bloodied, the appearance of true terror.

None of them said a word. No one even moved, instead staring at his body in disbelief. Disbelief that Dylan had done this, that he'd

killed himself, taken his own life just to escape the Animal.

Except for Riley. In that moment, staring at Dylan's blood, watching the kids' horrified expressions, she did what she'd never thought she would.

Riley laughed.

It was quiet at first, but then it grew, crazed laughter at the expressions of kids who'd learned what the monster they revered truly was. It was crazy, and she knew it. The Animal would slaughter her as well, but that was also why she did it. Laughing out of fear. So much tension built up twenty-five years of trauma that had to be released, and seeing Dylan's deathly look of confused terror had released it.

"Shut up!" Rhett screamed, pulling a knife on her throat.

But then, before he could attack her, they saw it. The shadow at the end of the hallway, moving without the sound of footsteps, features hidden in the darkness.

It moved in front of the window, standing motionless for a moment, watching them. Dim moonlight crept through behind it, just enough to outline its monstrous form, create a dark vision of the true horror.

It almost looked like them. Wolflike face, raised ears, dark fur. But even then, they all felt it.

Somehow, they knew, just as Riley always had. It almost looked like them, but it wasn't.

It was different.

Still stained in the blood of their friend, the kids shifted nervously, suddenly afraid of the monster they'd brought back. Afraid of the way it watched them, motionless from across the hall, not making a sound, seemingly not even breathing as it stalked them.

Instinctively, the kids moved behind the dogs, but not for long. Even as the kids told the dogs to charge, to attack, the dogs cowered in whimpering fear.

The German shepherd retreated to the left, running down another hallway, tripping over itself as it did, leaping onto the first door it came to, desperately trying to scratch its way in.

The husky, however, ran into the room behind them, throwing itself through the window, squealing as the broken glass cut into its flesh, howling in sudden agony as it was impaled on the spiked fence resting just outside, its body left hanging there, illuminated by the moonlight. A reminder of the truth Riley had always known.

There was no escape.

Then, as the kids turned from the dogs back to the monster, it happened.

Lightning flashed in the sky, the last desperate warning of what was to come, the earth itself illuminating the creature that had returned for blood.

The flash only lasted a second, but within it the kids witnessed the horrors they'd never imagined, and Riley saw the monster that haunted her dreams every night.

Black fur, hollow eyes, flesh ripped from wolves, it was covered in more dried blood than any of them had ever seen, shimmering in the flash of light, telling the story of its past. It hadn't just killed one wolf, it had ripped the flesh from countless, hiding itself within their monstrous features.

The next moment the flash of light was gone, but the haunting sight of it remained, and it would never go away. It wasn't just its appearance, it was the presence, the way it stood, the way the monster watched them.

Thunder echoed into the night, shaking the house, shaking their bones, the last cry of warning, as the night sky screamed in horror at what had returned.

The Animal.

As the last remnants of light faded and the cries of thunder stopped, everything changed. Still covered in the blood of their own, the kids froze in horror; everything they'd been planning was gone, and only one thought remained.

Run.

So they did. They looked to the dog still alive to their left, trying to claw its way to safety, bloodied paws staining the door as it did, and in a panic, they ran to join it.

Luke moved to grab Riley, but Rhett stopped him. "Leave her!"

One by one the kids ran, except for Gabriella, who stood frozen, still staring at what was left of Dylan's face, tears falling from her eyes.

It wasn't until she heard their screams that she finally snapped out of it and moved down the hall, leaving Riley alone in front of the approaching monster.

"No!" Riley screamed, watching the Animal move closer as she broke her wrist, trying to pull her hand free of the restraints, holding back the grunts of pain as the bones in her hand splintered apart.

But it wasn't enough. It would never be enough.

Hands bleeding but free, she fell backwards, into the room where she'd hidden all those years ago, back to the place where she'd first seen it. This time, it was her who slammed the door before backing up against the bed as though she was still a child, fighting the urge to hide underneath it as she watched the door, waiting for it to happen.

For the Animal to shatter the wood as it had before, and then hunt her, kill her like it had wanted to twenty-five years ago. Finally finish its prey and silence her screams.

But the moment never came.

At first, Gabriella moved slowly, still in a trance, unable to believe Dylan was dead, trying desperately to wipe his blood off her face, trying to forget his final horrified expression.

But then she heard her friends' screams echoing in front of her.

"Run!"

In shock she turned, seeing what was behind her, what they wanted her to run from.

The Animal hadn't gone for Riley. It was coming for her.

Horrified, she tried to run, listening to the cries of her friends.

"Run!"

But then, panicking, she didn't see the tripwire Riley had left, the one her friends had set off, and it caught her ankle, dropping her to the floor, body crashing hard on the wood.

She could feel the Animal behind her, moving closer with every second, and in front of her she saw her only glimmer of hope, the open door where her friends were hidden, and she reached out as if to grab it.

The door closed.

"Open it back!" Russel screamed.

"She won't make it in time," Rhett said, locking the door. "She's dead anyway."

"Open it!" Russel ordered again, moving toward Rhett, unwilling to leave his friend to die as easily as Rhett was, especially as they heard her cries echoing on the other side of the door, begging for help.

"The chain," Kelly said, pointing to the chain hanging from the doorway, noticing its length, its purpose. "It's too long. It must have been for her daughter to fit through."

Rhett's eyes met Kelly's and he understood her thoughts. Riley had designed the door to remain locked while leaving an opening for only someone as small as her daughter to fit through.

Gabriella was small.

With Russel still growling beside him, Rhett had no other choice.

The door cracked open once again, and Gabriella screamed for help, desperately stumbling on the floor as she stood up and ran toward safety, unaware of how close the monster was.

"Run! Now!" Russel screamed, seeing her through the cracked door, kept from opening further by the reinforced chain.

She reached the door and beat against it, realizing it wouldn't open. They had locked her out.

A chill crept down her spine as she felt it growing closer.

"Fit through!" Kelly cried out from within, and in that moment Gabriella understood. It was cruel, her own friends unwilling to risk themselves to save her, but she understood nonetheless. It was what she would have done.

Not looking back, not facing the Animal coming for her, she tried to push herself through a space made for a child, twisting sideways and grunting in pain as her flesh raked against the wood, until finally she could push no more.

But then, her friends grabbed hold of her, pulling her through the crack, finally getting her to the other side, unaware that it was already too late.

As her body finally moved past the door and into the safety of the room, for a brief second her hand was still exposed on the other side, and the Animal grabbed hold.

Suddenly, Gabriella felt its monstrous grip, bearing down on her wrist, almost crushing the bones within. Instinctively, she did what she always had. She pressed against her thumb and broke her hand, double joints allowing it to happen without pain. Then she backed up, shifting her weight, expecting the dislocated bones to cause her hand to slip through the monster's grasp and set her free.

But it didn't let go.

Its grip was too strong, digging down into her flesh, breaking the bones in her wrist in half, causing her to cry out in pain. Then, it pulled, lifting her body off the floor and slamming it into the door as it tried to rip her through the crack.

"Help me!" she cried out as her body crashed into the wood again and again, the Animal outside it thrashing her arm back and forth in a frenzy, not willing to let go of its prey, cracking wood as her bones struck it.

Crash.

Russel grabbed her, trying to keep her from being pulled back through the crack. Rhett and Luke pressed against the door, reinforcing the lock, keeping it as shut as they could, even as bones could be heard snapping in two.

Crash.

Over and over, she collided with the wood, wailing in agony as she tried to free herself from its grip, the splintered wood digging into her shoulder.

Crash.

Blood spattered as her body struck the wood again.

Crash.

Gabriella cried out, tears falling from her face, begging anyone to save her, trying with every ounce of strength she had to fight its grip and escape.

Finally, she gasped in torment one last time as it gave way, and she fell back from the door, free from the monster's grip, watching as they closed the door tight behind her.

It was over. She had escaped.

But soon the shock faded, and she saw the expressions of her friends: jaws open, eyes wide in horror as they stared at her, realizing what had been done. How she had escaped.

"What..." she stammered in confusion, the shock keeping her from feeling the pain, from knowing the truth.

Even then, her friends couldn't answer, instead only staring at her as if she was already dead.

Slowly, terrified of what she'd see, Gabriella moved her eyes from her friends to herself, screaming as she saw the torn flesh, the exposed bone, and the blood pouring down from her shoulder where her arm should have been.

CHAPTER FIFTY-ONE

She wouldn't stop screaming.

It wasn't even out of pain. Within seconds shock had set in, and much of the pain was kept at bay, but it didn't take away the horror of seeing the empty space where her limb had been ripped off, still feeling her hand, her fingers move, knowing it was a lie.

Kelly tried to cover Gabriella's mouth, scared that she'd lead the Animal to them, provoke it to crash through the wood and kill them all. But she couldn't stop the screaming.

Looking to the door, hands now shaking, Rhett nervously spoke. "We have to go, now."

"Where?" Luke asked, motioning to the locked door, which hid the Animal behind it. "We're trapped."

Gabriella screamed louder.

Panicking, Rhett tried to think. Luke was right, they were trapped. The door was the only way out, and if they opened it, the Animal would slaughter them all.

Cries of agony echoed through the house.

Then Rhett saw it. The dog, clawing at another door, so frenzied and desperate its paws were bleeding, leaving streaks of red flowing down the wood.

"Just kill me!" Gabriella begged. "Please!"

Rhett opened the door and saw what lay behind it. Another hallway, small, lined with white doors that made the darkness surrounding them seem vast, a claustrophobic path whose end was shrouded in a void of black nothingness.

It might lead to the stairs; it might lead to death. In the end, they had no other choice.

They moved to the hallway, Luke dragging Gabriella with them, covering her mouth but not silencing her cries of agony, her pleading for death as more blood left her mutilated shoulder.

As they stepped down it, slowly, barely seeing their path in the dark, Rhett's skin began to crawl.

The Animal could be anywhere. It could be waiting for them at the end, black fur and ripped wolf flesh hiding it in the darkness. Or it could even be within the walls, waiting to strike through the wood.

Suddenly, Rhett heard everything: every footstep, every breath he took, every time his heart beat, terrified it would alert the Animal. Terrified it would find him.

Grabbing the German shepherd by the collar, he tried to force it through the hallway, force it to walk ahead, bait for the lurking monster. But the dog wouldn't go, whimpering quietly, forcing itself back behind them, eyes frantically searching the wall.

Or it could come from behind, dragging them back into the room they left, their fingers leaving bloody trails on the floor as they tried to crawl away from the monster.

"Stop," Rhett whispered before motioning to Russel. He was the biggest, the strongest. If anyone had a chance, it was him. "Go in front."

"No way, man," Russel said, voice terrified.

"Go," Rhett growled, drawing his blade and turning to face where they had come. "I'll look behind us, you and Luke check in front."

For a moment Russel and Luke stood frozen, but then the desperate need to escape overtook the fear, and they moved, slowly stepping into the dark, the floor beneath them creaking with every step.

Further and further they went, almost feeling the darkness as it started to consume them, forcing them to move cautiously, unable to breathe for fear the Animal would find them.

Behind them, Rhett stared at the room from which they came, dimly lit by the moonlight seeping through the window within, light that betrayed the horrors left behind, the blood that stained the floor, even the walls.

Kelly stood with Rhett, wishing the room was dark, wishing the light was gone, because then she wouldn't be able to see the horror, see the monster if it came for them.

She'd glimpsed it for a moment when the lightning had flashed, and it had almost stopped her heart. If she ever saw it again, she didn't know if she'd even be able to run.

In the midst of them, not progressing to safety or watching for a monster, Gabriella stood in the middle of the hallway, right at the edge of the light, half of her body glowing in the remnants of moonlight, the other mutilated half now hidden in complete darkness. She was dazed; the blood loss had begun to steal her thoughts, glassing over her eyes and taking her voice. But still, a single thought broke through.

"Kill me."

Shaking in fear, unable to stop, Russel progressed further, hearing the dog begin to whimper behind him, signaling the monster was close.

Cautious, Russel reached out his hand, feeling the wall, using it to guide him, afraid of what could be lurking in front of him, afraid of his hands touching bloodstained fur.

The dog cried louder, trembling eyes searching for the horror.

Russel took another step, feeling Luke's breath behind him, quick and frenzied, causing Russel's heart to beat within his chest. The Animal would hear them. It would attack.

Horrific whimpering echoed as even the German shepherd desperately gasped for breaths that wouldn't come.

It's going to find us, Russel thought, on the verge of breaking down. *It could be right in front of me. This was a mistake!*

But then, his hand hit something, and in relief he saw he had reached the end of the path, for before him lay another hallway, which led to a window, to light. Soon, his breathing returned to normal, as he saw nothing was hidden in the darkness, no monster lurking in the shadows

He turned, calling out in a whisper, "It's safe."

"Let's go," Rhett told Kelly, turning to run down the hallway, escape the light that revealed horrors, praying for the darkness to return.

But then he saw Gabriella.

She was still standing in the middle of the hallway, at the edge of the light, moaning in confused pain as her eyes glassed over, desperately reaching her remaining arm across her body, trying to grab what was no longer there.

But that wasn't what scared Rhett, what caused a chill to creep over all of their bones. No, it wasn't Gabriella's pain. It was the dog.

It wasn't just whimpering anymore. It was wailing, pained screams escaping its shaking jaws as it stared at the monster it had found. The presence it felt, even through the wall that now held its gaze, forcing its twitching eyes to view the dark beast that none of them could see.

None of the kids could speak, unable to even cry a warning, as they saw where the dog was staring, where the monster was hiding.

Right behind Gabriella.

A monstrous arm covered in wolf's flesh burst through the walls, grabbing hold of Gabriella by the neck and pulling her back, through the broken wood, into the den where it slaughtered its prey.

Screams of terror and pain escaped from within the darkness of the cracked hole, horrible wailing, almost inhuman, as flesh was ripped and bones were snapped like glass.

They heard it all, every cry of pain, every tear of skin, until finally it stopped in an instant, and silence returned.

Cold, uneasy silence, signaling death.

But then Gabriella's corpse was thrown back through the wall, back to them, impacting the other side before falling to the floor, and they saw in horror that Gabriella wasn't dead.

Her bones were broken, flesh ripped, eyes white in her skull, and her body twitched in uncontrollable terror, screams of pain impossible because the Animal had taken her throat.

In mercy, they should have killed her, but they were too afraid to move, so they stood frozen as the blood loss finally overtook the pain and the living corpse lost its breath, dying in agony, a mound of distorted flesh that no longer appeared human.

Still, they couldn't move. Terror told Rhett to run, but to get to safety, he had to pass over the corpse, had to pass beside the broken wall that hid the Animal.

But then, something happened. The German shepherd, paws still bleeding, walked over to Gabriella, to its master, and saw her corpse. Smelled her blood.

For only a moment, rage took over, and the dog bared its massive teeth, growling for revenge as it leapt through the broken wall, hunting the Animal.

A second later it screamed in pain.

"Run!" Rhett said as he and Kelly darted through the hallway, eyes closed, not daring to look at the mangled remains of their friend left behind.

As they ran, they heard more cries of pain, more whimpers of fear.

Almost there, Rhett thought as they passed the splintered wood.

Bones cracked, and the cries were silenced.

Unable to breathe, Rhett and Kelly reached the end, seeing Russel and Luke, too afraid to run any further, hiding in a room, door cracked open to see if their friends made it.

Within the wall, a crash echoed from the broken flesh that hit the ground. The body of the dog. Then, a second crash echoed, revealing what the Animal had done to it.

Frenzied, Rhett dove through the door, Kelly behind him, and Russel locked it, their entire bodies shivering even as they backed away, scared of the Animal finding them. Scared of it breaking the wood and stepping inside.

Russel gripped his blade tightly. Kelly did the same.

"What are we going to do?" Luke whispered frantically. "We have to run. The stairs..."

"No," Kelly said, eyes moving, deciphering their location. "The stairs have to be on the other side, two hallways down. We'll never make it."

"We're gonna die," Luke said in fear.

Suddenly, they all turned to Rhett, looking for an answer, hoping for a way out. But he didn't see them. Instead, his eyes were down, staring at the wolf mask in his hands, looking into its eyes, its fur. The cracks left in it from the warehouse. The stains of blood from prey he'd slaughtered.

Dylan might have died.

Gabriella might have died.

But he wouldn't. They wouldn't. Suddenly his blood began to boil as his heart filled with rage. The Animal made them feel like they were nothing, but they weren't. They were predators. *He* was a predator.

Rhett wouldn't let the Animal take that away.

"We don't run," Rhett finally said. "We kill it."

"Are you insane!" Luke cried.

"We're not prey!" Rhett growled. "I won't just let it kill me like all the rest. We can kill it. *We* are the predators."

"He's right," Kelly said, sparks of madness coming back into her eyes.

567

"How?" Russel asked, hopeless dread still in his voice. "How do we kill it?"

"It didn't go for Riley," Rhett said, still whispering, afraid of making a sound. "It killed Dylan, not the girl. There must be a reason. If we can find them, maybe we can control it.

"Russel," he continued. "Find Riley. Kelly, find the girl." Rhett motioned to the hallway. "When we dragged Riley up here, I think I saw a safe room. Me and Luke will use that to try and kill it."

"How?" Luke asked, voice shaking.

"It's an Animal," Rhett answered, putting on his wolf mask, watching them do the same, taking on the image of predators once more, the last stand of a hungry pack.

"We just have to trap it."

CHAPTER FIFTY-TWO

Limping, Riley dragged herself down the stairs, desperate to reach the living room.

Everything was in pain: her shattered leg, her broken wrist, her still-bleeding side from when Rhett had forced her to scream. But she couldn't stop, she had to find Emma.

For a moment, when she had felt the monster's presence and heard her daughter's scream, she had thought it was over. She'd thought the Animal had taken Emma from her.

But then, when Dylan had screamed louder, there was a glimmer of hope, a small chance that it had spared the girl, for a reason she didn't understand. Maybe, since it hadn't killed her when it had the chance, it had left her daughter alive as well.

In her heart it didn't make sense. The Animal was a monster: no emotions, no thoughts, only bloodshed. Only hunting. It would never have spared its prey. She'd known that from the moment she had seen it as a child herself, and seeing it now, through the flash of lightning, she still felt it.

But to admit that meant admitting her daughter was dead, something she could never do. So she held out hope that somehow, her daughter had escaped the Animal. Escaped its monstrous grasp.

Which meant she had to find her. Protect her.

At the moment, however, limping in pain, blood pouring from her side, she couldn't protect anyone. At least, not without a weapon.

Which was why she stumbled across the floor, using the wall for support, and reached the cabinet where the folded flag still stood. A monument to war, a legacy left behind.

But what she was after was hidden in the cabinet underneath it. A medical kit, filled with bandages to stop the bleeding, ensure she didn't pass out, and beside it, a loaded shotgun: wooden handle, steel barrel.

She used the medical kit first, already feeling woozy from the lost blood. But before she could wrap it, she had to close the wound. The medical kit contained no sutures for makeshift stitches, not even adhesive glue she could use.

All it had to hold the wound shut was the clamps to the bandages—about two inches long, small metal spikes on either side designed to hold the material together.

It would have to be enough.

Raising her bloodied shirt up to the wound on her side, she bit down hard against her teeth and shoved the metal spikes into the wound, fighting back a scream before pulling the other side of torn flesh closer and driving the cold steel into it as well, bringing the open wound together.

Then, as tears of pain flowed down her face, mixing with lines of blood, she did the same to the other wound on her side, and the laceration on her leg.

Finally, still wincing in agony, she rested back against the wall for a moment and wrapped her side in the bandages, forced to tie them together, since the clamps had been repurposed.

Once she was done, she looked over to the flag still resting on top of the cabinet, grinning in nervous pain as she spoke.

"I told you I shouldn't have helped the kids."

Then, for the briefest moment, she felt calm, remembering everything she'd survived. But when she reached over for the gun, a voice stopped her, and the horrific reality returned.

"Don't."

Sighing, Riley cut her eyes to see a kid dressed up like a wolf, grey mask hiding his face from her view. But his size gave away his identity more than his voice ever could.

"Hey, Russel," she said, groaning in pain, realizing he was too close. By the time she could reach the shotgun, much less pump it, he would be on top of her. "I suppose I can't convince you to let me just walk away."

"Afraid not," he said, his voice less mad than the rest of the kids' and far less callous. He was a murderer, like all the rest, but apparently he still remembered what it felt like to be weak. Wasn't quick to murder injured prey.

"Well," she said, pain escaping with every word, "I guess I'll have to kill you, then."

Russel's laughter echoed from behind the mask, but then he raised the blade in his hand and rolled his shoulders, preparing for the attack. "I won't go for your injuries."

"Thanks," she replied, nodding slightly, waiting for the attack to come.

Finally, it did. Russel rushed, and she went for the gun, but he was on her before she could grab it, striking her face and swinging the knife at her shoulder.

Even dazed from the strike, she managed to block the blade, but a moment later he kicked her, the force from it knocking her back into the wall.

"I'm not trying to kill you," he said, almost sympathetically. "Just knock you out."

Riley spat out blood and attempted to rush him. It might have worked, had her broken leg not caused her to stumble in pain. Still, she managed to strike his face and shove him backwards, if only a foot.

In a burst of fury, she kept attacking, ripping the blade from his hand and trying to bring it down into his neck. She got close the first time, grazed it the second, but the third time he caught her hand and ripped the blade away.

Then she tried to kick his knee, but the moment she lifted her good leg, the other buckled, broken bone withstanding the pressure by itself.

The truth was, without a weapon, taking Russel down would have been difficult, even if she wasn't injured beyond repair. But with the broken knee, the shattered wrist, and the bleeding side, now on the verge of rupturing again, it was impossible.

Russel struck her face, bloodying her eye, before lifting her up and throwing her against the wall, its wood creaking from the impact. When her body hit the floor, she crawled toward the gun once more, but Russel grabbed her hair and slung her backwards, striking her again.

"What are you doing?" Russel asked, genuinely curious as he watched her struggle to stand up before shoving her backwards again, causing a loud crash to echo through the house as she impacted the glass doors of the cabinet, shattering it, forcing dozens of shards of glass to rip into her back as she fell to the floor.

When she did, she looked up at Russel, seeing the monster now looming behind him, and answered his question.

"Stalling."

"Stalling?" Russel asked, confused for a moment, until he felt the chill growing within his bones and turned to face the Animal, which had come for blood.

It was standing across the room, partially shrouded in the darkness, but its face was revealed. The face of a wolf, not a plastic mask or fake fur but the *real* face of a wolf. A face stolen from it, becoming the face of something worse. Something darker.

In terror, Russel realized he couldn't hear its breathing. Even in the darkness, he could see it move slightly with each breath, but it was silent, just as its footsteps had been. Unnatural, as if it wasn't even alive.

No sound, no warning.

Fear cried out inside of Russel, telling him to run. Run from the monster, away from his death.

Telling him if he stayed another second, he'd be slaughtered like all the rest.

But he also remembered running. Remembered what it had felt like, being forced to run away, living in fear of the torment inflicted by others. That wasn't him anymore.

If you ever stop moving, you die.

He was a predator now. He was what they ran from. So long as he could fight, he could kill it.

Then he remembered something else. What Riley had said about animals, about predators. They made no sound unless being approached by another predator. Another apex. Then, they growled.

Activating the tape recorder, growling himself, Russel waited to hear the Animal's growl. Its threatening message, its animalistic warning.

But it never came. Instead, the monster just stood there, silently.

Russel let the anger take over. It wasn't growling. It thought he was just prey that it could hurt, another victim to kill. It was wrong. He was bigger, he was stronger. He'd kill it.

Screaming, Russel charged the Animal, going for its head, attempting to strike it, kill it in one stroke.

The Animal took the blow directly to its eye, but Russel was the one who felt the sudden agony, a terrified expression growing underneath his plastic mask as he realized his mistake, seeing the monster didn't flinch, seeing that he should have run.

But it was far too late.

The Animal reached out and ripped the wolf mask from Russel's face. Before he could react, the monster reached its other arm out, grabbing his face, its tight grip cracking his skull before shoving him sideways, into the wall.

Before his body even left the wall from the impact, the monstrous creature was on him again, striking his face, further cracking the skull beneath his flesh before it then hit his back and threw him to the floor below.

As the Animal loomed over him, black fur haunting in the dark, looking down at its broken prey, Russel tried to run. Tried to crawl away, anything to escape the monster.

But he couldn't. He couldn't stand. He couldn't crawl.

He couldn't even move.

At first, he thought it was the fear. That terror was keeping him frozen. But then, as his eyes saw the blood dripping from the Animal's hand, Russel's heart stopped in horror as he realized the truth.

It hadn't just struck his back. It had broken his spine. Torn his flesh open and snapped the bones beneath.

Paralyzed, unable to move, unable to escape, Russel was forced to watch as the monster stood above him, his own blood dripping from its hands, a hollow expression gazing down at him, wanting bloodshed.

"Help!" Russel screamed. "Help!"

The bloodied prey screamed on the floor, looking up with terror in its eyes, body too broken to run away. Its head twitched, and its eyes lost their color, but its body couldn't move, its limbs couldn't run, couldn't crawl. It couldn't escape.

The crippled prey breathed quickly, heartbeat rising as it screamed louder.

The Animal listened to it scream for a moment longer, watching as it writhed on the floor, trying desperately to move even as its bones wouldn't allow it before finally lashing out and beating the prey to death.

The first strike broke its skull.

The second shattered it completely.

But the Animal kept going, striking it over and over, instinct causing it to beat its victim until there wasn't anything left to recognize, not even enough left for vultures to pick at, splattering its blood everywhere in a crazed frenzy.

Finally, it stopped, rising up slowly, breathing silently, now covered in the blood of the beast it had slaughtered, which shimmered in the moonlight that crawled through the windows.

The Animal turned its head, hearing footsteps upstairs.

There was more prey. More blood.

But then, it heard something else. The clicking of metal behind it.

The pump of a shotgun.

CHAPTER FIFTY-THREE

It was right in front of her.

The monster that had slaughtered her parents, murdered them without thinking, without caring, without remorse.

The Animal.

Riley held the shotgun up, hands shaking as she pointed the barrel at its head, its black fur and hollow eyes, mere holes that hid the face within. The face Riley didn't believe existed.

Standing here now, facing the Animal once more, nothing had changed. In an instant she became the terrified girl that she had been twenty-five years ago, helpless as the monster hunted.

It hadn't changed either. It was everything she remembered. The horror of its presence, the haunting look of its appearance. Even now, holding a shotgun inches from its head, she doubted the gunfire would kill it. Doubted the beast could be killed.

She could feel it in her heart. Even closing her eyes wouldn't make the terror go away, because it wasn't just the appearance, wasn't just the wolfskin. It was something else. Something that had crawled into her bones as it had moved closer, something that had stopped her heart from beating at its first appearance.

The forest had felt it, crying out in warning. The dogs had felt it, scrambling for their lives without even seeing it. Riley felt it too, the need to run, cry out in fear, try to escape it—escape the Animal.

But something stopped her. All the rage, all the sorrow came flooding back into her, drowning out the fear, the memories of a frightened child.

Her grip tightened on the gun, holding it steady against the monster's head.

It had murdered seventeen people.

Her finger found the trigger.

It had taken her parents from her. Slaughtered them like dogs.

The trigger inched back.

Maybe it could die. Even if it was a monster, maybe the gun could kill it. Maybe it could finally be over.

Every instinct she had screamed at her to do it. Pull the trigger, see the Animal's blood spatter across the room, watch it bleed out in a bloody mound of flesh like her parents had.

It didn't have a face. It didn't have a name.

Finally, she screamed, tears falling down her face, hands trembling as she tried to do it. Tried to end it. But she couldn't.

Because the Animal was going to let her.

It was standing there, facing its prey, seeing the hollow barrel inches from its head, yet it hadn't moved. Didn't try to attack her, didn't rip the weapon from her hands and tear her flesh open.

Instead, it just stood there, monstrous features staring back at her as if it knew what she had to do. As if it was going to let her.

No, Riley cried silently. *It doesn't get to do this. Doesn't get to be human.*

But there it stood, the Animal that had massacred an entire street, killed without remorse, not attacking her, not even twitching, or tilting its head.

Perfectly still, as if something was holding it back.

More tears fell as her grip tightened on the gun once more, and she asked the only question that still mattered. "Did you kill her?"

No response.

Her voice was broken. "Did you kill my daughter?"

The Animal said nothing. Didn't move. Didn't even breathe.

Riley couldn't take it. What if it had? Riley had heard her scream. What if Emma had been killed like all the rest? What if the Animal had taken her too?

But suddenly, she heard it. Another scream, echoing down from above.

It was Emma.

She's still alive!

It was a cry of fear, but it didn't matter. She was still alive.

Relief flooded over Riley as she realized the truth. The Animal had spared Emma. It had caused her scream, had heard the cry of its prey, but it hadn't silenced it. Instead, it had killed Dylan: the predator hunting her.

Then, it had passed over her. It had had every chance to murder Riley in that room, the same one it had attacked her family in all those years before, but it hadn't. It had let her live.

Maybe something was different.

Fighting the instincts screaming at her to end it, she lowered the gun, tears streaming down her face. She wanted to kill it, it was all she'd ever wanted, but she couldn't. Not like this.

For a moment longer, they both stood there. The Animal and the girl who survived, staring at each other, neither one attacking. Merely watching each other as rain and thunder echoed in the sky beyond the walls and moonlight glowed through the window, illuminating the space between them.

Soon, more footsteps echoed from above, more prey to be slaughtered, and the Animal moved away, back into the darkness, hidden once more.

Alone, Riley shed a final tear before kneeling down and picking up Russel's blade, ignoring the pain in her side, the agony of her broken leg.

The Animal would hunt the kids.

She had to find her daughter.

CHAPTER FIFTY-FOUR

Rhett ran.

The Animal hunted.

The trap was simple. Every predator in nature operated the same way. Once it began the hunt, everything else was removed from its vision. It couldn't see beyond its prey even if it wanted to.

Which meant that to trap an animal, all you needed was bait.

Rhett stumbled into the corner, hitting the wall as he tried to turn down the hallway, trying to reach safety. As he turned, he could see the Animal in the corner of his eye, hidden in the dark, a monstrous shadow moving closer, stalking in the night.

Twisted smile hidden beneath his mask as he ran, Rhett focused on the goal, the destination. The safe room hidden at the far end of the hallway. At first, he almost hadn't noticed it: a small parting in the wooden siding, a crack of darkness flowing out.

It was a false wall, a three-foot door that led to a safe room. The door appeared fully wooden on the outside, but inside it was lined with metal. Not even a monster could break it down. It also had a way to escape, a staircase within it that most likely led to the basement.

Rhett would be safe within the room, behind the door. He just had to get there without getting caught in the monster's grip.

With every step, he was cautious about the floor, afraid of more tripwires. If he tripped for even a moment, the Animal might catch him, and he'd be reduced to a screaming corpse, just like the rest, because so far, nothing it had caught had escaped with its life.

Which was why they had to kill it.

Glancing to his right, Rhett saw the door in the middle of the hallway. It led to a closet where Luke was now hidden, with a blade in hand.

With the Animal focused on Rhett, once it passed the door, Luke could burst out and stab it from behind. Shove the sharpened bone through its throat, spilling the Animal's blood and taking its life.

It had slaughtered Gabriella like she was nothing. Caused Dylan to feel unspeakable fear and take his own life. And if the screams that had echoed from below were any indication, a similar fate had befallen Russel.

But not Rhett. Rhett wasn't nothing; he wasn't just another kid the town would forget about, not another victim to be overlooked. He mattered. He was a predator, just as much as the Animal.

To prove it, he'd have to kill the monster.

Finally, he reached the false wall, panting in exhaustion, turning back to see the monster approaching. Looming in the darkness, death itself stalking him, pursuing him like prey.

But then it stopped. All at once, with no warning, the Animal stopped moving. Stopped hunting. Instead, it just stood there, body motionless as it tilted its head slightly, focusing on something. In a panic, Rhett realized what it was doing.

It was right in front of Luke.

In utter darkness, surrounded by walls that felt as though they were growing closer, Luke stood there, hands shaking as he gripped the blade, waiting to hear the Animal pass by him, just as Rhett had. But instead, he heard nothing, no footsteps, no movement.

But in his bones, he felt its presence, the looming shadow of death crawling over his skin, withering his skeleton into decayed fragments of fear.

The Animal was right outside.

Body shivering, heartbeat rising, he tried to remain quiet. Tried to control his breathing, but he couldn't. The monster was outside. It was watching him, stalking him.

Luke began to breathe faster, hearing each breath as though it were a scream, lungs struggling to get oxygen, but the fear wouldn't allow it. The air he gasped for didn't stop the horror, only making it worse. Every breath he took seemed to echo in his ears, causing him to shudder, terrified the Animal would hear him.

What if it heard the breaths? What if the monster attacked?

Each gasp for oxygen erupted in his ears until it was all he could hear. The fear, the search for air, his own body shivering, until he could barely grip the knife.

His father's words echoed in his head. *"Don't try to kill it. You can't!"*

He felt it outside, the beast seeing him through the wood, stalking him in the darkness, ready to attack. His father had warned him, but like an idiot he hadn't listened, too blinded by resentment, not understanding why his father could never move on, allowing himself to be talked into helping kill him because of it.

But now, Luke understood his father's fear.

"Don't try to hide, it will find you."

Gasping for air but unable to receive it, lungs choking themselves in desperate agony, Luke fought the urge to run like he should have from the beginning, wishing he'd run away from the monster the moment it had attacked and prayed it didn't find him. Didn't rip him in two.

It's going to find me! Luke finally stopped breathing completely, instinct forcing his body into silence, a desperate attempt to hide as his head became dizzy, unable to breathe, unable to think anything but horror. *It's going to kill me!*

But then, for a single second, as everything grew quiet and he listened in the silence, he allowed himself to hope. Maybe the Animal hadn't heard him. Maybe it wasn't lurking mere feet away, hungry for blood.

Maybe.

Wood shattered, and two fur-covered hands reached through the cracked door, grabbing hold of him and ripping him through the wood, cracking bones and tearing flesh as it did.

Not releasing its grip, the Animal pulled further, and Luke felt his ribs crack as his body was slung into the wall, like a rabbit caught in the mouth of a wolf, forced to scream in pain as the predator thrashed, snapping its prey's bones without loosening its grip.

Then, as he screamed in unbearable agony, the Animal began dragging him down the hallway, toward the end, toward Rhett, who had already locked the door, leaving Luke to die.

Desperate, being dragged like a corpse, legs leaving trails of blood on the floor, not daring to even look up at the Animal looming over him, Luke took the blade still in his hands and shoved it upwards into the creature's stomach, drawing blood, which poured down over him.

But the monster didn't stop.

Again and again, Luke stabbed, ripping flesh and drawing blood with every strike. But it didn't stop it.

Even as the blood poured out of it, the Animal didn't scream, didn't even flinch in pain, as if nothing Luke did would ever be enough to kill it, as if he was a rat trying to scratch a lion. The hollow strikes of prey doomed to be eaten, trying to fight the inevitable.

"No!" Luke screamed as they reached the end of the hall, and the Animal lifted him off the floor, shoving him against the wooden door that hid Rhett inside.

"Help me!" Luke screamed, not turning back to face the Animal behind him but feeling it looming over him all the same. Ready to massacre its prey.

"Please!" Luke begged, crying out, tears falling down his face.

"Help me!"

The Animal shoved its prey's face into the wall, cracking the wood.

The prey tried to scream again, words coming out slurred, broken.

Gripping the back of the prey's head, the Animal shoved it forward again, breaking the wall, splintering wood, revealing the metal behind it. But that didn't stop the slaughter.

The next strike broke the prey's mask, shoving the broken plastic into the prey's face, distorting it, cutting its throat, causing its cries for help to come out as wails of torment.

Again, the Animal crashed its head into the wall, this time breaking its skull. Then it did it again, breaking what was left.

Again, drawing only more blood and ending the cries of agony.

Over and over it went, even after the prey was dead, shoving the remains of its carcass into the wall, cracking wood and bending metal, until finally there wasn't enough left to grip and the prey dropped to the floor, a distorted mass of blood and broken bones.

The Animal stared in through the cracks in the wood, at the still-breathing prey that hid behind it.

Blood flowed down the wall, distorting what lay behind it, infecting the horrific image in a shade of red as the Animal watched him.

Rhett couldn't move, couldn't even breathe as he saw it. Not through a flash of lightning, or hidden within the darkness, but inches away.

The cracks in the wood only revealed glimpses of the monster. Flesh ripped from wolves, nothing like the plastic mask that still covered his face. Coarse black fur covered in the blood of its victims. Hollow eyes staring through the cracks, watching him, watching its prey.

Unable to think, Rhett felt his instincts forcing him back, away from the monster. Seeing it now, the monstrous Animal stalking him from behind the wall it had almost broken, Rhett felt the truth growing in his bones like a cancer, drowning out all other thoughts.

The doctor had lied. It wasn't human.

It couldn't be.

CHAPTER FIFTY-FIVE

Quietly, Riley moved through the house, searching for her daughter.

She had heard the screams of agony that echoed through the hallway across from her, felt the house shake as something was shoved into a wall, over and over again until nothing was left.

The Animal had taken more victims, slaughtered more prey.

But that didn't mean this was over. Not until she found Emma.

The screams had come from the safe room, which meant Emma hadn't hidden there. The door that held the chain had also been filled with screams, so she couldn't be there either. Which meant she was hiding in a normal room, with only a lock to protect her from the kids, the human monsters.

Riley moved to a door, dimly lit from the moonlight crawling through the window behind her. But as she turned the doorknob and peered at the room inside, she saw it was empty.

So was the next room, and the one after, both perfectly quiet, neither one containing any traces of life. But with every remaining room she checked, she felt the life draining from her own body. The blood loss, the broken leg; she might live through the injuries, but before long she wouldn't even be able to stand, much less protect Emma.

She checked another room. Empty.

Riley had to find her soon. She had to.

Then, she heard movement. A struggle. The scream of her daughter.

Downstairs, Rhett practically fell down the safe room's staircase as he crashed through the lower door and into the basement: a dark room hidden beneath the earth, a living tomb waiting to be occupied.

Have to lead it away from Kelly. It will kill her. It'll kill us all.

Rhett ran through the room, stumbling as he did, falling against a wall in the darkness and using it to lead him to the door. To safety.

Have to run!

Not injured but shuddering in fear, he moved closer to the exit, the stairs that led up to the house, to the way out, to salvation.

But then, the door crashed open, splinters of wood bursting through the room, fragments hitting Rhett's mask as he looked up in the darkness and saw a shadow looming above him. A dark figure outlined in the doorway, tilting its head as it peered down at its trapped victim.

The Animal had come for blood.

Riley limped to the origin of the scream, leaving a trail of blood behind her.

She was close. She could feel it.

Gripping the shotgun tightly in her hands, Riley took a deep breath, standing at the edge of the open door, almost scared of what she would find. What if she found Emma but couldn't save her? What if Emma saw her blood spill, just as she had witnessed her parents'?

But there was no choice to make, and so Riley moved into the room, raising the gun up and finding the life that was hidden inside.

Emma, hazelnut eyes that matched Riley's once filled with joy, now piercing with fright as she hung there: body leaning out of the broken window, hair blowing in the wind and rain.

The only thing keeping her from falling out of the window was the grip of a killer, holding on to her arm, keeping Emma precariously balanced between life and death.

Riley moved the shotgun's sights to the killer's mask, which hid the flesh and bone within.

"Drop it," Kelly's voice echoed out from behind the mask. "Or I drop her."

Lightning flashed in Riley's eyes, and she desperately wanted to fire on the girl who thought she could threaten her daughter. Wanted to watch the muzzle flash light up the room and stain the wall with Kelly's blood.

If she had just been holding Emma, Riley would have. From this distance, her aim would have been good enough to avoid her daughter and kill her target.

But Kelly was smart, holding Emma out the window. Even if Riley shot Kelly without hitting Emma, her daughter would still fall, and at this distance she wasn't sure she would avoid the metal spikes of the fence, which circled this side of the house closely, like the gate of an abandoned graveyard, trapping unfortunate souls in its cold ground, not willing for them to escape its hollow grasp.

She had no choice and lowered the gun.

"Unload it," Kelly said, smart enough to know Riley would just pick it up as soon as she let Emma go.

Not taking her eyes off her daughter, Riley cocked the shotgun, listening as the shell hit the floor. Then she did it again, and again, until there was nothing left inside.

Finally, she tossed the weapon to the floor as well, hearing its thud as it impacted the carpet, wanting desperately to move across the room, rip Kelly's mask off, and beat her to death with it.

But she couldn't. At least not yet.

"No!" Rhett screamed, turning away from the monster lurking above him and running through the darkness, heart racing, hands shaking as he tried to find a way to escape. A way out of the grave he had descended into.

No sound echoed as the Animal moved. No light revealed its features. But Rhett could sense it moving closer. In his bones he could feel it. There was no escape, no way to fight it.

It's going to kill me. I'm going to die here!

Desperate, unable to breathe, Rhett searched the basement, waiting for the hidden monster to strike, find where he was hiding, and rip his throat from his body, stealing his screams as it had stolen Gabriella's.

But then he saw it. A small sliver of moonlight, no more than a crack, streaming down from the ceiling in the corner of the room. The lining of doors, of a basement hatch.

Slanted doors leading outside. Leading to safety.

Rhett ran for it.

The wolf mask moved as Kelly looked Riley up and down, examining her new injuries: the cuts of glass, the bleeding head.

"Luke?" Kelly asked.

"Russel," Riley answered.

"Yeah, that makes more sense. Is he dead?"

Riley nodded.

"Aww, that's too bad. I liked him. Looks like he got you pretty good, though."

The bones within her leg were beginning to splinter out, cutting into the flesh of her knee, digging themselves deeper every second she stood, but she hid the pain. Just had to talk Kelly into letting Emma go, and then she could take the blade hidden in her boot and slit the girl's throat.

"So," Riley said, her eyes meeting Emma's for a moment, trying to tell her it would be okay. "What now?"

"I only need one of you as bait for the Animal," Kelly said. "So why don't you take the knife hidden in your boot and slit your own throat. Save me the trouble."

For a moment, Riley stood frozen, shocked at the request.

"Do it," Kelly growled, "or I drop her."

Knowing there was no choice to make, Riley took the knife and lifted it up in her hands, hearing Emma cry as she did, horrified as she watched what her mother was about to do. And as much as Riley knew what it might cost, there wasn't another way. She would gladly trade her own life for Emma's, without a second thought, a moment's hesitation.

But Kelly would just kill Emma anyway. Maybe she wouldn't drop her to her death, but eventually Kelly would kill her, either doing it herself, or by leaving her as an offering to the Animal, in the hopes of being spared.

Emma would die either way. There was no choice to make.

Riley gripped the knife tightly. "Do it."

"What?" Kelly asked, the shock in her face hidden by the wolf's mask.

"Drop her."

Riley knew it might kill her, that she might get impaled on the spike and cry out in pain. But she also knew her daughter was smart and would know to pull on Kelly's hand, keeping her from shoving her too far. Keeping her closer to the house, away from the fence.

The fall would still hurt, might break a bone, but it wouldn't kill her.

Confused, Kelly turned to Emma and then back to Riley, not knowing how to respond. "I'll kill her!"

Riley didn't answer, instead looking to Emma and softly nodding, telling her what she had to do if Kelly let go.

It was the only chance she had to save her daughter, and Riley found herself silently begging, hoping beyond reason that just this once, the one she loved would be saved from the monsters.

But then a sound echoed through the night and changed everything. It was the cracking of wood, the opening of the basement door. Even through the rain and the storm, Riley could hear Rhett's screams as he escaped the basement, terrified of what was coming for him.

"Rhett?" Kelly cried out, seeing him run through the grass below.

"Kelly!" he screamed, and even from a distance, Riley could hear the fear in his voice. The Animal had found him.

"What's wrong?" Kelly called out.

"It's after me!" he called back. "Stay in there. Don't come out!"

Then Riley saw Kelly's body language change, going from deranged to concerned. Almost terrified, but not of the Animal.

Terrified of losing Rhett.

In that moment, Riley realized the truth. They might not have cared about the dozens they slaughtered, might not have even cared about their friends, but they cared about each other. Tried to protect one another.

The revelation didn't bring sadness or even humanity to them. Instead, it filled Riley with dread, because she knew what was about to happen.

"Don't," she warned, but Kelly ignored her, knowing that her brother would be killed without bait.

"Take her," Kelly screamed, letting go of Emma, looking out the window as the child fell from the clutches of one monster into the grip of another.

"What about you?" Rhett screamed, drowning out Emma's cries. To Riley, it sounded as though he was covering her mouth.

"Don't worry about me," Kelly called back, turning to face Riley once again. "I can handle her. Just run."

"Good luck," he called out, voice regaining a bit of the sinister quality as he no doubt imagined his sister slitting Riley's throat.

Riley only hoped he stayed alive long enough to know what was about to happen to his precious *sister*.

"So," Kelly said, still cloaked in the costume of a wolf, mask tilted to its side, fur-covered arms revealing a sharpened bone hidden behind her back. "Any last words?"

Riley said nothing, instead looking over the room where they now stood. It was the first place she had gone after Hank had asked her to help the kids. On the wall behind Kelly were mounts of animals: coyotes, bobcats, bearskin. Marks of the predator.

On the wall behind Riley were the antlers of the whitetail deer she had hunted when she was nineteen, jagged horns jutting off in every direction. A symbol of prey.

"C'mon," Kelly said, activating the tape recorder in her costume, letting a growl echo throughout the room as she stood there, grey fur illuminated by the moonlight creeping in through the broken window, streaks of light dancing around both of them. "What's the matter? Can't you growl?"

Trying not to let the pain coursing through her show, Riley remained silent, standing tall despite the broken leg, shifting the antlers behind her from appearing behind her head to sprouting out her back like distorted wings.

Kelly laughed. "Fine, stay quiet. It will make the screams mean so much more."

Then, as if in a sign of warning, lightning flashed again, searing their eyes in its white glow.

By the time the flash was gone, Riley attacked, swinging her blade toward Kelly's head, not wanting to waste time by wounding her.

But Kelly was quick, far quicker than she had let on when they had sparred, and by the time the thunder arrived, she had grabbed Riley's wrist and forced the sharpened bone off its path.

No more lightning came, no more thunder, but still they fought, blades cutting the air as they went for each other's throats. At first, they moved surgically, attempting precise cuts in places they knew would bleed.

But soon, Riley felt the exhaustion setting in, the blood loss clouding her vision, and the broken leg beginning to not just erupt in pain from the pressure but buckle underneath it. She didn't have much more fight in her, and if she gave out before the girl, then she was dead, and Emma with her.

So Riley was careful. She held back and stopped attacking, instead letting Kelly attack her. The girl was vicious, attacking like she was possessed, swinging for Riley's throat, her eyes, even her heart.

But with every strike, Kelly grew wilder, a crazed predator whose prey was backtracking, growing tired of the hunt, ready to end it.

Riley kept waiting for an opening. A sloppy attack, a desperate lunge, anything to give her a chance to end it quickly. Finally, that opportunity came as Kelly leapt forward and attempted to drive the blade down into Riley's skull.

Then, Riley did what she had done to the predator at the safe house. She grabbed the mask, hard plastic covered in faux fur, and pushed it sideways, taking Kelly's vision. The price paid for the appearance of a monster.

Kelly screamed and stumbled backwards, appearing as a werewolf whose head was broken, trying to set the mask right again, when Riley unleashed what little fight she had left.

She swung her knife at the girl's neck, but instinctively, Kelly had held her arm up, deflecting the blade into her shoulder instead. But Riley didn't stop, pressing the knife in farther, hearing Kelly's screams, before she began to strike her in the face, fists colliding with the plastic mask over and over again until it cracked just like her brother's mask had.

Riley kept going, beating the blinded girl, until finally she ripped the knife back out of Kelly's shoulder and swung it at her neck, ready to end it.

But through the cracks of the mask, Riley saw Kelly's eyes and realized Kelly could see her too. By then, however, it was too late to stop it.

Seeing her opponent through cracked plastic and her own blood, Kelly blocked the knife before lifting her leg up and bringing her heel back down on Riley's knee. Her *broken* knee.

In an instant Riley lost her grip on the knife, and before she could even scream in pain she was on the floor, clutching her leg, feeling the distorted bone pressing against the skin, drawing blood from within.

The cry of pain came a moment later.

Kelly stood over her, ripping the cracked mask off her face and throwing it to the floor beside Riley. Her face was now covered in blood, cracks of the mask had cut her skin, and red streaks flowed down her face. Her blond hair crawled its way down to the grey fur that covered her shoulders, and despite the obvious pain, she flashed an evil grin as she watched Riley struggling on the floor, attempting to stand back up.

For a moment, it looked as though she would end it right there, slice Riley's throat while she was helpless, but then she had a change of heart. Just as Gabriella had watched the cat with broken legs try to escape, Kelly decided to watch her prey try to stand.

Tears flowed down Riley's face as she tried, planting her knee on the floor and trying to press up with the other foot, but the moment she did, she fell again.

"You didn't really think you could kill me?" Kelly asked.

Blood poured from her stomach as she tried again, but again the pain forced her back down.

"We killed dozens of people." Kelly grinned. "More than your *Animal* ever did. We're predators, just like it was. But you're still just the scared little girl who cried under her bed. We're predators, and you're just prey."

Wincing in pain, Riley planted her feet on the floor once again and whispered to herself, too quiet for Kelly to hear but loud enough to remind herself of the truth. That she was prey. Just like the deer had been. But...

"Even deer have horns."

In one final desperate attempt, Riley put pressure on the leg, wanting to scream from pain as tears fell from her face, but she didn't stop, forcing herself upwards, onto her feet once more.

Her broken leg cried out in pain, trying to drag her downwards. Her shattered wrist shook from where she had broken free from her snare. Blood dripped out of her side, where she had been made to scream, and four lines of red still streamed down her face, circling her eye, the wound from the dog's claws.

But still, she stood there, not backing down, not willing to die on the floor. Not ready to die at all.

She couldn't fight back. The moment she moved, she would hit the floor once more. She couldn't blind Kelly again; the mask had been removed. Her gun was lying across the room, unloaded, and her knife was now with Kelly, who was holding both of the blades, ready to strike.

Eventually, she did, lunging toward Riley, swinging both blades wildly, thirsty for blood, ready to kill Riley and prove she was special. That she was the predator she thought she was.

As she swung, Riley caught her left hand and, using the last bit of strength she had, pulled and spun, using the girl's own momentum to throw her backwards, into the wall behind Riley.

Into the antlers that hung there.

Then Riley collapsed onto the floor once again, looking up to the predator who was trapped against the wall, trying to move as blood poured down her chest and from her mouth.

For a moment, Kelly's eyes were filled with shock as she found herself unable to pull away from the wall's grip. But then she looked down and saw the horror. Sharp antlers, digging through her back and sticking out from her chest, keeping her in their grip, tearing through her lungs, taking away her breath.

In terror, she wanted to scream, but the antlers had taken that from her too, one of them reaching up to her neck, piercing her throat.

Even as her body started to shut down and death began to crawl over her, she couldn't drop to the floor, kept hanging there by the antlers, gravity pushing her further into them as her body went numb.

Slowly, Riley stood up from the floor once more and looked Kelly in the eyes, a flash of malice in her own eyes as she saw the girl impaled on the horns of the prey she despised, trying desperately to scream.

"What's the matter?" Riley asked. "Can't you growl?"

The girl's body started shaking, the grip of death growing tighter, and Riley saw the look in Kelly's eyes. Fear. Not of dying, but of doing so alone. Isolated from everyone else, like her parents must have made her feel, without even her brother by her side as she drew her last breath, bloodied corpse still hanging from the deer's antlers.

Riley breathed deeply, wincing in pain as she limped over to the shotgun, loading it once again before leaning against it, trying to take pressure off her leg, allow herself to move, to get to the forest.

The night wasn't over. Not yet.

CHAPTER FIFTY-SIX

Monsters exist.

Rhett knew that now, because one was hunting him.

Running through the forest, Rhett kept one hand gripped tightly on his blade and the other around the girl's hair, dragging her along with him, through the mud and the rain, passing trees that looked like hollow ghosts watching him in the night, waiting to see the slaughter.

The doctor had lied. She'd said it was a man. That it had a face, a name. But it wasn't human. Rhett had seen the monster through the cracked wood and the blood of his friend. It wasn't just a mask, wasn't just the flesh of the wolves. It was death.

Feet sliding in the mud, Rhett desperately leaned against the looming trees, trying to escape, trying to run as fast as he could, wishing to the sky above that he hadn't cut the tires of the cars to try and trap Riley.

As the forest seemingly began to move closer to him, branches cracking and dead leaves rustling, distorting the rainfall, Rhett wished he'd never come here, into this forest, the Animal's home.

But he'd had no other choice.

The girl tried to pull away, but Rhett held her tight. She was his last hope. If the Animal found him, maybe threatening the girl would stop it. Stop the slaughter.

Breathing heavy, Rhett felt as though he was suffocating within the mask. It was stealing his oxygen and corrupting his vision. So he took it off, losing his unnatural appearance for the sake of survival.

But he couldn't just leave it on the ground, tracks for the monster to find. So he placed it over the girl's head, taking away her vision as he dragged her farther into the heart of the woods.

Suddenly, the howling of wolves echoed in the distance, first to his back, then in front of him, then everywhere. Vicious howling directed toward the full moon, which shined so brightly in the sky that it slithered through the branches above, thin traces of light dancing around the forest, illuminating the fog of the night.

Even they seemed to be moving closer, attempting to strangle him in their glow, reveal him for the monster.

Where is it? Rhett thought as he continued to run. The monster had followed him, but without making a sound. No footsteps echoed. No breaths taken.

It could be right in front of him.

Hidden in the darkness, surrounded by traces of moonlight, rotting trees, and the howls of wolves, the Animal hunted.

Rhett thought he heard something. The cracking of a branch. In terror, he hid behind a tree, holding the girl close, hands shaking, heart racing.

Fear forced his eyes closed, not even willing to look through the trees, too afraid of seeing what lurked within them.

Too afraid of what could be stalking him.

Unable to control his nervous, horrified breathing, Rhett felt dizziness set in, almost causing him to stumble when he moved from that tree to another, attempting to hide, to grow further from the monster.

But every second he spent in the forest, whether hiding behind a looming tree with grisly bark or running through the wet mud and rain, he felt the Animal growing closer. In his bones he felt it stalking him.

The Animal slightly tilted its head, listening in the distance for the footsteps echoing through the forest as the prey ran through the mud, desperate to escape.

The prey would scream, like everything did.

Rhett ran to another tree, again stopping to hide behind it. He could feel it, the monster within the trees, waiting to rip him apart. In a moment of desperation, Rhett looked down at the blade in his hands, and for a single second, he considered it. Doing what Dylan had done, ending the horror before it got worse. Killing himself before the monster could.

But a second later, it was gone. He couldn't kill himself, not when the Animal was still out there, not when it might hunt Kelly next.

So instead, he ran again, hiding behind another tree, feeling its coarse bark dig against his back, shaking as the branches above him seemed to reach down, broken bark and withering leaves trying to grab hold of him.

Trying to keep him there forever.

Silently lurking in the dark within the forest, the Animal heard it breathing. Quick breaths of prey too afraid to think clearly. The Animal's hand twitched, waiting in the darkness, waiting to hear the prey scream, before silencing it forever.

It could be right next to me! Rhett thought, terrified. *What if it hears me breathing?*

Holding his breath, Rhett forced his eyes open, not letting fear take away his vision. If it attacked, he had to see it coming, had to be able to see the monster to run from it.

It was close. Very close. His skin crawled at its presence, and a chill swept over his back, piercing his spine, trying to freeze him in fear as his instincts cried out one last message.

Run!

So he did, turning from behind the tree, feet sinking in the mud as he tried to run, tried to escape the monster. But the moment he moved, his eyes saw it, and the mere sight brought him to the ground.

The Animal, right in front of him.

"No!" Rhett screamed, crawling backwards in the mud, looking up with panic at the monster looming above him.

Rain crashed down on its black fur, mixing with the blood still covering it. Moonlight escaped through the branches, thin cracks of distorted light revealing pieces of the beast. The head of a wolf. Fur ripped from flesh. The hollow dark holes where it watched him.

"No!" Rhett screamed again, crawling further until his back was against a tree. But the Animal did not move, only shifting its head, keeping its gaze on him.

A predator waiting for its prey to run.

Rhett ripped the mask off the girl, revealing her features. A child the Animal hadn't slaughtered. The child of its original prey. Rhett pressed the sharpened bone to her throat. "I'll kill her!" he screamed as he stood up from the ground, back still to the trees.

The Animal didn't move.

"I'll do it!" Rhett cried out, almost begging the monster to hear his cries, to let him go for the sake of the girl's life. But in his bones, looking at the Animal come for his blood, he knew it wouldn't happen.

It would never let him escape. Even if he got away now, even if he escaped the forest, the Animal would still hunt him. Nothing would stop it. Nothing could kill it. Eventually it would rip his throat from his body and end his life.

In that moment of haunting realization, Rhett felt his life already slipping away, felt the darkness calling him, a walking corpse just waiting for its blood to be spilled, waiting for the monster to attack.

To the monster, Rhett was just prey, as everything else had been. Just hollow breaths and blood-lined flesh, not human, not worth the struggle. Not even worth a growl.

In a sudden flash of anger, fear having left him because he was already dead, Rhett lashed out. He wasn't *prey*. He wouldn't let it slaughter him like he was. First, he would hear it growl. Growl as if it was growling at another monster: an equal beast.

"Growl," Rhett said, eyes piercing, blade against the girl's throat.

The Animal did nothing, only watching him from a few feet away, ready to spill his blood, but expressionless, emotionless, as if it wasn't even alive.

"Growl!" Rhett screamed, ready to slit the girl's throat right there before the Animal could reach him. "Or I kill her!"

No sound echoed.

"Do it!"

The Animal slightly turned its head, as if it was looking right past him.

"Growl!"

As his own scream echoed into the forest, Rhett finally heard it.

Growling.

It started off quiet, a low rumble, vicious and threatening. But then it grew, loud and animalistic, horrific growling accompanied by the snapping of teeth as monstrous jaws clicked together.

In horror, Rhett realized the growling was coming from behind him.

Slowly he turned, his eyes leaving the Animal and meeting the creature hiding in the shadows of the trees behind him: grey fur, sharp teeth, scarred face. The wolf from the game ranch.

It had escaped.

Before he could react, the wolf leapt on him, digging its teeth into his wrist, tearing enough flesh away to force the girl free of his grip. Rhett screamed and managed to throw the wolf off, ready for it to attack again and go for his throat.

But it didn't.

Instead, it crept back into the darkness, leaving Rhett alone with the Animal, without the girl in his grip to threaten.

"No!" Rhett cried as the monster moved closer, black fur and hollow eyes. It was going to kill him!

In a final desperate act, Rhett took the blade still in his hands and lunged forward, digging it into the monster's chest, piercing the Animal's heart.

But the Animal didn't die.

It reached out and grabbed Rhett by the throat, grip cutting off all oxygen, all blood flow as it dug its fingers into his skin.

Then, it began raising him up.

As the Animal lifted him into the air, its monstrous hand tight around his throat, Rhett cried in pain, and reached for the blade in the Animal's chest, pulling it out and stabbing the monster again.

Still, the Animal wouldn't die.

Rhett's feet lifted off the ground, hanging limp from his body as he stabbed the monster over and over again, drawing blood, ripping flesh from its chest, its shoulder. But its grip didn't loosen. It couldn't be killed.

Gagging, body seizing as it cried out for oxygen that wouldn't come, Rhett tried one final time and brought the sharpened bone down into the Animal's neck, the blade sinking down far enough that Rhett's hand was against the fur.

Blood poured from the wound, even as Rhett ripped the blade out and let it fall to the mud below, resigned to his fate. The Animal hadn't died. Hadn't even flinched in pain.

The monster couldn't die.

The Animal raised Rhett up further, grip crushing his throat as it kept him there, lifted into the air, blocking the moonlight from reaching its face, surrounded by the rain, and the flashes of lightning.

Then, in that moment, Rhett saw it. Far beyond the hollow eyes of the wolf's flesh, hidden behind the mask, the fur, he saw it. The true eyes of the Animal. Seeing it, he screamed out in horror, knowing the truth. That the eyes behind the mask were far less human than even the wolves' flesh it was covered in.

Now, as he screamed, unable to fight the Animal's grip and too scared to even try, Rhett waited for it to kill him. Waited to be slaughtered by the monster from the legends, the one more horrifying than they had ever told of.

The Animal held its prey up, listening to its cries for help, its screams of terror. It could even hear the prey's heartbeat, pulsing rapidly, choking itself on its own blood for fear of losing it.

It could feel the chill growing over the prey's skin, the trembling of its bones as the Animal held it there, ready to crush its throat. Feel its blood spill out onto the monster's hands. It could already hear the scream of pain, the cry of prey, as the child's life would be ripped from it.

But the Animal saw something else, buried deep behind the eyes of the child, the prey it was about to slaughter. Not just fear of dying, but something more.

The Animal hesitated.

"Do it," Rhett finally begged, choking, ready to die.

The Animal saw it then. The prey was already dead. Had already screamed, bled, and run. Now it just wanted to die. Die by the Animal's hand. The last resort to make itself into a predator.

In that moment, the Animal fought its need to hunt, its urge for bloodshed now replaced by a far different instinct. One it had learned long ago, from a monster whose heart it had ripped from its chest.

Cruelty.

The Animal released its grip, and Rhett hit the ground, gasping for air, crying in pain, before looking up at the Animal, outlined by the moon

It was massive, looming over him like death itself, an inhuman monster. But it didn't kill him. Didn't attack. For the briefest moment of confusion, Rhett allowed himself to hope.

But then he saw the eyes.

Glowing in the moonlight, revealing themselves behind the Animal, pairs of yellow eyes began to move, watching him from the darkness, a pack of wolves hungry for his flesh.

"No..." Rhett stammered, crawling away as the eyes moved closer, and the wolves behind them were revealed. Growling, mouths dripping with hunger as they snapped their teeth, approaching their prey. They moved past the Animal, which still stood there, watching Rhett as if it knew what was coming.

"No!" Rhett screamed, standing up from the ground and desperately trying to run from the pack, trying to escape with his life.

But then the sound of gunfire echoed in the forest, and Rhett felt the bullet pass through his knee, bringing him back down into the mud, now unable to run from the monsters.

As rain flooded from the night sky and thunder shook the trees of the forest, Rhett turned one final time to see Riley, leaning against a tree, holding the shotgun that had taken his leg. Staring at her for a moment, the girl who survived, the one they'd tried to kill, he felt his heart stop, knowing what Riley being there meant. She'd killed Kelly, killed his sister.

It was the last thought that crossed his mind before the wolves came and bit into his flesh, tearing it from his bones, ripping skin and spilling his blood into the forest, bringing with it screams of unimaginable pain.

Soon, the screams of agony stopped, replaced by the howling of wolves as they devoured their fallen prey.

CHAPTER FIFTY-SEVEN

The storm vanished as quickly as it had begun. The rain stopped, the lightning lost its flash, and the thunder echoed no longer, leaving the forest quiet, almost empty, as Riley saw her daughter.

She was still alive.

Riley fell to the ground as Emma ran to her, through the forest, through the trees, finally embracing her mother and hiding herself within Riley's arms.

As Riley held her, feeling the warmth of her daughter, tears fell down her face. Kneeling there in the forest, she couldn't let go, holding Emma tight, feeling the beating of her heart, hearing the breathing of her lungs.

Emma's still alive. The thought repeated in Riley's head, almost unable to believe it. After losing everyone else, Riley had always feared losing Emma too. But here she was, still alive, in her arms, her embrace.

Emma began to cry as well, fear from the night taking hold as the shock left her, and Riley held her tighter, almost afraid to let go, afraid the night would steal her away too.

They stayed there for a moment longer, both holding on to everything they had left in the world, scared to let it go. Even when they did, Riley just stared into her daughter's eyes, seeing the light still glowing within them, a final tear of joy falling from her face, which even the broken bones and bleeding side couldn't take away.

Emma had survived. That was all that mattered.

But then, looking back into her mother's eyes, Emma spoke. "It saved me."

For a moment, Riley was confused, until she saw her daughter's gaze focus on what was behind her.

Riley turned to see the Animal from her past, standing across the forest, covered in monstrous fur and the blood of its victims. For a moment, her heart stopped, and she became the frightened child once again. Afraid the monster would attack. Afraid it wasn't over.

But then, Emma's words sank in.

"It saved me."

As Riley watched it, still holding her daughter close, she saw it stumble slightly, and then she realized the truth. It wasn't covered in the blood of its victims. The Animal was covered in its own blood, and now that the hunt was over, the instincts gave way and the wounds took hold as the Animal fell, hitting the ground, its back resting against a tree.

It was dying.

Slowly, cautiously, Riley stood up, leaning against the shotgun's barrel, limping her way closer to the monster. Even now, every bone in her body shook, screaming at her to run, to try to escape.

But she had to know. She had to see it.

Dimly lit by traces of moonlight that twisted through the branches, Riley approached the Animal, kneeling down in front of it, feeling Emma still holding close to her back.

The Animal was shaking slightly, and Riley could see the blood now. Pouring from its chest, from its neck, no instincts to keep it alive. No adrenaline left to keep it hunting.

But it could still kill her. If it was the Animal she remembered, it could still slaughter her right there.

But she had to see its face.

Reaching over, ready for the Animal to attack at any moment, Riley's hand rested against its mask, feeling the coarse fur, the face of a wolf that had been taken from it. Slowly, she pulled the mask of wolf skin off, unable to breathe as she waited to see the monster that lay beneath it.

Then, she saw it. She saw *him*.

He had brown hair, just like her. Ten, maybe fifteen years older. A face filled with pain, years of horror and sorrow hiding behind his eyes, which looked at her, almost in fear. Afraid of what he had done to her. Afraid of the monster he'd become.

Tears streamed down her face as she saw it, the Animal who'd haunted her nightmares for twenty-five years, staring at her now, human eyes filled with more pain than she had ever imagined.

It wasn't a monster.

In the distance, police sirens echoed.

Riley knew what would happen next. Even after tonight, even after the truth about the kids came out, the town would still hold on to the legend, but it would change, adapt to the killings. The Animal would be the one who'd slaughtered the predators, the evil within the town, and in the end, after everything they had done, the kids would just be remembered as more of the Animal's victims.

Oliver would have liked that.

But Riley had never cared what the legends said. All she cared about was standing behind her. Emma, still alive, still breathing, and in front of Riley was the man who had saved her.

Riley moved her eyes slightly, asking without speaking. Maybe if the police came, maybe if they got to an ambulance quick enough. *Maybe.*

But the Animal shook its head, and she knew why. This was who it was, where it belonged. Where it should be allowed to die.

Riley held Emma close. She didn't know if the pain of that night would ever go away, or if she would ever be able to let go of what had happened. But still, in the heart of the forest, as the moon vanished behind clouds once more, Riley stayed there with it as it died.

The monster who'd slaughtered her parents. The Animal who'd saved her daughter.

Clyde.

THE END

ACKNOWLEDGMENTS

Firstly, I would like to thank my family for their continued support: my mother, my father, and my older brothers. It is so cool to know that when I finish a new story they will be waiting to read it. I couldn't do it without them.

Thanks also to MiblArt, who went above and beyond for this book. Not only did they design the awesome cover art, they also did all of the interior artwork along with the formatting, working closely with me to make sure everything looked as cool as it possibly could. It was a lot of artwork, and there isn't another company I would have trusted to work with on it.

In addition, I would like to give a special word of thanks to my editor, Eliza Dee, who did the copyediting and proofread. Not only did she do a fantastic job, she was also available on short notice, and if it wasn't for her help, this book might have not have been ready in time for its Halloween release date, which was really important to me.

I would also like to give a special word of thanks to my three beta readers for this novel: Ariel from *Reading and Whatnot*, Lezlie from *The Nerdy Narrative*, and Kayla from *Kayla Lezen YouTube Channel*.

Also, I would like to thank all the amazing booktubers, Instagrammers, and bloggers who reviewed my debut novel, *Nightmare*, and my second novel, *Shade*. Reviews are more helpful than you could ever know, so thank you so much for taking the time to review my stories.

Lastly, thank you, for reading this book.

Hope you read the next one too!

AUTHOR BIO

Chad Nicholas is a horror, mystery and thriller author, but if he's being completely honest, what he loves writing the most are unique stories with crazy plot twists, which can be seen in his debut horror novel, *Nightmare*, as well as his second novel, a crime thriller titled *Shade*.

When he isn't writing, Chad spends his time studying for his mechanical engineering degree, watching movies, and reading comic books. Chad was also ranked #1 in the world on the Teen Titan challenge map from *Batman: Arkham Knight*, a fact he is very proud of.

If you're reading this, it means Chad has finished writing his first slasher novel, *The Animal*, and is now working on his next book, a detective novel that he's been working on for a long time, and one that he cannot wait for all of you to finally read. It's going to be a special one.

Keep in touch with Chad via the web:

Instagram: @thechadnicholas

YouTube: Chad Nicholas

Website: thechadnicholas.com

P.S. DC Comics, I am asking you once again, please let Chad write a graphic novel about Scarecrow's origin story. His obsession with it has only grown worse since he completed his last novel, and the rest of us are starting to get concerned. He just keeps talking about how it would be the most terrifying Scarecrow story ever written, and how Jonathan Crane could be the greatest horror villain of all time.

Please, help make his ramblings stop.

I'm begging you...

Oliver's Journal

Riley
The Girl Who Survived

SUSPECTED OF:

ALIBIES:

MOTIVE:

NOTES:

☐ **DEFINITELY CLEARED**

☐ **POSSIBLE SUSPECT**

☐ **PRIME SUSPECT**

FINAL VERDICT:

Notes

Clyde
The One Who Found Tracks

SUSPECTED OF:

ALIBIES:

MOTIVE:

NOTES:

☐ **DEFINITELY CLEARED**

☐ **POSSIBLE SUSPECT**

☐ **PRIME SUSPECT**

FINAL VERDICT:

Notes

Kelly
The New Victim

SUSPECTED OF:

ALIBIES:

MOTIVE:

NOTES:

☐ **DEFINITELY CLEARED**

☐ **POSSIBLE SUSPECT**

☐ **PRIME SUSPECT**

FINAL VERDICT:

Notes

Rhett
The Protective Brother

SUSPECTED OF:

ALIBIES:

MOTIVE:

NOTES:

☐ **DEFINITELY CLEARED**

☐ **POSSIBLE SUSPECT**

☐ **PRIME SUSPECT**

FINAL VERDICT:

Notes

Luke
The Sheriff's Son

SUSPECTED OF:

ALIBIES:

MOTIVE:

NOTES:

☐ **DEFINITELY CLEARED**

☐ **POSSIBLE SUSPECT**

☐ **PRIME SUSPECT**

FINAL VERDICT:

Notes

Dylan
The Laughing Kid

SUSPECTED OF:

ALIBIES:

MOTIVE:

NOTES:

☐ **DEFINITELY CLEARED**

☐ **POSSIBLE SUSPECT**

☐ **PRIME SUSPECT**

FINAL VERDICT:

Notes

Russel
The Bullied Jock

SUSPECTED OF:

ALIBIES:

MOTIVE:

NOTES:

☐ **DEFINITELY CLEARED**

☐ **POSSIBLE SUSPECT**

☐ **PRIME SUSPECT**

FINAL VERDICT:

Notes

Gabriella
The Perfect Athlete

SUSPECTED OF:

ALIBIES:

MOTIVE:

NOTES:

☐ **DEFINITELY CLEARED**

☐ **POSSIBLE SUSPECT**

☐ **PRIME SUSPECT**

FINAL VERDICT:

Notes

Betty
The Helpless Prey

SUSPECTED OF:

ALIBIES:

MOTIVE:

NOTES:

☐ **DEFINITELY CLEARED**

☐ **POSSIBLE SUSPECT**

☐ **PRIME SUSPECT**

FINAL VERDICT:

Notes

Oliver
The Conspiracist

SUSPECTED OF:

ALIBIES:

MOTIVE:

NOTES:

☐ **DEFINITELY CLEARED**

☐ **POSSIBLE SUSPECT**

☐ **PRIME SUSPECT**

FINAL VERDICT:

Notes

Hank
The Old Sheriff

SUSPECTED OF:

ALIBIES:

MOTIVE:

NOTES:

☐ **DEFINITELY CLEARED**

☐ **POSSIBLE SUSPECT**

☐ **PRIME SUSPECT**

FINAL VERDICT:

Notes

Linda
The Good Doctor

SUSPECTED OF:

ALIBIES:

MOTIVE:

NOTES:

☐ **DEFINITELY CLEARED**

☐ **POSSIBLE SUSPECT**

☐ **PRIME SUSPECT**

FINAL VERDICT:

Notes

CONCEPT ART

THE
ANIMAL

David
Nicholas

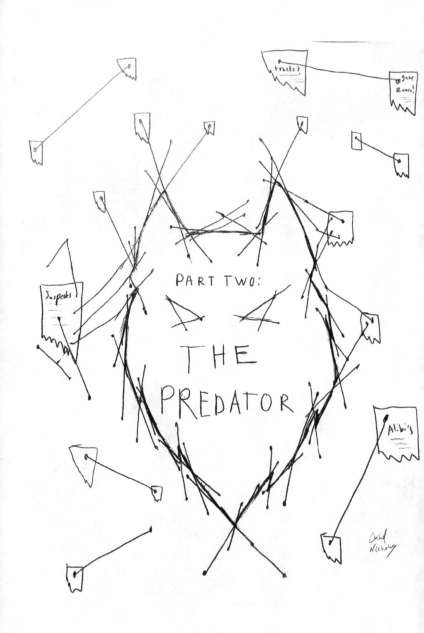

BOOKS BY THE AUTHOR
NIGHTMARE

SYNOPSIS

Had it come back? No, it couldn't have. He had buried it for good. Or at least that's what Scott told himself. But what if it had? Was that why the scarecrow now watched him?

But the more Scott tries to ignore it, the more the evidence begins to pile up. So do the bodies. Because sometimes, the dead don't stay buried. Sometimes the monster survives.

As the bodies mount, and the secrets of his past grow more haunting, Scott must do whatever it takes to save his family. But what if by doing so, they find out what happened all those years ago? What if they realize what he did?

Scott learns that there is no escape from his own past, or the crows that have crawled out of it. He can only watch, as his life is turned into a living nightmare.

REVIEW QUOTES

"A *Jekyll and Hyde* for the modern age."
—John Mountain, *Books of Blood*

"*Nightmare* is a psychological horror at its best!"
—Nichi, *Dark Between Pages*

"This book was a page turner—the story was so interesting and fast-paced that I almost read the whole book in one sitting. I thought I had it figured out so many times as far as where this story was going and I was wrong at almost every turn."
—Lezlie Smith, *The Nerdy Narrative*

"Chad might just be the plot twist master! Perfect pacing, great characters, extremely believable yet terrifying circumstances and amazing plot twists. This is now on my favorite horror novels list for sure!"
—Ariel, *Reading and Whatnot*

READ THE PROLOGUE NOW...

BY CHAD NICHOLAS

NIGHTMARE

Prologue

It was hard to breathe inside the grave. The cold touch of the soil surrounded him like a casket, numbing his body as he lay there motionless. Suddenly, he regained consciousness. He tried to breathe, but instead dirt poured into his mouth, gagging him. He opened his eyes, only to see complete and utter darkness. The ground above crashed down on him, causing his bones to crack under the weight.

He tried to fight his way upwards, but with every inch he gained, he could feel himself slipping back into unconsciousness. His lungs began collapsing, causing his chest to burn as if it was filled with hot embers. He could taste the rough, freezing dirt as it poured down into his throat, choking him. Still, he continued to crawl his way upwards, inch by inch.

Finally, he felt the dirt part above him, the chill breeze hitting his hand as it emerged from the dirt. He summoned what little strength he had left to pull himself up out of the ground.

He rolled over, coughing up the dirt. His lungs gasped for oxygen, his body shaking from the unforgiving chill of the night air. His eyes were still blurry from the dark, but he tried to see where he was. Finally, once the blurriness subsided, he could make out the moon above him, shining down on the tombstones around him. He struggled to find his footing, trying to stand. Once he did, he looked around the cemetery in confusion.

"Where am I?" he whispered to himself. The cemetery was quiet, with only the sound of his breathing cutting through the silence. He looked around at the tombstones, which seemed to stretch out for miles. Suddenly, the cemetery became dark as the moon passed behind an old oak tree. Its branches twisted, distorting the remaining moonlight that passed through them as it shone onto the cemetery.

Suddenly the flapping of a bird's wings tore through the silence. The man jumped in his skin in fear as he searched the sky for it. His breathing quickened as he desperately tried to find it in the darkness. Finally he spotted it, resting on a tombstone in the distance. The man stepped back in horror as he made out the bird's features. Its coarse black feathers were haggard, and its talons seemed like knives in the moonlight. Its head sat slightly askew, as if it was somehow disconnected from its body. It was a crow.

The man stared at the crow as his fear turned to dread. "No, you can't be here," he whispered to

himself. "You're just—" He stopped midsentence as the realization hit him. "No, no, no," he begged as his legs buckled under him and he collapsed to the ground. The fear had completely left him now as he leaned himself on a tombstone. Loneliness cascaded over him as tears streamed down his face. "Please, no," he continued to plead, knowing that it would make no difference.

As he leaned on the tombstone, staring out into the empty cemetery, he heard a horrific sound.

Sccrrreeee

It sounded as if a sawblade was being scraped across wood. The sound kept repeating. As he searched for its origin, he once again saw the crow, but it no longer perched upon the tombstone. It now rested upon a branch of the oak tree, scraping its talons against the wood. The scraping echoed through the night as the moon shifted up in the sky, further illuminating the tree. The man watched in horror, unable to breathe, as he saw the horde of crows that covered the branches. One by one, they joined in with the others, scraping their talons against the bark. The moonlight cast their shadows on the graveyard, covering every inch of it with their twisted reflections.

The man sat frozen with fear. He tried desperately to run, but he couldn't do anything as the crows lifted their broken, distorted wings to take flight. The sound of the flapping was

overwhelming, causing his ears to bleed as the crows tore through the sky, heading right for him. In an instant, they were on him, clawing into his skin, dozens at a time.

He tried desperately to scream, but he couldn't make a sound. He could do nothing but sit hopelessly as the talons tore through his flesh like razor blades. Finally the pain was too much, and he cried out into the night, but it made no difference. No one was coming to help him. He was alone.

BOOKS BY THE AUTHOR
SHADE

SYNOPSIS

All they had to do was catch him.

At first, it was just another case, another serial killer to stop. They had done it countless times before; this time shouldn't have been any different. But soon, days turned into weeks. Desperation set in, and the victims started getting younger. What were they missing? Why couldn't they save the victims? They would have given their own lives just to stop that monster, to finally put an end to his killing spree. In the end, they almost succeeded.

But then, eight months ago, everything went wrong.

From the aftermath of one monster, a new one is born: a killer more lethal than they could have possibly imagined, like something ripped straight out of their worst nightmares. With it comes a new potential victim, struggling with the skeletons in her own closet, the guilt of past mistakes. And the longer she waits for the new monster to find her, to kill her, the more she questions if, deep down, she wants him to.

The desperate hunt for a serial killer, an ex-soldier losing his grip on reality, and a victim who's not sure she's worth saving come together as past and present intertwine in this explosive psychological thriller, which begs the question:

Can you stop a monster without becoming one?

REVIEW QUOTES

"A tale of twisting psychological horror that can be mentioned in the same breath as David Fincher's *Seven*, and Michael Slade's debut novel, *Headhunter.*"
—John Mountain, *Books of Blood*

"A phenomenal crime thriller. Just when I thought I had predicted things, I was instantly proven wrong. It was brutal at times, and deals with some horrific topics, such as grisly murders and severe PTSD, but its handled brilliantly and vividly."
—Charles McGarry, *Bookish Chas*

"This crime story was filled with violence, gore, twists and turns that no matter how hard you look for, you'll never see coming. Chad Nicholas writes crack in book form, and I am so addicted."
—Lezlie Smith, *The Nerdy Narrative*

SHADE

ALL THEY HAD TO DO
WAS CATCH HIM

CHAD NICHOLAS

Chapter One

The six agents stood at the edge of the forest, guns shaking in their hands. The night was deathly quiet, and so dark and lifeless it almost appeared empty, with only the sound of their own breathing to remind them they were still awake, still alive. So far. To combat the all-consuming darkness, they clicked on the lights attached underneath the barrels of their weapons, each one projecting little glimpses of light within the trees, illuminating bark, leaves, and a trail leading into the heart of the forest.

A trail of blood.

One agent looked back, taking a final glance at the house behind him. Light shone through its white curtains, revealing the house within—the house they had been called to investigate. The house they had found empty.

As he turned back to the forest, his eyes once again stayed focused on the blood. He knew what it meant: something was waiting for them inside the

forest, within the trees. Something they wouldn't be able to escape from.

Deep down, they all knew.

Which was why they continued to stand on the edge, outside of the trees, outside of the danger—trained agents acting like children afraid of their own closets, for fear of the unknown horror that hid within.

Bulletproof vests draped over their chests, enveloping them in a shield of safety, and large black riot gear helmets mounted their heads, making them appear larger, more imposing than they actually were, just like a defenseless animal who tries to make itself look threatening so that maybe, just maybe, the bear won't devour it.

Defenseless, however, they were not. Armed to the teeth, each agent had a pistol holstered to their side as a backup, and either a Benelli shotgun or an AR-15 rifle rested in their hands; each weapon was equipped with a tactical flashlight as well as a green laser sight, and they carried enough ammo to fend off a small army.

But it wouldn't be enough. Not if they found what they were expecting in there. Not if they found him.

"Eyes up." The words came from the agent in charge—code-named Alpha—who tried to force himself to sound calm. "We don't know for sure what's in there, so no one shoot until we have confirmation." He wanted that part to be clear at least. They didn't know what was in there. They knew who, and they thought they knew why, but they had to be sure. 'Maybe we're wrong,' the agent thought. 'Maybe the blood doesn't mean what it appears to. It's possible. Sure, we could be wrong.'

He prayed they were.

"Let's go," he finally said, taking his first cautious step forward. The rest followed, and soon, they had entered the dark forest, their boots crunching the brittle leaves beneath them. Hollow trees seemed to stretch on forever, surrounding them like vultures ready to witness a slaughter and take the carcasses for themselves.

They followed the trail of blood as best they could, but it was scarce. More distance was growing between every crimson-painted leaf, and the trees seemingly began inching closer together, as if the forest itself was trying to suffocate them, keep them from progressing, from moving farther into its heart.

Alpha drew a deep breath. If they continued at this rate, they wouldn't find anything until morning, and if they were right about what was in there, it would be too late by then.

If it wasn't already.

"Split up," he said. "Groups of two. Delta, take Echo, sweep right." Delta was a big guy, practically a giant, highly trained and fearless. Alpha tried to hope that it would make a difference. "Charlie, you're with Foxtrot." He pointed left, knowing it was unlikely that the blood would lead that way, hoping they would find nothing. Charlie was tough, rugged, not easily put down, whereas Foxtrot had the quickest draw time Alpha had ever seen, almost as if he was a gunslinger pulled straight from the old west. But they were also young, inexperienced. If they found what they were looking for, it would be a massacre.

The agents turned to look at him, trying to hide the fear in their eyes behind the black visors of their helmets. But he saw it nonetheless.

He didn't blame them. He heard it too, the voice in his head telling him to run while he still could. But he also knew it wasn't a choice they could make. They had to find him before something worse happened. Before he did what they thought he had come here to do.

Bravely, he took one step forward, signaling to the agent on his left, Bravo, to follow him. "Stay on coms. Check in every minute. If you find blood, say something, and we will move to your location. And if you see him, don't engage. No matter what, don't engage."

His voice managed to come out strong; years in the field had granted him at least a calm voice in the midst of terror. But the same didn't apply

to his hands. He fought hard to control them, but they were shaking so badly it was causing the light to flare back and forth, distorting their path even further.

"Sir?" Bravo asked, concerned.

"I'm fine," he lied, keeping his eyes on the ground as they progressed further, looking for any hint of blood, anything to lead them to him. Because it wasn't just about finding him. It was about finding him before he did it—what they thought he had come here to do. Because maybe, if the line hadn't yet been crossed, they would be okay. Maybe then they could talk him down. But if not?

If not, he didn't think they would be leaving the woods.

Jagged pieces of bark sliced at his shoulders, trying to grab him in the darkness as he moved between the trees. Suddenly, there was a noise to his left. The faint crackling of a branch. From the low volume of the noise, he knew it was just a small animal, most likely a squirrel, but his adrenaline was racing, borderline spiking, as was that of the agent beside him. They both swung around, training their guns on the perpetrator, seeing that their instincts were right. It was just a squirrel, bent over a fallen branch, unaware of the carnage that was about to ensue.

"Sir," Delta's voice whispered over the speaker, "I found something."

"What?"

"Blood, sir. It's everywhere."

The two agents stared at the blood, their feet frozen in place.

"Stay where you are," Alpha instructed over the coms, and they would have been happy to oblige had it not been for the breathing they heard in front of them.

Slow and methodical, it almost sounded like wind twisting through the trees, calling to them. They looked at each other and slowly nodded their heads in agreement. They wouldn't go far, just enough to investigate the breathing. Truth be told, they thought it was in their imagination.

It wasn't.

Both carrying shotguns, they kept the barrels up, watching as the combination of light and lasers crept through the forest, crawling over the trees. They progressed slowly, both fighting the urge to run back, out of the woods, away from whatever they would find in front of them.

The further they progressed, the louder it got, until finally they saw the trees in front of them. Light gray bark appeared almost white in the light of their flashlights, contrasting sharply with the red stains spattered across it. They knew the smart thing to do would be to wait, to tell their commanding officer what was on the trees and wait for their backup. But if the breathing was loud enough for them to hear, he was close. Close enough to hear them if they spoke, and help would never arrive in time.

So they had no choice. They each took a deep breath and continued on, catching only glimpses of what lay beyond the trees. As fleeting as the glimpses were, they were enough. They saw him.

They stepped forward, their guns trained on his back as they entered the small clearing, barely fifteen feet wide, seemingly disconnected from the rest of the forest. That was probably why he was there, kneeling in the dirt, hunched over something they couldn't see, not even acknowledging their presence.

The agents stared at his back, unable to speak for a moment. They couldn't see his face, but they knew it was him. Their lasers remained trained on his head, limiting the flashlights to revealing only the top few feet of him, leaving everything below his shoulders shrouded in darkness.

Finally, Delta found the strength to speak. "Agent Shade?"

No answer came. He just stayed there, like a wolf guarding its kill, his head twitching slightly. The two agents started to move, walking on opposite ends of an imaginary circle as they made their way around him. Slowly, as they moved

forward, their flashlights revealed more, bringing the grisly picture before them into focus.

They could see his face now. It was bruised and covered in blood, but there was no mistaking it. It was him. Shade.

In his hands was a knife, so soaked in blood that the silver glint of the blade couldn't be seen. His black coat was also stained red, and torn to shreds. Someone had fought back.

And even now, with the flashlight in his eyes, Shade didn't acknowledge their presence. Instead, his eyes moved back and forth wildly, following a seemingly random pattern, as if he was staring at monsters that only he could see.

"Agent Shade, where is she?" Delta asked, but still no answer came. Shade just continued to look into the distance, and the agents came to a horrifying realization, one that either fear or hope had hidden from them. The blood that covered him. It wasn't his own.

Delta nodded to his partner to keep his gun trained on Shade's head while he himself lowered his, the flashlight creeping down Shade's body, revealing what had been shrouded in darkness only a moment ago.

Seeing it almost caused him to drop his gun. What was lying in front of Shade, what he was hunched over, was a woman.

Dark red hair appeared to climb up from the mud and onto her head, surrounded by pale skin. Her navy-blue T-shirt now appeared purple, and her blue eyes stared up at the moon, unblinking, lifeless. Her throat was slit, and her stomach was opened, with so many stab wounds the agent couldn't find a single piece of remaining skin.

No longer realizing what he was doing, Delta stepped forward. "What did you do?" he asked as he moved his gun back up toward Shade's head. "What did you do?!"

In his shock, he took one step too many.

A bloodcurdling shriek echoed through the woods. "Delta?" Alpha frantically asked over the coms. "Delta, Echo, what happened?"

No answer came.

His feet began running, despite his mind telling him to turn around. He knew by the time they got there it would be too late, but he ran anyway, as did the agent beside him—through the forest, through the trees, over the footprints heading in the opposite direction.

"Delta!" he screamed as he passed the trees stained in blood and emerged on the other side. He swung his gun around, searching through the

darkness for the bodies, until finally, he found them.

The two agents lay in the dirt by the edge of the trees, their limp bodies about ten feet apart. Despite knowing they wouldn't answer, he called out to them. No reply. Desperate, he ran to them, checking for a pulse, praying he would find one.

He did.

They were still alive. Unconscious and bleeding, but still alive. For a single moment, Alpha allowed himself to hope. If they were still alive, maybe the line hadn't been crossed yet.

That was until he heard the nervous voice behind him. "Sir?"

"What?" he asked, turning around to see his fellow agent, Bravo, a man who had seen countless horrors just like he had, who was now so white with fear he could almost be mistaken for a ghost. "What is it?" After receiving no reply, he was forced to follow Bravo's hollow gaze down to the dirt, where the horror he had feared was finally revealed.

Staring at the woman's mangled body, he fought the urge to vomit. He'd seen countless crime scenes in person, countless more in photographs, but this was the most horrific corpse he had ever laid eyes on. Except for–

Behind the body, something moved in the trees. A dark figure, too large to be an animal. He tried

to follow it with his gun, but in an instant, it was gone. Knowing he still had two agents left out there, he issued a single warning over the coms.

"He's here."

Fifty yards to his left, Charlie and Foxtrot walked back to back, their guns shaking as they held them up in front of them. They walked slowly, in tandem with one another, making their way to the sound of the shriek, trying not to let their imaginations get the best of them, when suddenly, Charlie saw something shimmer between the trees, too far away to see clearly, but close enough to instill fear. He moved his laser to it, watching as the light reflected back off into the forest, askew at first, until whatever it was began to turn, forcing the laser's reflection to creep back across the trees, until finally it stopped, right on Charlie's chest. For a breath, the object remained still, and in his terror, he thought it looked like a claw.

The knife flew through the air, impaling his chest via a razor-thin opening within the lining of his vest. Blood crept out of his mouth as he dropped to his knees, his gun falling to the ground, sinking down into the mud below it.

Foxtrot felt him fall away from his back. "Are you okay?" he asked, not daring to turn around.

He told himself that it was because he had to continue to watch his side, and that his partner had merely stepped away—anything to justify not turning around and facing reality. But when he heard the sound of his partner's body colliding with the ground, he knew he had no choice.

As he spun, his gun turned with him, the light piercing through the darkness like a bolt of lightning, revealing the figure standing only inches in front of him.

Gunshots rang through the forest. The thick wall of trees hid their flashes from his sight, but Alpha knew where they had come from. "Report in," he pleaded desperately over his coms, waiting a moment for an answer he knew he wouldn't receive. He turned to Bravo, whose face had finally regained color. "It's just us now. Keep your gun up."

They both readied their weapons and began walking back into the thick of the forest, leaving what was left of the body behind them. Whereas before, the agents had heard nothing but silence from the forest, now they could hear every branch that cracked, every leaf that scraped against the rough bark of a tree as it fell, every gust of wind that blew through the night air, whispering to them softly. And with every new noise, they pointed their guns toward it, until soon their

flashlights were moving so quickly, desperate to reveal something, anything, that they ended up revealing nothing.

Finally, Bravo saw a figure standing in the darkness, watching them. He started to fire his weapon when the flash went off. A flash that didn't come from his own rifle.

Almost as quickly as the bullet had torn a hole in his stomach, his legs gave way beneath him.

Hearing the shot, Alpha turned to fire his weapon, but the figure in the woods had vanished. All that was left was his fellow agent, lying on the ground, the blood from his stomach mixing with the mud below.

He moved Bravo's hand aside, seeing his stomach, trying to find the entry wound.

The bullet had hit right below the vest, in a place that would cause enough blood loss to incapacitate him, but maybe not kill—not if he got medical attention in time.

As Bravo grunted, beginning to lose consciousness, Alpha picked up his gun once again and started spinning it wildly, looking for the figure in the woods, the monster who had done this. The light went back and forth across the trees, searching for something. For someone.

"Where are you!"

Something pulled against his throat from behind. Instinctively he tried to bring his gun up to fire, shifting the barrel so it rested on his shoulder, pointing backwards, but it was knocked from his hand as the thing gripping his throat began to cut off the oxygen to his lungs. In a last-ditch effort, he gathered all the strength he had left and began trying to pry it off, to remove the hold on his neck.

But he couldn't.

His feet left trails in the leaves as he was dragged backward by a force he couldn't see. His eyes began to lose their sight, and the sound in his ears grew fuzzy and distorted. Finally, he allowed his body to go limp; it was no use fighting against the force. They had lost. Now all he could do was hope the figure allowed him to live. As the world began fading from his vision, he managed to speak a single question.

"Why are you doing this?"

He received no answer as his world turned to black.